JUL 1 5

D0762406

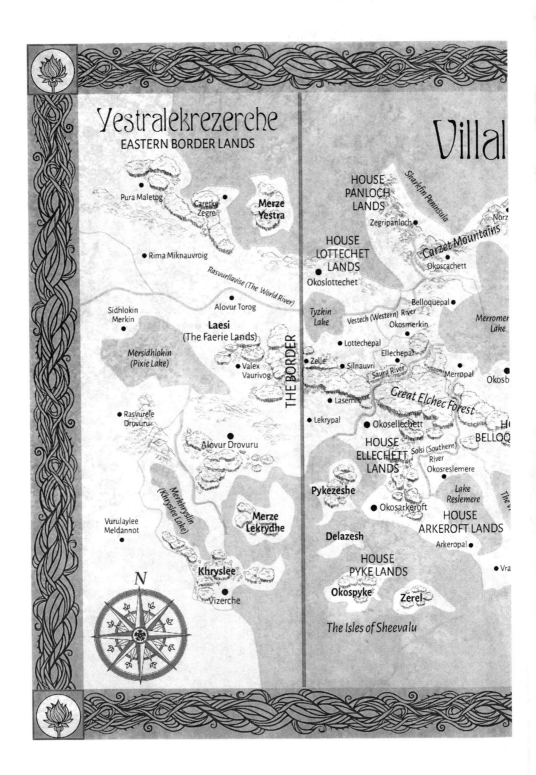

Yestralekrezerche
EASTERN BORDER LANDS

Pura Maletog

Caretke
Zegre

**Merze
Yestra**

Rima Miknauvroig

Rasvurliavise (The World River)

Alovur Torog

Sidhlokin
Merkin

Laesi
(The Faerie Lands)

Mersidhlokin
(Pixie Lake)

Valex
Vaurivog

THE BORDER

Rasvurele
Drovuru

Alovur Drovuru

Mehhryslin
(Khryslee Lake)

Vurulaylee
Meldannot

**Merze
Lekrydhe**

Khryslee

Vizerche

N

Villal

HOUSE
PANLOCH
LANDS

Sharkfin Peninsula

Zegripanloch

Norz

Carzet Mountains

HOUSE
LOTTECHET
LANDS

Okoscachett

Okoslottechet

Belloquepal

Tyzkin
Lake

Vestech (Western) River

Okosmerkin

Merromer
Lake

Lottechepal

Ellechepal

Zelle

Silnauvri

Saura River

Merropal

Okosb

Great Elchec Forest

Lasemir

Lekrypal

Okosellechett

**HOUSE
ELLECHETT
LANDS**

Solsi (Southern)
River

Okosreslemere

H
BELLOQ

Pykezeshe

Lake
Reslemere

Okosarkeroft

**HOUSE
ARKEROFT LANDS**

Delazesh

Arkeropal

Vra

**HOUSE
PYKE LANDS**

Okospyke

Zerel

The vi

The Isles of Sheevalu

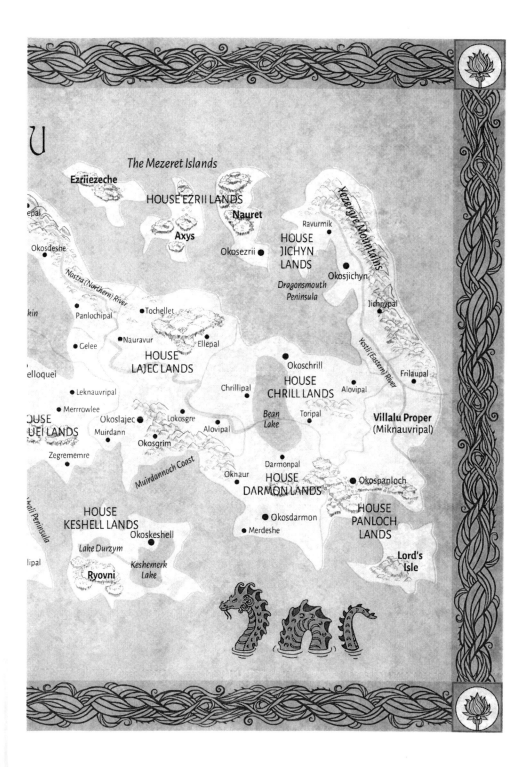

the SIDhE

THE HEART OF ALL WORLDS, BOOK ONE

Charlotte Ashe

interlude press

For Link, who never allowed me to
stop calling myself a writer.

"Yesterday we obeyed kings and bent our necks before emperors. But today we kneel only to truth, follow only beauty, and obey only love."

— Khalil Gibran

PROLOGUE

Ⅰт started in Villalu. In Ravurmik, to be precise, a tiny fishing village on the innermost lip of the Dragonsmouth province.

It was precisely fifty thousand years since the final day of *Es Muchator*, the Great Change, not that the people of Villalu were aware of it. Such things had not survived in their history books, and the little oral tradition that had been preserved from the Age Before the World had been distorted into nonsense over the millennia that had elapsed.

Yet it started. And no one noticed a thing.

No one noticed a restless twelve-year-old boy by the name of Brieden Lethiscir creeping out of his bedroom to stare in wonder at the full moon and to check whether pails of honeysuckle left on the back steps were empty.

They were.

His eyes went wide at the discovery. The village around him slept as he followed a vague but distinct trail of crumpled petals into the forest.

No one saw when a sharp breeze snuffed out his candle, leaving only the moonlight to guide him. And no one saw him pause at the forest's edge, swallow a gasp and go completely still as he beheld the Yestli river on the other side of the clearing.

He knew of the creatures, in a theoretical sense; the honeysuckle had been left for them, after all, and he'd never doubted his grandmother's stories. She had told him of The Sidhe since he was a tiny boy, pressing seashells and blossoms into his palms as she explained the sorts of gifts they liked best. They were noble and powerful people, she said, who were to be respected, but also feared for their unpredictability. They were beautiful, magical and elusive, and catching a glimpse of one meant good luck until the next new moon.

But none of her stories—not one—had prepared him for what he beheld in the clearing that night.

The sidhe, and it couldn't be anything but a sidhe, was so beautiful that Brieden could barely look at him. His pale, wet skin glistened like stars as he slipped up the riverbank, illuminated by the pregnant moons. His naked body was long and lithe, his hair was midnight-blue and his ears were perfect delicate points. When he ran across the clearing, his steps were so light he barely seemed to touch the ground. The sidhe passed near enough to his hiding place that Brieden could almost make out the color of his eyes, dark and bright, before he disappeared, laughing like music, into the forest.

It was a good five minutes before Brieden moved a muscle.

He was not merely overcome by the sight of the beautiful elf he had just seen. He was also overcome by the fact that he suddenly understood himself in a terrifying new way; because he finally understood why he had never noticed the girls in the village the way the other boys did.

Yes, it started in Villalu. In Ravurmik, to be precise, on the innermost lip of the Dragonsmouth province. But no one—least of all the twelve-year-old boy sitting at the forest's edge, looking up at the full moon over the river and crying silent tears— noticed a thing.

No one human, anyway.

THE SECOND TIME BRIEDEN SAW A SIDHE WAS MORE THAN A year later. He was at the market with his mother and saw a woman draped in silk and beads, trailed by one of the beautiful elves.

The sight stopped him in his tracks, but not because he was captivated.

It was a female sidhe this time. Her beauty had been blunted by a loose burlap dress, lank violet hair and dull lavender eyes. Around her neck, she wore an iron collar attached to a delicate silver chain that looped around the wealthy woman's wrist.

"Mother, what... that's a sidhe, isn't it?"

"Yes," his mother said in a tight, clipped voice. Brieden was not the only one staring at the pair, and the wealthy woman wore a satisfied expression that chilled Brieden in a way he couldn't quite place.

What he *could* understand was that the sight was upsetting his mother.

"What... but why is she like that? What's wrong with her?" he whispered.

His mother paused, eyes fixed on the woman and the sidhe, then turned to face him. "She's a slave, Brieden," she answered softly.

Brieden stared at her in silent shock. He didn't know where to begin.

Over the next few weeks, Brieden managed to extract more details from his mother, who seemed reluctant to acknowledge the ugliness of the situation to her son.

He learned that, although The Sidhe wielded incredible natural power, they had been captured and traded as slaves for generations in Villalu. Their powers were suppressed with iron collars or by injections of verbena tincture, and they were status symbols among royalty and the very rich. Sidhe were rare to find and difficult to catch, an unusual sight to behold in any poor region, let alone one as far from The Border as Dragonsmouth.

There was, however, quite a lot that his mother did not tell him.

She never told him about the flesh markets. She never told him exactly what so many of the cultured, aristocratic men with cold, hard eyes liked to do with their sidhe slaves. She never told him how bad things actually were.

When he arrived in Villalu Proper in his sixteenth year, as the recipient of a coveted scholarship to attend the Royal Service Academy, he heard whispers of such indecencies for the first time. And what he didn't hear spoken he deduced when his own sexual awakening began to reveal previously hidden social truths.

Sexual relations between men were as officially taboo in Villalu Proper as they had been in Ravurmik, although here the official stance was accompanied by a nod and a wink, and Brieden had no trouble finding willing partners at the Academy. Although he had never thought himself unusually handsome, he couldn't deny that he had often caught the eye of one village girl or another in Ravurmik. He possessed the dark eyes, glossy black hair, full lips, lean yet muscled frame and chestnut-colored skin inherited from his father, who had always been considered a very attractive man. It appeared that the tastes of the boys in Villalu Proper were not so very different.

And so he allowed himself to indulge with other boys, delighting in the freedom and the pleasure of it, without any true fear of getting caught. Those boys who did get caught received a gentle scolding, belied by laughing eyes, from their housemasters and instructors; a short lecture on the importance of working it out of their systems while they were young and unmarried; and the advice that they be more discreet in the future.

It was a different matter altogether with The Sidhe, though.

Among the very wealthy, and royalty in particular, it was commonly accepted for men to purchase sidhe for sexual use. The gender of the creature was socially irrelevant. The elves were not human, and therefore nothing done with them was of much importance. Half the wealthy married men in Villalu Proper seemed to own a sidhe, and a man using his sidhe for pleasure was considered no more scandalous than using a horse for transportation.

At first, it had sickened Brieden—had quite literally made him lose his supper.

It still sickened him, he supposed, but he had learned to tamp down the queasiness, had accepted it as a grim social reality because there didn't seem to be any other option.

A handful of Brieden's classmates had been given the use of their fathers' sidhe when they turned seventeen, the traditional passage into manhood. A couple of the wealthier boys had even been given a sidhe of their own. Brieden would try to change the topic of conversation and disguise how truly uneasy the subject of sex with a sidhe made him become, but evasion was useless.

This was Brieden's world now. There was no getting away from that. The entire purpose of Brieden's work at the Academy was to gain employment with a noble household, where the presence of sidhe slaves was downright ubiquitous.

So he allowed himself to grow slightly numb. But just slightly, in the end. Because sometimes sorrow hit him afresh when he saw one of the proud elves with defeated eyes, limping along, luminous flesh marred with bruises.

Sometimes he still cried silent tears in his bunk at night, embarrassed by his own childish incredulity that the world could be so cruel.

Of course the world was cruel. Brieden had known that for a very long time.

He knew it when his grandmother was murdered in her bed during one of the many Frilauan raids on his village.

He knew it when his mother spent the day after one such raid sobbing and curling into a ball while Brieden brought her clean rags to lie on. He exchanged them for the blood-soaked ones he would then take to wash in the river.

He knew it when, nine months later, his mother gave birth to a baby boy who could not possibly have belonged to Brieden's father, and when, a month after that, his father ran off with a barmaid.

His mother made him compete for the Academy scholarship not because she saw the promise in him, but because she simply could not afford to feed both Brieden and his brother any longer.

By the time he left home, his mother's eyes reminded him uncannily of that first sidhe slave he had seen in the market all those years ago.

But still, all that pain had not hardened him against the flesh markets; against the slave traders who looked as though they could have been men from Brieden's own village.

Many would think him ungrateful for regarding it all with such secret disgust. Being selected to train for royal service was an honor, after all, and the fact that he had been chosen to serve the House of Panloch's crown prince was a greater honor still. But the mere mention of the honor was sour on his tongue.

He had been in Prince Dronyen's employ for close to two years now and had quickly become one of the prince's favorite servants. He had already been named steward of the castle's eastern wing, and the fact that the prince had selected Brieden to accompany him to the flesh markets to select a new "toy" had earned him the envy of the palace staff.

Dronyen seemed to use up his "toys" pretty quickly.

Brieden hated him.

But only a little bit more than he hated himself.

Dronyen yawned broadly as the next sidhe was ushered onto the platform, this one a female.

"This is honestly the worst batch I have ever seen," Dronyen muttered. "If I don't find something new today, you'll need to fetch me some options from the brothel tonight, Lethiscir."

Brieden cringed, but silently hoped that he would be assigned that dreadful chore. At least the whores got paid to endure Dronyen's cruel appetites, although no amount of copper or even gold could be payment enough for a night in the prince's bedchamber.

"Yes, Your Maj, of course." He tried not to look at the stage. The flashes of anger buried in the defeated eyes as one magnificent being after another was offered up for abuse and degradation haunted his dreams every time he saw them.

But something outside of his control or understanding tugged at him on this particular day, and when Dronyen shot up in his seat with a delighted gasp, Brieden couldn't help but look.

And the world stopped.

Because on the platform was the most breathtaking creature he had ever laid eyes on in his entire life.

The sidhe was tall, supple and lithe, as all sidhe tended to be, with milk-pale skin that glowed like moonlight over lean, taut muscles. Like all the others before him, he was naked, giving potential buyers a full picture of what they were bidding on.

And he was extraordinary, head to toe.

His chin-length hair was violet-red and it gleamed in the afternoon sun. His lips were pink and delicate with a pronounced bow, his nose had a narrow, smooth slope and his eyes...

His eyes.

It wasn't that they were the most incredible color imaginable: a storm of deep, contrasting, impossible greens unlike any Brieden had ever seen. And it wasn't that they were large and almond-shaped beneath a fan of plum-colored lashes.

It was that they were full to the brim with *life*.

Never before had Brieden seen a sidhe slave with such lively and expressive eyes, even as he stood for auction. Those eyes were not dull or defeated in the slightest. Wary, yes, and utterly devoid of trust, but also *blazing*.

Blazing like the eyes of that sidhe Brieden had seen at the riverbank when he was twelve years old—the only free sidhe Brieden had ever had the chance to behold.

The elf stood on that platform as if he owned it. As if he were judging every human man before him, and not the other way around.

He tucked a lock of hair behind a delicately pointed elfin ear, then jutted his chin to reveal a chiseled jaw that contrasted beautifully against his tender features.

And though he knew it was insane, Brieden was quite sure that he was in love.

He also knew, beyond a shadow of a doubt, that Dronyen was going to purchase this elf.

Even so, he was not prepared for how painfully his heart constricted when Dronyen, eyes alight with blind, unmasked hunger, shot out of his seat to begin the bidding.

The bidding began higher than usual and reached astronomical heights. Brieden wasn't surprised; if he had never seen anyone so beautiful, none of these men had either.

When the bidding was down to three, as was traditional, the men were allowed to touch before finalizing their bids. Rage surged through Brieden's body as he watched their meaty hands paw at the sidhe as if he was nothing more than livestock, stroking his perfect skin, inspecting the inside of his mouth, the pads of his feet, between his buttocks.

But even worse than the sight of their hands on the elf was the look in his eyes as he endured their touch. No matter how defiant or proud the sidhe's eyes may have been, there was no disguising the fear that now shone through as well. It was raw and unmasked, utterly gut-wrenching. That look of fear tore into Brieden and made him want to charge the platform and throw himself between this perfect being and these repulsive swine who actually felt entitled to touch him.

Brieden began to die inside when Dronyen placed the winning bid.

The elf rode with Dronyen on the journey home, flush against the front of his body. The sidhe had been outfitted in breeches, a jerkin and leather slippers, and even as Brieden rode his horse behind them, torn between deep sorrow and boiling fury, he was grateful that the sidhe had at least been granted the temporary dignity of clothes.

Brieden lay awake in his bunk that night, staring at the ceiling and trying to believe that Dronyen's new slave was not suffering. He knew it was an empty hope. Brieden knew Dronyen far better than he would have liked, and Brieden had seen how Dronyen looked at this particular sidhe. Dronyen had seen something of what Brieden saw in him, and Dronyen valued what he saw, for the worst possible reasons.

Dronyen didn't just see a pleasing way to pass the time. He saw the fierceness in the sidhe's eyes. The pride. The strength. The resolute refusal to be broken.

Dronyen was a true sadist. This Brieden knew.

Many aristocratic men would be shocked to hear what they did to their sidhe described as rape. Their slaves were simply there for their pleasure, and *consent* was an alien concept. Most of these men were ignorant of their own cruelty. Some had probably even convinced themselves that their victims liked the attention.

But Dronyen? Dronyen probably *loved* the fact that he was commiting rape. Brieden imagined it must have thrilled him to the core.

Dronyen didn't just keep slaves for pleasure and status. He liked *hurting* his slaves. He liked breaking them. And the elf he had just purchased was a challenge that he wouldn't even try to resist.

Brieden bit his lip and glanced out his bedroom window. It was late, late enough that Dronyen had probably sent the sidhe to the slave quarters for the night.

He told himself he wasn't going to do it. He swore he wouldn't. But even as his brain denied it, Brieden found himself moving through the castle, creeping past guards and sliding around corners until he was at the hallway that led to the sidhe's cell.

It wasn't guarded. Why would it be? The elf's veins were surging with verbena, effectively nullifying any threat he may have posed in his natural state.

Let alone in *this* state.

The sidhe was in a corner curled up against the stone walls; the thin blanket and small straw mattress on the other side of the cell seemed untouched. Moonlight seeped through the bars at the window onto his pale, glowing skin, which was now purpled with bruises. His face was pressed into his knees, and he was sobbing. *Sobbing.* Brieden had never heard a sound of such pure, musical, tortured pain. It somehow managed to sound horrifically lovely and it was utterly soul-shattering.

Maybe, despite who he had become and what he had allowed himself to grow accustomed to, maybe he hadn't lost his soul quite yet.

And Dronyen? Dronyen had no soul. Dronyen was able to hear these sobs and go about his life. More than that, he took pleasure in trying to break something beautiful.

But Brieden was not Dronyen.

And Brieden wouldn't allow this creature, this sidhe, this *exquisite man* to be broken. He wasn't sure what he was going to do, but he was going to do something. He may not have had the power to change the slave market, but he could change the future for one slave. It was risky, but not impossible.

He had to do it soon. But it wouldn't do either of them any good if Brieden were executed for trying to free the elf, so he needed a good plan. If there was even the smallest chance that Dronyen could dull the light in those bright forest eyes, Brieden would never forgive himself.

When he returned to his bunk, Brieden tried to sleep. But instead he tossed and turned and whispered feverishly, hoping that he could somehow will the enslaved sidhe three floors below to hear him.

"I love you," he whispered.

And, "I'll save you."

And, "I'm sorry."

"I'm so, so *sorry*."

No one, least of all Brieden, knew that it had started ten years ago in that clearing by the riverbank. That it had started in Villalu, on the anniversary of the Great Change.

But Villalu was not where it would end.

CHAPTER ONE

"**L**ETHISCIR!"

Brieden halted, heart pounding as he slipped the small object in his hand into the pouch on his belt.

"Yes, Maj," he responded calmly, turning toward Dronyen as the prince approached, his new slave at his heels. The prince narrowed his eyes at Brieden.

"What business did you have in the trophy room?" he demanded.

"I was assessing its condition, Your Maj." Brieden lowered his head. "I thought you might like to show Lady Brissa the tokens of your House's many accomplishments. The room is quite in need of dusting, and some of the older medals are in need of polishing." He forced himself not to look behind Dronyen at the sidhe, who was clad in a blue silk loincloth and decorated with jewels around his neck, wrists and ankles. His bruises were mostly faded and he was looking better-fed, no doubt for the benefit of the Keshells. Lady Brissa, second-eldest daughter of the House of Keshell, was to marry Dronyen, and their engagement party was to take place within the week. The castle had been a bustle of activity in anticipation of her arrival, and Brieden had wasted no time in using the distracted state of things to his benefit.

He spared a glance at the sidhe's distant, rage-filled eyes. *Soon.*

Dronyen clapped Brieden on the back and smiled. "Excellent thought, Lethiscir. It is actions such as this that make you my favorite. See that your staff tend to it."

"Yes, Your Maj."

"Walk with me, Lethiscir. I have a task for you and I must impress upon you how vital it is that you do not disappoint me." Brieden closed the door to the trophy room and accompanied Dronyen down the corridor toward the prince's rooms.

"When my lady arrives, I will have little time for the elf." Dronyen paused, turning toward the sidhe and stroking a hand down his fine-boned cheek. Every visible muscle in the elf's body tensed at the touch. "I don't want the poor thing to think I'm neglecting him, and he'll need meals, exercise and someone to bathe and dress him. I may call for him at a moment's notice, and he must look as lovely as possible for our guests at all times." Dronyen let his hand wander down the sidhe's pale chest. "I have heard that the Keshells are... not entirely comfortable in the company of elves, but I imagine we can change that, can't we, lovely thing?"

The sidhe glared at him.

"Forgive me, Maj, but I was under the impression that Cerade was tending to the sidhe's needs," Brieden cut in before Dronyen could reprimand his prisoner or force him to answer.

"He was." Dronyen turned his stony expression away from the sidhe as he began to walk down the corridor again. "But Cerade has proven himself less than trustworthy. He does not understand that the elf is my property, and that I do not share my property with those that are paid to do my bidding." Dronyen's eyes slid to the side to observe Brieden. "I trust that you have no trouble understanding the concept?"

"No, Your Maj. I understand completely."

13

"That is excellent. I would hate to see you suffer a fate similar to that of Cerade, after all."

Brieden suppressed a shudder. "Of course, Your Maj."

In Dronyen's rooms, he showed Brieden the trunk full of fine fabrics and jewels with which he enjoyed bedecking his slave. "I will have this sent to your rooms, along with instructions and a schedule. I expect you to notify me immediately of any problems. Leave the larger punishments to me, but if he misbehaves, you may correct him, just as long as you are careful not to leave marks. Report anything more serious than routine disobedience to me rather than attempting to handle it yourself. Do you understand?"

Brieden clenched his hands behind his back, made himself breathe deep and nodded once. "Yes, Maj," he said.

"Very good. Other than that, you are not to touch my property, except as necessary to see that he is bathed and dressed. Is that also clear?"

"Of course, Your Maj." Brieden glanced at the sidhe, who was staring at the sliver of sky visible through the window across the room. He appeared lost in thought, as if imagining himself to be anywhere else at all.

The Keshells arrived three days later, and Brieden found himself in the nerve-wracking clutches of a golden opportunity.

Money... that part was, surprisingly, the easiest so far. Dronyen wouldn't think to look for some of the older medals and trophies anytime soon. They fetched an impressive price at market, of course, but finding trustworthy buyers took time that Brieden scarcely had to spare.

Being tasked with the sidhe's care was a boon in more ways than one: Brieden knew Dronyen's taste. He had sold the silks and jewels from the sidhe's wardrobe that the prince was less likely to request on the occasions when he called for the elf to sit beside him on a little velvet pillow for the evening meal.

Slightly more difficult had been securing transportation. A carriage and horses had been outfitted according to specifications that had made the merchant raise an eyebrow and hold out his palm for more gold, but Brieden had paid handsomely enough to avoid unnecessary questions. Brieden had also begun to purchase maps and to collect drinking water and food that would keep. He slipped the bundles into the carriage when he could finagle a trip into town and fought the uneasiness in his gut whenever the carriage merchant's heavy gaze landed upon him. But Brieden handed him more gold at each visit and assured him that he would not have to look after the horses and carriage much longer. He only hoped that the words were true.

He had the carriage. He had the money. He was building a cache of supplies. Now all he needed was a good escape plan and the sidhe's trust.

That last thing proved to be the most difficult.

The sidhe refused to speak to him.

For the first week, Brieden simply focused on bringing the elf small comforts, like soft blankets and warm water with which to bathe himself and soft leather moccasins to save the soles of his feet from the cold stone palace floors. Brieden turned his back respectfully while the elf bathed and gave him extra space when he stared up at Brieden with tear-stained cheeks and hate-filled eyes on the mornings after Dronyen had called the sidhe to his bedchamber. He tried to engage the sidhe in conversation once or twice, but stopped when he was firmly ignored.

Brieden tried not to panic. He had time. Not in excess, but he had it, and he would need patience if they were going to survive.

One morning in the second week, Brieden awoke to the scent of honeysuckle wafting through his bedroom window and was reminded of his grandmother. She had always told him that honeysuckle was a favorite food of The Sidhe, and he had nothing to lose by testing the theory.

The pail of flowers earned him his first ghost of a smile, as well as his first taste of the elf's voice.

"Thank you."

Brieden rolled the words back and forth across his mind, relishing the voice: sweet and soft and almost as delicate as the honeysuckle itself, it was balm for Brieden's ears. It was an oasis in the midst of the gruff, harsh, booming, bellowing male voices that usually surrounded him.

It was the best thing Brieden had ever heard.

At the beginning of the third week, Brieden dared to ask the elf his name.

"Why do you wish to know?"

"I... so I know what to call you. I'm Brieden."

"I thought your name was Lethiscir."

"That's just my surname. But Brieden is what my friends call me. Um. I... what I mean..."

The elf looked away. "You wouldn't be able to pronounce it."

"Well, what do humans usually call you?"

"They don't."

"Well... what can *I* call you?"

When the sidhe looked back at him, his eyes were throbbing with desperate, angry pain. "What do you want from me?" he whispered.

Brieden looked around him, making sure that they were alone. He leaned as close as he dared.

"I just want to help you."

The elf stared at him, and Brieden had never felt so utterly naked and vulnerable. He forced himself to look back, putting everything he had into that look, doing everything he could to make the sidhe *see*.

I'm safe, he willed his eyes to communicate. *You can trust me. I won't hurt you. I want to set you free.*

The elf looked away again. Brieden had lost him. Maybe all of this was hopeless, perhaps he'd been a fool to truly believe—

"Sehrys."

"Pardon me?"

"My name... you really wouldn't be able to pronounce it. But you could call me Sehrys. It's a shortened version, kind of a pet name that members of my feririar used to call me."

"Your fer...?"

"Feririar. I suppose you could say it's like my tribe. Village? Flock?" Sehrys sighed. "The people I came from."

He sounded so wistful that Brieden almost hated himself for having asked the question.

"Sehrys," Brieden repeated. "That's lovely. I've never heard anything like it before."

Sehrys shrugged. "My full name is prettier."

"What is it? I mean... even if I can't say it, could I hear it? Maybe? If... you want to tell me. You don't have to."

Sehrys studied him, his face still uncertain. Brieden offered him a nervous smile.

Sehrys almost—but not quite—smiled back. "*Sehrys Silerth Valusidhe efa Naisdhe efa es Zulla Maletog Feririar ala es Fervishlaea efa es Vestramezershe,*" he said, the words rolling off his tongue like a lilting melody.

He was right on both counts: There was absolutely no way Brieden would ever be able to pronounce it.

Also? It was beautiful.

Brieden smiled. "Pleased to meet you, Sehrys."

Sehrys's expression darkened.

"Don't do that," he said flatly and turned his back on Brieden.

"Don't do what?"

"Pretend we're friends. Or even friendly. Pretend you see me as more than an animal. Pretend you don't know what your prince does with me at night when he's finished courting his lady."

Brieden swallowed hard. He didn't know what to say.

Sehrys walked to the single barred window and looked out over the courtyard. Brieden had always found it odd that the cell had one of the best views in the castle, when the cell itself held so few comforts. Besides the threadbare straw mattress, and the tin chamber pot and the washtub tucked in the corner, there was nothing to distract from the rough stone and iron bars that surrounded Sehrys for so much of his days. It was hard to imagine the window as a kindness. Perhaps it was less that Sehrys would have a nice view and more that the entire court could catch a glimpse of the prince's prettiest possession.

"Sehrys, I do see you as more than an animal. In fact, I see you as more than human, if I'm to judge by most of the humans I have met."

Sehrys didn't turn around.

"And... I'm sure that Dronyen has never asked you what you wanted, which leads me to believe that he's probably been doing things *to you*, and not *with* you. And I understand the difference, Sehrys, truly I do." Brieden swallowed, unsure if Sehrys was listening, but unwilling to stop before he'd said all that he needed to say.

"Sehrys, I... I also know that what he does to you isn't your fault. It doesn't change who you are, and it doesn't make you any less... perfect."

Sehrys slumped against the window sill, but continued to look outside, eyes cast firmly away from Brieden.

After a few moments more, Brieden stepped out of the cell and walked away, feeling deflated.

He didn't see the tears in Sehrys's eyes.

BRIEDEN FOUND DRONYEN IN THE GARDENS WITH BRISSA later that evening to report on Sehrys's care.

"What is it, Brieden?" Dronyen asked him, voice unnervingly gentle but also firm and edged with exasperation, as if he had not specifically told Brieden to meet him there during his evening stroll.

"Forgive me, Your Maj. I was hoping to report on your elf, but I see that you are keeping company with your lady. Perhaps we can speak after you've finished your walk?"

"That is entirely up to my lady," Dronyen replied, taking Brissa's lace-gloved hand and bowing slightly. "Although I would not presume to speak of such matters in her presence, it's my understanding that she rather enjoys keeping abreast of palace affairs."

Brissa whipped open a delicate paper fan, then raised it to hide her demure smile. "Thank you, my prince. I would love to hear of the elf's condition. Although I admit The Sidhe unnerve me, they also fascinate me greatly. And he is to be my slave as well, is he not?"

"He is," Dronyen replied, barely managing to conceal his irritation. "So what have you to report? Is he taking food and drink? No signs of slave-madness, I hope."

Brissa gasped at the mention of madness, although she was clearly interested.

"No, Your Maj. The elf is well. He appears to be sleeping through the night, and his appetite is good. He has not misbehaved, and his mind appears clear. He does... spend quite a bit of time at his window, however. I believe he would enjoy some fresh air, if you would give me leave to take him for a walk out of doors."

Dronyen narrowed his eyes. He glanced sidelong at Brissa, and then plastered on a jovial smile.

"Of course. You may take him for a stroll in the gardens tomorrow as a reward for his good behavior. And please be sure to tell him that it is a gift from me for his obedience."

Ignoring the gooseflesh that rose on his arms at the words, Brieden nodded. "Very good, Your Maj. I will retire now, if it pleases you."

Dronyen waved him off, and Brieden bid goodbye to the pair. He paused to take one last look around the gardens—just beginning to bloom in the gently warming springtime air—and his gaze fell upon the picture that Brissa and Dronyen made, side by side against the setting sun. From this distance, they looked like a beautiful and happy couple; Brieden rarely thought of Dronyen as attractive, given the poison in his soul, but, on the surface, he was a handsome man, tall and lean with creamy beige skin that spoke of a lifetime of luxury and good sleep, alert slate-gray eyes, a neatly trimmed beard and close-cropped nut-brown hair.

Standing almost as tall as Dronyen, Brissa had the darkest complexion Brieden had ever seen, nearly coal-black and luminous. Though her hands were dainty, her lean frame was defined by a surprising hint of musculature. Thick glossy black curls cascaded down her back. Despite her blushing giggles, she had shrewd, thoughtful eyes and already carried herself like a queen.

Dronyen would destroy her.

Brieden turned away from the false beauty spread before him against the golden-pink sky and headed toward the castle.

The following afternoon, Brieden's heart soared at the expression on Sehrys's face when he led him to the gardens. It was a gorgeous change from the look of razor-edged shame in the sidhe's eyes that very morning; his arms and thighs seemed freshly bruised when Brieden brought him his breakfast.

"Oh!" Sehrys said softly, with something like a shadow of delight in his voice as he approached a lilac bush. "I love these. I'd never seen them before I came to Villalu, but the last person who purchased me had them in her garden. They're delicious."

Brieden smiled. "Help yourself."

"I—are you sure Dronyen won't—"

Brieden pulled his dagger from his belt, cut a panicle of white blossoms from the bush and handed it to Sehrys. "Don't worry. Brissa's ladies have been cutting fresh flowers for her rooms nearly every day. He'll never miss them."

Sehrys smiled and popped a blossom into his mouth, then closed his eyes and chewed with a pleased sigh. "Thank you for bringing me here, Brieden. I don't know what you did to get Dronyen to agree to it, but simply walking on the grass again, and seeing the sky... I can't tell you what it means to me."

"It wasn't anything, really." Brieden demurred. "He actually said you could consider it a gift from him. For your *obedience.*" Brieden rolled his eyes.

And then instantly wished he could take it back.

Sehrys dropped the lilac to the ground. "Bring me back inside," he said, voice flat.

"But—are—you just said—"

"Bring me back inside."

"But Sehrys—"

"I know that you don't have to bring me back inside. You don't have to do anything I say. But I am asking you, Brieden, *please,* to bring me back to my cell."

"But the lilac—"

"I don't want it."

"But—"

Sehrys turned to Brieden; his eyes flashed with the kind of rage he hadn't directed at Brieden for some time. "Survival is not obedience." He very nearly snarled. "I want no gifts from that man. If you refuse to take me back to my cell, that is your choice, but know that I am no longer enjoying myself."

Brieden swallowed. "Of course. I'm sorry. I'll bring you inside."

There was no further conversation or eye contact from Sehrys that night, and Brieden couldn't blame him. A fresh swell of anger rose up over Brieden: anger at Dronyen, at himself, at the entire situation. Why did he continue to wait? The carriage was ready. Sehrys was suffering. It was time to figure out exactly how he was going to manage the escape.

He walked back to the gardens, picked up Sehrys's fallen lilac blossoms and cradled the panicle as he tried not to cry. If only he hadn't said—

"I thought you'd be back for those."

Brieden whipped his head up at the voice that came out of nowhere. It belonged to a woman he did not know. She wore a tunic and breeches, which was strange, and the tight black curls on her head were cropped close. She had the dark skin and lilting accent of a Ryovnian, which would most logically make her one of Brissa's attendants, but he didn't recognize her.

"Who—"

"Never mind that. You need my help, so I'm offering it. If you want to get the elf out of here, your best bet is the night of the wedding."

Brieden's heart plummeted into his shoes. He couldn't even swallow, let alone come up with anything close to a response.

"By the old Gods, *blink.* I promise I really am here to help you, and you're damn lucky I am. That greedy bit of filth who sold you your carriage had a big mouth, and it's nothing more than blind luck that I got to him in time."

"I don't—Dronyen has simply tasked me with—I don't—"

"Save your precious breath. If you don't listen to me, you may have little of it left. Your carriage is now in my possession. On the night in question, I will advise you where to find it. If you are very smart and very fast, you may actually manage to flee the kingdom. And if you are extremely lucky, you may even make it to The Border."

Brieden narrowed his eyes. Nothing about this felt right, but he could not for the life of him conceive of her angle.

"And what do you expect in return for your assistance?" he demanded in a harsh whisper, as his eyes darted around the garden.

"I expect you not to fail. I expect you will not get caught. I expect you to keep Dronyen very distracted."

"But *why?* What on earth could you possibly hope to gain—"

"I need him distracted."

"And why—"

"You don't require any further information. Now, are you in or are you out?"

"I—" Brieden knew he shouldn't trust her. He also knew he would be an idiot to pass up such an opportunity. "I hope I am not a fool for agreeing to this."

A wide smile split the woman's face. "So you're in?"

Brieden sighed. "I'm in," he answered, accepting her outstretched hand in a firm shake.

THE NIGHT HAD COME, AND BRIEDEN COULD NOT SIT STILL. He had spent the entire week since his first meeting with the mystery woman looking over his shoulder; his heart hammered during every conversation.

So very much could go wrong, and there was no turning back.

First, there were all the things he had stolen from the palace. From Dronyen.

Then there was the fact that he had sold most of them on the black market.

And, the carriage that was waiting for him somewhere in the forest outside the city walls? The one with all the maps to the Faerie Lands and the stolen supplies from the palace? Yes, there was that, too.

And the fact that the man who had sold him the carriage had been found dead in his shop only a day before Brieden had met his strange new accomplice.

The wedding had been almost unbearable to endure, even in a service capacity, but it was the best night to make his escape. Dronyen and Brissa had already left for their honeymoon at the Panloch holiday home on the Isle of Lords, and it was up to Brieden to see that the household ran in good order while they were away.

Brieden's mystery woman had ensured him that she would take care of the palace staff and guards at the agreed-upon time, and he was relieved to see that they hadn't been "taken care of" as the carriage merchant had. The servants were occupied in late-night revelry with the plentiful leftover wine, and the guards who weren't celebrating were out cold with flasks, most likely spiked with sleeping draught, propped against their sides.

The time had come.

His heart pounding in his chest, Brieden moved quickly through the palace. This had to work. It simply *had* to. Sehrys's life, as well as his own, depended upon it. As he crept through the corridors, his heart leapt into his throat at the shadows cast by his own movements in the light of the torch in his hand. He had memorized the place where the carriage was supposed to be. He wondered—not for the first time—whether this entire arrangement might be an elaborate trap. If he incurred the risk of getting Sehrys out of the castle, after all, what was to stop the woman from slitting his throat and stealing Sehrys? Brieden swallowed hard and clutched the sword at his hip tightly.

This *had* to work. He would see to it that it did, no matter the consequences.

But when Brieden reached Sehrys's cell, he suddenly forgot himself, the plan, the urgency, the risk, all of it, helpless to do anything but *behold.*

Sehrys had used the blankets Brieden had brought him to make a nest atop his sparse straw mattress and was curled up in a pool of moonlight. He wore the freshly laundered breeches and tunic that Brieden had supplied; the lacing at his throat was loose and falling open. His lips were parted slightly, and he was so gorgeous that Brieden could barely stand to watch him.

It was the first time Brieden had seen him look anything close to peaceful.

Brieden spoke hesitantly.

"Sehrys."

No response.

Brieden repeated his name a little louder, and a little louder still and then made a thoroughly embarrassing attempt at Sehrys's full name, which he was glad Sehrys didn't awaken to hear.

He wasn't sure what to do when the elf continued his unbroken slumber. He didn't want to walk into the cell and shake him. After the sidhe had been manhandled and hurt and *raped* by Dronyen and others before him for God only knew how long, Brieden certainly wasn't going to risk touching him without permission.

Brieden drew a sharp breath and then broke the deafening quiet by rapping his keys against the bars, hard.

Sehrys jerked at the sound, sat up with a start and clutched the blanket to his chest in a white-knuckled grip.

"Sehrys," Brieden whispered. "It's me."

Sehrys gave a small, strangled noise; his bright green eyes were impossibly round with fear and confusion.

"It's Brieden." He clarified in what he hoped was a soothing tone. "Look, I know that you've just woken up and you're probably frightened, but we need to leave right now."

"I... Brieden?"

"Yes."

"Is this a dream?"

"No."

"I don't understand."

"We... we need to go. Now. Escape. Leave this place. So you can be free."

Sehrys stared at him.

"You want me to go... with you."

"Yes."

"Why?"

"Because I can't stand to see you like this. Because this life is making me into a horrible person and I've been allowing it to happen. Because—I don't know, I suppose because it would mean I was finally doing something I could be proud of."

Sehrys looked unconvinced. "*How?*"

Brieden sighed irritably. "Time is somewhat of the essence right now, Sehrys. I have been planning this for weeks. I just need you to come with me. Do you trust me?"

"No."

Brieden laughed. Right. Of course. Why in the Five Hells would Sehrys trust him? How could he have been so presumptuous?

"Do you at least trust me more than you trust Dronyen?"

"I don't know."

Oh. Well, there it was. Brieden had hoped that he'd gotten a bit farther along with Sehrys, but he clearly didn't understand how little reason the elf had to *ever* trust a human man.

Brieden fidgeted. All right then. If this really was about freeing Sehrys, and not about Brieden running off with some beautiful boy that he had convinced himself he was in love with, Brieden had to prove it—to himself as well as to Sehrys.

"Look, Sehrys. I have a carriage waiting outside the city with maps to the Faerie Lands. Dronyen and Brissa have left for the Isle of Lords, and all the palace staff are either well and truly preoccupied or in a drugged sleep, but I'm not sure how long that will last. If you want to, you can come with me, and we can try to get you home." Brieden pushed the door to the cell open slowly, wincing at its loud creak in the stillness. He began to make his way inside, but stopped abruptly when Sehrys narrowed his eyes.

"Or you can stay here," Brieden added, holding up a placating hand, "if you don't want to go. Or, you can allow me to help you escape, and you can go off on your own and never see me again as soon as we leave the province. Although I hope you might at least consider staying with me until the verbena is out of your system because you would definitely be safer that way. But the decision is yours alone. I am not going to force you to do *anything*." Brieden took another tentative step toward Sehrys; the elf's eyes were bright in the light of Brieden's torch and impossible to read. "But I will say this—if we are going to leave, we must leave right this very minute because I have a feeling that once things begin to unravel, they are going to unravel fast."

Sehrys continued to stare at him. "All right," he said finally. "Let's go."

REACHING THE COURTYARD WAS EASY, CROSSING THE PALACE walls more difficult. They discarded Brieden's torch before leaving the castle and stayed crouched in the shadows for some time, study-ing the movements of the patrolling guards—who, apparently, had not partaken of the same drink as those within the castle walls—before they were brave enough to continue. A small gate about three hundred yards from the main entrance was used primarily by groundskeepers and the like. It was barely big enough for a single person to fit through, and if their timing was good, they could slip through unnoticed.

Brieden pushed what he believed to be the appropriate stolen key into the lock on the little door.

It didn't work.

Panic rising in his chest, Brieden began to fumble through key after key; his eyes darted wildly.

He heard a delicate gasp, and saw Sehrys press back into the shadows just as Tepper, one of the night guards, approached carrying a torch.

"Who—Brieden?"

"Um, yes. Hello, Tep. I was—I couldn't sleep, so I was going for a walk in the forest."

Tepper furrowed his thick brows and came closer. "Huh."

Brieden managed a weak laugh as Tepper's long, thin face came into closer relief in the torchlight. He was about Brieden's height and quick with a sword, but very much on the slight side, and certainly the smallest of the guards. Brieden had always thought he kept his beard especially bushy as an attempt to add more bulk.

"Sometimes I just need to escape the palace walls," Brieden said with a shrug.

"Without a torch?"

"I... prefer to go walking without a torch at night on occasion. Helps to keep my reflexes sharp."

"Even so, why are you using *this* door?"

"I didn't want to bother anyone with opening the main gate."

"How did you get a key?"

"His Maj gave it to me. He wanted me to have access to everything I might need in his absence."

Tepper continued to advance; his eyes grew ever more skeptical.

"What—wait just a moment. Isn't that His Maj's sl—"

It happened so fast, Brieden almost couldn't believe it himself. As soon as Tepper was within range, Brieden threw the keys to Sehrys and shot his hand out, hitting Tepper hard in the temple with the heel of his hand.

Tepper crumpled to the ground. Brieden reached down to grab him under his armpits. Sehrys managed to unlock the door.

"Hurry!" Brieden whispered.

Brieden dragged Tepper through the gate. Sehrys stamped out Tepper's fallen torch before he followed and locked the door behind him.

"What are you going to do with him?" Sehrys whispered.

"Gag him and tie him up. I don't want anyone finding him until we are *very* far away."

"Why don't you just kill him?" The question was delivered without emotion.

Brieden looked at Sehrys "Tep's not a bad person. He... he just doesn't know any different, Sehrys. It isn't as if he deserves to *die*."

Sehrys snorted and turned away.

"What?"

"Nothing. It's just... interesting how much reverence you people seem to have for *human* life, that's all."

Brieden almost opened his mouth to reply but then decided better, and instead simply leaned over to hoist Tepper over his shoulder. He broke into a run, leading Sehrys as far away from where the carriage was hidden as he could manage without losing too much time.

Both moons were slender but visible, providing enough light to guide them through the thinner outskirts of the forest, but not so bright that Brieden didn't slow and stumble as the canopy above their heads grew denser and began to blot out the sky.

"My eyes are better in the dark than yours." Sehry's voice came from beside him. A firm but gentle arm steadied him when his toe caught on a twisted root. "I can guide you if you will point me in the right direction." His hand on Brieden's shoulder was a small but real comfort, and Brieden allowed himself to relax ever so slightly.

They moved deeper into the forest and stopped only when Brieden was confident that they were far enough from the gate. He sent Sehrys to find some strong vines while he ripped the sleeves off his own shirt, stuffing one into Tepper's mouth and using the other to tie it in place. When Sehrys returned with the vines, Brieden tied Tepper to a tree, trying to place him in as comfortable a position as he could manage.

It might be a day, perhaps even two, before he was found. But he *would* be found. When it became clear that Prince Dronyen's prized possession had been stolen, the palace guard would be combing these woods.

After Tepper was secured, Brieden took a deep breath and cast his eyes skyward. "This is the tricky part," he said to Sehrys softly. "We can't leave a trail, so try your best to stay off the ground."

They stepped on rocks and tree stumps until Brieden stopped at the base of a particular tree and motioned upward.

Brieden had his doubts as they began to climb up the branches, but when they reached the treetop, it became clear that the mystery woman had not led him astray. There truly was a pathway of thick branches from tree to tree in the canopy, and the moonlight was bright enough to guide their way. Sehrys rose to his feet and strode ahead along the canopy path when he understood where they were headed, nearly as graceful and sure-footed as he was on land.

Brieden, on the other hand, crept along slowly on his stomach, gripping the branches with his arms and thighs, willing himself not to fall. They didn't travel far, but it was as if a tiny eternity had passed before he heard the soft nickering and shuffling of horses ahead of them.

When Brieden finally spied the carriage, its headlamps glowing soft but sure against the darkness, he paused. "Wait here," he whispered. "I... I need to check that it is safe to proceed."

Brieden climbed down as nimbly as he could and pulled his sword from its scabbard as soon as his feet touched the ground. Body poised to react, he crept toward the carriage slowly. The ink-black forest air pressed into him from all sides. He could neither hear nor sense the presence of anyone besides Sehrys and himself, but he wasn't willing to risk being wrong. Slowly, he reached his hand out toward the handle on the carriage door. The door swung open on its own, and he leapt backward. He braced himself; his posture was defensive, and his sword was held aloft.

Brieden's mystery woman looked out at him, her cocky eyebrow somehow still distinct in the darkness.

"There you are. I was beginning to think you might have been intercepted. Or perhaps found your courage lacking."

Although her voice was almost a whisper, Brieden nearly flinched at how loud it sounded in the near-silence of the forest.

"I'm here," Brieden replied without lowering his sword.

"Did anyone see you?"

"One. But... it's been taken care of."

The woman narrowed her eyes at Brieden. "Is that so?"

"He has been detained. Please, there is no need to kill him, I—"

"I believe it would be best to allow me to be the judge of that. Where is the elf?"

"He is near."

"Near."

"Near. And that is all I will tell you until I have determined this is not a trap."

"You believe I devised all of this to trap you?"

"Perhaps to... to set me up. To make it look as if I tried to steal the sidhe, so that you could kill me and steal him yourself."

The woman stepped out of the carriage. "That would be a good plan," she conceded. "Were I interested in turning a profit in the slave trade, I might have considered it. But that is not my motive, and I have no designs on your elf."

"He isn't *my*—"

The woman sighed. "We are wasting time. What do you require, boy, a blood oath? I have never pretended that this is an act of altruism, at least not entirely. I need you gone, and I need you gone soon if I'm to have enough time to forge a false trail. You aren't any good to me if you get caught, especially this early on."

Brieden swallowed.

Do you trust me?

No.

He couldn't ask Sehrys to take a greater risk than he was willing to take himself, no matter how little he trusted this woman.

"All right. Sehrys!" Brieden called. "If you would still like to accompany me, we must leave now."

After a pause that was just long enough for Brieden to question whether Sehrys had continued on his own path through the treetops and left Brieden behind, the sidhe dropped neatly to the ground beside him, considering both the woman and Brieden with curious eyes.

"Do not worry, *esil kryshi*, I will be on my way," the woman said, offering Sehrys a slight bow. "This one will bring you to safety," she added, gesturing at Brieden. Sehrys raised his eyebrows and looked as if he were about to speak, before changing his mind and closing his mouth. A thoughtful expression lingered on his face.

"You understand the route?" she asked Brieden. He nodded, pushing his curiosity away for the moment.

"All right then. Make haste."

She was gone, barely making a sound as she sprinted into the night.

Brieden motioned with his head for Sehrys to climb inside the carriage and then circled it to make sure that all was in place.

Brieden concentrated on taking deep breaths as he prepared the horses. A broad skirt of weighted horsehair attached to the back of the carriage would wipe their path clean. They wouldn't be following any formal trail, but the hand-drawn map given to Brieden by the woman outlined a tricky, winding path that would take them to a road far outside the city walls, nearly outside the province. They had planned as much as possible. Now they had only luck and divine providence on which to rely. Brieden disrobed quickly, eager to put distance between himself and the kingdom he had chosen to betray.

When Brieden opened the carriage door, Sehrys saw that he was clad only in his underthings and gasped; a look of dread and dawning comprehension moved across his features.

Brieden's eyes widened. "Oh! No... I... I have to change. This is only going to work if people think that you... that I own you." Brieden flinched at his own words. "I have to appear to be a wealthy man. I have some things in here. Could you please pass me that satchel?"

Wordlessly, Sehrys did so.

Also wordlessly, Brieden dressed.

He took a deep breath before turning back to Sehrys and addressing him with far more confidence than he felt. "Sehrys, I am going to get us as far away from here as possible. These are fast horses and I am going to drive them hard. When we have put enough distance between ourselves and Villalu Proper, we can take a break, but until then, why don't you go ahead and get some sleep? And you may as well keep this with you, just... just in case." He handed Sehrys a finely crafted dagger in an oiled leather sheath.

Sehrys simply took the dagger and nodded, settling back into the plush velvet seat.

Brieden climbed to the perch at the front of the carriage and grabbed the reins.

This was it.

He was leaving.

And Sehrys was coming with him.

Brieden gave the reins a firm pull, and they sped off into the night.

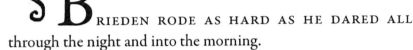

CHAPTER TWO

BRIEDEN RODE AS HARD AS HE DARED ALL through the night and into the morning.

He didn't want to wreck the horses, but he didn't want to get caught either. He couldn't be sure how soon the palace guard would come after them, no matter how convincing a false trail his accomplice laid. He didn't know how hard Dronyen would pursue them once he discovered what Brieden had done; the prince went through quite a lot of sidhe slaves, after all. He used and abused them until they were either too permanently injured for him to enjoy, or until one day they were simply, discreetly gone.

Killing one's property wasn't illegal, though it was considered quite crass to draw attention to it.

But Sehrys was different. And Brieden was denying Dronyen the pleasure of breaking him.

It was possible that Dronyen would pursue them hard. It was possible that he might realize how rare and precious Sehrys was, even if it was for the most horrific reasons.

And then there was Brieden. Dronyen would most likely be *shaking* with rage at the audacity of his betrayal. A peasant, given a plum position at court, positioned to become Dronyen's next right-hand man. And now this.

Dronyen would want to set an example. If Dronyen or any of his men ever found them, they would kill Brieden. Pure and simple.

Or not so pure and simple. In all likelihood, Dronyen would prefer to kill him dirty and complicated.

Dronyen would publicly torture him, and it wouldn't surprise Brieden if it lasted for weeks. But Brieden had known this from the very start, from the instant he had decided to free Sehrys.

Brieden prayed for one thing and one thing only: That they wouldn't be discovered before the verbena had left Sehrys's blood. Even if they caught and killed Brieden, even if they broke his mind, body and soul into a million jagged pieces, they wouldn't be able to touch Sehrys at full power. They wouldn't even get close to him.

He didn't know why he was prepared to die for Sehrys. It didn't make sense, even to himself, but he couldn't remember ever feeling anything more real.

Brieden drove until he could barely keep his eyes open, until his stiff muscles were screaming with pain. He followed the course that had been set, bringing them along what he hoped would be the least likely route to attract Dronyen's men.

When they had finally gone far enough, when he believed that neither he nor the horses could take any more, he led them off the dirt road into the woods. He found a suitable clearing and eased himself from his perch; his knees buckled as soon as his legs touched the ground.

Brieden allowed himself to simply lie like that. He was fairly certain he even dozed a bit. Sounds and images flashed across the periphery of his consciousness and he couldn't feel his body at all, which had definitely become a blessing.

After an indeterminate period of time—a moment? an hour? two? five?—Brieden roused himself; his head was spinning with everything he needed to do.

It was full daylight, and the horses were grazing on grass and drinking from a stream at the edge of the clearing. The tent he had packed was pitched between two oak trees, and that warm, woody smell *hadn't* just been part of a vivid dream because Sehrys had started a crackling fire. The elf leaned over a bubbling cauldron; an incredibly appetizing smell mingled with the wood smoke.

And—was that?—yes. Brieden was wrapped in a blanket.

He sat up slowly, testing his ability to move. He groaned when he attempted a stretch, and Sehrys turned to look at him.

His eyes held a softness that Brieden hadn't seen before. Brieden's breath caught and his head spun.

"Hi," Brieden managed, grinning widely.

"Hi." Sehrys didn't return his smile, but the softness in his eyes remained. Brieden had broken through, just a little bit.

"You... you didn't have to do all this. I was going to—"

"Keel over and die? Yes, you were. I can't believe you pushed the horses that hard. They were barely in better shape than you. Poor things."

Brieden sighed. "I had to get us as far away as possible."

"I understand that. But Brieden, can we please stay here at least until tomorrow? The horses need to rest. You need to rest. You're no good to me if you can't even stand up on your own."

Brieden tried to mute his excitement, reel in his smile. Sehrys still looked wary and wound tight, but...

"So, you're planning on staying with me then?"

Sehrys quickly returned his attention to the cauldron. "Yes, for now, if your offer still stands. You're right about the verbena. As weak as I am right now, I wouldn't last a week out here on my own. I would get caught and sold again, and the next owner might be even worse than Dronyen."

"I don't think that's possible," Brieden replied; his voice was hard and quiet.

Sehrys was silent for a moment.

"Even so. I think I'm quite done with being treated like the property of human men."

Brieden couldn't bear to meet Sehrys's eyes. "I'm sorry, Sehrys," he said. He sounded broken even to his own ears.

Sehrys's gaze lingered on him. He offered a nod of acknowledgment before turning back to the cauldron.

Sehrys had made an incredible stew from dried herbs that Brieden had packed, as well as vegetables and roots that he had found in the forest while Brieden had slumbered.

"Why didn't you use any of the dried meat or fish I packed, Sehrys?" Brieden asked, as he tucked into the meal. "There's plenty."

Sehrys looked down into his bowl for a moment, almost afraid, as if he expected to be slapped.

"No... I didn't mean—it's perfect the way it is," Brieden assured. "I just wanted to make sure that you realize you can use whatever you need. Help yourself. All of this is as much yours as mine."

Sehrys glanced at him uncertainly. "Thank you, Brieden, but I prefer not to eat animal flesh."

Brieden raised his eyebrows. "Oh. But you always—"

"I always ate what I had to eat in order to stay alive. I've done many unpleasant things in order to stay alive. But my body doesn't digest it well, and to be honest, it pains my heart to eat it. So if it's perfectly all right with you, I think I won't."

"Of course it's all right. I just... I didn't know. I hope I brought enough other things."

Sehrys smiled. "I'm very good at finding plants, and there are many things that I can eat that you cannot, so keep the meat for yourself and we should be fine."

"What kinds of things do you usually eat?" Brieden asked. "When you were—before you were—"

"Enslaved?"

"Yes."

Sehrys shrugged. "Leaves, mostly, and flowers. Roots and grasses, fruits on occasion. For example, this"—Sehrys plucked a leathery-looking leaf from the shrub beside him—"would suit me fine." He popped the leaf in his mouth and ate it with relish.

Brieden smiled. "What's your favorite thing to eat?"

"Honeysuckle."

Brieden almost clapped his hands. "I knew it! My grandmother—she *told* me sidhe love honeysuckle. We used to leave baskets of it on the back steps at the full moon so they would bless our home."

Sehrys looked intrigued. "*Where* exactly are you from?"

"Ravurmik. It's a small village on the Dragonsmouth peninsula, northwest of the kingdom proper."

Sehrys nodded. "I've heard of it. There are some nomadic feririars in that area. Not much of a slave trade, as I understand it."

"No. I didn't even know about the slave trade until I was thirteen years old. The first sidhe I ever saw was free."

Sehrys smiled. Brieden's heart jumped.

"He was beautiful..."

Brieden tried to stop himself. He did. He truly did. But he couldn't.

"...Like you."

Iron gates crashed down behind Sehrys's eyes, locking him up tight. That one perfect smile that Brieden had finally managed to coax from him disappeared without a trace. Sehrys wrapped his arms around his torso and clenched his jaw before turning his face away from Brieden.

Brieden swallowed. "I'm sorry, Sehrys, I shouldn't have—"

"What do you want from me, Brieden? Please tell me the truth."

"I just want to help—"

"Stop." Sehrys turned back to Brieden, fierce eyes burning into him with such intensity that Brieden nearly jumped. "I don't want to hear about your desire to help me, and how you want to be a good person, and how this is some twisted path to redemption for you. I want you to tell me *why* you are doing this, and I want you to tell me right now."

Brieden stared into that deep, flashing green and felt the demand down to his very core, as if Sehrys were siphoning the truth out of him with his eyes.

"Because I'm in love with you."

Sehrys's eyes widened. "Oh, Gods," he whimpered.

"I'm sorry! I—it's true, Sehrys. From the first moment I saw you, I—"

"It isn't true."

"Yes, it is! Sehrys, I—"

"You *don't* love me, Brieden," he spat, curling his arms around himself more tightly. "You love the *idea* of loving me. You barely even know me. You see me as some frail, delicate creature to rescue, and then what? I'm supposed to give myself to you? And it's *different* than Dronyen paying for me and keeping me like a possession because you view it as some sort of romantic tale? Because you *deserve* me? Because you've cast yourself as the noble hero?"

"Sehrys, No! That's not—"

"Fine," Sehrys said, his voice growing dangerously honeyed and his eyes sparking with malice. "Because I'm *not* a frail and delicate creature, Brieden. As I said before, I do what I have to do in order to survive. And this is nothing new. I understand. You are doing something for me, so I should give you something in return."

He crawled over to Brieden and climbed onto his lap. Brieden froze.

"So, you're the romantic sort. What will it be? Kisses and sweet nothings beneath the moonlight? *Love*making, slow and gentle and face to face?" Sehrys purred.

He kissed Brieden on the lips. A jolt slammed Brieden back into the present moment. He leapt to his feet, sending Sehrys tumbling.

Brieden touched his fingers to his lips, overwhelmed by the confusion swirling in his gut. How was it possible for something to feel so wonderful and so utterly wrong all at once?

"No," Brieden whispered, voice shaking, as he looked down at Sehrys. "I don't want *this,* Sehrys. I don't."

Sehrys stared up, eyes like an electric storm. "Then... then *what* do you *want* from me?" he wailed before collapsing into tears.

The intensity of his breakdown surpassed even those gut-wrenching sobs Brieden remembered from Sehrys's first night at Dronyen's castle. Sehrys's face fell into his hands and his elbows fell onto his knees. Brieden crouched and very, very gingerly touched Sehrys's shoulder. When Sehrys flinched, he withdrew his hand.

So Brieden sat down beside him and waited.

Sehrys cried for a long, long time. There was rage in it, and there was pain in it too, but mostly there was deep fear.

Brieden wanted to hold him so, *so* badly.

When the tears finally began to subside, Sehrys looked at Brieden through bloodshot eyes, his question still hanging between them.

"I don't know what to say, Sehrys," Brieden sighed. "Maybe what I'm feeling isn't true, I don't know, but I believe it is. And what I *want* is for you to be free and happy, even if I have to die to make it happen. And what I *don't* want is for you to kiss me, or... or touch me in any way, unless it's what *you* want to do. Not because you think you owe me or I expect it, but because you want it. And if you never want it... that's all right too."

Sehrys tucked his knees to his chin, looking miserable. "I don't think I can believe you."

Brieden shrugged. "Maybe I haven't earned that yet. I hope I do, eventually." He smiled at Sehrys. It was a careful smile, and to his surprise, Sehrys actually smiled back. It washed over Brieden like a warm bath.

"I hope so too," Sehrys replied softly.

That night, they slept on opposite sides of the tent.

Brieden slept fitfully and found himself gazing at Sehrys between patches of slumber. It was hard to see him in the darkness of the tent, but Brieden could make out the outline of his body, the rise and fall of his chest. He could hear the near-musical soft breathing, and the comfort it gave him was overwhelming.

Brieden didn't realize that he wasn't the only one with open eyes in the tent.

He didn't see Sehrys sneaking gazes of his own when Brieden's breathing evened into sleep. He didn't see him tracing the curve of his body, from shoulder to hip, with his eyes. He didn't see him falling asleep with a smile on his lips when he had finally stared so long that he could no longer keep his eyes open.

And he did not realize that, for the first time in many, many years, Sehrys slept without fear.

CHAPTER THREE

BRISSA AWOKE TO THE SMELL OF THE SEA.

For the tiniest of moments, she could almost believe that she was at home on Ryovni, that she could look out her bedroom window and see Cliope sitting on the perch outside her own bedroom window, examining the stars.

It was certainly a night for it. The greater moon was a thin, curved blade in the heavens above, the dwarf moon barely visible at all where it trailed behind.

As slowly and gently as possible, Brissa lifted Dronyen's arm where it lay heavy across her chest. She twisted free of the sheets and lowered her bare feet to the cold stone floor. Every cell devoted to silence, she moved toward the narrow, open window across the room.

If it hurts too much, sister, look at the stars. I promise I will be looking at them too.

The sea lapped gently on the little beach below, and she knew that this would be far easier than she could possibly have imagined.

Only two guards had accompanied them on the ship, after all, and her ladies had seen to them. No one but she was awake on the whole of the estate. She could feel the truth of that in her very lungs.

It shouldn't have surprised her. The Panlochs had been too long in power, and none had challenged them in ten generations. What need had they for a night watch at their holiday estate?

Brissa did not take a torch as she made her way through the tower and down to the lower level. *Island girls do not fear the dark.* She did not take a torch as she slipped outside and made her way down to beach. *Even the blindest island girl can find her way to the sea with a sure and graceful foot.*

When her feet sank into the cool wet sand at the shoreline, she nearly wept with relief. She bent to cup the icy water, running it over her arms and embracing the salty gooseflesh that arose in response.

"Island girls have salted blood," she whispered into the night, voice a papery echo against the gently breaking waves. "Island girls serve no mortal thing." She touched her cool fingertips to her forehead, anointing herself with drops of seawater. "Island girls serve only the sea and the lines of ley and the sands that carpet the world."

Brissa pulled her nightgown over her head and tossed it onto the dry sand before wading deeper.

"Guardian, cleanse me," she whispered, with almost no breath; her lips barely formed the words, and the tears that had threatened to fall for so long finally began to gather behind her eyes. For the first time since her wedding night, she allowed her shoulders to relax, let her body feel the pain that wouldn't subside and allowed the tears to flow.

She dove beneath the water, raced into its pure embrace with strong limbs born of years of daily swimming. When she surfaced, her tears were still flowing, but she did not bother to fight them away. Instead, she allowed them to warm her face as she floated on her back and breathed deep, her lungs like something freshly born.

She was queen.

Brissa floated in the sea and looked up at the stars and felt small.

Chapter Four

FOR THE FIRST TWO WEEKS OF THEIR JOURNEY,
they kept to back roads and wooded paths. Eventually they would
have to venture into a more populated area to gather supplies, but
both men hoped to put that off until it was necessary. Even so,
skirting the edges of civilized society did not mean they wouldn't
encounter other travelers, and they could ill afford the suspicion
of strangers, especially this close to the capital.

Brieden needed, above all else, to keep up the ruse that he was a
wealthy man. And wealthy men did not walk about with knotted
balls of misshapen fuzz upon their heads.

And so he found himself battling frustration as he sat by the
creek beside which they had set up camp early one evening, trying
to force his hair into some semblance of order. He had just begun
to debate whether shaving it off without a proper mirror was wise
when Sehrys approached, carrying the basket he used for gathering
roots and flowers.

"May I?" He settled beside Brieden in the grass and pulled their
mortar and pestle out of the basket, along with a handful of what
looked like small, dirty stones and some glossy flat brown leaves.

Brieden furrowed his brow and lowered his hands from the
embarrassing nest that was his hair. "May you...?"

"I belonged to Lady Jichyn for perhaps two years." Sehrys dipped his feet into the creek and bent to scrub the little stones clean with his fingers. "The Jichyns control the Dragonsmouth province; I believe that is where you are from?"

Brieden swallowed the lump that pulsed in his throat; Sehrys had been so close. "Yes. I remember when she died. It wasn't terribly long ago."

"It wasn't," Sehrys agreed and began squeezing the little stones one by one, revealing their true nature as tubers when their tough skins gave way to soft, oily pulp, which Sehrys began scraping into the mortar with practiced hands. "It was her son who put me to market when Dronyen bought me. She was the least cruel master I had by far, and thankfully not a Frilauan. She even provided me with a bed."

Brieden tried to smile, with limited success.

"I was mostly tasked with seeing that her skin stayed soft and supple, that her baths were always hot and fragrant and that her hair always fell in glossy curls." He smiled. "Few others thought to let their sidhe put their knowledge of plants to use. Not that she ever suggested it to those in her social circle; she quite enjoyed having the most beautiful hair in eastern Villalu."

Brieden laughed. "You're not suggesting that you can tame this wild nest, are you?" He gestured at his own head.

Sehrys smiled. "You'd be amazed at some of the magic I can work, even without my powers."

Brieden swallowed, throat suddenly dry, as he watched Sehrys squeeze the leaves in his fists before adding them to the mortar, slowly turning the substance within into a thick, shiny paste.

"Wet your hair," Sehrys instructed, as he dipped a finger into the bowl and rubbed the paste between his thumb and forefinger, looking satisfied at the consistency he found.

Brieden did, then allowed Sehrys to settle behind him and begin working the paste into his hair. The heat of Sehrys's body against his back, the soft breath on his neck and the long, nimble fingers working their way gently into his hair were reassuring and more than a little bit overwhelming. Brieden allowed his eyes to drift closed, as he took in the earthy scent of the plants Sehrys massaged into his tangled locks.

"You don't..." Brieden murmured, trying to force himself into a sense of conviction. "You shouldn't do slave things for me. I don't—"

"Hush," Sehrys admonished, tugging a lock of Brieden's hair for emphasis. "This isn't a *slave thing*. I used to do this for my sister when we were young and for my betrothed when I was older. It isn't a slave thing unless choice and intent make it so."

"But you had no choice—"

"I always had a choice. I could have chosen to let her beat me. Or sell me to someone far worse. Or hang me to set an example for the others. I chose to obey and to make myself useful. But that isn't the choice I am making at this moment, Brieden. I am choosing to share a kindness with you. It may be the same act, but it isn't the same thing at all."

"And your intent?"

"With her, my intent was to keep myself safe. With you, my intent is to make you happy. Could you please pass me the comb?"

Brieden bit back a smile as he peered into the basket Sehrys had brought, finding within it a wide-toothed wooden comb that the elf must have carved. Brieden winced, steeling himself for the painful tug of it forced through his tangled, wiry locks. But the pain never came.

"How—are you actually managing to get that through my hair?"

The warm sound of Sehrys's laugh washed through Brieden pleasantly. "Yes. It's a crime that people in your region, with thick hair like yours, haven't discovered this treatment yourselves, though I imagine some must have; cochut pods aren't good for much else."

Sehrys combed through Brieden's hair slowly, then tied it back in its usual style.

"Leave that in for at least two hours," Sehrys instructed as he rinsed his hands and the comb in the creek.

"Thank you," Brieden said, as he turned to face the elf. "That was so kind of you, really, you didn't have to—"

"I told you I wanted to," Sehrys assured him with a slight roll of his eyes. "It's for my own benefit too. I do have to look at you every day."

Brieden's cheeks flushed as he laughed. He glanced down at the mortar, seeing that there was still quite a bit of the paste left inside.

"Could I... would you like me to... do yours? You certainly don't need it the way I did, but if you'd like?" Brieden shrugged.

"I—" Sehrys closed his mouth as quickly as he'd opened it; his face became contemplative.

"I just thought you might—"

"Yes."

"Oh. Um. Yes?"

Sehrys fixed Brieden with a smile that could have lit up the entire forest. "Yes. It's been a long time since anyone else has tended to my hair like that. Thank you."

"Of course." Brieden watched Sehrys step into the creek and bend to wet his hair.

Smoothing the paste through Sehrys's silky locks was entirely different but just as pleasurable as having his own hair tended. The feel of Sehrys's wet hair between his fingers sent an unexpected pulse of contentment through Brieden's body, and he could feel the other man relax, letting out the tiniest sigh of pleasure as Brieden massaged his scalp. Sehrys's hair was even more captivating than usual in the fading afternoon light; streaks of plum and scarlet and violet glinted like ropes of precious jewels.

"Tell me of your life before?" Brieden asked, as he worked his fingers through Sehrys's hair. "You said you have a sister? And a... betrothed?" Brieden's throat felt thick as he swallowed around that last statement, but he did his best to keep his voice even.

"I *had* a sister," he corrected wistfully. "I had a betrothed. But he... I don't know what I have any longer. It's been so long since..." Sehrys sighed. "I was born a twin, but my sister fell ill when we were very young. She was a child when she died."

"I'm so sorry," Brieden whispered, biting his lip.

"It was a long time ago. But thank you. It... it's somehow reassuring, sometimes. I still miss her every day, but at least I know what's become of her. There's nothing left to wonder about."

"You won't have to wonder about anyone else for long."

Sehrys turned to look at Brieden over his shoulder; his hair slipped from Brieden's hands.

"I suppose not, if luck is truly with us. I have you to thank for that, Brieden, and I... I do want you to know that I am truly grateful."

Brieden shook his head and lowered his eyes. "No. I—you were right, before. This isn't some romantic tale, and I'm not a hero of any sort."

"Brieden." Sehrys turned around to face him completely. When Brieden looked up, Sehrys's lips were quirked into a smile, his eyes were cool but gentle. "I did not say you were a hero. I simply said I was grateful. Take it for what it is, rather than what you wish it to be."

Brieden returned Sehrys's smile. "I don't wish you to see me as a hero."

Sehrys raised an eyebrow.

"I *don't*!" He insisted with a laugh. "I do wish I weren't so skilled at always seeming to say the wrong thing to you, and I cannot help what I feel, but I truly don't see you as a prize I wish to win."

Sehrys stared at him for a long moment, with droplets from his wet hair running lazily down his pale skin. "Who was that woman?" he finally asked.

"Who—"

"That woman. The one who met us at the carriage on the outskirts of the city. She spoke to me in Elfin."

"Oh. I honestly don't know."

"The two of you seemed acquainted."

"She approached me about a week before we made our escape. She never told me her name, but she said she wanted to help us."

Sehrys sighed. "I need you to understand why it is difficult to trust you when you tell me things like that."

"But it's *true*."

"It doesn't make any sense."

"That doesn't make it any less true. I was... I was already planning this, but apparently the man who sold me the carriage betrayed my trust. That may be how she found out about me, but I never told her I was planning to free you." Brieden took a deep breath. "I think she killed him."

Sehrys's eyes widened. "The carriage merchant?" Brieden nodded. "But why?"

"I... I know you probably don't believe me, but it didn't make any more sense to me than it makes to you. She said I didn't need to know why she was doing it, just that she needed Dronyen distracted."

"Which could mean we are no more than pawns in some greater scheme."

Brieden shrugged. "As long as we are pawns who make it to The Border, I can't say I'm terribly concerned. She doesn't know the route we're taking now that we've left the capital."

"She looked familiar," Sehrys mused. "Definitely Ryovnian, if I were to wager a guess, but she didn't look like one of Brissa's ladies."

"Brissa brought quite an entourage," Brieden pointed out, recalling how Dronyen had paled at the sheer number of them as they entered the palace gates. "I've never seen a lady with so many attendants. If the woman who helped us had disguised herself as a proper serving woman—"

"Perhaps," Sehrys murmured, head cocked to the side and eyes lost in thought.

"What did she call you?" Brieden asked. "Before we left?"

"*Kryshi*. It means sibling, though not always in a literal sense. But it isn't something one would normally call a stranger."

"That... that's a good sign, isn't it?"

"She wanted me to trust her," Sehrys replied. "It doesn't mean that I should. And it doesn't mean that you should either. We may have served our purpose for her, or there may be more to come. We cannot let our guard down because of something that seems like no more than a stroke of luck."

Brieden rolled his eyes. "We're on the run from the law, Sehrys. At best, this woman has used us as bait, and I'm surely a wanted criminal by now. I would hardly say that our guard is down."

"Perhaps it isn't up high enough," Sehrys said, his voice slightly clipped. "Particularly for me. I'm not going to lie to you, Brieden. You still seem to be hiding things from me. Why would two humans at court risk their safety to set me free?"

"Sehrys, I told you—"

"I know what you told me." Sehrys sighed. His eyes were suddenly tired and sad as he pulled himself to his feet. "Don't touch your hair until after dinner. I picked some greens and mushrooms earlier that will make a nice soup with some of the things we already have. I'll get started on it."

Brieden nodded, heart lodged in his throat. "I'll collect some wood for the fire," he offered to Sehrys's already-retreating form.

He pulled on his boots and headed into the forest, grateful, if nothing else, for a bit of space to think.

In truth, Brieden didn't know what he wanted.

He did wish Sehrys would trust him, of course, but he understood the cost to the elf of placing his trust a human man. But what Brieden truly wished...

His grandmother had told him that love wasn't selfish, and as with everything she told him, Brieden believed her. But he couldn't pretend there was no selfishness in his motivation. Brieden *did* want something from him, although it may not have been what Sehrys feared.

He wanted to see Sehrys running up a riverbank, laughing and strong and free. He wanted the truth of Sehrys's life to match the truth in his eyes.

But more deeply than that, selfishly, Brieden wanted to greet death eye to eye when it came to claim him, rather than lowering his gaze in shame. Rescuing Sehrys had been the first true choice Brieden had made since his decision to creep out of his cottage that night at the age of twelve. Sehrys had jolted him out of the passivity of overachievement he'd settled into: He had been an excellent student as a boy, and so offered the sort of educational opportunity at the Academy of which few of his social class dared to dream. The Academy wasn't the only option his academic achievement afforded him, but it was the most prestigious, and it was the one his mother had insisted upon.

And so he went. He had a good mind for the running of a household, an innate sense of how to appear trustworthy to his social betters and an excellent hand with a sword. He had graduated at the top of his class and had been offered a place with Dronyen

Panloch, the man who would be crowned king as soon as he settled on a bride.

And so he went, even though he was well aware that the Panlochs were strident Frilauans, that it had likely been Dronyen's father who had ordered the raid on Brieden's village that had bloodied his life beyond repair. Although Brieden knew he would likely be much happier in service to the Lajecs or the Arkerofts, the House of Panloch was considered the pinnacle of achievement for a man of his training. Brieden did not even consider it a choice. He went.

And then he had laid eyes on Sehrys, and just like that he *had* to make a choice. A wild, reckless, dangerous and utterly illogical choice. One that gave him nothing but a future of vivid, urgent choices, each more terrifying than the next. And one that put the luxury of passivity far beyond his scrambling grasp, perhaps forever.

Ever since he had made that choice, his heart had become something freshly born. It hammered in his chest, strong with certainty; his muscles felt more at ease than they ever had, even as they tensed at every unexpected sound, even as he reached for his sword far too many times during each day. If he perished in his mission, freeing Sehrys would still be the most perfect decision he had ever made.

"What I want from you," he whispered, listening to the quiet sounds of Sehrys preparing dinner off in the distance, "is to give you the very thing you have given me. What I want is to give you your freedom."

.

CHAPTER FIVE

THEY HAD BEEN JOURNEYING FOR ABOUT THREE weeks when Brieden finally asked about it.

They were driving along at a reasonably mellow pace. The trees that lined the dirt road dappled the sunlight as the scent of oak and pine trees drifted by on lazy winds. It was a warm and pleasant day; they had recently taken food and drink; and Sehrys was feeling pleased at his decision to name the horses. They were steadfast and devoted companions, after all, and Sehrys couldn't imagine where they would be without them. He had happily pronounced the coal-black mare Raven and her equally black gelding companion Crow, and Brieden had professed to liking the names very much.

Sehrys was driving. They had both agreed that it would look odd if Brieden were holding the reins instead of this "slave" if another human crossed their path. Brieden had joined Sehrys on the perch, however; their arms occasionally brushed lightly as Sehrys handled the reins.

"Sehrys," Brieden began, his sweet, deep voice a pleasant complement to the birdsong in the trees around them. "I was wondering... I—I mean, you don't have to answer me if you would rather not talk about it, but I was, um, wondering... I mean..."

Sehrys smiled. He had found himself smiling more in the past few weeks than he had in the last six years. Brieden was quite endearing when he became nervous and flustered.

"It's all right, Brieden, you can ask me. If I don't want to answer you, I won't."

Brieden smiled back. "I was only wondering when, and maybe how you were... you know, caught?" Brieden blinked and fixed his eyes on the road ahead as soon as the question left his lips.

Sehrys took some time to consider the request. He wasn't sure if he wanted to talk about it. Then again, his third elder had always told him that the Gods created language to heal the soul. Sehrys hadn't spoken to anyone about his experience. His owners obviously hadn't cared to hear it, and what few other sidhe he had been allowed to converse with from time to time didn't want to talk about the horror that was their capture and enslavement. They wanted to talk about their old lives, their true lives. They wanted to speak in their native tongue with another being just to remind themselves that it hadn't been a dream, that life hadn't always been about desperation and raw survival.

But Sehrys still didn't know quite what to think about this strange man who had sacrificed everything to help him. He, in equal parts, wanted to trust Brieden and wanted to decipher his scheme. Was Brieden really planning to sell Sehrys to someone else? If so, why the good-natured ruse, when all he would have to do was bind him in iron and throw him in the back of the carriage? Was he simply toying with him? Had he been dishonest about his lack of expectations? And if so, how exactly did any of this benefit Brieden?

One thing was certain. Brieden was either unimaginably kind or unimaginably cruel.

Sehrys forced himself to consider the possibility that Brieden was in fact a cruel man, even though he couldn't muster the ability to believe it. He wasn't sure if his growing faith in Brieden was comforting or terrifying. And if Brieden were actually in love with Sehrys as he claimed...

Sehrys had heard that not all human men in Villalu looked down upon The Sidhe. He had never experienced this lack of prejudice personally outside of the border cities, and it was more than a little unnerving. But Brieden didn't merely view Sehrys as his equal. He had been taught by his elder to *revere* The Sidhe. Sehrys had also heard about that; he knew that things had been quite different in the long-ago. But the long-ago for The Sidhe was the very, *very* long-ago for the human race, whose lives were so short they treated the stretch of a single generation like an eternity.

Sehrys, not for the first time, wished that he'd made the effort to learn more about human society before his Rite. If he had known more, he wouldn't have let himself fall asleep in that clearing, completely at ease, as if nothing in the world could touch him.

It had been his first journey into Villalu. He hadn't made it back for his wedding the following day.

"Well," Sehrys finally began, his voice soft and a bit shaky. Brieden blinked, startled, and turned to face him. He probably hadn't expected Sehrys to answer him after such an extended silence.

"Sehrys, you don't ha—"

"Brieden, hush. This isn't like asking me about a trip to the market. It's going to make me upset. Are you going to be able to withstand that?"

Brieden swallowed, but nodded when Sehrys looked at him out of the corner of his eye. Sehrys returned his attention to the road ahead, barely able to endure the weight of Brieden's eyes on him as he spoke. A sweet twist of breeze made the trees around them rustle and soothed him. Grounded him. The world around him may have been nothing like the prismatic forests of his homeland, but there was something essentially familiar nonetheless.

He focused on the reins in his hands, the loamy smell of the air, the patterns that the sunlight made on the road before them, and spoke.

"All right then. It was about six years ago, I believe, I'm not entirely sure. I try to pay attention to the seasons and the moon, but I was in a dungeon for, I believe, a few months at one point, which threw off my orientation a bit."

"S-six *years?* A dungeon... oh, Sehrys..."

"I was on a traditional trek called the Nuptial Rite. All young sidhe must complete the Rite on the day before they are married. We journey to one of several sacred sites, and we are supposed to... hmmm... we call it soul-walking? A bit like meditation, I suppose, but with the aid of a mild hallucinogen. The point is to take stock of oneself, of one's betrothed. The soul-walker takes the journey alone, speaks to no one, and then returns to officially declare the intent to marry or the intent to withdraw from the union. It's usually more of a formality than anything else, but I..." Sehrys swallowed a lump that had presented itself in his throat and took several deep, slow breaths.

In the distance, the babble of a stream grew more pronounced as the foliage around them grew increasingly dense. The thick-trunked trees with broad, round white-green leaves had begun to overtake oak, evergreen and maple as they moved westward into the Darmon lands, and it suddenly occurred to Sehrys that he didn't know what they were called.

"So they trapped you while you were med—uh, soul-walking?" Brieden prompted gently.

Sehrys sighed. "No. The site is on protected ground. But the journey from my village to the site took me through Western Villalu, just for a few miles. And I... I was incredibly stupid. I was incredibly young and incredibly stupid, Brieden, and that is how I got caught."

"Sehrys, it wasn't your fault. You can't think—"

"No, it wasn't my fault. But it could have been avoided. I actually stopped and took a nap on Villaluan soil!" Sehrys laughed harshly. "I had just finished the Rite, I was on my way home and I was ready to marry him. Everything was just so perfect. It was a beautiful day, much like this one, in fact, and I stopped to rest and eat some sweet grasses. I fell asleep, and when I woke up there were men throwing iron chains across me."

Brieden looked at him with enormous brimming brown eyes.

Those eyes had an effect on Sehrys that he didn't understand.

Sehrys wasn't sure whether he should share this next part. Perhaps it was too intimate, perhaps simply too much. But he had never said it out loud, and perhaps it was time that he did.

"That first night..." Sehrys took a deep, shaking breath, his eyes fixed hard on the road ahead and not on Brieden.

"I... I had never been intimate with anyone before. My wedding night was going to be my first time. But they... they just passed me around and did what they liked. Most of them just grabbed at me and—but one of them..." Sehrys shook his head as if it could clear his mind of the memory. "Gods, it was so terrifying."

Sehrys hated that he had started crying again. He hated that Brieden was probably crying too. He hated that the story made him sound like such a weak, pathetic victim.

Brieden gently took the reins and pulled them to a stop.

"Sehrys, may I hug you?"

The sweetness and formality of the request just made Sehrys cry harder, but he found himself nodding because he hadn't been hugged in six long years.

Brieden gently pulled Sehrys to him and wrapped his arms tenderly around the sidhe's trembling body. Sehrys leaned into the embrace, rested his head in the crook of Brieden's neck and allowed himself to fall apart completely as Brieden stroked his back gently, just holding him, as Sehrys stained his tunic with a flood of tears.

The pale green hue of the sunlight through the broad, thin leaves of the trees around them somehow seemed like an added embrace unto itself; the call-and-response birdsong was a reminder that, no matter what else befell him, he was as safe as possible in this moment, in this man's arms. He was free.

They stayed like that for a long time.

Finally, Brieden spoke. It was a murmur, so soft that Sehrys wouldn't have been able to hear it if he hadn't been so close.

"How were they never able to break you?"

Sehrys sniffled. "They did."

"No, Sehrys, they didn't. Your eyes... they aren't like the others. Your eyes look free. In six years, you never let anyone take that from you. I cannot—you are simply amazing."

"I... I feel broken, Brieden." Sehrys's voice was very small. Brieden hugged him tighter.

"Of course you do. But you're not. You're strong and fierce and alive and *whole*. I can see it even if you don't, Sehrys. It's what made me fall in love with you."

Sehrys tensed, and Brieden loosened his grip, but Sehrys didn't push him away. After a moment, Sehrys relaxed back into the embrace.

"It wasn't that I thought you were frail and weak," Brieden said. "It was that I *knew* you were incredible and powerful and full of fire. No matter what they did to you, Sehrys, and no matter what they made you think you were *choosing* to do to stay alive, they never really touched you. I doubt that they even got close."

The wind picked up slightly, and Sehrys shuddered despite its warmth. "Dronyen got quite close," he whispered. "If you hadn't—I don't know how much more I had left in me, Brieden. I think he truly wanted to destroy me."

"He did," Brieden agreed through gritted teeth. "But he won't."

Sehrys took a deep breath against the steady thrum of Brieden's heartbeat. "I truly hope this is all real, Brieden. I hope you aren't just a different variety of sadist from Dronyen. Because I'm going to tell you something right now, and it's going to leave me completely defenseless."

Brieden inhaled sharply, but didn't speak.

"I... I think I trust you. In fact, I know I trust you. And if you betray me now, it *will* break me. Utterly and completely."

Sehrys lifted his head from Brieden's chest and looked him in the eye.

"You have the power to break me, Brieden," he repeated. "And that... that is all I wanted to say."

Sehrys looked away, overwhelmed by the intensity in Brieden's eyes. A spray of golden petals danced past them on the breeze, several catching on the horses' manes and tails. Sehrys studied the lovely contrast of rich yellow against mirror-black, realizing all of a sudden that he knew them. They were cassia blossoms. Smaller than the ones he recalled from his boyhood, but unmistakable in appearance and scent. He hadn't tasted them in years.

Brieden's hand softly cupped his cheek.

"I promise that I won't betray you, Sehrys."

Sehrys closed his eyes, melting into Brieden's touch. He felt loved and safe in a way that had only lived in ghostlike memories, gathering cobwebs in his heart, for far too long.

"Thank you," Sehrys breathed. "For... I—thank you."

Brieden smiled as Sehrys lay his head back down in the crook of his neck.

"Thank you for trusting me," he replied.

✦✦✦✦✦

THAT AFTERNOON, THEY FOUND THEMSELVES RIDING through the first unavoidable village of their journey. They stopped to feed and water both the horses and themselves, and to replenish what supplies had dwindled. It was a small village, and clearly not a wealthy one, as evidenced by the simple clapboard homes, modest one-story shops and the single dirt road that swept through the center of town.

All eyes were on Sehrys. Brieden had to treat him like a slave, and Sehrys had to treat Brieden like his master. Anything out of the ordinary might become a story worth telling, and that was simply not an option.

It was a disconcerting arrangement, especially after the sweetness of their conversation earlier that day.

Brieden barked orders, telling Sehrys what to fetch for him and making Sehrys carry heavy bundles on his own when Brieden could easily have helped him. Brieden did his best to apologize with his eyes whenever a chance presented itself, and Sehrys replied with silent looks of sympathy that let Brieden know things were going to be fine between them.

It wasn't until they were sitting on a wide bench near a cluster of shops, enjoying the sun, that the man approached them. Sehrys was eating an apple and Brieden was eating a chunk of cheese with a piece of bread.

The man sidled up to them, smooth and smiling, his dark blue eyes hard as rock. He seemed to be about forty, with oiled and swept-back sandy hair; his stained, calloused hands and well-polished belt and boots suggested the modest wealth of a tradesman.

"Hello, sir, Grade's the name. I don't believe I've had the pleasure of making your acquaintance."

Brieden glanced up with a practiced look of irritable boredom. "Jor," he said. "Just passing through. On our way to Chrillipal."

"Pleasure to meet you, Jor. Say, that's a mighty pretty elf you got there. May I?"

Grade's hands were poised to touch Sehrys.

"Rather you didn't," Brieden said, trying to keep his voice even. "Not for sale."

"I understand that," Grade said, resting his thick hands across his broad stomach. "Creature like this you want to hold on to for a while. But some pals and I might be able to rustle up a bit of coinage if you're of a mind to rent. You staying in town tonight?"

"No," Brieden answered firmly. A little too firmly. "Got to get back on the road. Nice to meet you, though, Grade." Brieden got to his feet and motioned Sehrys to follow him.

Grade reached out a stocky arm and closed his hand around Sehrys's wrist. Brieden spun around and yanked Sehrys's wrist free.

"What can I give you for fifteen minutes with it, Jor?" Grade pleaded. "Have a heart. We don't get much in the way of quality sprite flesh around here."

Brieden grabbed Grade by the lapels and slammed him against the bench.

"I'm sorry, Grade, but do I look like a man who needs your money?" he hissed. "Do I look like a man who likes to share his toys?"

He shoved Grade down onto the bench, hard.

"Let's go," Brieden muttered to Sehrys. "We need to get the hell out of here *now*."

"Oh, it's like that, is it?" Grade called after them. "You're just a couple of boys up from Khryslee, aren't you? I don't want your filthy wild elf anyway, you bloody abomination!"

Sehrys and Brieden made it back to the carriage in record time. Sehrys took the reins and drove them east out of the village. Out of view of the town, they followed a wide circle until they were westbound once again.

Neither man said anything for a good long while.

Finally, Brieden spoke: "I'm sorry, Sehrys."

"You say that quite a lot, you know."

"I feel like I should."

"Brieden, you have nothing to apologize for. I'm just glad we've left that horrible little place. Small human villages are among my least favorite places in the world. You do realize that it's considered poor manners not to rent out your slave for a fair price, though?"

"Fine. Then I have poor manners. At least I have a soul."

"That you most certainly do." Sehrys smiled, trying to melt some of the tension that Brieden was clearly still carrying from the confrontation.

Brieden smiled back, relaxing a bit.

"Sehrys?"

"Yes?"

"Do you know what he was talking about? Khryslee?"

Sehrys was quiet for a moment.

"Yes," he finally replied.

Brieden waited for Sehrys to continue. When he didn't, Brieden pressed.

"What is it?"

"It's a place."

"That much was fairly obvious. What did he mean? What sort of place is it? I don't think I've ever heard of it."

Sehrys sighed and pulled the carriage over.

"Get one of your maps. One that shows a bit of Laesi."

Brieden furrowed his brow. "The Faerie Lands," Sehrys clarified. "Laesi is what The Sidhe call them."

Brieden fetched a map, and Sehrys leaned in.

"See... there?" Sehrys traced what looked like a narrow strip just past the entrance to the Faerie Lands. "It's quite near The Border, as you can see. It requires a bit of travel through the Eastern Border

Lands after you have crossed, and then there you are. They are highly protected lands. Of those who desire to live there, only some are welcome. But it's the only place I know of where…"

"Where…?"

"Where… unconventional pairings are accepted." Sehrys did not look at Brieden as he said it.

Brieden's heart began to pound in his chest. Could Sehrys be telling him… did he mean…?

"Yes," Sehrys replied to the question that hung between them as he looked up to meet Brieden's eyes, "Humans and sidhe live there as lifemates, but others do too. Humans who wish to make a life with another human of their own sex, sidhe couples in unblessed pairings…" Sehrys shrugged. "It's supposed to be a beautiful place."

"It sounds beautiful," Brieden murmured, his voice wistful.

Sehrys laughed. "I was referring to the *landscape*. It's said to be quite lush. But it's rare for anyone to see it unless they are planning to relocate there. Permanently."

"Would… do they let people in on their own?"

Sehrys raised his eyebrows.

"I only meant… once we get you home, I'm going to need to figure out a plan for myself. I can't stay in Villalu, and I have a feeling I won't be particularly welcome in Laesi…"

"That feeling would be correct," Sehrys confirmed.

"So I wonder if… maybe I could go to Khryslee. I think I could stand to live in a place like that."

Sehrys studied him. Brieden had grown proficient at reading many of Sehrys's expressions, but not this time. This look was an utter mystery.

"I don't know, Brieden, but I think you should try," he said finally, picking up the reins and continuing them on their way.

IN THE VILLAGE OF OKNAUR, A ROYAL MESSENGER DELIVERED a scroll to the steward. The steward hung it in the window of the general supply store, where all important notices were put on display.

On his way home from the tavern, still feeling frustrated and irritable from an incident earlier that day, a man named Grade stopped to study the scroll.

One of Prince Dronyen's courtiers had apparently run off with quite a lot of palace gold, as well as one particularly high-quality sidhe slave. The palace was offering a reward for any information that might lead to the man's capture.

Grade read the physical description of the criminal at large.

He smiled to himself.

CHAPTER SIX

T HEY SAT BY THE FIRE OF THEIR CAMPSITE AND watched the sunset fade into blue.

Sehrys was stationed on the grass, which was still wet from an earlier rain; Brieden sat on a rolled-up blanket with a second blanket draped around his shoulders because Sehrys had insisted. He had been feeling a bit under the weather, and Sehrys was doing his best to tend to him with warm blankets and hot broth and soothing touches to his cheeks and forehead.

Brieden certainly wasn't going to complain.

But after nearly a month of traveling, Brieden had to know. He couldn't avoid the question and ignore the inevitable any longer, no matter how much he might prefer to do exactly that.

"Sehrys?"

"Yes?"

"How long... when will the verbena be flushed from your system?"

Sehrys fiddled with a blade of grass.

"I don't really know. I've never been given the opportunity to find out. But I've heard it can take a fair while."

"Will you know when it happens? Will you be able to tell?"

Sehrys smiled slightly, still staring at the blade of grass between his fingers. "Brieden, if you had shackles on your wrists and ankles for six years and then one day someone took them off, would you be able to tell?"

"Oh. It's like that?"

"It's like that."

"Do you remember what it feels like?"

"I remember that it feels *more.* I remember that it feels less isolated, more like I'm a part of everything around me."

"That sounds incredible."

Sehrys sighed and leaned back on his elbows. "It is."

"When it happens, Sehrys, you won't need me anymore. You should probably just…"

"Let us cross that bridge when we come to it, shall we?"

Sehrys lay back on the grass, knees bent and feet flat on the earth, staring into the fading day. He tucked his hands behind his head. Brieden started to lie back as well, but Sehrys glared at him.

"Don't, Brieden. You clearly caught a chill when we stopped in Naurasvu, and your frail human constitution won't be helped by lying on the cold, damp ground. In fact, you should probably move closer to the fire."

Brieden smiled. He loved how bossily nurturing Sehrys had become. He was clearly starting to care about Brieden, although Brieden still didn't know what it meant for them, or if it was enough to keep Sehrys by his side until they reached The Border.

"Sehrys?" he asked, looking out across the darkening plain spread before them. They had spent the better part of a week traveling through a narrow belt of hills along the Muirdannoch coast, and now the sea was at their back. The view from their hilltop campsite was both breathtaking and sobering; they had come so far already.

They still had so very far to go.

"Yes?"

"Can I ask you something… sort of personal?"

"Have you ever asked me anything else?"

Brieden smiled again. "I suppose that's fair enough. But before... when you said you were going to get married, it kind of sounded like... like the person you were marrying was a man."

Now it was Sehrys's turn to smile.

"More like a boy, really, we were so young. But yes. His name was... is... his pet name, anyway, is Firae."

Brieden was silent for a moment, allowing Sehrys's words to sink in. He watched points of light begin to reveal themselves across the plain below them, a rough map of the cities, towns and villages they would need to navigate and avoid as they pushed forward into central Villalu. He wondered how many men like him lived in those places, married to women they could not love, perhaps fumbling with secret lovers beneath this very moonlight while their families slept. He wondered how many of their wives did the same.

"I... I didn't know that sidhe did that. Do women marry each other too?"

"Yes, if that's their preference; there are many types of acceptable unions and pairings. Sidhe culture is by no means perfect, but we don't have the same sort of taboos that you humans do. I think that may be your biggest problem."

Brieden laughed. "Oh, I don't know, Sehrys. We have so many problems to choose from."

"That may be true, but when men don't control women, and love isn't about dominance, and the powerless aren't used to satisfy the repressed cravings of the powerful..." Sehrys gave a small shrug. "I do think that takes care of quite a few problems."

Brieden mulled this over; it was too simple to make as much sense as it did.

"As I said, The Sidhe aren't perfect, Brieden," Sehrys continued, sitting up and draping his arms across his knees. Both moons were visible now, the greater moon full and pregnant with light, the dwarf moon a soft little half-coin below it. Between the fire and the moonlight, Sehrys's eyes nearly glowed, contemplative but sharp. "Some of our social shortcomings can be almost as disturbing as yours. But no one marries because they need to in order to survive, or in order to be taken care of. It is a choice, and it isn't a choice that everybody makes."

"But it is a choice that you made."

Sehrys was silent for a moment. He drew his knees closer to his chest, lifting his gaze from the fire to look out across the plain. Were it not for the plain, their campsite would feel cozy, a tiny clearing surrounded by a dense forest of silver-trunked tochet trees on all but one side.

"Yes," he said, although it didn't sound like a pure yes.

"But...?" Brieden ventured.

"It's... no, we loved each other very much. There was just a bit of pressure for us to marry young. Perhaps more than a bit, in fact."

"How come?"

Sehrys sighed.

"It's—sidhe culture is different, Brieden."

"Do... do you still love him? Firae?"

Sehrys turned to look at him. "I don't know. It's been years. I don't even know if he's the same. *I'm* certainly not the same. But he was a dear friend, and I've known him since I was a child. I know I still care for him, I just don't... I suppose I don't know what that really means anymore."

Brieden wanted to ask: *Is he handsome? Did he deserve you? Did he make your body shiver when he kissed you? Could you ever love me the way you loved him? Am I less of a man if I hate him a little bit, even if he made you happy?*

Instead, Brieden said, "I hope you get to see him again." It was a true statement, but barely.

"Me too," Sehrys said, his voice little more than a sigh of longing.

Brieden looked away and his heart clenched as if being stabbed.

OVER THE NEXT FEW DAYS, BRIEDEN'S HEALTH DECLINED. When Sehrys crept closer to Brieden in the tent one night—as he had found himself doing from time to time when he woke from terrible dreams—he was startled to hear loud, shallow wheezing. He pressed his ear to Brieden's chest and his lungs sounded thick. He touched Brieden's forehead and it felt like fire.

Sehrys swallowed hard. This was far more than a chill. Brieden was *not* well.

The next day, Brieden almost fell off the perch while Sehrys was driving, and Sehrys nearly upended the carriage when he lunged to catch him. Brieden was sweating, his eyes were glazed and he was breaking out in boils. Sehrys wrapped him in blankets, carried him to the carriage and folded him onto the seat.

"Sehrys? What—where—"

"Just sleep, Brieden," Sehrys soothed.

Brieden sighed and burrowed into the blankets.

"I love you," he murmured, already half asleep.

"I know," Sehrys whispered, allowing his hand to linger on Brieden's cheek a little longer than necessary.

When Brieden awoke, Sehrys had already begun to ease him out of the carriage.

"I can walk," he grumbled irritably. "I'm a grown man."

"Of course," Sehrys agreed, and stepped back to let Brieden climb to the ground on his own and assess their situation.

Brieden squinted at the street lamps through the drizzle of rain around them, utterly confused. "Where are we?"

"We are in Okosgrim, at an inn. We are going to sleep here tonight."

"Sehrys, no. It's too—"

"Brieden, yes. I don't care if it's risky. You aren't well. You need a hot bath and some strong broth and a warm, dry place to sleep. I don't want to hear another word."

Brieden groaned, but allowed Sehrys to lead him toward the inn. As they approached the door, Sehrys hung back deferentially and cast his eyes to the floor in the manner of a slave.

They walked into a warm and softly lit dining area, where a few men were nursing mugs. One particularly burly man sat in front of a pegboard full of keys, his feet up on the table in front of him.

"Pardon me," Brieden rasped, and Sehrys winced at the effort it clearly took him to keep his voice steady, "but we... uh, *I*... would like a room, please."

The man glanced up at them, his eyes settling on Sehrys. "Hmmm," he responded lazily, "Thing is, son, I'm not sure we *have* any rooms open just now."

"But your sign said you have vacancies!"

"*Did* it, now? Strange. Must have forgotten to change that."

Brieden shook his head. "Let's go," he muttered, turning to leave. He clearly didn't have the energy to deal with this obstacle.

"Well, now, wait a minute," the man said, stroking his thick brown beard with a rich grin. "I think I might have *one* small room in the back. But it's going to cost you a bit of time with your elf. That's fair, right? See? I'm not a bad sort."

"No," Brieden answered flatly and pulled Sehrys toward the door.

"Brieden," Sehrys whispered and pulled his arm back slightly. "Stop."

Brieden stopped. He was barely able to walk, let alone stand, and his chest was heaving with the effort of moving a few paces. Sweat ran down his face, and his lips were distorted with sores.

"Brieden. Just... take the room. We need the room."

Brieden stared at Sehrys, but Sehrys met his gaze without flinching. He had made up his mind.

"You cannot be serious," Brieden whispered.

"One last time isn't going to break me, Brieden," Sehrys replied, as gently as he could, hating the pain that flared in Brieden's eyes. "Please let me do this. I know his type, and he's most likely after something quick and simple, so he can say he's been with one of us. I'll be fine. I *promise* you I will be fine."

"No."

"Brieden, *please*. I'm not going to watch you die."

"No."

Sehrys sighed and touched Brieden's arm with his free hand. His eyes flickered back to the innkeeper, who was watching them with just a little bit too much interest. He let his gaze fall back to the floor and his shoulders sag. He didn't want to do this. He didn't want to manipulate the one person who had been entirely honest with him in the past six years. But they needed that damned room.

"Brieden, I need you. If anything happens to you, there won't be anyone to protect me. If I have to do this again, I'd rather it be for one night than... I can't be a slave again, Brieden. I *can't*." He didn't look at Brieden as he spoke. He couldn't.

Brieden let go of Sehrys and strode to the innkeeper as fast as his straining lungs would allow him.

"I'll pay double the rate."

"I believe I already named my price."

"Triple."

"Son, what *is* it with you? You sweet on your slave or something? I'm offering you—"

"Jaren!"

The innkeeper swiveled around just in time to be smacked on the head by an older woman with wiry gray hair and eyes like steel. He flinched.

"What in the Five Hells do you think you're *doing?*" She stared at Sehrys with disgust. "You want a slave, you get up off your ass and work for a change, and you *buy* yourself a damn slave. If you give away one more room for free because you can't stop thinking with your cock for five minutes—"

"Ma! Come on! I wasn't really going to—"

"Get your ass in the back!" she spat. "Do something useful for a change!" She gave him another solid smack to the back of his head, causing him to yelp and scurry away.

"Now," she said, fixing Brieden with a shrewd eye. "I believe I heard you say something about paying triple our usual rate."

Brieden collapsed onto the floor.

Sehrys ran to him and knelt to feel his pulse. It was steady. Shakily, Sehrys rose to his feet.

"Ma'am," he said, voice carefully submissive as he stared at the floor, "I apologize for addressing you directly, but my master is very, very ill and I need to tend to him. I assure you that he will be happy to pay triple your usual rate, and I would like to request a hot bath and some supplies so that I may attend him, which he will of course pay for as well."

The woman took a split-second to glower at Sehrys before addressing the semi-conscious heap on the floor.

"Tell your elf to make a list of the supplies you need, and I'll send up a girl. That is, if it can write."

Yes it can, you miserable wench. "That won't be a problem. Thank you," Sehrys said.

"We have a suite with a private bath," she said, continuing to pretend she was addressing Brieden instead of Sehrys. "There's even a pump installed, feeds the bath from an underground hot spring. Isn't cheap, though. And at triple rate—"

"He'll take it," Sehrys said, working very hard to sound calm as he dug into Brieden's purse.

"Very well," she replied, after carefully counting out the gold Sehrys had dropped into her cupped palms. He didn't know the usual rate, but whatever he had given her appeared satisfactory. She emptied the coins into a deep pocket in the front of her apron and headed for the staircase in the far corner of the room. "Follow me."

Sehrys scooped Brieden up and followed the woman. Brieden didn't complain about being carried, but he did whimper.

His pulse had started to fade.

Sehrys put Brieden down on the bed and quickly drew up a list of supplies that they would need. He handed it to the innkeeper. She snatched it, refusing to look at Sehrys, and left without a word.

Sehrys started the bath and then headed to the stables to fetch some herbs and stones from the carriage. When he returned, the supplies he had requested had been placed in a neat pile on top of the dresser, and a young girl was in the process of building a fire. She only turned to look at Sehrys briefly before finishing her task.

When the bath was ready, Sehrys undressed Brieden carefully, trying not to let his eyes linger.

He did let his eyes linger. But only a little.

When Sehrys eased him into the bath, Brieden's eyes opened, and he gazed up at him with untempered adoration. He didn't speak, but continued to stare at Sehrys as he bathed him, his fever-bright eyes full of wonder.

After his bath, Sehrys dried Brieden and slipped him into a soft linen dressing gown. He gently placed him on the bed. Perhaps a bath and some broth and a warm, dry bed would do the trick after all.

Sehrys was preparing the broth when he heard a crash behind him.

Brieden had collapsed onto the floor.

And this time he had completely lost consciousness.

He wasn't asleep. He wasn't half-conscious. This wasn't temporary. His pulse was faint and he was barely breathing.

Sehrys stared wildly at all of his supplies, as if anything there would help Brieden. He took a deep breath, fighting to calm his racing heart. He had exactly one option left, or Brieden was going to die.

Sehrys's body shook in spite of his efforts. If he did this... would Brieden know? What would he do? How would it change things?

It would change everything.

But if he didn't do it—

Sehrys pulled a small pouch from among the healing herbs arranged on the dresser, sat on the floor, laid Brieden across his lap and kissed his forehead. He opened the pouch and pulled out seven small gray stones, carefully placing six of them upon Brieden's torso to form a circle.

Sehrys closed his eyes and let out a deep sigh. Pounds of tension fell from his shoulders as he placed the seventh stone in the center of the circle. His skin and Brieden's both began to glow a bright gold where they touched the stone.

The glow spread outward in thin tendrils to each stone in the circle, and then outward still, wrapping around Brieden's body like threads of diffused sunlight. The glow began to pick up depth and richness and covered Brieden completely. It rose to envelop both men, deepening into amber and ochre and finally shifting into a vibrant leaf green.

The room smelled like a forest in springtime.

They were buried inside the glowing aura, and it was buried inside them. It permeated Brieden's organs, gently nourishing them with pure, clear, concentrated vitality. It sank into his skin, drawing out the poison and replacing it with roiling life. It chased the darkness away and bathed every cell in light.

When he awoke the next morning, with sunlight streaming into the room through the rain-streaked window and Sehrys sleeping sweetly beside him, Brieden had never felt better.

Chapter Seven

"I CAN'T BELIEVE IT, I TRULY CAN'T! IT'S SIMPLY *amazing,* Sehrys. I don't know how you did it!" They had left the inn several hours ago, but Brieden couldn't stop bringing up how fantastic he felt, especially since he'd been so sick the night before. He had never experienced anything like it in his life.

"I told you, I'm a very good caretaker." Sehrys said, his eyes fixed on the road ahead. They had reached a chain of small villages around the outskirts of Okoslajec, the largest town in the Lajec region, and more than a few curious faces were peering out at them from cottages and farmhouse windows as they drove past.

"Yes, but... I don't even know how it's possible. Last night I was at death's door, and now..."

"It was probably a virus that ran its course."

"But I don't just feel better, I feel *incredible!* I feel like I could run for days on end!" Brieden bounced a little in his seat.

"I gathered that. You haven't been able to sit still since breakfast."

Brieden frowned at Sehrys's dry tone, but settled down as he noticed another carriage about to pass their own. He exchanged polite smiles and nods with the older gentleman on the passengers' side of the perch; a flaxen-haired young sidhe slave was at the helm. "I just... I've never even *heard* of anything like this," he continued softly, after the carriage had passed. I thought I was going to die last night. I could barely even breathe. And now—"

"Yes, I know. It's a miracle," Sehrys muttered, his eyes still trained straight ahead even as they reached an empty stretch of road bracketed by rolling wheat fields. "The Gods will be singing your tale across generations. I can't *believe* that cow actually charged us triple the rate. How many decent humans do you have in this country? Four?"

"Sehrys, what is wrong with you?" Brieden looked at him with an arched brow.

"Nothing!" Sehrys snapped, and immediately flinched. "I mean, nothing is wrong," he said more softly, finally turning to look at Brieden. "I was just very worried about you last night. I suppose I'm still a little bit tense."

"But Sehrys, I feel ama—"

"Amazing, I know." Sehrys smiled as he returned his focus to the road. "Just... I think you should accept it, Brieden. Don't worry too much about why it is."

Brieden grinned at him. "I do remember you taking care of me, though, Sehrys. Parts of it, anyway. You—it was so sweet."

Sehrys blushed; his pale features utterly failed to hide it. "I wouldn't get very far on my own without you, would I? It wasn't an entirely selfless act."

"Yes, but..." Brieden furrowed his brow, a fragment of a hazy memory from the night before hovering at the edges of his mind. And then he snapped his head up and stared at Sehrys as it came back to him vividly, all at once. "Wait a minute, Sehrys! You—"

Sehrys swallowed hard and glanced at him.

"You were going to—with that innkeeper. Just—just so I could get the room! Sehrys, I *never* want you to think you have to—"

Sehrys slipped the reins into one hand and used the other to pat Brieden on the knee. "Brieden. Let us change the subject. *Please.*"

Brieden grinned. That was fine with him. He was so happy, he didn't think he could concentrate on being upset with what that disgusting innkeeper had almost done to Sehrys—not when the sun was shining and his skin was tingling and every taste and smell and sight and sound was crisper and more perfect than ever before. Not when the air was sweet and grassy, the rippling of the wheat fields in the breeze as lulling as the sound of ocean waves. Everything was clear and rich and impossibly beautiful.

Especially Sehrys. It wasn't that Sehrys had gotten more beautiful; it was that he could *see* how truly beautiful Sehrys was for the first time. It was as if his eyes had been cleansed of dust and grime and haze and a fog that he hadn't even known were there. He easily picked out details that he had never noticed before, like the smattering of barely-there freckles across Sehrys's nose, which were only completely visible in full sunlight, and the rich varieties of color in Sehrys's hair, the rainbow of wine and rose and vermillion and orchid and indigo; the perfect jut of Sehrys's collarbone against the polished-pearl skin of his beautifully sculpted chest...

Well, maybe he *had* noticed that last part before. But that didn't make it any less beautiful.

And his eyes... Brieden was careful to take only small, measured glances into his eyes. They were too breathtaking to bear. And the way Sehrys *smelled*. Just like a forest in springtime. How had Brieden never noticed that?

Brieden sighed into a broad smile. He could still feel the ghost of Sehrys's touch on his knee.

Even the light drizzle that started as the morning gave way to afternoon couldn't mar Brieden's spirits. He tilted his face up into the cool spray. What a blessing it was to feel gentle rain on his skin! He laughed, just because he could.

"I suppose that *is* changing the subject, in a way," said Sehrys, arching an eyebrow and offering the faintest hint of a smile.

THAT NIGHT, BRIEDEN WAS ROUSED FROM A VERY PLEASANT dream by what he at first incorrectly surmised was an even *more* pleasant dream.

"Brieden," Sehrys whispered his name and rubbed his upper arm.

"Mmm, Sehrys..." he murmured, pulling him close.

"*Brieden*!" A sound smack to the chest. Oh. Definitely *not* that kind of dream. Brieden's eyelids flew open and he opened his mouth to speak, but Sehrys placed a finger against his lips and jerked his head toward the clear sound of advancing men's voices.

Brieden sat up wordlessly and moved to the edge of the tent. He grabbed his sword and handed Sehrys his spare.

"You know how to use this?" he whispered. Sehrys rolled his eyes.

"*Yes,* Brieden," he muttered. "Humans are hardly the only swordsmen in the world."

They crept out of the tent as quietly as possible, moving in a wide circle through the trees that surrounded their campsite. When they finally got close enough to hear what the men were saying, they crouched low.

"I'd say it's *definitely* him. Makes sense, west through Oknaur and Okosgrim, that's aimed right at the border cities. Fit's Dronyen's theory."

Sehrys and Brieden's gasps swallowed one another. They exchanged horrified looks.

"All right, better go let the others know. Let's close ranks, make this fast and clean."

"Brieden," Sehrys whispered. "Run."

Brieden stared at him, frozen to the spot.

"Hey, did you boys hear somethi—"

"Brieden! *Run!*"

Sehrys grabbed Brieden's hand and bolted into the forest. He dodged trees and roots with liquid grace; he pulled Brieden to his feet with unnatural strength whenever he stumbled. The shouts increased behind them, and Dronyen's men were hot on their trail, less sure-footed but utterly relentless.

Brieden's eyes shot to the sky when a flare bloomed red across the heavens and temporarily exposed them as if in daylight. They ran through a small clearing and then stumbled to a halt.

Because now the men weren't just behind them. Now the men were *all around* them. And there were dozens of them.

Brieden's breath caught in his throat. He and Sehrys released one another's hands, as if by silent communication, and stepped back into each other, backs touching and swords held aloft. The light of the full moon exposed the gleeful expressions of the men that surrounded them. Brieden recognized several of them. These were Dronyen's best. Hand-picked. Just as he had been.

"Look at that! Isn't that *adorable*!"

"Is it true love, boys?"

"Hell, His Maj is right. The pervert *is* taking that thing to Khryslee!"

"Give it up, Lethiscir. Even you aren't stupid enough to think you can actually get out of this."

"His Maj is very disappointed in you. In *both* of you. So come with us nice and civil, and he'll go easier on you. Marginally. *Maybe*."

Laughter all around.

Deep, cold fear settled into Brieden's gut. What had he done? It would have been better if he'd died at that inn. Then maybe Sehrys could have gotten away. Maybe he would have done better on his own, hiding in trees and sleeping under the open sky. Maybe he would have been better off without Brieden from the very beginning.

This couldn't be happening.

Brieden knew two things for certain. First, he wasn't going to live through this confrontation. He could let Dronyen's men kill him, but he wouldn't give Dronyen the pleasure of breaking Brieden himself.

And second, he would go down fighting. He would put everything he had into that minute, infinitesimal chance that Sehrys might somehow get out of this, alive and free.

Because if Dronyen ever got his hands on Sehrys again...

"Frankly, boys, I'm finding your strategy of standing there and making cute comments at us a little less than threatening," Brieden called out, his voice strong and clear and unwavering.

"Sehrys," he whispered. "Over there, south by southwest. You can get out if you don't hesitate. As soon as they come for me, let those feet fly."

"Brieden," Sehrys whispered back, "I'm not going to—"

"Yes, you are. They just want to kill me. They want to give you back to Dronyen so he can break you. If I have to die to keep that from happening, then I die. It's my last wish, Sehrys. You can't deny me my last wish."

Sehrys inhaled sharply. Brieden thought he heard the edge of a sob.

"So, how many of you boys have been bending over for Dronyen now that his slave is gone?" bellowed Brieden. "Thought your gait seemed a little off, there, Sinchett!"

The man he had singled out flew at him with a scream of rage, widening the gap Brieden had pointed out to Sehrys.

"*Go!*" Brieden screamed.

They both took off like arrows.

Sinchett ran at Brieden with murder in his eyes.

"No! Sinchett! We're supposed to save him for His—"

Brieden stopped in his tracks and turned to Sinchett, glaring hard and bright, laughing at his rage, making him boil. He had picked Sinchett for a reason. His anger was his undoing, and his impulsive charge at Brieden had every other man distracted.

Brieden held his sword defensively to block the first jab. Sinchett was going to kill him, he was sure of it, but maybe he could at least get in a few good licks.

Sinchett flew at Brieden and raised his sword.

And then Brieden was thrown from his feet and the world came apart at the seams.

It took Brieden a minute to realize that he was alive and on the ground, even if the very ground was moving in violent waves all around him. Men were falling down as far as he could manage to see, and try as he might, he could not secure his footing on the throbbing earth.

And then the screams began.

Brieden rolled to the side just as a cluster of thick vines exploded from the ground beside him. They were as tall as trees and moving with clear intent. Something hot and sticky dripped onto his face, and he looked up to see Sinchett, held high in the air by one of the vines; his tortured features were sharp and bright against the full moons and some other unearthly source of light, and that vine was squeezing the life out of him. Brieden could hear the sickly crunch of bones breaking, and he finally managed to scramble to his feet to get out of the way before even more blood rained down.

Brieden was only vertical for a moment before the shaking ground claimed his balance once again.

But in that moment...

Oh, that moment.

In the middle of the clearing, incandescent with a light that made the entire forest glow in response, was a being of such incredible beauty and power that it took Brieden's breath away.

He took Brieden's breath away.

He knew it was Sehrys, but he had to take a moment to fully grasp what that meant.

He was Sehrys, and there was nothing containing him. Nothing weakening him. His skin glowed with pulsing colors: amber-gold and leaf-green and sky-blue and blood-red and pure, blinding white. He stood upon the roiling ground as if it were as still as stone. His eyes blazed with deep green fire.

And those eyes were trained directly on Sinchett.

Brieden had never seen such rage in Sehrys's eyes. He had never seen such utter homicidal malice. Sehrys wasn't simply killing Sinchett. He was eviscerating him.

Just as Brieden lost his footing again, he heard the tortured scream and horrible ripping sound of Sinchett being torn in half.

Brieden crawled away blindly, rolling and swerving to avoid the flailing vines that pursued the desperately fleeing men all around him. "*Sehrys!*" he screamed raggedly as the ground burst open, and he felt himself sliding helplessly into the newly-formed cavern. Just as Brieden was about to fall screaming into the earth with two other men, a vine wrapped itself around his waist.

And he wasn't afraid.

Even though he couldn't explain it, the vine *was* Sehrys. That uncanny truth was undeniable. He had a sense of being held safe in Sehrys's strong arms. Brieden stroked the vine affectionately as it gently lifted him and placed him on a high, thick branch of a tochet tree on the edge of the clearing, outside the fray. And when he touched the vine, he knew that his instinct was true. Because as he let his hands slide across the smooth flesh of the plant, Sehrys looked up and their eyes locked. Through the dark fire, Brieden saw nothing but pure affection.

He leaned his head against the rough bark of the tree as the vine slipped away and watched the spectacle below.

A few of the men had the good sense to run away, but not most. These were Dronyen's best men, hand-picked, and they had been trained to see nothing beyond the mission. Neither death nor dismemberment could deter them.

And Sehrys seemed more than happy to dole out both.

Some of the men tried hacking at the vines, but it was like hitting solid steel. Brieden saw one particularly delicate-looking vine curl itself around the hilt of a fallen sword and begin spearing men through the hearts as effortlessly as a knife through butter.

Two men ran at Sehrys from behind carrying iron chains. Brieden's heart clenched, but a scream of warning hadn't made it to his lips when the men dropped the chains with howls of pain. With staggering rapidity, the chains glowed red-hot and then began to melt, filling a slight indentation in the earth with molten metal. A single vine caught both men, wrapped around them tightly, thrust their faces into the liquid iron, and held them there.

And all this without Sehrys even bothering to turn around.

Vines crushed the bodies of men into pulp, tore off their heads and limbs, littered the ground with flesh and blood and bone. It was horrifying to behold, but Brieden was barely looking at the carnage.

He was looking at Sehrys.

True, pure, unbridled Sehrys.

When the work was finally finished, when the only living soldiers had long since escaped and, presumably, gotten as far away as possible as fast as they could, the earth went still. Eyes still glowing, Sehrys calmly proceeded to the edge of the clearing. He leaned against the tree where Brieden was perched.

Brieden heard a faint roar, which quickly grew in volume. His eyes widened as a rush of water, as though a dam broke, approached the clearing.

Sehrys remained still and watched the water come.

The water flooded the clearing; an invisible wall seemed to shield it from the line of trees where Sehrys stood. It moved in strange patterns, swirling and tugging at objects, pulling things down into the openings where the vines had already retreated. When the last of the water swirled, whirlpool-style, into the caverns, the earth shifted once more, and the caverns closed. The meadow looked slightly soggy, but otherwise the same as before the confrontation.

Brieden noticed a rustling beside him, and a branch from a neighboring tree bent itself into what looked like a three-pronged hand, palm cupped, waiting. He climbed into it.

The tree bent with a gentle creak and set Brieden on the ground next to Sehrys.

Brieden stared at him.

The fire in his eyes was gone now, and the glow—Sehrys still had his usual pale moonlight glow, of course, but the pulsating colors had faded away.

Sehrys looked down at his hands, and the look on his face couldn't have been more dissimilar from the expression he had just worn. He looked frightened and vulnerable, and the fact that he wasn't meeting Brieden's eyes was clearly by choice.

"So..." Brieden said carefully. "The verbena. About a month, then, to flush it out?"

Schrys continued to study his hands. "More like three weeks," he mumbled.

"Sehrys." Brieden tried leaning to catch his gaze, but Sehrys turned his head slightly.

"Sehrys, please look at me."

"No."

"Why not?"

"I don't want to look in your eyes and see what you think of me."

"Sehrys... you know what I think of you. Now that I've seen your power, I—"

"I'm a monster."

"No. You're a survivor."

Sehrys finally lifted his head and met Brieden's gaze.

85

"I didn't just kill them, Brieden. I... I—"

"You were a slave for six years. I think you're entitled to a bit of catharsis."

Sehrys gave a tiny, bitter laugh before moving his gaze back to his hands.

"Sehrys... that's how I got better so fast, isn't it? You healed me." Sehrys nodded.

"I... thank you. But I don't understand. Why did you lie to me?"

"Brieden, don't," Sehrys begged softly.

"Don't what?"

"I... I can't."

Sehrys brought his hand to his face, and his shoulders began to shake with sobs. Brieden simply looked at him. After a few moments, Brieden moved toward Sehrys gingerly and reached out to touch him. He half-expected Sehrys to flinch away. He did *not* expect Sehrys to catch the sides of Brieden's face in his hands and pull him close, so close that their breath mingled into one heat. So close that they were almost touching.

"Brieden, I'm—I'm terrified."

"Sehrys, what is it? *Please.* I want to help you."

"Brieden, I don't know what you're doing to me."

Brieden breathed in deep. "Sehrys," was all he could manage to say.

"When you said before... that I wouldn't need you when I got my power back. That was absolutely terrifying. Because I *do* need you. I don't want you to leave me."

"I'll never leave you. Not unless you want me to." Brieden's voice was a fierce whisper as his own tears stung his eyes.

"And I... I don't know what to do. When I think about going home, I think about you being there with me. But you won't be there. I can't have you there. And I can't stand it and it scares me *so much.*"

86

"Sehrys…" He wanted to say, "Come with me to Khryslee. Be with me forever," but he couldn't do it. He couldn't use Sehrys's vulnerability like that. So instead he said, "You don't have to decide anything right now, Sehrys, but I'm here for as long as you want me."

Sehrys's grip on his face tightened as he choked back a sob and whispered, "I want you so badly that sometimes I can't even breathe."

At that, Brieden's hands shot out and clutched at Sehrys's biceps and held on tight because it was the only thing he could do to keep his knees from giving out entirely.

Sehrys slid one hand to the back of Brieden's head and laced his fingers into his hair, and then moved that whisper of distance toward him. Their lips met. No hesitation. Sehrys leaned his body into Brieden's and kissed him slow and hard and deep, and he didn't let Brieden fall. And as soon as Brieden realized that *yes, this is real, yes, this is actually happening,* he won back a bit of control over his limbs. He wrapped his arms around Sehrys and surrendered completely.

Sehrys tasted like a summer garden.

CHAPTER EIGHT

ⒾT WASN'T A DREAM.

Sehrys traced the contours of Brieden's face. They lay on a blanket near the bank of the small pond where they had made their camp, and the hand that wasn't moving gently across his features was clasped in Brieden's own. They had started out watching the sun rise, but now they just watched each other.

They hadn't been able to sleep—hadn't even tried. They hadn't attempted much in the way of conversation either; there was too much to say. The few things they'd said were simple and laced with sweetness, like what Sehrys said now: "You're the most beautiful man I've ever seen."

Brieden smiled, then softly kissed Sehrys's thumb as it trailed across his lips.

"For a human, you mean."

"No, Brieden. For a *person.* You take my breath away."

Brieden caught Sehrys's lips with his own. They pulled each other closer.

They had been doing that quite a bit in the long stretches between words.

It never stopped seeming like the right thing to say.

Brieden was nearly delirious with adrenaline and sleep deprivation and whatever it was that Sehrys had done to him when he healed him, and so it really was necessary to keep reminding himself that he wasn't dreaming.

Because he couldn't be.

Because even the best dreams he'd ever had didn't capture the way Sehrys's lips fit so perfectly with his, the way Sehrys's tongue felt as it lapped tentatively into his mouth, the way Sehrys tasted, the way he made Brieden's skin buzz with every touch.

Sehrys ran his hand down Brieden's back and slipped it under his tunic. He trailed his knuckle up against Brieden's bare skin.

"*Sehrys,*" Brieden moaned against his lips. Sehrys's hands were like pure silk, and Brieden could only imagine how the rest of his skin might feel.

"Brieden," Sehrys whispered breathlessly, "touch me."

Brieden stiffened. One hand was on Sehrys's clothed arm and the other was threaded through his hair; the sensation was thrilling but innocent. Safe. But what Sehrys was asking for was anything but safe.

"I... I..." he stuttered.

"I'm not going to fall apart, Brieden. I just want to feel your hands on my skin. I want to feel nice. Doesn't this feel nice?" Sehrys moved the hand under Brieden's tunic to his chest, stroking gently, fingers slipping over a nipple.

"Y-yes," Brieden managed, "but Sehrys... I..."

Sehrys pulled his face back just far enough for their eyes to meet. "What is it?"

"I don't want to hurt you. Everything you've been through, I couldn't bear to—"

"Brieden. Do you trust me?"

"Completely."

"Are you sure? I know I lied to you about the verbena, and—"

"Sehrys." Brieden cupped Sehrys's chin and kept their eyes connected. "*Completely.*"

"Then trust me when I say I want you to touch me. Trust me when I say I want *you*."

"I know, but... what if I get carried away and—"

"Would you get too carried away to stop if I asked you to?"

"No. Of course not."

"Then I really don't see a problem, Brieden. Unless—"

"Unless what?" Brieden asked softly.

Sehrys averted his gaze.

"Unless you don't want to touch me, after... what I've been used for."

"Sehrys, *no*." Brieden stroked Sehrys's jaw. "I think I'm scared of how *much* I want to touch you. But I... I don't want you to feel like I'm just another man who wants you because of who you are. Or, um, because of *what* you are." Brieden traced the pointed tip of Sehrys's ear and fixed him with a shy smile.

Sehrys gave a tiny gasp of pleasure and returned Brieden's smile. "Brieden, the first time we ever really spoke, you told me that Dronyen was doing things *to* me and not *with* me because I didn't want him and I never gave my consent. I had been living that way for so long that I'd almost forgotten that." He paused to place a tender kiss on Brieden's lips. "And the truth is, I've never been *with* another man before. Don't you think that maybe... after everything I've been through... that I deserve to be?"

Brieden's smile broadened despite the sheen of tears in his eyes. "Oh, Sehrys, of *course* you do."

"And now I'm finally here, with a man I actually want, and he's afraid to touch me because he thinks he's going to traumatize me. How is that fair?"

Brieden laughed. "All right, I understand. But I need you to promise me that you'll tell me if it becomes too much, and you want me to stop. I'm not saying I don't trust you, Sehrys, but—"

"You need to hear me say it?"

"Yes."

"Brieden, I promise that I will tell you if I want you to stop. And I trust you. And I want you to touch me very, *very* much."

They both laughed into another kiss as Brieden moved his hand to Sehrys's waist. He slowly slid his palm beneath Sehrys's tunic and up the soft bare skin of his back as the sidhe's muscles shifted beneath his touch.

"Breathe," Sehrys whispered. Brieden let out a ragged exhale, eyes closed, his trembling fingers splayed across the curve of Sehrys's back.

Sehrys kissed each of Brieden's eyelids before sitting up just enough to pull his tunic over his head then toss it aside, which prompted Brieden to open his eyes and stare up at him in wonder. The invitation, the *want* painted across Sehrys's face eliminated the few traces of doubt Brieden had managed to hold on to, and all he could do was raise his arms in surrender and allow Sehrys to pull off his tunic as well.

They took a moment to simply stare, cheeks pink and eyes bright. Everything was new. Their bodies were beautiful together, both in similarity and variation: Sehrys, lean and pale and defined, with tiny silver-pink nipples surrounded by sparse wisps of hair nearly the same color as his pale, luminous flesh. Brieden, brown and broad-shouldered and muscled, with a smattering of dark curly hair across his chest and trailing down his stomach.

Sehrys smiled almost shyly, wound his arms around Brieden's neck, and kissed him. They moved together as a matter of instinct, Sehrys lowering himself onto his back as Brieden followed. They kissed, chest to chest, skin to skin, heartbeats melting into one another as if shared, all the while carefully holding their hips at a distance.

Unable to resist all of the soft, bright skin and firm, yielding muscle beneath him, Brieden kissed a trail from Sehrys's jaw to the hollow at the base of his throat. He looked up at Sehrys and received a nod of encouragement before allowing his lips to continue on their path. He kissed one of Sehrys's nipples, and then licked it. Sehrys gave a small squeak of pleasure and arched his back into the wet warmth. Brieden smiled around the nipple, and then licked and sucked it thoroughly before moving to the other one. Sehrys had begun to squirm and sigh beneath him; the responses raced through Brieden's blood and waked every nerve, made his groin ache with arousal.

Sehrys slid one palm up and down Brieden's back. His other hand was buried in Brieden's thick, dark hair, holding him close. Brieden kissed across Sehrys's chest and stomach, pressing his lips to every inch of skin possible, trailing his tongue in small, lazy patterns.

Sehrys moaned softly and whispered his name. Whispered how lovely it felt. Whispered, "Please don't stop." And Brieden didn't. As he shifted slightly, kissing a line above the waist of Sehrys's trousers, Brieden became abruptly aware of just *how* good it really must have felt. Clearly he was not the only one who was aroused.

Nerves overtaking desire, Brieden moved back up Sehrys's body, kissing his lips before moving onto his back and tugging Sehrys on top of him. However much Sehrys might trust him, Brieden still needed to offer him some control.

Taking control was not a problem for Sehrys. He rose to his knees and swung a leg over Brieden, leaning down to kiss Brieden hard as he hovered above him on all fours, their lips the only place where their bodies met. Sehrys's hair fell against Brieden's cheeks and tickled him slightly when the breeze made it dance. Brieden sighed with pleasure and traced the perfect point of an elfin ear.

And then quite nearly forgot his own name.

Sehrys had eased his hips down onto Brieden's so their erections pressed together through their thin trousers. Brieden threw his head back and groaned deeply, losing Sehrys's lips in the process.

Sehrys used the opportunity to press his mouth to Brieden's neck and suck gently as he began to tentatively rock his pelvis.

Brieden wasn't sure when his hands found their way to Sehrys's hips, when his fingers ventured carefully across the perfect swell of his rounded buttocks, but before he knew what he was doing, he was *squeezing*. He froze for a moment, but Sehrys was making soft sounds of unmistakable pleasure, so Brieden let himself relax into the moment, the contact, the undeniable fact that Sehrys's body was on his.

"*Brieden,*" Sehrys groaned, his voice huskier than Brieden had ever heard it but no less musical, as he settled himself on top of Brieden and reached behind himself to spread Brieden's hands over his backside.

"I love you," Brieden whispered, and Sehrys's lips fell onto his as their bodies moved together.

They rutted against each other slowly at first, savoring the slow build overlaid with sharp jolts of toe-curling pleasure whenever they rubbed together *just* the right way. Brieden lost himself to it, allowed Sehrys to set the pace and guide Brieden's body with his own. Before long, Sehrys's thrusts had grown hard and hungry, and he slid his palms beneath Brieden's back, fingers curling up over his shoulders and holding tight.

Brieden kneaded Sehrys's buttocks in time with the rocking of their bodies, moans mingling as their chests slid together, lubricated by a thin film of sweat. He buried his face in Sehrys's neck, kissing the smooth skin between ragged gasps. The sounds Sehrys was making were so delectable Brieden could almost taste them with his tongue as they vibrated through his slender throat.

Feeling his climax sidle up, winding through his belly and groin, Brieden rolled his eyes back and let the delicious friction unravel him completely as he came with a breathless wail.

As Brieden rode out his orgasm, Sehrys thrust against him and followed soon after with a piercing cry. He collapsed on top of Brieden; his entire body shook more and more violently with each moment, but before Brieden could summon any concern, he realized that Sehrys was shaking with laughter. Near-delirious laughter, in fact, and it was nothing less than a sound of pure joy.

Sehrys wiped his eyes and sat up, bringing Brieden with him and pulling him into a crushing hug. "Oh, Brieden, that was *fantastic,*" he said and sighed.

Brieden nestled into the warmth of Sehrys's chest. Everything was beautiful and pure and perfect, and Brieden couldn't remember ever feeling so happy. When they finally pulled away, the smiles that they fixed on one another outshone the sun.

They ate something. They bathed in the pond. They changed into clean clothes. And then they slept the morning away, faces close and limbs intertwined.

THAT AFTERNOON, THEY WERE BACK ON THE ROAD. BRIEDEN had argued in favor of staying at the campsite for a few days. After all, they had nothing to worry about from Dronyen anymore.

Sehrys, however, had begged to differ.

Even though he was as inclined as Brieden to delay the journey that could probably only end in heartbreak, he knew that Dronyen wouldn't simply surrender and leave them to their respective destinies. The game had changed, no doubt of that, but it was far from over. Sehrys had been caught before and he could be caught again; he was fairly certain that Dronyen was far more familiar with the limitations on sidhe power than Brieden was.

Some of Dronyen's men had escaped. Dronyen would no doubt discover what had happened before long, and he would know exactly what he was dealing with: an angry sidhe at full power with a vulnerable and lovestruck human at his side. Brieden had become the one who needed protection, and it was more than likely that Dronyen would figure out exactly what Brieden meant to Sehrys.

If the idea of breaking Sehrys had excited Dronyen before, the notion of breaking him at full strength would have him absolutely *salivating*. And the easiest way to do that now would be for Dronyen to get his hands on Brieden.

Beautiful Brieden.

Brieden, who was all Sehrys wanted to think about. Brieden, whom Sehrys couldn't let himself think too deeply about. He would let himself feel because he had no choice, but every time he began to think too much about what it all meant, he would push his thoughts away and concentrate on the sweetness and the peace and the urgency and the heat that Brieden set to swirling in Sehrys's gut every time he looked at him. Because Brieden made him feel... *more* than he'd felt in a very long time. Or perhaps ever.

But no, that was too close to thinking. And he couldn't let himself think. Because they still had some time before they got close to his homeland, and Sehrys wanted to enjoy the journey as much as possible. He would let his body have this bliss, even if it was just for a heartbeat in the long life of a sidhe.

Because he needed it. Because the pleasure was like a balm for his wounds. Because Brieden made him feel as if he was pure and fierce and beautiful and unblemished and deserved to be loved.

Sehrys glanced at Brieden, who was gazing at him, his serene smile in place. He passed Brieden one of the reins and laced their free hands together, resting their joined hands between them. Right now, they were here and Sehrys was happy. Right now, no one was trying to hurt them and no one was trying to take Brieden from him. Right now, Brieden was looking at Sehrys as if he was the most perfect being in all creation.

Right now they had each other.

They drove on.

95

CHAPTER NINE

"THE PIGEONS ARRIVED THIS MORNING."

"How far?"

"Just shy of Merrowlee. They're probably into Belloquei territory by now."

Dronyen swore a blue streak at the news from his advisor. Brissa looked up from her needlepoint with a furrowed brow. Mister Bachuc had certainly appeared grim and urgent when he arrived at their rooms, and she knew how seriously Dronyen took the news of his steward's betrayal and the loss of his slave.

Still, it was more than a little bit startling to see how single-minded his obsession had become. His recent coronation had brought him no apparent satisfaction, and all were instructed to interrupt him, no matter what he was doing, if any news of the boy and the slave arrived. The last advisor to suggest that he simply go to the flesh markets and procure a new slave while his men continued the search had ended up with a black eye, and Brissa had a few bruises of her own as a result of the king working out his frustration.

"Convincing Belloquei to help will take time we don't have," Dronyen growled as he paced the room. "He probably doesn't even have any decent men trained. You know what a coward he is. How many are left?"

"Of those you sent? By the relief team's account, eight in good health. Herrett survived but is badly wounded and may not make it, and another four—" Bachuc swallowed heavily and raised his hands in a helpless gesture.

"Another four *what?*" Dronyen demanded. "Out with it, Bachuc. Dramatics don't suit you."

"It's just—they are physically sound, but by all accounts they are not mentally stable enough to be of any use. The things they report having seen are *horrific,* Your Maj. The creature tortured over fifty of your best men to death. Are you quite certain you want to—"

"If you are going to advise me to leave Lethiscir to successfully abscond with my property, Bachuc, I would advise you to hold your tongue. If he is not made an example, where does that leave me? The House of Panloch has ruled Villalu for ten generations, and that rule shall *not* end with me."

"Of course not, Your Maj. I mean no disrespect. But this creature is very dangerous and very powerful, and I fear that your forces will be weakened beyond repair if you continue to risk good men to pursue Lethiscir. There are other ways, Your Maj. Perhaps Lethiscir has family that could be used to set an example?"

"Forgive me, husband, but I agree," Brissa cut in softly, lowering her eyes but continuing to speak. "You should not pursue the criminal or the elf yourself. It is far too dangerous. You are newly king and we are newly wed. My heart would ache were you to make a widow of me already."

"My dear, this matter is no concern of yours," Dronyen replied, voice cold and even. "The danger is mine to face and the risk mine to take. But I thank you for the suggestion, for I believe I *will* pursue them myself." Dronyen's eyes glittered with an excitement Brissa had not yet seen. "Bachuc, send word to the relief team that I shall reach their station by morning, and that I will need more relief stations manned through to Merrowlee. Ready a carriage and the six best men that remain within the palace walls. Lethiscir will face me himself, and the elf *will* be suppressed. It is my duty as king and as a Follower of Frilau to see that it is so."

Bachuc nodded once, bowed to both king and queen, and made a brisk exit.

Brissa swallowed. "Will you not at least wait until morning? The forest is full of perils at night—"

Dronyen chuckled, walked over to where she sat and tipped her face up into a swift kiss. "I do not fear the perils of the forest at night, sweet queen. Fear not. I shall return almost before you have noticed me gone, and I shall bring home our pretty slave."

"You are bringing him back *here*?" She could not keep the shock from her voice. "But you heard what Mister Bachuc said. He has tortured and killed dozens of men. How am I to feel safe in my own home?"

"My dear, I assure you that he will be safe and submissive upon his return. I will not bring him back until he is harmless as a kitten. I would not risk you or the sons you will bear over a slave."

Brissa frowned, but nodded. "Yes, Your Maj. I can't claim to understand how you will make it so, but I trust you."

"As you should. Breaking wild creatures is a particular skill of mine," he assured her, and his smile chilled her to the marrow of her bones.

Her hands shook as she watched him go.

CHAPTER TEN

After much debate, Brieden and Sehrys decided to veer off course in the hopes of throwing Dronyen off their trail. They would have preferred not to stop at all, but the horses needed reshoeing, and they needed some items that were outside of Sehrys's ability to produce from the earth with a flick of his wrist. So instead of northwest to Okoslajec, they made their way northeast toward Lokosgre. It was a small town, although one with a very good market; it sat on the border between the lands of the House of Lajec and the House of Chrill, making it a popular destination for trade in the region, and one not unaccustomed to strangers and travelers. If they were lucky, they wouldn't draw attention.

Neither Sehrys nor Brieden knew exactly where they stood now with regard to Dronyen. Obviously, he had known where they were headed, and by now he might know about Sehrys's restored power and the fact that Sehrys chose to stay with Brieden.

And the fact that Sehrys was willing to kill to defend him.

Sehrys brushed his fingers across the dagger in his pocket more than once as they crossed the river bridge into the city. The sound of splashing and children laughing along the banks did little to calm his nerves. It wasn't until they had made their way down the cheerful cobblestoned streets into the heart of town that he let himself breathe a sigh of relief at the lack of guardsmen bearing the Panloch crest.

They dropped the horses and their carriage off with the farrier and wheelwright before making their way to the bustling open-air market in the town square. Sehrys kept his eyes down despite the bright colors, interesting smells and ringing voices around them, and he flexed his fingers against the urge to tuck his hand into Brieden's. The change in their dynamic had undeniably affected their ability to play the master-and-slave roles.

"We could drop the charade altogether," Brieden murmured, glancing down at where their knuckles, not quite grazing one another as they walked, may as well have been oceans apart. "Surely you could destroy anyone who would dare challenge us, after all…"

Sehrys smiled at Brieden's suggestion, but shook his head. "It will be different when we reach the border cities, Brieden. No one would dare parade a sidhe slave so brazenly anywhere close to the Faerie Lands, but we're still too far east. We would just attract more attention to ourselves than we already are. And…" Sehrys chewed his lip and scanned the crowd. "Just because Dronyen's men aren't about doesn't mean Lord Chrill or Lajec won't send their soldiers if they get word we are here. If they found us, it would put everyone around us in danger, Brieden."

Brieden sighed. "I know. But I hate treating you like a slave."

Sehrys's mouth twitched into a small smile. "You're the reason I'm not a slave any longer. And this is only temporary. We'll be alone again soon enough." Brieden didn't reply; the crowd around them was beginning to thicken and they couldn't risk taking their clandestine conversation any further, but the weight of Brieden's longing settled over Sehrys like a blanket, and it was almost as nice as holding his hand.

When they reached the heart of the market, Brieden immediately ran for the first dairy stall he saw. Brieden had stopped eating flesh, had traded away every bit of dried meat and fish he had. Sehrys had never asked him to do it, but he was touched by the action nonetheless. Brieden had made it very clear that he was *not,* however, about to give up milk and cheese and eggs, and he relished any opportunity to enjoy them. He was guzzling a jug of milk in an almost obscene fashion when another stall caught Sehrys's eye.

"Master, may I...?" Sehrys asked, eyes averted and tone demure.

Brieden attempted to disguise his wince before waving him off dismissively and barking out a gruff: "Stay where I can see you."

Sehrys went over to the stall. His eyes raked the wares laid out on the long, silk-draped table before he picked up the beautifully crafted set of panpipes that had first caught his eye. He wanted to see if they sounded as lovely as they looked, but the merchant behind the table fixed him with a suspicious glare. He looked like the sort who would scream about not being able to sell pipes that had been covered in elf spit, rather than the sort who would try to take Sehrys to bed in exchange for them.

Not that the two sorts never overlapped.

Just as he was sure the merchant was going to demand that he put the pipes down, Brieden whispered, "Do you play?"

Sehrys turned to Brieden and nodded, blushing at the admission. He was hardly a gifted musician, but he had enjoyed making music around the community fire at night as a boy, and seeing the pipes had awoken a longing deep in his gut to create beauty simply for the sake of it. Brieden smiled and took the instrument from his hand.

He talked to the merchant and returned with not only Sehrys's pipes, but a long-necked lute as well. "We should play together," Brieden said softly, as they walked farther into the market. "It would be nice. I've been too long without music."

Sehrys smiled and wanted to hold his hand and kiss him, but settled for "accidentally" brushing his hand against Brieden's thigh.

Brieden responded with a raised eyebrow, which only made Sehrys want to do *more* than hold his hand and kiss him.

"How long will it be until the horses are ready?" he whispered to Brieden.

Brieden licked his lips. "Too long."

THEY FOUND AN INN.

"This is absurd," Sehrys mumbled between kisses, as Brieden pulled him toward the bed. "The horses will be ready in a couple of hours, and you shouldn't spend money on—"

"*Our* money, Sehrys. And there's plenty. I stole it from Dronyen. I can't think of anything *better* to spend it on." Brieden pulled Sehrys flush against him and licked his ear slowly, from rounded lobe to pointed tip. "Can *you*?" he whispered, voice rough against the warmth of Sehrys's ear.

Sehrys swallowed hard, knees wobbling. "N-no, I suppose not." He dropped onto the edge of the bed, leaning down to unlace his boots and pull them off of his feet along with his socks. When he had finished, he stood back up and unlaced the top of his tunic, and then slid it over his head. Blushing slightly, he caught Brieden's eye before nervously working at his belt and pulling down his trousers and undershorts.

Brieden watched, mesmerized, until Sehrys was naked before him. He let out a faint whimper at the sight.

Sehrys smiled, and then bit his lip and averted his gaze. In case he was feeling vulnerable while Brieden stood there fully clothed, Brieden proceeded to remedy the situation.

Sehrys seemed to relax after Brieden was naked too. He reached his hand toward him, fingers lightly touching Brieden's stomach.

"Brieden, is it all right if I...?" Sehrys asked, trailing his fingertips very slowly down the trail of dark hair there. Brieden opened his mouth to say yes, but when all he could manage was a sort of strangled squeak, he simply nodded emphatically.

Sehrys cupped Brieden's hardening length very gently, and Brieden fell against him with a moan.

"Brieden," Sehrys murmured. "You feel so... I want to..."

"Anything," Brieden groaned. "*Anything* you want, Sehrys. Please just—God, I just *want* you."

Sehrys kissed him, still holding Brieden's cock, tracing its contours with his thumb.

"I want us... I want to make love with you, Brieden. Can we... I mean is it all right if we do that?"

Brieden was utterly distracted by the slender fingers and wandering thumb on his erection. He was, however, mentally present enough to find it odd that Sehrys didn't know the answer to that question.

"Sehrys, I... yes, I..." Brieden took a deep breath, forcing himself to move Sehrys's hand away from him, bringing it to his lips to kiss his knuckle. "I'm sorry, I just really can't have a conversation with you while you're doing that."

Sehrys looked sheepish. "Oh."

Brieden smiled. "Not that I'm complaining. It felt really nice." He took Sehrys's hand and sat down on the bed. Sehrys followed his lead.

"Sehrys, of course that's all right. Did you honestly think I'd say no?"

"No. Yes. I don't know. I—"

"Did you want to be the one to make love to me? Is that it?" Brieden ventured after it had become clear that Sehrys wasn't going to continue. "Because that would be amazing."

Sehrys shook his head and looked at his hands. "No, Brieden, I... no. I want *you* to... I want you to."

"That would be amazing too," Brieden assured him, as his thumb rubbed circles over the fluttering pulse at Sehrys's wrist.

"It's... it doesn't mean I liked it. Before, when... I don't want you to think... oh, *Gods,* Brieden."

Sehrys sighed. Brieden laced their fingers together. After a moment, Sehrys looked back up at him.

"Brieden, you've... you've had men *fuck* you, haven't you?" He said the word quickly, pushing it out and then scuttling away from it.

Brieden nodded. "Yes, I have."

"And you... you like that?"

"I do."

"It feels good?"

"It can. When it's done properly, it feels fantastic."

Sehrys squeezed his eyes shut; his whole body trembled. Brieden pulled him into a hug.

"It... the physical act was done to me so many times that I feel like I should never want it again," Sehrys explained, voice cracking slightly. "I feel like there must be something very wrong with me for wanting it. But... I... I need to see what it *can* be. What it *should* be. Does that make any sense at all? Or am I just so damaged that—"

"*No!*" It came out much more loudly than intended. Brieden took a deep breath. "No," he repeated, softly. "There is nothing wrong with anything you want. There is nothing wrong with *you.* Of course it makes sense."

Looking a little embarrassed, Sehrys pulled back and smiled at him. Brieden smoothed the tears from Sehrys's cheeks with his thumbs and kissed him softly. "Sehrys, I'm honored," he whispered, "to be the first man to make love to you. I'm the luckiest man in the world."

Sehrys sighed happily and leaned back for another kiss.

They let the kiss gather heat, and Sehrys pushed Brieden back onto the bed, shifting with him until they were lying across it properly and Sehrys was draped over Brieden's body completely. Brieden ran his hands up and down Sehrys's sides, over the perfect roundness of his bottom, down the backs of his thighs. His skin felt so incredible, like silk and rose petals and the finest velvet.

This was the most important thing Brieden was ever going to do. He would do everything he could to make this absolutely *amazing* for Sehrys. To make Sehrys feel safe. To show Sehrys that making love was different from being taken by force, different in every way that could possibly matter.

Brieden rested his hands on Sehrys's lower back and gently stilled their movements.

"Sehrys… I may need to go down to the kitchens to find some… um… oil or something, for…"

Sehrys lifted his head and gave a smile that couldn't be described as anything other than impish. "I've got something better," he said. He climbed off of Brieden and went over to the dresser, where a jug of water had been laid out along with drinking cups and a wide, shallow bowl for washing. Sehrys poured a bit of water into the bowl, and then dipped the tips of his fingers into the water to produce a soft golden glow. He pulled his fingers away and the water continued to glow, as if by its own volition. A tiny green shoot popped up. It continued to grow and unfurl, until it was a tiny shrub with white-gold branches, pale green leaves and six large, round, crimson flowers. Sehrys looked immensely pleased with himself.

He plucked one of the flowers and brought it to Brieden. Brieden sat up and peered at it; it was definitely a flower, but the petals were tightly closed, their pointed tips twisting together into a spiral. Sehrys placed it in Brieden's palm and began to carefully unwind the tips of the petals until they sprang open. Inside, the base of each petal joined with the others into a smooth wall of plant flesh, creating a cup that held a small pool of glistening liquid. A delicious and utterly alien scent drifted up, sweet and floral but somehow pleasantly sharp at the same time.

Sehrys dipped his middle finger and forefinger into the liquid, and then held them up to Brieden's mouth. "Taste," he commanded softly.

Brieden took Sehrys's fingers into his mouth and sucked gently, finding the taste intriguing and not at all unpleasant. The consistency was very similar to the plant oils he was familiar with, and it tasted tart and fresh and almost effervescent. It made his tongue tingle. In fact, it made his entire mouth tingle.

Sehrys laughed softly at Brieden's expression and dipped his fingers back into the flower. Sehrys trailed the liquid over his own lips, and then kissed Brieden. And... *wow.*

It was as if the kiss were ten kisses all at once. Every part of Brieden's mouth was pulsing with sensation, and when Sehrys's tongue found its way into his mouth, Brieden groaned loudly and fell back against the pillows, pulling Sehrys down on top of him. Sehrys managed to catch the flower before it fell from Brieden's hand, placing it on the nightstand before returning his full attention to the man beneath him.

And for a few moments, Brieden forgot all about making love. Because this, *this* was possibly the most incredible sensation he'd ever felt. The wet warmth of Sehrys's mouth, the soft, plump lips slicked with oil, the talented tongue—Brieden had never felt like *this* before. It was almost too much to bear. "Sehrys, what *is* that?" he gasped when Sehrys pulled away, breathless and smiling down at him.

"It is called *hubia rija* in Laesi. It heightens sensation and is highly prized by lovers."

"I can see why," Brieden murmured, and then the full meaning of Sehrys's words actually sunk in. *Highly prized by lovers.* Which meant...

"Oh, my *God*," Brieden groaned; his entire body spasmed at the implication.

Brieden's lips still tingled with sensation. He pulled Sehrys's lips back against his own, and gripped him around the waist, moving them until Sehrys was lying on his back. He paused to coat his fingers in oil from the flower, and then moved his hand between Sehrys's legs.

He nudged Sehrys's legs apart gently, and then let his fingers slide across that delicious spot behind his testicles, between his cheeks, across his already-pulsing entrance. Sehrys gasped, and Brieden paused.

"Keep going?" Brieden asked. "Or...?"

Sehrys stared at him through eyes like a storm-tossed sea. "Keep going," he whispered, voice rough.

Brieden moved his fingers as Sehrys gasped and emitted breathy moans at the intensity of sensation, and Brieden nearly choked on his own breath with arousal. His fingers were so unbelievably sensitive from the oil, he could feel every nuance of the hot, tender flesh against them. Sehrys looked simply delicious with his head thrown back, his eyes half-lidded, his lips parted and his back arched.

Brieden removed his fingers briefly and dipped back into the flower for more oil. When he put his fingers back at Sehrys's entrance, he began to tease, circling gently and then more firmly before slowly pushing a finger inside.

Sehrys tensed. "*Oh!*"

Brieden paused, both to let Sehrys adjust and to give him an opportunity to change his mind.

Sehrys relaxed around him, and Brieden began to move his finger, overwhelmed by the tight, hot texture surrounding it. He inserted a second finger when Sehrys seemed ready, pausing again until Sehrys relaxed before moving the fingers with and against one another, gently stretching.

"Wh-what are you doing?" Sehrys gasped.

"Getting you ready," Brieden said, not liking the look of confusion on Sehrys's face.

"Hmmm," Sehrys murmured. "So slow. So... *oh.* Feels so *nice.*"

Brieden did not want to cry. He did not want to make Sehrys cry. But the thought that no one had ever done this for him before... something so simple, so easy, to lessen the pain...

No. Now was not the time to think about that. Now was the time to make Sehrys feel good. Now was the time to make Sehrys feel *incredible.*

Brieden let his fingers begin searching. Sidhe physiology seemed similar enough to that of human men, so it would be nothing short of a cruel joke if Sehrys didn't have—

"*Oh, Gods, Brieden!*"

Well. It appeared he did.

Brieden stroked the nub as Sehrys cried out in pleasure and writhed against him. Sehrys didn't even tense when Brieden slipped a third finger inside of him, stroking in and out, spreading his fingers against the softening rings of muscle.

It was nearly time. Sehrys's cock was hard and thick, nearly the same violet-red as his sweat-damp hair, and fluid had gathered at its tip. Brieden licked a stripe down the length of it, pausing at the base for a quick nuzzle. Sehrys's sparse lavender pubic hair was as soft as down, and Brieden had never felt anything like it.

"*Brieden,*" Sehrys whimpered. "I... *please.* I want you. I want *all* of you."

Brieden didn't need to be told twice.

He pulled his fingers out and guided Sehrys into a sitting position with his other hand. Brieden shifted so that he was sitting against the headboard, urging Sehrys to climb on top of him. "I think...

this position might be nice," he suggested, voice rough even to his own ears. "If you want to try it."

Sehrys smiled, allowing Brieden to maneuver him so that he was straddling Brieden's lap. "All right," he agreed, excitement evident in his voice.

Sehrys picked up the flower and drizzled most of the remaining oil over Brieden's length. He pumped Brieden slowly with his hand, and Brieden almost choked at the excess of pleasure. God, he hoped he could last long enough to make Sehrys come first.

Sehrys moved onto his knees, hovering above Brieden. Their eyes locked, and Brieden couldn't help but say, "I love you" before he kissed Sehrys and lined himself up, one hand settling on Sehrys's hip. Sehrys smiled, finally allowing himself to sink down, and took Brieden inside in one slow, smooth motion.

There were no words. Simply no words.

Brieden clutched Sehrys to him, gasping for air, because this was *Sehrys,* and this felt unbelievably good. The excess of sensation was almost more than he could physically take.

Sehrys made a noise that was both soft and gut-deep, and it brought Brieden back, his face falling against Sehrys's neck, his hands moving to Sehrys's hips. He guided him in a steady rhythm, slow to make this last, thrusting up into him each time he slid down.

"*Sehrys,*" Brieden whispered. "Sehrys, you feel amazing. You feel *amazing.*"

Brieden moved his knees up behind Sehrys, feet flat against the mattress, shifting his body until Sehrys gave the strangled yelp of pleasure that meant Brieden had hit the spot he was looking for.

And then they began to move faster.

Sehrys wrapped his arms around Brieden's neck and worked his hips up and down, moaning and gasping and occasionally breathing Brieden's name into his ear, hot and damp and urgent and so desperately intimate it made Brieden's heart throb. Brieden managed to grasp the flower and pour what remained of the tingling liquid over Sehrys's flushed cock, while stroking Sehrys in time to his upward thrusts. Sehrys cried out, moving his hands to clutch at Brieden's shoulders and letting his forehead fall against Brieden's neck.

Sehrys shuddered, and it wasn't until he felt the wetness against his neck that Brieden realized he was sobbing.

"Sehrys..." Brieden said softly, stilling the hand on Sehrys's length and bringing it up to cup his face.

Sehrys shook his head and looked into Brieden's eyes. "No..." he whispered, voice wrecked, but lips crooked into a damp smile. "They're good tears, Brieden. *Good* tears."

Sehrys kissed him and guided Brieden's hand down to his cock. They sped their movements again. Sehrys kissed Brieden over and over, the fingers of one hand digging into Brieden's hair while the other clutched at his back, sobbing and shaking and making sounds of intense pleasure.

All Brieden could do was hold on. He clutched Sehrys's hip with one hand, stroking him fast and firm with the other, and God, he wanted to come. He was unbelievably close, but he had to hold on, he couldn't let go, not until Sehrys did.

And then Sehrys did. He tensed around Brieden; his entire body went rigid. He pulled Brieden's hair without meaning to and screamed Brieden's name.

That did it for Brieden: knowing that when Sehrys lost control and surrendered to pleasure, Brieden was the only thought on his mind and the only word on his lips.

Brieden let go. He came so hard he thought he might lose consciousness. He came so hard he was half-convinced he might never be able to come again. And when he came, he called out

Sehrys's name because Sehrys was the only thought in his mind and the only word he wanted on his lips.

Sehrys's arms were wrapped around him; his face was buried in Brieden's neck and his tears were subsiding.

Brieden wrapped his arms around Sehrys as well and held him, and waited for Sehrys to be the first to speak.

Finally, Sehrys sat up straight, wiped his eyes with the back of his hand and looked down at Brieden with an expression of overwhelming sweetness. "Thank you," he whispered. "That... that was... it was incredible. I've never... I didn't..." he swallowed, and shook his head. "I. Just. *Thank you.*"

"Thank you," Brieden echoed, just as lost as Sehrys for the words to properly convey how he felt about what they had done. "You're amazing."

They kissed, and then Sehrys carefully climbed off of Brieden, letting out a small gasp as Brieden slipped out of him.

Brieden gazed at him with a look of pure euphoria and trailed a finger across the sticky residue on Sehrys's chest without thinking. He brought the finger to his lips to taste. His eyes went wide.

"Sehrys! Oh, my—that's *delicious!* I've never tasted—it's like *ambrosia!*" Unable to contain himself, Brieden leapt at Sehrys, pushing him onto his back and lapping hungrily at his stomach and chest, while Sehrys giggled uncontrollably.

"You're never tasting mine," Brieden mumbled against him. "*Never.* It's disgusting. You... God, *everything* about you is just so... incredible."

Sehrys let his hands fall against the back of Brieden's head and gave a happy little sigh. "You're pretty incredible too, you know."

THEY STAYED AT THE INN. AFTER DINNER, SEHRYS PLAYED HIS pipes and Brieden played his lute, and they fell into easy melodies with one another, finding songs they were surprised to know in common and songs from deep in childhood that they laced together into something new. Brieden sang, and Sehrys was impressed with the fine, clear timbre of his voice.

Later, they lay beside each other and enjoyed the comfort and novelty of a bed to sleep in. They touched each other gently, feeling none of their earlier urgency. Just comfort. Just bliss. Brieden gazed at Sehrys with heavy eyes, smiling.

"I love you," he murmured sleepily, while Sehrys stroked his cheek and watched his breath become slow and even. His features were lovely and delicate in the pale moonlight.

Sehrys couldn't sleep. He waited for Brieden to drift off and then walked to the window, looking out over the village with his arms wrapped around himself. He let his forehead slowly fall against the window pane.

"I love you too," he whispered; the words made him shiver despite the warmth of the room, as a thick rope of fear curled its way around his chest.

Because this was bad.

This was very, very bad.

CHAPTER ELEVEN

IT HAD BEEN NEARLY TWO WEEKS SINCE THEIR night at the inn. Sehrys and Brieden found a beautiful grove of willow trees, too lovely to resist, and stopped earlier in the day than they should have to set up camp.

They spent hours in the tall soft grass together before they even thought to free Raven and Crow from their tethers. Brieden whined slightly when Sehrys remembered the horses and jumped to his feet, the sunlight sparkling on his naked skin, to give them some water and allow them to graze.

Propping himself up on his elbows, Brieden sighed. "I should probably put up the tent," he conceded. Brieden dressed, leaving his boots off so he could feel the warm grass between his toes. Sehrys had put only his trousers back on, and Brieden admired the way his back muscles worked as he untethered the horses. He had memorized Sehrys's body, and he loved partnering the sight of him with the memory of how it felt to touch him. When Sehrys strained his arm so the curve of his bicep came into focus, Brieden remembered the sensation of trailing his tongue across it. When he stretched his neck and the tendons stood out, Brieden remembered tracing their lines with his fingers while Sehrys's throat vibrated with moans.

Tent. Right. Tent. Brieden needed to set up the tent.

Utterly absorbed in one another, they had been traveling at a slower pace since the night they had first made love, taking far less care in selecting their campsites and lingering in their now-shared sleeping space each morning, as well as stopping whenever the desire to touch became too much.

Brieden had just finished stringing the tent between two trees when Sehrys walked over to him, still shirtless, and wrapped his arms around Brieden's waist. Sehrys's skin was sun-warm, and Brieden leaned back against the tree behind him and sighed as Sehrys kissed him.

It was perfect.

Until it wasn't.

Too late, they heard the rustle of leaves above them. Too late, they moved as they realized that something had fallen.

Or rather, that something had been dropped.

The chains hit Brieden soundly on the head, the pain so sharp that he barely registered the sound of Sehrys screaming and the faint smell of iron before the world bled to black and he crumpled to the ground.

THE FIRST THING BRIEDEN BECAME AWARE OF WAS PAIN. His head hurt so badly that he almost vomited. He opened his eyes, tried to sit up and promptly passed out again.

Brieden was more careful the second time. He gave himself a few moments to take stock of his body before he opened his eyes. He wasn't terribly uncomfortable; he was on something soft, perhaps a bed. His arms hurt. He wriggled his hands experimentally. His wrists seemed to be shackled to something, and his legs were bound as well. He opened his eyes to lamplight. Slowly, he began to raise his head. A wave of dizziness washed over him, and he groaned.

"Brieden?"

Sehrys. Sehrys was here. Whatever else might be happening, Sehrys was here. Brieden sobbed. He turned his head toward the voice, and his sense of relief quickly vanished, making space for dread.

Sehrys was directly in his line of sight. The elf was chained to the wall; he sported a black eye and a bloody lip, and his skin had taken on a waxy pallor. He sat with his head on his bent knees and his arms wrapped around his calves, and he was draped in iron chains.

"Sehrys," Brieden croaked. "What—where are we? What happened?"

"We got careless," was Sehrys's flat reply. The defeat in his voice was like a knife in Brieden's heart.

Brieden closed his eyes and inhaled sharply, biting back tears.

They had been so close. If they had paid more attention, traveled a little faster, remembered how unsafe they still were...

"What are we going to do?" Brieden whispered.

"What *can* we do, Brieden? We've been caught. It's over."

Brieden opened his eyes and stared at Sehrys. "No. It can't be over. Schrys, you *know* it isn't really over."

Sehrys's eyes welled up, and he dropped his head.

"I'm so sorry, Brieden. You never should have rescued me."

"Don't say that."

"You shouldn't have. If you'd just left me there with Dronyen, you would be free now. And I'd be in exactly the same position I'm in right now."

"It was worth it, Sehrys." Brieden stared at him, willing him to meet his gaze. "Even if it gets me killed, it was worth it... to be with you."

Sehrys met his eyes then, smiling sadly. "It wasn't worth it if it gets you killed, Brieden. I'm not worth that."

Brieden shifted to his side to face Sehrys. A link in the chains that bound him reflected the lamplight on the wall. Sehrys stared at the link. "Brieden," he whispered, wide-eyed. There was something in his voice. Something that made Brieden's heart skip a beat.

"Your chains... they aren't iron?"

Brieden flexed slightly and inspected them. "No. Bronze, I think? I suppose they'd rather not waste iron on humans when bronze will work just as—"

"Brieden." Sehrys's eyes darted to the doorway and then back. "Please listen carefully because I might not have time to repeat myself. When I... when I healed you back at that inn in Okosgrim, I may have left you with a little something."

Brieden's eyes widened and he opened his mouth, but Sehrys held his hand up as much as his shackles would allow.

"I had to. It's just... just a *little* bit of my power, and it's only temporary, so please don't be upset. But if you can... if you can find an anchor, we may actually be able to get out of this."

Brieden swallowed hard, not daring to let hope rise in his chest. "Anchor?" He asked. "What—"

"You need to anchor the power in something essential to make it work. An element. Earth, fire, water—"

"—air?" Brieden asked hopefully, looking around them.

Sehrys sighed. "No, unfortunately. Air is a conduit, not an anchor. But if you can get your hands on—there!" Sehrys stared at something above and behind Brieden's head. Brieden craned his neck. On the wall above the headboard was mounted an oil lamp: a strong flame burning inside an open-mouthed glass ball.

Fire. That had been Brieden's least favorite option of the three. "What do I... how?"

"The only problem is going to be getting your hands on it. If you can somehow get your—"

At that moment, the door burst open. Dronyen walked in.

Flanked by his guards, Dronyen looked thinner than Brieden remembered in tight black leather riding pants and a belted wine-colored tunic. His eyes were sunken and his skin was sallow, but his shoulders were squared. He wore a look of smug triumph.

"Leave us," he commanded, voice lazy. The guards departed, and Dronyen walked to the middle of the room, crossed his arms over his chest and looked at the two men. His eyes gleamed nearly as brightly as his freshly polished boots.

"So. Boys. We've been having a fun little adventure, haven't we?" His tone was admonishing, laced with a snide mockery of affection. "You know, I've been looking *all over* for you boys. And when I finally thought I had you, you went ahead and destroyed some of my best men, and then disappeared all over again." He clucked his tongue as he rounded the bed and made his way to Sehrys.

Brieden's thumb caught on a loose nail in the headboard, and he immediately set to work attempting to free it with his fingers.

"But I don't mind," Dronyen continued softly. He knelt before Sehrys and stroked his cheek gently with the back of his hand; his dark eyes fixed the elf with a hard stare. Sehrys tried to look away, but Dronyen grabbed his chin and forced Sehrys to look at him. "Actually, elf, it was quite thrilling. I knew you were something special. I didn't think Lethiscir had it in him, but this couldn't have turned out better. I just *knew* that you would be the best I've ever had."

Brieden stilled his hands as Dronyen turned toward him. "You know, Lethiscir, I might actually let you live," Dronyen mused, standing and walking over to him. "He had a bit of wildness to him when I bought him, after all, but after six weeks with you, I believe he's gone positively *feral*." Dronyen growled slightly on the last word, tossing Brieden a lecherous grin.

"And, you really do need to work off all those lovely things you stole from me. Some of those trophies were centuries old, you know. And we'll also need to calculate a fair price for your use of the elf.

How many times *would* you say you've used him?" Dronyen sat beside Brieden on the bed and began to stroke his leg.

Brieden couldn't bring himself to speak because everything he could think of would make Dronyen happier. His hurt, his anger, his need to protect Sehrys—all of it would strike Dronyen as amusing and delightful, and anything that *didn't* strike him as amusing and delightful was likely to make Dronyen hurt Sehrys.

Dronyen continued to stroke Brieden's leg before allowing his hand to trail up Brieden's hip bone, beneath his tunic and across his stomach. His hand came to rest upon Brieden's bare chest.

"So I'm sure we can think of some way for you to pay off your debt, can't we? Because to be honest, you boys are both so scrumptious, I'm not even sure where to start." He watched Sehrys as he spoke, obviously enjoying the fear and horror in the sidhe's eyes as he watched Dronyen touch Brieden.

"What do you think, elf? How about I do everything to him that I've done to you, and let you watch the show? Would you enjoy that?"

"Please don't," Sehrys whispered.

Dronyen threw his head back and laughed. Sehrys gave an involuntary whimper; his entire body was trembling.

Brieden swallowed. "Sehrys, it's all right." He wasn't sure why he said it. It was an insane thing to say because clearly *nothing* could be less right than this.

Dronyen laughed again, patting Brieden's chest firmly before he stood up and clapped his hands. "Oh, you boys are *fun*." He walked over to Sehrys. "So, elf, I believe we may need to establish a few things if I'm going to keep you. Now, I believe we were having a bit of trouble with our first lesson before you left. So let's get back to it, shall we?" Dronyen leaned close to Sehrys. "Who am I to you?" He asked in a soft, private tone as though speaking to a lover.

Sehrys was silent. Dronyen grabbed him around the throat.

Brieden bit his lip so hard it bled while furiously working at the nail in the bed frame.

"I am your final master, elf. Say it."

Sehrys averted his eyes as he struggled to breathe. Dronyen smiled broadly and pulled a dagger from his belt. He held the tip to the tender underside of Sehrys's chin. "Say it, elf, or I'll slit your pretty throat."

"*No!*" Brieden cried out.

Sehrys closed his eyes and sighed deeply. He didn't speak.

Dronyen smiled again and reached out to ruffle Sehrys's hair. "Very well, then. Let's try this a different way." He swung around to face Brieden, who quickly let his hands drop limply behind him.

He strode to the bed and pressed the dagger to Brieden's throat. "Killing him would mean nothing to me."

Sehrys's eyes flew open.

"Now say it."

"Master," Sehrys said without hesitation. "You are my final master. When I die, I will die in your possession. There will never be another."

Dronyen roared with laughter. The dagger bounced against the skin of Brieden's throat and pierced it slightly; beads of blood welled up. "I thought so."

He ignored the blood trickling down Brieden's throat and put the dagger back into his belt, then moved to fetch something from the small table just inside the door. Brieden exhaled heavily and tried to convey reassurance to Sehrys with his eyes. Sehrys simply shook his head and cast his eyes down.

Dronyen returned with a clouded glass syringe heavy with brownish green liquid. "Now, elf, I am going to be kind. I have a proposal for you. I am going to allow you to choose to stay with me, and it is a choice you are going to make."

Sehrys clenched his jaw, his eyes burning with hatred.

Brieden pulled the nail free. Its rusted edge cut his thumbnail to the quick, and he bit his lip to keep from crying out.

"If you choose to stay with me, I will let Lethiscir go. I will personally see to his safe exit and I will let him keep the carriage and horses that are rightfully mine. You'll never see him again, of course, but he will be safe."

Sehrys looked back up at Dronyen, waiting for the rest of it.

"Or... I can keep Lethiscir instead. I will probably end up killing him within the year. Humans are much more delicate stock, as I'm sure you know, but I'm sure I'll have the chance to enjoy him before it comes to that. And if I keep Lethiscir, *you* can go. I'll even see to your safe return to the Faerie Lands. Two hundred years from now, you won't even remember him." Dronyen smiled.

Brieden worked the nail in the keyhole of his handcuffs.

Dronyen held out the syringe. "If you take the first option, I'll even let you inject yourself."

Sehrys reached for it.

"Sehrys, *no*!" Brieden wrapped a fist around the nail and thrashed against the chains, as if that would do anything besides make Dronyen laugh.

Sehrys looked at him, his expression pure misery. "Brieden," he said softly, "he's right. You wouldn't survive."

"Sehrys, he's lying! He's trying to break your spirit. He's going to do whatever he wants! Do you honestly think he would ever free either one of us?"

"Would you like it in writing?" asked Dronyen, staring down at Sehrys. "Witnesses? I'm being perfectly sincere."

Brieden worked the lock furiously.

Sehrys took the syringe.

"Sehrys, I'm not worth it!"

Sehrys took a breath and looked deeply into his eyes. "Brieden, yes, you are. You're worth everything. I—"

Brieden wrenched his arms free.

Dronyen hurled around just in time for Brieden to swing a now-loosened chain and hit him squarely in the jaw with a heavy bronze handcuff.

Dronyen hadn't hit the ground before Brieden picked the lock on his ankle cuffs, desperately trying to keep his hands from shaking. Finally free of all his chains, Brieden jumped up on the mattress, bracing himself against the wall when a wave of dizziness washed over him.

"Brieden!" Sehrys's voice was choked with shock. "Are you—"

"I'm all right," Brieden insisted, taking a deep breath. When he was steady, he unscrewed the globe of the lamp, yelped at the heat as he pulled it free from its base and twisted around to drop it. Dronyen pulled himself to his feet. Without thinking, Brieden hurled the globe at him. The hot glass met Dronyen's temple with a sickly crack. He fell to the floor with an aborted scream.

Brieden turned back to the wall. He stared at the naked flame before him.

"Sehrys, what do I do?"

"Take it and hold it in your hands."

"*What?*"

"Brieden." Sehrys all but hissed, as Dronyen started to stir. "Do it. You *can* do it. You just have to know that you can."

Brieden reached toward the fire, but jerked his hand back when the heat became too intense.

"*Brieden!*" Sehrys's voice was shrill. "You have to know that you can. Not believe it, *know* it. Know it the way you know your own name."

"Sehrys, I can't—"

"Do you trust me?"

"Of course I—"

"Then trust what I'm telling you right now, Brieden. You can do it if you know that you can, the way you know that... that..."

The way I knew that I loved you the moment I first laid eyes on you. Brieden reached into the fire and picked it up.

Cradled in his palms, the flame curled itself into a ball. It wasn't hot, but it was warm, and it felt like a fluttering ball of feathers.

Dronyen once again began to rise.

"Melt my chains!" Sehrys blurted.

"How—"

"Focus your intent. See them melting. See them melting faster than you've ever seen anything melt. Faster than I did it that night in the clearing. Almost too fast to see at all."

"Sehrys, I don't want to burn y—"

"Brieden! I'll be fine! Just *do it*!"

So Brieden did.

It was amazing; the chains softened more and more until they slid off Sehrys like slinky fabric, leaving no residue save for uncomfortable-looking pink marks where they had touched his skin.

Dronyen was fully alert now. Blood poured down the side of his head where the hot glass had smashed against him. He looked at Brieden and spat out some teeth.

And then he looked at the syringe on the floor.

"Brieden!" Sehrys called and held out his hands.

Brieden understood immediately. He threw the ball of fire to Sehrys just as Dronyen reached the syringe and lunged for the elf.

When Sehrys caught the ball, an orange glow lit his entire body; the syringe flew from Dronyen's hand and smashed against the far wall.

Dronyen looked wildly back and forth between the two men, and then pulled out his dagger, obviously deciding to charge at the one he knew was weaker.

As if he had not offered Brieden's life in exchange for Sehrys's freedom, knowing exactly what Sehrys would choose.

As if he had not heard recounted, in vivid detail, exactly what Sehrys had done to the last man who had tried to kill Brieden.

As if he stood a chance in the Five Hells against any sidhe at full power, let alone this one.

Before he could reach Brieden, a ring of fire shot up around Dronyen. The chest-high flames were thin and controlled.

And for the first time, Brieden saw genuine fear in the man's eyes. It suited him.

Dronyen screamed for help. The door burst open. Six guards barreled in and then froze when they saw what was happening.

Sehrys fixed the men with eyes full of dark green fire.

They ran.

Dronyen stared at the open door; his eyes were awash with horror and confusion at being left to fend for himself for the first time in his life. When he finally found his voice, it came out as a plea.

"You—you wouldn't kill me like this, would you? Not like *this*. Look at me; I'm pathetic. I'm helpless. I'll leave you alone, I—you've won, all right? You've *won*. Please, I—"

"What's my name?" Sehrys asked softly.

"I... I..." Dronyen looked up at Sehrys in utter defeat. "Master?" He asked tentatively. "My—my final master. When I d—"

Sehrys snorted. "No, Dronyen. I'm asking you what my name is. You bought me, paid for me, tortured and raped me, tried to break me. I would at least have expected you to learn my name."

Dronyen was silent.

"What is it?" Sehrys asked again, as the flames closed in.

Dronyen sweated profusely. "I... I don't know," Dronyen sobbed. "Please don't kill me."

"I've killed better fleas than you."

Brieden stood quietly behind Sehrys, avoiding Dronyen's desperate gaze.

"Brieden... please—"

Brieden simply shook his head and walked to the other side of the room. He had nothing to say. He couldn't think of anyone who deserved to decide Dronyen's fate more than Sehrys.

Dronyen met Sehrys's eyes. Sehrys didn't look away.

"Please. I'll give you anything. Gold, horses, a castle—titles? You can both have titles! You'll be the only elf in Villalu with a title, it would be..." He swallowed. "I'll give you anything," he repeated desperately.

"Fine," Sehrys said. "Give me back the last six years of my life."

And with a slight flick of a slender wrist, Dronyen was utterly consumed by the flames.

CHAPTER TWELVE

THE FIRE BEGAN TO SPREAD.

Sehrys still held the original ball of flame in one hand. He walked calmly to a stunned Brieden and reached out to him with his free hand.

"We should leave before this entire place, whatever it is, burns to the ground."

"Couldn't... couldn't you stop it?" Brieden asked, accepting Sehrys's hand.

"I could," Sehrys agreed simply, leading Brieden out of the room.

Brieden shot him silent glances as they walked. Sehrys's eyes were still bright with magic, sparkling in the darkened corridor.

No one stopped them as they strode down the long hallway. They were in a mid-sized house of some sort, probably one belonging to a common family and commandeered by Dronyen.

Brieden pulled Sehrys to a stop.

"Sehrys, no. This is someone's home. It could be all they have. We can't let it burn."

Sehrys didn't meet his eyes. "That *someone* let Dronyen use it to torture us. They probably knew exactly what he was doing, and offered up their home as a service."

"Sehrys," Brieden said quietly. "Please look at me."

Sehrys looked at him, eyes so full of green fire they were nearly blinding. Brieden refused to flinch. "This is what I am, Brieden. Do you really expect any sort of mercy from me?"

"Yes," Brieden answered softly. "And you shouldn't feel bad about what you did to Dronyen. He would never have stopped coming after us if you had let him live."

Sehrys snorted. "I'm not a human being, Brieden. Do you honestly think I feel the least bit—"

"Yes. I do. You're not a monster, Sehrys. You're kind and compassionate and you can't convince me otherwise. Do you honestly think you won't feel terrible if you let this house burn? You won't even eat animal flesh. And the way you care about Raven and Crow..."

Sehrys averted his gaze again. "Horses aren't humans, Brieden."

"No," Brieden agreed, "but I am. And... what if this were *my* home? With my children living in it? Or what if I were a servant here?"

Sehrys turned back toward Brieden. The fire faded from his eyes; his lower lip trembled.

"Brieden, you don't understand," he whispered. "With Dronyen, I... I *enjoyed* it. I had to make myself kill him just to stop myself from torturing him. I'm... I'm—"

"You're nothing like him."

"But what if I am? What if that's what he did to me? What if he didn't break me? Maybe he just poisoned me and... turned me into someone like him."

"He didn't. You are *nothing* like him. I wouldn't love you if you were, and the way I feel about you has not changed. Sehrys, stop the fire. Let's leave this place and find somewhere safe and then we can talk, all right?"

Sehrys sighed and nodded. They walked back to the room. Sehrys appeared to do no more than look into it before the flames stopped, simply winking out of existence in a single instant. The room itself had seen much better days; large portions of the floor and walls were charred black, and the bed linens and curtains on the windows had been reduced to singed shreds. There was also a very unpleasant-looking mound of what had once been Dronyen between the bed and the far wall.

Guilt rising in his eyes, Sehrys turned to Brieden. Brieden kissed him. "Let's go," he said gently.

They walked out the front door, hand in hand, Sehrys still clutching the ball of fire.

As they stepped out into a peach-colored sunset, Brieden's eyes widened. He grabbed Sehrys and pulled him down just in time to avoid an iron chain swinging wildly in their direction.

Sehrys looked up, eyes once again alight, and melted the chain in mid-air. A yelp of pain rang out from the guardsman who had been holding it.

A smattering of Dronyen's guards stood circumspectly in the yard in front of them, holding an assortment of weapons. Even through the green fire, Brieden could tell that Sehrys was tired.

Brieden looked at the guards and let his voice ring out loud and clear. "King Dronyen is dead. I understand your desire to avenge him, but if you try, you will be killed."

The men did not lower their weapons.

"This man," Brieden continued, motioning to Sehrys, "has destroyed all of His Maj's best men, as well as the king himself. We are offering you exactly one opportunity to go. Go and tell your erstwhile king that he is king once more. Tell him that his son is dead and that we are responsible. Let King Drayez send more men after us if he will. But at least some of you must live to carry the message, and any who fight will die tonight." Brieden tried to catch the eye of each man. "You have five minutes to leave or you have five minutes to live. It is your choice."

The men exchanged looks. Part of their oath was to defend their king to the death, but clearly that point had passed, at least with this particular king. Slowly, one by one, they departed, until only two remained, side by side.

"I am not a coward, to run cringing from a glorified peasant and a slave!" yelled one, sword aloft.

"Nor I," called the other. Sehrys looked as if he was going to cry.

"Sehrys, can you get their swords away from them?"

The ground rumbled slightly; cracks opened and vines shot up to grasp both swords and toss them at Brieden's feet before slithering back into the ground, radiating the same exhaustion that seemed to be rolling off of Sehrys in waves. The men cried out but stood firm, and then one of them began to advance.

Brieden picked up one of the swords and walked over to the man who was moving toward them.

"Go," he said softly, pressing the point of the sword to the man's chest.

The man swerved and then crouched and lunged at Brieden's legs in one smooth motion. Brieden let the man take him to the ground before wrenching his legs free and kicking him in the face. The man fell on his back. Brieden scrambled to kneel above him and place a knee on his ribcage.

He hesitated for only the barest second before plunging the sword into the guard's heart. He pulled out the sword and swiveled, ducking to avoid the second man's lunge. The man stumbled, and Brieden thrust forward as he sprang to his feet and buried the sword in the second guard's throat.

The man spasmed; horrible gurgling and choking sounds fell from his lips before he finally collapsed beside his dead comrade.

Brieden pulled the sword free and threw it to the ground. Then he walked back to Sehrys, who watched him with wide eyes.

"Now we have both killed today," Brieden said. "Shall we see if we can find our horses?"

Sehrys nodded, and Brieden picked up the second sword. He had awoken in this place without his own sword, and it would be helpful to have one around, preferably one that was not covered in blood.

They found the stables, and Brieden was relieved to find their carriage and horses. Sehrys gasped and immediately ran to the horses. "Oh, darlings," Sehrys breathed, burying his face in Raven's mane and reaching out a hand for Crow to nuzzle. "I was so worried that they would hurt you, just to hurt us. Are you terribly hungry?"

Brieden smiled at the comfort Sehrys took in the horses. He allowed them a few moments together, while he rifled through the contents of the carriage to see what had been taken.

Pilfering their stores must not have been a priority for Dronyen's men. Most of their belongings remained. Brieden lifted one of the benches, happy to see that their food stores did not seem to have been disturbed at all, nor had the stash of gold in the hidden compartment beneath the floorboards. He fetched a few apples—some of the only fresh food they had, but certainly not a waste if they would make Sehrys smile.

Sehrys was delighted by the apples; something almost like peace settled in his eyes as he quietly fed them to the horses.

When Crow and Raven finished the fruit, Sehrys used the fire in his hand to light the headlamps, as it had grown close to full dark, and they prepared the horses in silence.

Brieden looked up at the sky, attempting to orient himself. "So, that direction should be west... and we were headed northwest last I knew, but I'm not sure where we are right now, so..."

Sehrys pointed. "That way. Home is that way."

Brieden looked at him. "How can you tell?"

Sehrys smiled and threw the fireball up into the air. The flames fanned out spectacularly before winking out of existence. "Because I can feel it."

THEY RODE FOR A FEW HOURS BEFORE FINDING A SECLUDED clearing to make camp. Now that Dronyen was dead, the sovereignty would revert to his father, Drayez, at least until one of Dronyen's younger brothers was married—most likely to Dronyen's widow— and crowned. And while the elder Panloch would certainly send men before long, it was unlikely that they faced any immediate danger. Drayez kept a far cooler head than Dronyen, and he would be well-aware of the extent of Sehrys's power and the danger it posed.

Still. They had learned the hard way that it paid to be more cautious rather than less. They pitched their tent beneath the scant light of the waning moons, forgoing a campfire and making a meal of dried fruit and forest greens. They didn't need to attract any undue attention, and there had been more than enough fire in their day as it was.

Sehrys curled up on the far side of the tent almost as soon as he was inside. He had been quiet on the ride, and making his bed so far away from Brieden had barely been a conscious decision. He had just needed a bit of space to mull over everything that screamed in his mind, even though he knew it hurt Brieden to see him pull away.

Brieden hadn't asked about or protested the distance, and lay on his back, his eyes fixed on the canvas ceiling, his brows knit tight as he chewed on his lip. Sehrys watched him out of the corner of his eye in the thin light of their small lantern.

They were steadily getting closer to Laesi, and Sehrys was becoming more and more comfortable with the overwhelming amount of blood on his hands with every obstacle they faced along the way.

No matter what Brieden said, he didn't want to think about how much damage he might cause without this sweet, earnest human to hold his heart.

But that was exactly the problem. Because he *couldn't* let Brieden hold his heart for much longer. And what would happen then? What would Sehrys become when he finally let Brieden go?

Brieden sighed, perhaps more loudly than he intended, and nothing mattered except the pain in that sound. Sehrys crawled across the chasm between them in the tent and slipped into Brieden's arms, then kissed his cheek and, when Brieden turned to face him, his lips.

"Brieden, thank you," Sehrys whispered.

"For what?"

"For saving me from myself. For seeing what was happening inside of me when I couldn't even see it myself."

Brieden opened his mouth to protest, but Sehrys shook his head. "Don't argue. It's true."

Brieden swallowed. "You're welcome."

Sehrys lay his head on Brieden's chest, stroking his abdomen slowly through his tunic.

"I'm sorry I was so... withdrawn after we left. I needed some time to think."

"I understand. But I was afraid..." Brieden drew a deep breath, blinking up at the ceiling. "I was afraid I was losing you."

Sehrys lifted his head to kiss him again, slow and soft. "No," he said. "You're not losing me."

He settled his head back on Brieden's chest. "I don't enjoy killing, Brieden," he murmured, drawing strength from his lover's warmth.

"I know that."

"I just... it scares me sometimes. I haven't been able to properly express my anger in years, and I haven't been able to use my power in years, and then the two rise up together and I don't feel like I have control, and I... I can't stand my own cruelty."

"Sehrys, you had to kill—"

"I know, Brieden, but I didn't have to enjoy it."

"Sehrys, after what those men have put you through, it's only hu—" Brieden stopped himself.

Sehrys laughed. "You were going to say it's only *human,* weren't you?"

Brieden laughed too. "I suppose I was. What I meant to say is that I think it's only *natural* to feel some relief, and probably even enjoyment, in destroying those who have spent so much time and energy trying to destroy you. But it isn't who you are. And you *will* get control. You haven't had your power back a month. And... in the meantime... I can be kind of like your anchor, Sehrys, if it gets too intense. If... if you want me to be."

Brieden's cheeks went pink. Sehrys clutched him tighter, his heart swelling with joy at the simple offer that meant more than Brieden could possibly understand. "You already are," he whispered, and for that moment, all was right with the world.

Sehrys snaked his hand under Brieden's tunic and began playing idly with his chest hair. Every touch, every physical connection between them, strengthened the places where Sehrys felt frayed and stretched thin.

"Those last two men, Brieden, I—"

"I know."

"I couldn't do it anymore. The violence, it was just—"

"I know," Brieden said, running his hand up and down Sehrys's back.

They lay in silence, hands continuing to gently soothe one another's bodies.

"I quite like your chest hair," Sehrys murmured, mindlessly, lost to the sensation of wiry curls and soft skin, to the rise and fall of Brieden's chest.

Brieden laughed. "That was a rather extreme change in topic."

Sehrys smiled against him. "I can't say your body is a topic that's ever terribly far from my mind." He twirled a tuft of hair at the edge of Brieden's nipple, eliciting a soft hum of pleasure. "Sidhe men have very little body hair, and there's something so... *sexy* about how different your hair is."

"Mmm," Brieden replied, slipping his hand under Sehrys's tunic and sliding it up his bare back. "I feel the same way about your skin."

Sehrys moved to kiss Brieden's ear. "I like your ears too. They're so cute and round."

Brieden leaned over to kiss Sehrys's ear as well. "I *love* your ears," he whispered. "They drive me wild." He took the tip of Sehrys's ear into his mouth and sucked gently. Sehrys moaned.

"Brieden? How tired are you?"

"Never too tired for you."

Sehrys gently pulled away from Brieden and crawled toward the entrance to the tent.

"Get undressed," Sehrys said. "I'll be right back."

Sehrys turned his face to the moon as he stepped out of the tent, breathing in the warm summer air. He could sense the change already, the flavor on the breeze from The Border's proximity. It was heady and electric.

For six years, it was all he had dreamed of. Catching that scent again, letting it draw him home by any means necessary. But now...

Sehrys shook his head and knelt to summon from the earth the flowers he needed. Brieden was waiting for him. No matter what the future might bring, Brieden was waiting for him tonight, and he didn't intend to keep him waiting long.

When Sehrys returned to the tent holding two large *hubia rija*, he paused in the entryway. Brieden was lying on top of the blankets, eyes closed, naked and stretched out. His arms were bent, his hands were underneath his head, and a soft beam of moonlight fell across him from the open flap of the entryway.

He was simply stunning.

He opened his eyes and beamed up at Sehrys. "What are you doing?"

"Looking at you," Sehrys murmured. "You're extraordinary."

"Come here," Brieden whispered. Sehrys's lips tilted into a smile and he joined Brieden on the blankets, undressing along the way. They pressed their bodies together, savoring the differences in build, texture and scent, and let their hands roam freely.

Sehrys unfurled the tip of one of the flowers and dribbled a bit on his tongue. He snaked his way down Brieden's body, taking him into his mouth and moaning softly at the feeling, at the taste of him, at the delicious sounds of desperate pleasure he tore from Brieden's throat as he began to move up and down the silken shaft with his tongue lapping softly behind the firm ring of his lips.

"Oh, *God,* Sehrys," Brieden choked, lacing his fingers through Sehrys's hair.

As Sehrys continued to work Brieden over with his mouth, he allowed his hands to wander, cupping Brieden's testicles and squeezing gently, tracing the smooth skin behind them. His heartbeat picked up as he allowed his hands to continue their path, to do what he had been thinking about, wondering about, *wanting* to try. Tentative and trembling, he brushed his fingers between the tight, round cheeks of Brieden's buttocks.

Correctly reading Sehrys's hesitation, Brieden spread his thighs. "G-go ahead, Sehrys, if you want to," he gasped.

Sehrys pulled his mouth fom Brieden's erection and sucked in a deep breath before dipping his fingers into the flower. He let his fingers trail slowly from behind Brieden's testicles to his entrance, grazing across it lightly and then trailing his fingertips back to massage it with added pressure. Brieden gave a yelp of pleasure at the sensation, writhing at the pressure of Sehrys's fingers, every nuance of Sehrys's touch intensified by the oil.

Sehrys could only stare, overwhelmed by the responsiveness of his lover. Brieden was beautiful: head thrown back and biceps straining as he twisted his fists into the blankets beneath him; cock hard against his trembling stomach; muscled thighs spread wide and toes curled.

"Sehrys... I'm close... I—"

Sehrys pulled hand away; his own arousal was slightly tempered by nerves. "Brieden, do you think I could try... I mean, would it be all right if..." his eyes darted down to where Brieden was damp and slick between the legs.

"God, yes," Brieden groaned, spreading his legs wider at the mere suggestion.

"It's just that I've never... I don't want to make a mistake, or hurt you."

Brieden took a deep breath to clear his mind. "Follow your instincts, Sehrys. I'll help talk you through it."

Sehrys bent his fingers and submerged them completely in the liquid inside the flower before moving them to Brieden's entrance. The oil dripped everywhere; little patches of tingling sensation bloomed across the flesh where it landed. Sehrys eased a finger inside of Brieden, and Brieden threw his head back and whimpered.

"All right, so h-hold it still for a minute, Sehrys, it's b-been awhile," he rasped.

Sehrys did as Brieden asked, using his free hand to stroke the insides of Brieden's thighs until they were gleaming with oil.

"You can start to m-move it a bit, now. S-sort of in and out and a-around and... *oh*, Sehrys, j-just like that, that feels *so good...*"

Sehrys watched with nothing short of fascination as Brieden's eyes rolled back in his head and he writhed beneath him.

135

"Y-you can add an-nother one now…"

Sehrys did, surprised at how good it felt just to have his fingers inside Brieden. He moved them in the same way that Brieden moved for him, slowly stretching.

"Brieden, how do I find that spot that feels so nice?"

Brieden panted. He swallowed hard, speaking slowly and deliberately, as if only remembering how to speak with each individual word and instantly forgetting afterward. "C-crook your f-fingers to the f-front a bit, and sort of f-feel it out… it might take some time, but you'll find th-this little—*Sehrys! Nngghh! Oh… Oh…*"

Sehrys gasped at the sheer magnitude of Brieden's reaction.

Brieden bucked against him, giving cries of pleasure, and Sehrys fought to maintain a steady, patient focus on the task at hand. He was so turned on that he could barely see.

"Brieden, do you feel ready for me to—"

"Yes! *Please!* Now!"

Sehrys drizzled himself with oil from the flower, coating himself with a few strokes. He positioned himself in front of Brieden, and slowly pushed inside; a whimper escaped his lips at the incredible sensation that seized his body. Brieden wrapped his legs around Sehrys's waist, pulling himself closer to get better leverage, and Sehrys sank down on his knees a bit more, pulling Brieden so that his lower back rested on Sehrys's thighs.

When Sehrys leaned forward to kiss Brieden, they both moaned deeply at the involuntary thrust the movement created, burying Sehrys even more deeply inside.

"You feel so incredible," Sehrys whispered against Brieden's lips.

"So do you," Brieden gasped. "Don't ever stop."

Sehrys kissed him again, shifting their bodies until he was leaning over Brieden. He held Brieden's hips and began to thrust slowly, shivering and moaning as his body tried to process the sheer volume of pleasure Brieden's body was giving him. He let the deep, gorgeous sounds that Brieden made guide his movements, pulling almost completely out before pushing back in to the hilt; his pace built steadily and his thrusts got harder all the time, as he memorized the angle that made Brieden clutch at his ass and scream.

When he realized that his eyes had squeezed shut, he forced them open, because he could not allow himself to miss this, to give up a chance to watch this gorgeous man completely unravel beneath him. And when Brieden reached for the flower, Sehrys beat him to it, stopping his hips momentarily, snatching up the flower and drizzling Brieden's cock. Sehrys stroked Brieden as he resumed pumping into his body, trying to do both in perfect rhythm, but having to settle for a slightly erratic one.

The erratic rhythm seemed fine with Brieden; he had begun chanting Sehrys's name raggedly; his eyes glazed over, as if in a trance; his chest and forehead glistened with sweat. Sehrys felt drunk on the sight and the feel of Brieden clenched around him. He began to pump Brieden faster with his hand, feeling Brieden tense beneath him, until Brieden threw his head back, screamed and came spectacularly across his chest and stomach. His muscles clenched around Sehrys while he watched it happen, and it was the best thing that Sehrys had ever felt or seen in his life, and he came too, calling out Brieden's name, desperately fighting back the urge to scream "I love you."

Sehrys collapsed onto Brieden, both of them panting, their bodies a mess of sweat and skin and oil and come.

"I love you," Brieden whispered into Sehrys's ear, because he could. Because he was brave. Because he had nothing to lose by saying it.

Sehrys managed not to cry. Instead of answering Brieden, he reacted in his usual way. He kissed him.

"Come on," Sehrys said. "Let's wash."

"How? There's no water source here, and I don't think we have enough to spare in our flasks."

Sehrys kissed Brieden on the nose. "Have you forgotten who you're here with? Come on."

He eased himself out of Brieden's body, rose unsteadily to his knees, crawled over to his satchel, and pulled out a cake of soap. He then helped Brieden to his feet and led him outside. They walked to the middle of the clearing, naked under the open sky.

At the first drop of warm rain on his shoulder, Brieden looked up, startled. "You made it rain?" he asked, voice a soft rush of wonderment. He laughed with the delight of a child, closing his eyes and tipping his face up into the slender column of warm rain around them; his long black eyelashes glistened like jewels in the moonlight. Sehrys beamed; even after what they had endured that day, and no matter what the future held for them, Brieden's face was awash with simple joy, and Sehrys had made it happen.

They took their time washing one another, scrubbing themselves clean of the day behind them, paying no heed to what might lay ahead. By the time they finished, the full weight of their combined exhaustion had settled across them in earnest.

They walked back to the tent, drying themselves halfheartedly with clean cloths before collapsing back onto their decidedly less-clean nest of blankets.

"We should really wash some of our things tomorrow," Brieden murmured, as his fingers twined through Sehrys's damp hair.

"Mmm," Sehrys agreed. "But let's take them to a washerwoman, shall we? I'm sick of hand-washing, and we should be arriving at the first of the border cities tomorrow."

Sehrys couldn't hold back the excitement in his own words, knowing the greater measure of safety the border cities could provide, but he couldn't ignore the way it made Brieden tense in his arms.

And even as Sehrys drifted off to sleep, he could feel the lingering tension in his lover's shoulders as Brieden lay in the tent, eyes open, staring at the canvas ceiling above him once again.

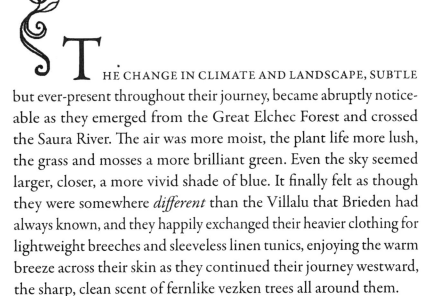

CHAPTER THIRTEEN

THE CHANGE IN CLIMATE AND LANDSCAPE, SUBTLE but ever-present throughout their journey, became abruptly noticeable as they emerged from the Great Elchec Forest and crossed the Saura River. The air was more moist, the plant life more lush, the grass and mosses a more brilliant green. Even the sky seemed larger, closer, a more vivid shade of blue. It finally felt as though they were somewhere *different* than the Villalu that Brieden had always known, and they happily exchanged their heavier clothing for lightweight breeches and sleeveless linen tunics, enjoying the warm breeze across their skin as they continued their journey westward, the sharp, clean scent of fernlike vezken trees all around them.

The west was different in more ways than Brieden had ever understood. He had heard tales of the four border cities as a boy: exotic, godless places where black magic flowed like water and witches feasted upon the souls of wicked children. He had long since dismissed such tales as nonsense designed to scare children into obedience, but the cities had remained by and large a mystery to him, with only scraps of genuine information making its way to those of his class who lived in the east.

"Brieden, you may notice a... shift in how people regard us when we get to Silnauvri," Sehrys told him as the city's walls came into view, barely visible over the rolling green hills spread out before them.

"Slavery is outlawed, yes?" Brieden asked, unable to contain his excitement.

"Slavery is outlawed, yes, which is possible because Silnauvri considers itself to be its own republic apart from Villalu. Though I am sure that Drayez would beg to differ."

Brieden frowned. "And the Lottechets allow it? This is their land, is it not?"

Schrys shrugged. "I believe the House of Lottechet does own the surrounding lands, but the border cities have been here longer than I have been alive. I don't imagine it would be any small feat to overtake them. Though from what I have heard, the Lottechets are only as loyal to the House of Panloch as they must be in order to keep their lands. They certainly don't make any attempt to block entry to the cities."

Brieden considered this. For reasons both religious and political, the House of Lottechet had been among Dronyen's less favored of the twelve royal houses in Villalu. But he had never realized the true magnitude of the Lottechets' defiance.

"But Brieden, House politics aside, I need you to hear me. When we enter the city, you should... well, just make sure you stay close by me, all right?"

"That won't be a problem," Brieden murmured, shifting his head slightly to kiss Sehrys's neck.

Sehrys laughed softly. "Not just for the usual reason. I think you'll find that there might be a bit of a shift in how others... approach us."

Brieden moved his head off of Sehrys's shoulder and looked at him. "Sehrys, what are you trying to say?"

Sehrys sighed. "Things are a bit different in the border cities. Most humans who live in them have... something of an attachment to The Sidhe."

Brieden's eyes twinkled as if he was repressing a slightly lewd comment, but he waited for Sehrys to continue.

Sehrys glanced at Brieden, looking uncomfortable about what he was going to say.

"There is… it's not exactly slavery. But there are many sidhe who like to keep humans as… as pets. Playthings. Some even like to keep a collection. It isn't tolerated in the feririars or in Khryslee, but it is very much the normal way of things in the border cities."

Brieden shrugged. "I suppose if the humans are willing—"

Sehrys shook his head. "They do keep a kernel of free will. A kernel. But many sidhe are gifted with the ability to compel others, especially creatures such as humans, to obey and believe it is their own true desire. And even those who don't possess the power naturally can purchase it easily enough on the black market."

Brieden stared at Sehrys in shock. "Sehrys, can *you*—"

"No. I can't compel, and I wouldn't want to."

"I didn't know that sidhe power can differ from one person to the next."

Sehrys laughed so bitterly that it was startling. "It varies quite a bit, Brieden."

"So… does that mean we should pretend that I'm your… um… pet?" Brieden asked.

"No. We're fine just being… ourselves together. But you're quite a bit lovelier than I think you realize, and I wouldn't want some less noble sort of elf to compel you to them."

Brieden flushed. "Sehrys, if I'm left with even a kernel of free will, no one could take me from you."

Sehrys smiled. "That's very pretty, Brieden, but I don't think you really understand. Just please stay close to me."

Brieden slung his arm across Sehrys's shoulders and kissed him on the cheek.

"Like I said, Sehrys, that really won't be a problem."

Neither man noticed the figure cloaked in blue and silver that watched them with interest from the forest.

SEHRYS WANTED TO STOP AT THE FIRST OF THE RUINS, NEAR the gates to Silnauvri.

He stepped down from the carriage and moved to the overgrown remains of the crumbling statue, tracing it gently with his fingers and looking at it with a mixture of reverence and deep sadness. "B!Nauvri'ija," Sehrys murmured. "*Esil supalin vormikente nau'at.*"

"What's that?" Brieden approached Sehrys from behind.

"*B!Nauvri'ija,*" Sehrys repeated, turning to look at Brieden. "Sacred Weaver of Blossoms. Guardian of Trees. This was Her shrine, but now..." Sehrys sighed. He placed his hand on a tangle of vines covering the remains. Tiny purple flowers popped up one by one. "An offering," he explained to Brieden.

Brieden watched him with a furrowed brow. Something tugged at the edges of his memory, but he couldn't quite place it.

"This... this is a sidhe God?" he asked.

Sehrys nodded.

"But it's in Villalu."

"There are free sidhe in Villalu. Not nearly as many now as there once were, but this is the ancestral home to many feririars, and some choose to stay, no matter the danger."

Brieden moved closer to the statue's remains, trying desperately to clutch at the elusive familiarity of it. "I know. I've seen... there was that one sidhe I saw back in Ravurmik, and my grandmother said—"

Brieden tilted his head. "Sehrys, do... did humans ever worship sidhe Gods?"

"I believe so," Sehrys responded. "I'm afraid I don't know as much as I should about human history, but I know... things used to be different than they are now."

"Is there a God... um... His name is something like Kraaflevina?"

Sehrys raised an eyebrow. "Pardon me?"

Brieden looked sheepish. "Um, He was... blessed something... I think it had to do with shells, or carpets, or... sand?"

Sehrys stared at him until a dawning look of comprehension spread over his face and he burst out laughing. Brieden blushed and looked at his feet.

"Brieden, do you mean *L!Khryauvni?*"

Brieden squinted.

"Blessed Guardian of the Sands That Carpet the World?" Sehrys added.

"Yes, that's it!" Brieden was excited. "I think... I think my grandmother took me to a ceremony, or a ritual, or *something* for Him once. I don't remember that much about it, I was so little, but people brought flowers—"

"Lilies," Sehrys supplied.

Brieden's eyes widened at this freshly unearthed detail. "*Yes!* And... shells?"

"Bivalves, still connected by their ligaments."

Brieden gave a victorious-sounding yell and threw his arms around Sehrys with abandon.

"*Sehrys!* I can't believe I forgot! It was—I remember it was supposed to be a secret. She would talk to me about Kraa—you know, *Him,* and we'd collect shells and pick lilies, and we'd leave honeysuckle out so that the forest sidhe would bless our home, and we—"

Suddenly Brieden froze. "Oh, God," he whispered.

Because something had hit him that wasn't exactly a memory. It was one of those cognitive experiences that begin as a memory from deep in childhood, but then the cracks in comprehension are filled in by lessons learned with age.

His grandmother had been murdered when Frilauan fundamentalists raided his village. This raid had been a bit different than the others, though. The raiders had a figure. It was supposed to look like a person—no, it was supposed to look like a *sidhe*, but it was really sort of like a scarecrow—slung up high in a tree. It wore a crown of lilies and a chest piece of shells. There had been a lot of yelling, and the raiders had burned the figure, and his mother had taken him into the cellar to hide. The next day, his grandmother was dead, along with several others, most of them very old.

All the people they killed had been at the ceremony with Brieden and his grandmother. His mother had told him never to speak of the Sand God again.

And he never had. Until now with Sehrys, at the crumbling ruins outside the rebel city, near the western border of Villalu.

Brieden fell to his knees.

Sehrys crouched beside him.

"Brieden... what is it?"

Brieden swallowed. "Let's... let's get out of Villalu," he said, voice shaking.

SILNAUVRI WAS EASIER TO ENTER THAN BRIEDEN HAD imagined, especially given how imposing the city was; its high stone walls extended for miles in either direction. They presented themselves at large bronze-plated gates, each at least a foot thick and as high as the tallest tree Brieden had ever seen. Guards stationed in turrets on either side of the gates called upon Sehrys to demonstrate that his powers were not being suppressed and he was not Brieden's slave before they were permitted to continue to the second set of gates, which were smaller and made of thick dark wood. Their carriage was thoroughly searched before they moved to the third set of gates, which consisted of polished brass bars, through which was visible the bustle of the city. At the barred gates, they were asked for payment. Brieden began to reach for his purse, but Sehrys smiled and shook his head, selecting a glass jar and candle from an assortment of objects that the guard presented to him.

He scooped the flame from the candle into his hand, and then stretched and shaped it into a squirming ball. He then rolled it into a thin tendril and poured it into the jar as if it were liquid. Sehrys stoppered the jar and handed it back to the man. The guard bowed in thanks and opened the final gate, admitting them to Silnauvri, the easternmost of the four border cities.

"What was *that*?" Brieden asked, when they had ridden out of earshot of the guard.

"They prefer to be paid in magical essence. Much higher market value. Unaccompanied humans trying to gain passage to Khryslee will practically sell limbs to get their hands on a jar like that."

Brieden stared. There was clearly still much that he didn't understand.

Reading his confusion, Sehrys continued. "The Faerie Lands are protected by very strong and very old magics, Brieden. A human being cannot simply cross The Border and stroll in. They can't even force their way in. The simplest way by far to gain entrance is to be led through by a sidhe. If that is not an option, a fresh bottle of magical essence will usually get one through, if the sidhe who provides it is powerful enough. Which I am." Sehrys shot Brieden a rather satisfied smile. "The third option involves complicated spellwork, but from what little I know of that option, it's rarely successful, and is more likely to kill the human who tries it than to actually penetrate the barrier."

"Wow," Brieden murmured. It was dawning on him that they were now in a territory that Sehrys understood and he did not. He was utterly dependent on Sehrys, and the feeling both thrilled and terrified him.

As they rode into the city, Brieden couldn't stop staring. He had never seen anything like it, and he caught himself begging Sehrys to slow down so he wouldn't miss a thing.

The houses were a strange hodgepodge of traditional Villaluan stone-and-wood constructions and structures that looked like giant mounds of leaves, grass, moss and flowers. The mounds were dotted with windows and doors that looked like completely organic and naturally occurring portals, and the only feature that made the dwellings look like something other than bizarre natural phenomena were the neatly stacked stone chimneys emerging from their centers.

"Sehrys! Are those... sidhe houses? Did you live in a house like that? What are those bushes out front? Are those—Oh, my God, those are our red flowers! Growing right out front where everyone can see them! Do people realize... I—wait, what do those houses look like inside? Are they really made of plants? Is there regular furniture, or is it... kind of grown out of the ground, like the houses are? Oh, my God, what is *that*?"

Sehrys's laughter was pure delight as Brieden reacted to everything he saw. More than anything else, Brieden was amazed by what looked like a dragonfly the size of a small goat, dozing in a patch of sunlight on top of one of the sidhe houses.

"Oh," Sehrys breathed when he saw it, warm and wistful. "Yes, Brieden, those are sidhe homes. No, the... structure I grew up in was a bit different, but there were many houses like these in my ancestral lands. Yes, those are our flowers, and yes, everyone knows what they are for. Sidhe culture has no understanding of sexual shame. The dwellings *are* made of living plant matter. The furniture inside is a mixture. Some of it is crafted and some of it is grown with magics. And that," he said, gesturing to the large dragonfly creature, "is a grimchin. There must be a hive nearby: They rarely cross into human lands. That one is probably a pet."

Brieden continued to stare as Sehrys guided the carriage to a sidhe-run inn. A slip of an elfin boy appeared almost as soon as they had arrived to lead Crow and Raven toward the stable.

Brieden watched, captivated, as the youth bounded off.

"I've never seen a sidhe child before," he mused. "How old do you think he is?"

Sehrys glanced back at the boy. "Probably no more than twenty," he said.

Brieden stared at him, open-mouthed. "*Twenty?* Sehrys, that's almost as old as *I* am! How... how old are *you?*"

Sehrys pursed his lips. "Hmm. I was fifty-six when I went on my soul-walk, so probably... sixty-two?"

Brieden was stunned. "But you... you look so *young.*"

"I *am* young, Brieden. I'm less than a century old."

Brieden did not want to ask the question. If he asked the question, he would have to think about what it meant. He would have to think about how much more complicated it made things than they already were. He would have to face the inevitable truth.

He asked the question.

"How long do sidhe usually live, Sehrys?"

Sehrys looked away. "A long time," he said. But before Brieden could seek more information, Sehrys turned back to him with a slightly forced smile. He pulled Brieden close and kissed his breath away.

"It's nice that we can do that out in the open, without fear, isn't it?" Sehrys asked softly, stroking his cheek.

Brieden nodded. "It is."

Sehrys took his hand and tugged him forward. "Come on, I remember this place from when I visited Silnauvri as a child, and I know you're going to love it. You'll never want to stay at a human-run inn again!"

Brieden allowed himself to be temporarily placated by the whimsical beauty of their lodgings. The inn was a grouping of mounds similar to those Brieden had seen on his way into town, but smaller. The innkeeper lived in a large main house. She was an ageless-looking sidhe woman who conversed rapidly with Sehrys in language that sounded like music, then led Sehrys and Brieden to one of the mounds and showed them inside.

The inside of the mound was a single-room dwelling, simply furnished, the walls a woven tapestry of leaves, moss and blossoms. Some of the blossoms emitted a lovely golden glow, and lit the dwelling as if by sunlight. Brieden saw a woven table, reminiscent of wicker, that seemed to grow directly out of the ground, flanked by two carved wooden chairs. The floor was carpeted with impossibly soft and smooth moss, and the room smelled like flowering sweet peas and roses.

Brieden furrowed his brow. He saw folded blankets, but... "Sehrys... where is the bed?"

Sehrys smiled. "Ah, but that's the best part. Come here."

Sehrys led him to a corner of the room where the moss seemed to be of a different texture and consistency than the rest of the floor. Sehrys lowered himself onto his knees, bringing Brieden with him.

They sank into the most luxurious cloud of comfort Brieden had ever felt. The moss formed a deep bed, hugging the contours of Brieden's body and radiating a slight warmth that soothed the aches in his body. He let out a deep sigh.

"*Gods,* I've missed a proper bed," Sehrys groaned, lacing his fingers with Brieden's and letting silence settle over them. They lay there quietly, drinking in the comfort and sense of safety around them.

And in the silence, Brieden couldn't stop the questions from creeping in.

It had been close to half a year since he had first laid eyes on Sehrys.

And it had been well over a decade since he'd last laid eyes on his grandmother.

He wondered if Sehrys would suddenly be reminded of his flash of time with Brieden, centuries from now, the way Brieden had suddenly dredged up the long-buried memory of his grandmother's Sand God.

How long would it take Sehrys to start to forget him?

How strong would the emotion be if he chanced to remember him?

Would he remember him at all?

Sehrys eventually began to press soft, sleepy kisses to Brieden's neck. Brieden turned to him and kissed him fiercely, willing Sehrys to remember his body, his skin, his touch, the passion between them. Sehrys allowed Brieden to lead, let him to play his body like a lute, drawing music from his throat as they came together once again.

And this time, when they made love, it was Brieden who cried.

Chapter Fourteen

BRISSA SAT ON THE COOL MARBLE BENCH AT THE center of the room and stared at the wall of ashes.

The irony could not have been more profound.

The bodies of all deceased Panlochs were burned in the Frilauan tradition. Their favorite slave was cast into the fire, bound to their master even in death. Heavy black urns lined the wall on smooth stone shelves; the empty spot where Dronyen's urn would sit appeared cavernous to Brissa's eye.

Brissa shivered, wrapping her arms around herself despite the stuffy air of the mausoleum. Dronyen's remains were on their way back to the palace. His favorite slave was not only unavailable for burial, but was directly responsible for his demise.

"My, but this place is depressing."

Brissa cast a shadow of a smile toward her twin sister, who stood in the doorway. "It's a tomb, Cliope. What did you expect?"

Cliope shrugged and strode into the room. She leaned down to examine the row of urns shelved closest to the floor. She was a handsome woman who preferred to wear her curls short and her face bare, unlike Brissa, but none who met the two of them could truly be surprised that they were sisters. They shared the same broad nose, twinkling golden eyes and full, dark lips, after all, although Cliope had a smaller stature and a slightly lighter complexion.

"I don't know. Flowers, I suppose?" Cliope responded and shrugged. "A little fish pond? Something more like to the burial grounds on the island."

Brissa sighed. "We're not on Ryovni any longer, sister dear."

"Don't remind me," Cliope grumbled as she straightened up and turned to face her sister. "I have not encountered a decent seaweed platter in months." She sighed. "I miss Mother's cooking."

Brissa could not help but purse her lips. "Mother does not cook. She assembles."

"Be that as it may, she does know how to assemble a delicious platter."

"With ample help from the kitchen staff, I suppose that's true." Brissa's smile was melancholy, and her heart gave a short, painful lurch of yearning for her homeland.

Cliope chewed her lip as she studied her twin's downcast gaze. "They've reached the border cities."

Brissa whipped her head up, fixing Cliope with a hard stare. "When did this happen?"

"Not long ago. The pigeon arrived not twenty minutes ago. We... lost sight of them for a bit, but they're definitely in Silnauvri. Apparently flitting about the place like a pair of lovesick children, barely a care in the world."

"You clearly lost sight of them for longer than a *bit* if they're already in Silnauvri, Cliope," Brissa snapped, pulling off her gloves and twisting them in her hands. "They're too close. You won't reach them in time."

"They are lingering, Brissa. Please trust me. I have eyes and ears from here to The Border and I *will* reach them, but I must leave today."

"Of course." Brissa softened. "Thank you. I—please take care of yourself. I couldn't bear it if anything happened to you."

Cliope rolled her eyes. "Island girls have salted blood. It will take more than a sword or a bit of magic to take me down."

"But still. Be careful."

"You as well," Cliope replied seriously. "Are you sure—Drayez is due to arrive with Dronyen's ashes before long. If you would prefer I stay with you, I am certain Lapyse could handle—"

"No, Lapyse will need you there. They all will. Just—make haste. Do not let them cross into the Facric Lands."

"You have my word, Your Majesty," Cliope vowed, giving Brissa an exaggerated bow. Brissa laughed and rose to her feet; she brushed dust from her skirts before pulling her sister into a tight embrace.

CHAPTER FIFTEEN

On their first morning in Silnauvri, much to Brieden's surprise and delight, Sehrys showed him another feature of their plant-mound inn. Each of the mounds had a path behind it and each of the paths led into its own clearing in a thickly wooded grove.

Their path brought them to the most incredible thing Brieden had ever seen. It was too impeccably constructed to have occurred in nature, but too natural and perfect to have been crafted by human hands. It was a small pond in a little clearing surrounded by dense growth that created a sense of complete privacy. The far side of the pond was fed by a lightly trickling waterfall cascading down gently sloping rocks. The source that fed the waterfall was too high to see. Shrubs and flowers, including large red flowers with tight, closed petals that spiraled to a point, dotted the rocky slope.

Brieden laughed when he saw them. "God, there's no pretense at all, is there?"

Sehrys quirked his lips into a playful smile. "Absolutely none."

The pond was crystal-clear. When Brieden dipped a hand into it, he found the temperature deliciously mild.

The only feature that looked out of place was a polished wooden wardrobe nestled between two trees. Inside the wardrobe, they found everything they could desire for bathing, as well as clean, soft robes.

They each undressed and chose some things from the wardrobe, and then walked over to the pond and slipped in. The water reached Sehrys's navel and Brieden's midriff. The bottom of the pond was carpeted with soft white sand.

The sands that carpet the world.

Brieden forced away the flush of sadness that came over him. Now was not the time to give himself over to pining. Not when they were in a beautiful place like this. Not when Sehrys was looking at him like *that*.

"Brieden," Sehrys said softly, "I think you need a shave."

The tone Sehrys used was so tender, his eyes so soft with longing, that it made Brieden chuckle.

"I'm serious," Sehrys continued. He was holding a brush and a small wooden bowl with some cream-colored powder at the bottom. He dipped the bowl into the water, and then stirred the mixture with a brush to form a rich lather.

"Hold still," Sehrys murmured, still looking at him with eyes that spoke of languorous touches at sunrise. He applied the lather to Brieden's face and throat. He gently lifted a straight razor from the bank and unfolded it.

"May I?" Sehrys asked. Brieden smiled and nodded.

Sehrys shaved Brieden with slow, steady hands. Brieden could nearly feel the intensity of Sehrys's focus, and his breath was close and rhythmic on Brieden's tender skin. He caught Brieden's eyes each time he paused to rinse the blade, and his affection made Brieden's heart throb at the simple, timeless domesticity of the exchange.

When he had finished, Sehrys ran his hands over Brieden's smooth face and bent for a gentle kiss.

"Much nicer," he sighed. "I was starting to get scratch marks on my thighs."

Brieden blushed. "Sorry," he muttered. "I'd offer to return the favor, but you never seem to need it."

Sehrys rubbed his own chin and sighed. "No, sidhe men rarely grow beards, especially not at my age. I do find them... intriguing, but I think I prefer you with a smooth face." Sehrys ran the back of his hand across Brieden's cheek, and gazed at him fondly. "I like being able to see every last bit of it."

Brieden caught the hand in his own and kissed Sehrys on the palm. "I like being able to see every last bit of *you,*" he returned. "Have I told you how unbelievably gorgeous you are?"

Sehrys flushed a radiant rose pink across his pale skin. "Yes, Brieden," he replied, his smile coy. "But that doesn't mean you need to stop."

Brieden kissed him hard. When he pulled back, he covered Sehrys's neck, shoulders, and chest in kisses, pausing between each press of lips to breathe, "*Gorgeous,*" and "*Beautiful,*" and "*Immaculate,*" and "*Perfect*" into Sehrys's silken skin. Sehrys allowed Brieden to walk him backward until he was pressed against the moss-covered rocks with the trickling waterfall cascading gently down Brieden's back.

The water was shallower here, only reaching Brieden's thighs, and the spray from the waterfall misted over their bodies. Sehrys pulled Brieden to him and kissed him roughly; Brieden pushed him further into the rocks. The damp softness of the moss slid comfortably behind him as they rocked together.

Something different was building between them: their usual softness was replaced by a raw urgency, as if anything too tentative or gentle might make them disintegrate. They grabbed at one another desperately, and Sehrys instinctively slid his mouth to the spot where Brieden's neck and shoulder met. He bit down and Brieden gave a rough cry, grabbing Sehrys behind one knee and lifting his leg, grinding into him hard.

Sehrys's hand flew back and groped blindly behind him, coming back with two large red flowers. Not even bothering to unfurl them, he thrust them between Brieden's chest and his own, crushing them, smearing the oil and petals across their bodies, feeling it drip down to their groins and thighs. Sehrys rubbed Brieden's oil-slicked nipples with his thumbs, and Brieden jerked against him with a scream.

"Gods, Brieden, I want you inside me," Sehrys gasped, and Brieden responded by locating the branch from which Sehrys had torn the first two flowers and plucking a third.

As little in the mood for delicacy as Sehrys was, Brieden crushed the flower between his hands, soaking his fingers and palms with tingling sensitivity. Using one hand to rub his length together with Sehrys's, he moved the other to Sehrys's entrance, stretching as slowly and gently as he possibly could, although he was literally *shaking* with need. His ministrations were abruptly halted when Sehrys pulled both hands away and stared at him with dark, hungry eyes. Sehrys placed his hands firmly on Brieden's shoulders.

"Catch me," he growled, using Brieden's shoulders as leverage to jump up and wrap his legs around Brieden's waist. Brieden caught him around the thighs, pressing Sehrys forcefully back against the rocks and thrusting up into him while letting him drop slightly, burying himself deep inside. Sehrys screamed his pleasure, heels digging into Brieden's ribs, his head thrown back against the moss-covered rocks.

There was almost *too* much sensation. Every part of them that touched seemed to be saturated with oil from the flowers, every nerve ending blazing, and all they wanted was *more*.

Brieden's brain had short-circuited, which is why he didn't stop himself from whispering into Sehrys's ear, "Don't forget me. Please don't ever forget me."

"Never," Sehrys gasped out. "I could *never* forget you. Gods, Brieden, *harder,* please!"

Brieden began thrusting harder, very nearly slamming up into Sehrys with the kind of raw passion he'd been afraid of, not wanting to hurt him, not wanting to make him think this was anything other than an act of love.

But it wasn't *other* than an act of love. It was more.

It was need, and desperation and the unspoken understanding that *now* was all that existed because now might be all that they had.

Brieden squeezed Sehrys's trembling thighs, pounding into him and panting nonsensical attempts at verbal expression, as Sehrys let his head roll back, eyes half-closed and utterly unfocused, groaning in pleasure and belting out strings of Elfin words until his entire body shuddered and he came without a touch from Brieden's hands.

And Brieden felt it, saw it and then lost himself completely with one last hard, slow thrust, sliding Sehrys up the rocks farther than he'd thought possible.

Panting hard, Brieden leaned against Sehrys, touching their foreheads together. They stayed like that for a moment, wrapped tightly together, before Brieden pulled out of Sehrys and eased him down to his feet.

Brieden reached a hand to Sehrys's stomach to coat his fingers in a slick mixture of Sehrys's ambrosia, flower oil, petals and sweat. To Brieden's surprise, Sehrys reached a hand to Brieden's stomach to do the same. They didn't break eye contact as they tasted.

"That was... intense," Brieden ventured, after he'd licked his fingers clean.

Sehrys nodded, smiling. "I liked it," he said, almost timidly. "Quite a bit, actually."

"It wasn't too... rough for you?" Brieden asked, his gaze darting away from Sehrys.

"It was what I wanted, Brieden. Was it what *you* wanted?"

Brieden looked back up at him. "Yes."

"Good," Sehrys said, touching Brieden's cheek.

THEY STAYED IN SILNAUVRI FOR ALMOST TWO WEEKS.

Sehrys did long to see his feririar again, and he knew that he was needed at home. The possibility of Drayez's men finding them in one of the stretches between border cities, not to mention at the cusp of The Border itself, still loomed. They still weren't sure that Brieden would be accepted into Khryslee, and Sehrys had no idea where Brieden could go if he wasn't. If another safe haven for humans existed in Laesi, he wasn't familiar with it. Not even the border cities would be safe for Brieden without Sehrys to protect him. The rebel cities may have provided a glimpse into a perfectly melded sidhe and human world, but Sehrys knew that was largely an illusion. And this city, like the others, was definitely not Khryslee.

The air of amicable tolerance and coexistence was tainted by the flesh trade and the black market. Humans desperate to gain passage to Khryslee were willing to do anything to get there, and there were sidhe who had been expelled from their feririars and cast from their ancestral lands for immoral uses of power. The human governments of the rebel cities gave tacit permission for their sidhe residents to indulge their power, no matter how unsettling the manifestation, because these sidhe also used their power to reinforce the city walls and keep them safe from the rest of Villalu.

But as was true in all the border cities, on the surface, Silnauvri was quaint and peaceful and beautiful. And if Sehrys had anything to say about it, that was the only version of Silnauvri that Brieden would see. Sehrys knew that the safety they felt was very much temporary and imperfect, but as long as Brieden stayed close to him, it was also quite real. For the first time since fleeing Villalu Proper, they could relax.

And, then, of course, there was Brieden himself.

He had seemed so sad since discovering how ill-matched his own lifespan was to Sehrys's. Some part of Brieden had really believed that Sehrys would live with him in Khryslee.

"Please don't ever forget me." It broke Sehrys's heart.

They deserved this. *Brieden* deserved this, to step outside of time, to live a handful of days in which all they had to do was bathe and feast and make love and play music and walk hand in hand exploring a beautiful new city. They still had plenty of money, and when they crossed into the Faerie Lands, it would cease to have value, so they indulged.

Brieden and Sehrys both very much enjoyed a particular café. It had menus for human patrons, and its tables were set among lush gardens. The sidhe patrons were given baskets to fill with leaves, flowers, grasses and fruits they chose from the bounty that grew around them. Sehrys never tired of the honeysuckle, and Brieden tried a new kind of cheese each day.

There was an amphitheater where human and sidhe musicians performed, and Sehrys and Brieden attended the performances nearly every night. They also played together in their little leaf-mound domicile and in the clearing around their private pond, Sehrys on his pipes and Brieden on his lute. Once Sehrys put down his pipes and sang while Brieden played, and Brieden stood and clapped so enthusiastically when the song was finished that Sehrys ducked his head with a blush and a grin.

They bought beautiful and useless things at the open-air markets, adorning one another with blushes and shy smiles. For Sehrys,

Brieden picked out a brooch with delicate tendrils of bronze wrapped around deep green stones that reminded him of his eyes. For Brieden, Sehrys selected a pendant, a chocolate-colored translucent slab of stone on a gold chain that glittered in the sunlight and that matched *his* eyes. He slipped it onto Brieden's neck and kissed him tenderly, in the middle of the busy marketplace, in front of everyone.

Brieden was clearly in heaven, and Sehrys was determined to keep it that way.

Although he did take pleasure in speaking his native tongue and being around others of his own kind, the city sidhe of Villalu were not to be trusted. Sehrys had known that simple truth since his very first trip past The Border as a child. He gripped Brieden's hand tightly whenever they were in public, kept his eyes trained on the crowd around them and fixed those whose gaze lingered on Brieden with a possessive glare, making it perfectly clear who the beautiful boy with the sweet smile and the shining eyes belonged to.

It wasn't until the end of their stay that Sehrys was directly approached by another sidhe on the subject of Brieden. They were at their favorite cafe, and a fellow patron broke away from her table of fawning humans to stroll over to them. She was taller than Sehrys, and clearly older as well, and her platinum hair was pulled back into a short braid that was tied off at the nape of her neck. She was attractive, as were all sidhe (at least as far as Brieden was concerned), but not nearly as beautiful as Sehrys. She licked her lips as she looked at Brieden and addressed Sehrys.

"Charmed," she said to Sehrys in a lazy drawl, speaking Villaluan, as was standard practice among sidhe in Silnauvri.

Sehrys forced a tight, insincere smile in return. "Yes, hello. Enjoying your meal?"

"Mmm, not bad. A bit weary of the company, though. You have a lovely boy. Do you ever rent him out?"

Brieden's jaw dropped.

"No," Sehrys answered forcefully. "And he's not mine. He's here of his own free will."

The older sidhe laughed musically. "Shame. He looks delicious. But if you're not using him..."

The sidhe stepped closer to Brieden, cupping his chin and leaning her face close to his. She looked into Brieden's eyes.

And suddenly Brieden realized how beautiful this woman truly *was*. Why hadn't he seen it before? She was at least as beautiful as Sehrys. And he could sense the kindness, the *goodness* within her. Brieden felt his heart swell with emotion.

Was it possible to be in love with two people at the same time?

No. He loved Sehrys. He wanted Sehrys.

But Sehrys didn't love him. And Sehrys probably wasn't going to stay with him. This sidhe, on the other hand—she lived in Silnauvri, and Brieden very much liked Silnauvri. He had never imagined that he could love a woman before, but he had never met *this* woman before either. Brieden could stay with her in Silnauvri and she would never leave him because she hadn't left the other humans that were with her at the cafe, and they all looked so *happy...*

Brieden was jarred out of his reverie by the sound of angry voices speaking Elfin. Sehrys and the female sidhe stood and faced one another, gesturing to Brieden and appearing as if they were about to come to blows. Sehrys's eyes blazed with green fire, and the new sidhe's eyes crackled with gold. The woman turned to Brieden and advanced toward him; Brieden smiled fondly.

Sehrys grabbed the other sidhe's arm and yanked her roughly away from Brieden. His grip seemed to pulse with green light, and his eyes flashed like lightning.

The stranger's eyes widened. With fear.

"Y-you—" she stuttered in Villaluan.

"Esil dronafalt nau'at esil esvish. Nau ria lek gerrila com esilat sed nau fala terevishente enoch," Sehrys cut in, his voice harsh.

"What... what are *you* doing here? With a *human?*" The other sidhe gasped.

"Esil debi nau'at lek mikabdor, lek esil debi nau nauefa malinan. Ablas eslogat nuhup. Esil lek conosupalin silco," Sehrys answered, and released her arm.

"I... I didn't know," the older sidhe said weakly. She stumbled backward, and then glanced at Brieden. His stomach suddenly dropped; the haze of pseudo-love dissolved in an instant.

What in the Five Hells had just happened?

The sidhe hastily made her way back to her own table, her eyes darting back to them furtively from time to time.

"Sehrys..."

Sehrys looked at him nervously, but said nothing.

"What was that?" Brieden finally asked.

"She compelled you. She thought I was weaker than her, and she figured she could take you."

"But... you're not weaker than her."

"No."

"Sehrys... what did she mean, when she asked what you were doing here with a human?"

Sehrys sighed and looked down at the table. "Sidhe with my... particular range of power don't usually consort with humans, that's all."

"Why not?"

"It's complicated."

"Try me." Brieden had never allowed such an edge into his voice before when speaking to Sehrys, and Sehrys looked at him with surprise.

"It's... sidhe politics, Brieden. I wouldn't even know where to start."

Brieden threw his hands up. "Sehrys, we've been traveling together for months. I don't *care* how complicated it is, please tell me. I tell you *everything*. But you—all you give me are half-answers and cryptic implications and I just..." Brieden looked squarely at him. "You're not coming to Khryslee with me, are you? There's not even the smallest chance, is there?"

Sehrys sighed. "No."

Brieden stood up. "Then I guess it doesn't matter. None of it matters."

Sehrys looked up at him helplessly, eyes bright with unshed tears. "Brieden, I never said—"

"I know. You never promised me anything. But I suppose I had hoped that this... between us... that it meant something. To you."

"It does," Sehrys whispered.

"What?" Brieden asked. "What does it mean? What do *I* mean to you, Sehrys?"

Sehrys looked back down at the table in silence.

Brieden felt as if he was going to be sick. He threw a few coins onto the table.

"I'll see you back at the inn." His voice was hollow even to his own ears.

As he walked away, he heard Sehrys sobbing.

He didn't turn around.

Chapter Sixteen

SEHRYS DIDN'T LET HIMSELF FALL APART FOR LONG. After Brieden left, he took only a few moments to pull himself together, to start thinking clearly enough to register one very important fact.

Brieden had left the café. On his own. In Silnauvri.

Sehrys bolted from the table and ran out the gate.

His heart pounded as he scoured the streets. Brieden hadn't been gone long; how far could he have gotten?

He couldn't believe he had let this happen. This wasn't just any human loose in a border city. Brieden had been compelled so easily it was almost stunning, although it shouldn't have been. He was compelled easily because he trusted easily, because his heart was open... Sehrys swore under his breath. In Brieden's current raw state, all it would take was a glance. A glance from a sidhe looking to trade or acquire a new pet, and Brieden would be gone.

Sehrys was going to be sick.

He ran back to the inn as fast as he could. Brieden was not in their little leaf hut, and he was not at the pond. The woman who ran the inn had not seen him. The stable boy had not seen him. The other guests had not seen him.

Sehrys searched the woods around the inn, calling for him. He went to the amphitheater, the market, the public gardens. The more places he visited, the more he began to panic.

Someone had Brieden. He was sure of it. He could feel it in his blood.

Sehrys may have had responsibilities waiting for him at home that were bigger than his own happiness, bigger even than Brieden's happiness. But nothing was bigger than Brieden's freedom.

Sehrys was going to get Brieden to Khryslee. He was going to do everything in his power to give Brieden a good life, even if he couldn't be a part of it. And he was *not* going to allow Brieden to become anyone's toy.

Sehrys ran back to the markets to the stall where he and Brieden had bought their trinkets. It was a long shot, but it might be the only shot he had.

He found a pendant with a clear chocolate-brown stone that glittered in the sunlight. The pendant itself differed slightly, but it was definitely the same sort of stone that had been on Brieden's necklace. And because they were being sold by the same craftswoman, at the same stall, they might have been cut from the same stone. Sehrys bought the pendant and walked back to the inn. He would need privacy.

Inside the leaf hut, Sehrys sat on the floor, closed his eyes and breathed deep. He held the pendant in his hands and concentrated. On the stone. On glittering deep brown eyes. On reuniting that which had been broken.

After a few minutes, the stone begin to glow, and his heart leapt. He allowed his consciousness to follow the thread of connection, slowly navigating the winding path and dimming his awareness of the other pieces of the stone that lingered around the city. All he wanted was *that* one. The one on the thin gold chain, hanging below Brieden's throat. *If* Sehrys was lucky and Brieden was still wearing it.

With a jolt, the connection hit him. The stone. The eyes. The skin. The thoughts and feelings, fuzzy with another's control.

Sehrys's eyes snapped open and he leapt to his feet. He ran to the stables to ready the horses.

BRIEDEN KNEW EXACTLY WHAT WAS GOING TO HAPPEN WHEN the stranger approached him.

That first time, at the cafe, Sehrys had anchored him, had kept him from drifting too far, even as he had tasted the ease of simply letting go.

But Sehrys was gone. Not yet, not literally, but their time together had been nothing but a means for Sehrys to heal some wounds and have some fun. Brieden had welcomed it and he didn't regret it, but he couldn't do it anymore, because Sehrys had told Brieden that he had the power to break him, but Brieden had never told Sehrys that the reverse was also true.

The sidhe who approached him on the way to the inn tried a smooth line to get Brieden to look into his eyes. Brieden knew exactly what he was trying to do.

He raised his head, met the stranger's eyes and let it happen.

SEHRYS SPED ACROSS THE COUNTRYSIDE, FOLLOWING THE pull of the pendant around his neck. The stone actually lifted from his chest, straining forward with sheer determination to join with its other half.

Sehrys was grateful that Raven and Crow had had such a good long rest. They had been well-cared-for at the inn, given plenty of exercise, good food and clean water. He felt bad about pushing them so hard on their first time back in harness, but he had to get to Brieden. He *had* to.

The man at the western gate recognized the description. A few bottles of essence coaxed all the details out of him that he could muster: Three sidhe had left the city with Brieden, heading for Lasemik to "do some trading." They had several attractive young humans with them, and their intent was clear, although they claimed to trade in tableware.

That was the game. That was how it was played.

Lasemik was the largest of the border cities, about seventy miles southwest of Silnauvri. Sehrys sincerely hoped he could reach Brieden well before Brieden reached the city gates.

The sidhe who had taken Brieden would have several days with him before they reached Lasemik. Sehrys prayed that they preferred women and Brieden was not to their taste, and then instantly despised himself for allowing such thoughts to creep in. How dare he wish that kind of illusory, counterfeit consent on another, just so the man he loved could be spared?

In some ways, what The Sidhe did to their human pets was even more terrible than what the humans did to their sidhe slaves. At least Sehrys's mind had always been his own, no matter what had been done to his body. When Brieden had come to him, after six years of slavery, Sehrys had *chosen* to go with him. Chosen it because he could. But after six years of compulsion, any kernel of free will would be gone, rendering a human pet incapable of choosing to leave its master. His true desires, his very self, would simply have burned away and died over time.

Sehrys pushed the horses harder. The pendant strained against his throat.

THE ONE BRIEDEN LOVED HAD NOT TOLD HIM HIS NAME.

"Just call me sir," he had said in a tone that might sound cold coming from anyone else. Coming from him, however, it sounded authoritative but gentle. It sounded lovely.

Sir. His Sir.

The first night they spent on their journey to Lasemik was agreeable, even though Brieden didn't get as much to eat as he would have preferred. The sidhe slept in tents and Brieden and the other humans slept outside, and it was a little cold, especially without blankets, but that was all right because it was what Sir wanted. Brieden slept huddled close with the other humans.

He dreamt of bright green eyes.

He woke up feeling troubled. Sir didn't have green eyes. Sir's eyes were violet. He knew that because he awoke to those very eyes peering down at him.

Sir's hand was on his arm. It was still dark, the moons were high, and Sir tugged him to his feet.

"Come along, Brieden. I have something nice for you to do."

Brieden smiled up at him and rose to his feet. He followed Sir to one of the tents. It wasn't Sir's tent. It belonged to the female sidhe. He followed Sir inside.

She lounged on a pile of pillows and blankets, her pose and eyes seductive. Brieden supposed she was beautiful, with piercing blue eyes, long silver hair and a willowy frame. Her come-hither approach had no effect on him, of course, and Brieden turned to look at Sir in confusion.

"It's all right, Brieden," Sir said with a smile. "Go ahead and take your pleasure with her. It isn't disloyal to me. I want you to."

"As do I," she added, with a musical laugh.

As much as it pained Brieden to argue against Sir, he felt the need to make himself clear.

"But I... I prefer men. *Only* men. I'm sorry." He turned to the woman. "You are very beautiful, but—"

Sir boomed with laughter. The woman scowled.

Sir grasped Brieden's chin between his thumb and forefinger and tilted his face up toward him, and Brieden gasped with excitement.

"Brieden," Sir said in a rich, mellow voice, staring deeply into his eyes, "you want this. You want to be with her. Whatever your past inclinations, you can't resist her. Perhaps you can't explain it to yourself. That doesn't matter. Go to her. Now."

Brieden turned toward the woman. She *was* lovely. Brieden thought about kissing her. It didn't seem like such a terrible idea. Her skin was gorgeous, and it glowed like pale moonlight...

Like Sehrys's skin.

Brieden was suddenly seized by a sharp jolt of pain tearing through his heart. He choked back a loud sob and covered his face with his hands.

Sehrys.

When he looked back up, the two sidhe were staring at him in surprise.

"I... I can't," Brieden managed to utter.

Sir sighed. "All right, then. Go back to sleep with the others." He sounded annoyed, which was very upsetting. Brieden lingered, staring at him.

The woman looked indignant. "What do you mean, go back to sleep with the others? You aren't trying hard enough. Force him!"

"No," Sir said, voice stern. "It's still early on and he could break away completely if I push too hard." He stroked Brieden's cheek. "Give him time."

The woman made a noise of frustration. "But what if he isn't completely yours before we get to Lasemik? You know he will be snapped up as soon as we put him to market. Just look at him! I *want* him. He's magnificent."

Sir smiled. "Don't worry. He will be mine. And then he can be yours for a night. Patience, my lady."

Sir turned back to Brieden. "Go back to sleep with the others, Brieden," he said, his voice more forceful.

Brieden did as he was told.

SLEEPING WITHOUT BRIEDEN WAS MISERABLE.

Sehrys didn't realize how much he had come to depend on his warm body beside him to feel safe. He slept clutching Brieden's sword, sitting bolt upright at the smallest sound.

He did sleep, but not much. Not steadily. The tent was cold and empty and far too large. Sehrys would have preferred not to sleep at all, to press on through the night, but he knew he needed his strength. Brieden was with three sidhe, and it would take all the power he had to overcome three.

How had he ever slept without Brieden? How was he going to be able to spend the rest of his life without it? Without him?

Could he?

Had one of the sidhe taken Brieden to bed with them by now? He clenched his jaw with rage at the thought of someone subverting Brieden's will and touching him without his consent. At the thought of anyone else touching Brieden at all. For any reason. Ever.

For the first time, Sehrys allowed himself to think about whether he could leave Brieden, sacrifice his own happiness for the greater good. He would lose Brieden eventually, of course. He could extend Brieden's life—sidhe did it in Khryslee all the time—but only for so long. Brieden would die first, and Sehrys would have to spend a very long time without him.

But before that, he would be able to spend a very long time *with* him.

Sehrys pushed the thought away. When he returned home, he would be in a position to change things. To make a difference. To save lives. He couldn't dismiss that simply to spend a couple hundred years with the man he loved.

Could he?

No. He couldn't.

Sehrys fell asleep with tear-stained cheeks, his hand placed lightly over the pendant at his throat.

He dreamed of clear brown eyes.

CHAPTER SEVENTEEN

SIR ASKED BRIEDEN ABOUT SEHRYS.

"I *do* love you," Brieden assured him.

"But you love him too."

Brieden sighed. "I love you too much to lie to you. Yes, I love him. But he doesn't love me."

Sir smiled, and something in it gave Brieden a small and temporary pang.

"But you know that *I* love you, don't you, Brieden?" His voice was silken, the words like a healing salve. Brieden had ached for those words for so long, and Brieden knew that Sir was telling him the truth.

"Yes. That's why I'm here with you. I need to be with someone who loves me as much as I love him."

Perhaps it was odd that he didn't desire Sir the way he remembered desiring Sehrys. It wasn't that Sir was unattractive; Brieden had never seen a truly unattractive sidhe, and Sir was objectively lovely with his emerald hair and violet eyes. But the sight of him did not make Brieden's heart pound or his skin tingle.

But perhaps not every sort of intense love was accompanied by intense desire. He had, after all, desired many men that he hadn't loved. It stood to reason that the reverse could be true.

It was evident that Sir did not desire Brieden either; he had taken Kessa, one of the female humans who traveled with them, into his tent several times, but shown no desire to spend the night with any of the rest of them. He also remained adamant that Brieden should make love to the one they called Madame. Brieden wasn't quite sure why Sir wanted this so much, but Brieden wanted to please him. And so on the third night, he tried.

He had allowed Madame to undress him and kiss him and touch him, but he couldn't make himself respond to the touch. He had tried kissing her back, touching her, running his hands over her, everything.

There was a moment when he thought it would work. He was running his hand down the back of her knee, and as he squeezed her sweat-dampened thigh, he was thrown into a memory.

The memory of silken skin and trembling thighs beneath his hands. The body against his own sliding against slick, moss-covered rocks, head thrown back, gasping his name. Brieden felt himself start to harden. "Sehrys," he groaned, burying his face in Madame's neck.

But it was only a moment. Because she smelled nothing like Sehrys. Because he could feel her breasts pressing against his chest. And because she really hadn't seemed to enjoy being called Sehrys.

And so now Sir was asking him about Sehrys, while Madame glowered at them from a distance.

"What is it that makes you hold onto your love for this other elf when you know you were just his plaything?"

Brieden cringed. "I don't think… it wasn't like that."

"No? Didn't you tell me that he rejected your love? That he only wanted to use your body?"

"I wouldn't say *use*—"

"Brieden, I love you for *who you are*. I don't need your body. Do you understand that?"

Brieden wasn't entirely sure that he did, but when he looked into Sir's eyes, it all made perfect sense.

"Yes," he said.

"What I can't understand is why you choose not to take pleasure with our lovely Madame. She is most hurt by your rejection."

"I... I didn't mean to hurt her. I just... I've never wanted a woman in *that* sort of way. I tried, Sir, I really did, but I—"

"Brieden, I can't help but think that if you really loved me, you would feel the desire I tell you to feel," Sir said with a gentle smile.

Brieden gazed into his eyes. "I'm sorry," he whispered. "I'll try harder."

SEHRYS WAS FAIRLY SURE HE WAS LOSING HIS MIND.

It had been four days since he'd left Silnauvri, and he'd seen no sign of Brieden. The pendant continued to tug him in the right direction, and he could feel Brieden's essence mingled with the stone it sought. But he seemed to be getting no closer. It was maddening.

Sehrys strained to close the distance between them, stuffing leaves into his mouth while he drove rather than stopping to eat, sliding to the ground on road-weary legs to slip in a few hours of sleep in the evenings. Sometimes he slept far longer than he should, but he never slept well and he never felt rested. He was haggard and sore and exhausted and knew he needed to take better care of himself, not to mention Crow and Raven, if he was going to overpower Brieden's captors.

But he couldn't stop. He hated sleep. Because they had Brieden, and if Sehrys didn't reach him in time, it would not be only Sehrys who lost Brieden. The *world* would lose Brieden. And Sehrys couldn't do that to the world, no matter how much he hated it sometimes.

Sehrys loved Brieden so much it ached. He loved him so much it burned. He couldn't spare enough feeling to be furious with himself for falling in love with a human because just thinking about it made the love swallow the anger whole. But he had allowed Brieden to get caught. He had allowed himself to wallow in self-pity long enough for Brieden to be taken prisoner, and it was completely Sehrys's fault. And nothing could swallow the fury he felt toward himself for that.

So he pushed ahead, praying to the Gods that he wouldn't be too late, that someday he might be able to forgive himself for what he'd done.

ON THE EVENING OF THE FOURTH DAY, THE SIDHE RATIONED out their water. Milord, the third among them, had complained about how little they had, and asked Brieden how long humans were generally able to live without it. Brieden asked him why he didn't simply summon a column of rain as Sehrys had.

They all looked at him.

"I... thought you said that Sehrys healed you?" Sir asked in an odd tone.

"He did," Brieden said proudly. "He even left me with some residual power, so I could melt iron chains. It was incredible."

The three exchanged nervous glances.

"Brieden," said Sir slowly, staring hard into Brieden's eyes, "you need to tell us *everything* you saw Sehrys do."

Sir was being mature and gracious about Sehrys, even though it must be painful for him knowing that Brieden still loved him. He was clearly impressed with Sehrys's power, just as Brieden had always been. Brieden couldn't hide his excitement when he told him about the night in the clearing when Sehrys had destroyed Dronyen's best men.

"I'm sorry, Sir," he finally said, when he realized that no one else had spoken a word for quite some time. "Is it... painful hearing me talk about Sehrys? I'm sure your power is very impressive too. I'd just never seen a sidhe use their power before I met Sehrys."

"It's fine, Brieden," Sir said shortly. Brieden noticed that the others were busy packing the wagon.

"Are we leaving? But we just arrived."

"We're leaving. We will ride through the night to Lasemik. Now help the others."

"But—"

"Don't ask questions!" Sir roared. "Just *do as you're told*!"

Brieden stumbled backward and then ran to help pack the wagon.

The pendant was absolutely vibrating. If Sehrys hadn't replaced the delicate chain with strong cord before leaving Silnauvri, it would have flown from his neck by now. It strained against the cord, digging into the back of his neck. He couldn't stop for the night as he'd planned. Not when Brieden was so close.

He could almost feel him. Almost feel his skin and see his eyes. He could nearly taste him in his very bones.

"*Huppah!*" Sehrys cried out with all the strength in his lungs. The horses reacted as if the ground was on fire, surging forward so hard that the carriage was temporarily lifted into the air.

"I'm coming, Brieden," Sehrys whispered.

They were almost ready to go when Brieden felt a tug at his neck. He looked down to see his pendant glowing, straining forward of its own volition. He reached up to touch it.

"What's that?"

He looked up to see Madame standing in front of him, eyes fixed on the pendant. "It's a necklace. It just started doing this. I'm not sure—"

"Where did you get it?"

Brieden stroked the stone with his thumb. It was warm. "Sehrys bought it for me."

Madame screamed something in Elfin, then ripped the chain from Brieden's throat so hard that he jerked forward and nearly fell. Sir and Milord ran over, and the three sidhe began shouting rapidly in a language that sounded much less like music than Elfin usually did.

Sir was trying to push Brieden toward the wagon, whereas Milord was trying to pull him back. Madame kept gesturing with the pendant; her eyes were full of fear.

Finally Sir prevailed. He hurried Brieden toward the wagon with the other two close behind, bellowing for the group of humans to *move their asses.*

Brieden saw a faint glint against the moonlit sky as Madame hurled his pendant out of the back of the wagon.

They moved toward Lasemik at incredible speed.

SEHRYS PULLED THE CARRIAGE TO AN ABRUPT HALT.

The pendant had begun pushing back *against* him, as if trying to burrow into his flesh.

As if he had passed the thing it was looking for. He stood up and turned around, and the pendant strained forward again.

He turned the carriage around, guiding the horses into an easy walk. When the strain of the pendant became too strong, he pulled them to a stop and hopped down from his perch.

Sehrys walked slowly around the clearing. It had obviously been abandoned recently; the embers of a fire were still warm in their makeshift pit, and tent-sized patches of grass were still flattened.

Suddenly, the pendant struck him in the chin. He looked up.

Above him, tangled in a low branch, was Brieden's pendant. The chain had been snapped, and the stone was trying desperately to reach its counterpart at Sehrys's neck.

Sehrys pulled a dagger from his belt and sliced the cord free. The pendants flew together, and Sehrys fell to his knees.

A SMALL WOMAN IN THEIR PARTY NUDGED BRIEDEN AWAKE as they reached the gates of Lasemik.

They all muttered their consent to be traveling with the sidhe, and the sidhe among them were instructed to show their power to prove that they weren't enslaved. Brieden watched in fascination as Sir caused a flower to sprout from between the cracks in the cobblestone, Madame summoned that same flower to jump into her hand and Milord caused it to burst into flames.

The three sidhe paid their way with essence and rode into the city.

Brieden didn't see as much of Lasemik upon entering it as he had Silnauvri. Here he was only able to crowd with the other humans and glimpse the scenery through the back of the covered wagon. It was a much busier city, and the smell of cooking food made him clutch his stomach and breathe deep. He hoped that Sir would allow them to explore the markets and sample the local cheeses after they had reached their destination.

They stopped at what appeared to be an inn, although Brieden was disappointed to see that it was a human-run establishment built of stone and wood. Inside, his first impression was that it wasn't particularly nice, or even clean, but when Sir looked at all of them fondly and asked, "Isn't this a *lovely* inn?" they all realized that it was. Why hadn't he seen that at first? Perhaps he was just a bit cranky because he was so thirsty and couldn't remember the last time he had had something to eat.

The sidhe led them upstairs to a dusty, sparsely furnished room with greasy windows.

"This is where you will be staying," Sir said to the humans. "We will be staying across the hall. Brieden, would you come with me, please?"

Brieden smiled. Sir wasn't asking for Kessa. Sir was asking for *him*.

Sir led Brieden across the hall to a considerably cleaner and more pleasant room. Madame and Milord were already there.

"Brieden," Sir said, looking him deeply in the eye. "I want you to desire Madame. That is my deepest wish. Can you do that for me?"

"I..." Brieden faltered. He didn't want to disappoint Sir, or to give Sir cause to doubt his love, but he wasn't sure if he could force his body to respond.

"I do love you," Brieden said desperately. "I just..."

Sir sighed and turned to the others. "We don't have time for this. He's too entrenched. We'll have to stipulate males-only."

"But a caveat like that will bring the price down!" Madame objected.

"We're hardly in a position to worry about *that!*" Sir grated. "That damn *busix* could figure out where we are before we can make any kind of sale at *all*."

"If you recall," Milord interjected coolly, "I did suggest we cut our losses and leave him in the clearing. Then we wouldn't have to worry about any of this."

Brieden wondered what they were talking about. None of it made any sense to him.

Sir barked out a harsh laugh. "Look at him. Even at a reduced price, he's still worth more than twice what any of the others are." He turned to Madame. "I'm sorry. We have to stipulate."

She stomped her foot in frustration.

He then turned to Milord. "There is, however, still the little matter of his hang-up on our many-talented friend. So... perhaps you can help him work that out."

Milord looked at him with pleasure and surprise. "Really?"

Sir laughed. "Of course. We're stipulating, aren't we? No point in deconditioning that little boy-quirk of his now. Just make sure he can't remember the little *busix*'s name when you're through."

Milord smiled as his eyes bored into Brieden. Madame laughed. "Still wish we'd left him in that clearing?"

Milord snorted. "I think you can leave now."

Madame threw her head back and sauntered out, casting one last lingering gaze at Brieden before slamming the door behind her. Sir touched Brieden's cheek and looked into his eyes.

"Brieden, I know that you cannot desire Madame, and I understand. But it would mean very much to me if you would desire Milord. He wants very badly to make love to you, Brieden, and it is my sincere belief that you want him to as well." Sir tilted Brieden's head so that he was looking squarely at Milord.

Milord was really quite handsome: that much had been evident to Brieden all along. But he had never realized *how* handsome. His hair was golden-orange and his eyes...

Oh. His eyes were green.

He looked to be around Sir's age, definitely older than Sehrys, although Brieden couldn't have said how much older. His skin was darker than most of the other sidhe Brieden had seen, and it gleamed gold.

Brieden could do this for Sir. He knew he could.

Milord walked over to Brieden and kissed him, and Brieden shuddered at the pleasure that shocked through him at the contact. He gave a soft groan and leaned closer, his body responding with enthusiasm as Milord deepened the kiss and walked him backward toward the bed.

He heard Sir laughing behind them. "Come see me when you're finished, boys," he said in a playful tone and shut the door behind him.

Chapter Eighteen

After Sehrys got past the gates to Lasemik, finding the inn wasn't difficult.

A covered wagon full of young human women and men and led by three sidhe wasn't the kind of thing that escaped notice, even in a city like Lasemik. Sehrys had only needed to put a few coins in the right palms to find himself at the proper destination.

He walked inside, finding the place dingy and in need of a good day's scrubbing. The air was stale, and the walls were yellowed with what was surely decades' worth of pipe smoke. The middle-aged human man at the front desk eyed him critically.

"You wanting a room, son?"

Sehrys smiled as he approached him. "Actually, I'm looking for someone. I thought you might be able to help me."

The man turned his gaze from Sehrys and began shuffling some papers. "I'm not in the business of putting my hands in other people's dirty laundry. Folks come here, they get their privacy. I'll offer the same to you if you want a room."

Sehrys sighed. "This is very important. I have reason to believe that a dear friend of mine might be here against his will, and I need to find him."

The man frowned. "We don't tolerate slavery around here, son. Our sidhe are free. You should know that."

Sehrys pinched the bridge of his nose and closed his eyes, giving himself a moment to breathe. "All right, look," he said, voice sharp. "I'm not an idiot and I know that three sidhe came in here with a group of humans under compulsion. You probably stuck them in your dirtiest room for triple the rate. Now, I am willing to offer you two choices: You can tell me what room they are in, or I can burn your absolutely *disgusting excuse* for an inn to the *Gods-blasted ground.*" On these last words Sehrys's eyes flashed like lightning, causing the innkeeper to blink.

"Second floor, fourth door on the left. Room twelve," he said quickly.

By the time the man had finished speaking, Sehrys was already climbing the stairs.

Sehrys found room twelve and pounded on the door.

"Who is it?" came a calm, sweet woman's voice with an Elfin accent.

"Housekeeping," Sehrys answered through gritted teeth.

"Oh, I think we're all s—"

Sehrys pulled the dagger from his belt, picked the lock with practiced ease and flung the door open, almost hitting a beautiful female sidhe in the face. Sehrys scanned the room desperately, barely sparing her a glance. The woman was there with a male sidhe—oh, and he was *definitely* the one with the power to compel. That much was clear from the way the eight or nine humans in the room gazed at him.

None of whom were Brieden.

"Where is he?" Sehrys demanded.

"I'm sorry, but *who* are you looking for?" the male sidhe asked smoothly.

"You know *exactly* who I'm looking for. *Where is he?*"

The two sidhe exchanged baffled glances.

Oh no. Had he been following the wrong people? Was Brieden somewhere else entirely? Sehrys felt panic rise in his throat. What if Brieden really was gone? What if he was never going to find him? What if—

"No... just slow down for a moment... *please*—"

The plea was barely loud enough to be heard in the hallway. And the voice was unmistakable.

Sehrys whipped around, hurling himself at the room across the hall. The two sidhe from room twelve advanced on him quickly, and Sehrys pulled out his dagger and held it before him, slamming the backside of his body against the shoddy door to the room that held Brieden. He burst through the door backwards, stumbled to the floor, but managed to hold onto his dagger. He scrambled to his feet with incredible speed and turned to the bed.

Brieden was pinned beneath a handsome male sidhe with cold eyes. The man froze, staring at Sehrys. Sehrys had arrived just in time; both men were already stripped down to their undershorts.

It took a moment before Sehrys could speak. He stared at Brieden, unsure whether he should scream or cry. Brieden stared back at him, his eyes thick with the clouds of compulsion.

And then they flickered. "Sehrys?" he asked, voice small.

"Brieden," Sehrys groaned, choking back a sob. He turned his eyes to the man on top of Brieden. "Get off him," he snarled.

"Or what?" the man sneered.

Sehrys glanced around the tiny room. There was no anchor to be found. They were on the second floor of a human-made structure, and there was no water for washing or drinking in the room. There were no candles or lamps burning. There were no plants or earth, save for what little their boots had tracked in. All three of Brieden's captors wore looks of smug triumph.

Sehrys reached into his pocket and pulled out a small glass jar. It was swirling with fire threaded with streaks of green.

His own essence.

"Or I'll fucking kill you," Sehrys responded.

The man leapt off of Brieden as if he was made of hot coals. He looked at Sehrys as he edged his way out of the room. When he got to the door, he flat-out *ran*. The woman had already fled, probably the second she saw the jar.

Brieden sat up, staring between Sehrys and the sidhe who had compelled him.

Sehrys turned to the other sidhe, who remained standing between Sehrys and Brieden.

"Let him go," Sehrys demanded.

The man looked at him, his lips curling into a slight smile. "No."

"Do you want me to—"

"I'm not afraid of you," the other sidhe cut in, his violet eyes hard as amethyst. "I know what this boy is to you and he isn't just your pet. And if you make a single move to uncork that little jar of yours, I will destroy him."

Sehrys's blood went cold. The man had him.

Only two people can break a compulsion: the person under compulsion and the sidhe who cast the spell. And until the compulsion was broken, the sidhe who controlled Brieden had the power to snap his brain like a twig, to drive him permanently and irreparably insane.

Sehrys swallowed hard and moved past the other sidhe toward the bed, putting the jar back into his pocket.

"Brieden," he said, "please come with me."

Brieden's eyes darted to the other elf. "But... Sir... I'm with Sir now, Sehrys. He loves me."

The other sidhe smiled comfortably, making no move to stop Sehrys from moving closer to Brieden, clearly not seeing Sehrys as a threat.

Sehrys sat down on the edge of the bed. "No, Brieden, he doesn't. He's controlling you."

"No one is controlling me, Sehrys. I chose this." There was a resolute edge to Brieden's voice that surprised Sehrys.

"Brieden, you want to go to Khryslee, *remember*? You want to be free. To be yourself. That's so important to you... you aren't meant to be someone's pet."

Brieden looked away. "I'm staying with Sir, Sehrys. Please leave."

Sehrys stared at him. He didn't seem to be fighting the compulsion. Why wasn't he fighting it? Where was his spark?

"I believe the boy asked you to leave," the other sidhe said.

"I believe this *man* is in no position to know *what* he wants," Sehrys snapped.

"You know, he's telling you the truth. He did choose this."

Sehrys snorted.

"It's true. He knew exactly what he was doing when he looked into my eyes. It was as if he *wanted* to give up control. Easiest conquest I've ever made, to be quite honest."

Brieden had shifted his position on the bed and was now sitting with his back against the headboard and his knees up against his chest. He didn't look at either of the sidhe.

"Brieden," Sehrys said. "Please fight this."

Brieden didn't react.

The other sidhe sighed loudly and strode to Sehrys, grabbing his arm roughly.

"All right, I've had about enough of this. The boy won't want you unless I tell him to want you. So I believe we've reached an impasse. Unless..."

Sehrys turned to look at the man as he jerked his arm free.

"Unless you would like to discuss a fair price."

Sehrys's jaw dropped. "I'm not going to *buy* him from you!"

The other sidhe laughed indulgently. "I don't see why not. You're looking to obtain, and I'm looking to trade. And it isn't as if you can't afford him. He's already told us what you are. The only thing to settle is how *much* essence—"

Sehrys's eyes flashed. "He's not property!" Sehrys roared. "I won't treat him like property. I wouldn't *ever* do that to him." He turned back to Brieden, heart thumping. "Brieden," he begged, "*please. Please fight this. You're strong, I know you are. I don't understand why you won't fight this. I want you to come with me. Please come with me!"

Brieden murmured something into his knee.

"Brieden? What—"

Brieden lifted his face and looked at Sehrys through the clouds in his eyes. "You don't love me," he said simply, his voice like the sound of heartbreak itself.

Sehrys stared at him. He swallowed hard.

"That's not true, Brieden," he answered softly. And that's when he saw it. The flicker in his eyes, the lick of fire parting the clouds.

"Sehrys," Brieden said, his voice shaking. "Do you... what do you mean?"

"He means he's trying to manipulate you," Sir said. "Brieden, look at me."

Brieden ignored him. He continued to look at Sehrys.

"Do you love me, Sehrys?"

Sir lunged. He threw himself between Sehrys and Brieden, taking Brieden's face in his hands and staring at him hard.

"Brieden, listen to me. *I* love you. I'm the only one who loves you. This man betrayed you, and you can never forgive—"

Brieden gave a whimper of pain, twisting to free himself of Sir's grip. Sehrys pulled the other man from Brieden and shoved him from the bed, hard. Both sidhe jumped to their feet.

"Get out," Sehrys snarled.

The other sidhe laughed. "Or else what? I believe we already had this little discussion. If you so much as—"

Sehrys punched him. Hard. In the throat. The force of the blow sent Sir to the ground, gasping, and Sehrys whirled, grabbing Brieden's hand to pull him off the bed.

"Brieden, we have to go. Now. *Please.*"

Brieden held his hand, but resisted the pull. He stared into Sehrys's eyes. "Do you love me?"

"Brieden, we have to—"

"Do you love me?"

Sehrys tried to keep his breath steady. "It doesn't change anything," he said.

Brieden's eyes were almost completely clear. "I didn't ask if it changed anything. I asked if you love me."

Sehrys's heart was pounding so hard it could be heard across the city. "I love you."

Brieden blinked once, and the clouds were gone.

Sehrys heard Sir struggle to his feet behind him. Without breaking eye contact with Brieden, Sehrys reached into his pocket and took out the glass jar of essence, fiddling the cork with his thumb.

There was a pause, and then the sound of footsteps rapidly disappearing behind them as the other sidhe fled the room.

He had seen Brieden's eyes, too. And he knew that his control was over.

"Sehrys," Brieden choked out, his eyes filling with tears, "please tell me you meant that. Please tell me you weren't only saying it to break the compulsion."

"I meant it, Brieden," Sehrys assured him, allowing himself to look at Brieden the way he'd been wanting to look at him for months, his heart in his eyes and nothing withheld. "I love you." Sehrys reached for Brieden's hand, and Brieden responded by squeezing so hard Sehrys was surprised he didn't break his fingers.

Brieden's face broke out into the most radiant smile Sehrys had ever seen. "Say it again."

Sehrys laughed, bright and pure. "I love you!"

Brieden was laughing too. "Say it—"

Sehrys pulled Brieden to him and kissed him. Brieden responded by throwing his arms around Sehrys's neck and surging forward, causing Sehrys to fall backwards and Brieden to land on top of him.

It was a long time before they broke away, kissing each other as though their lives depended on it, as if it was more essential to their survival than gravity or air. Sehrys reached his hands up to cup Brieden's face, pulling back just far enough to whisper it again and again against his lips.

They fell back together, crying and laughing and kissing, neither one sure how long it lasted because time itself seemed like a trivial detail in the face of the joy they were feeling.

When they finally did pause to get some air, Brieden frowned. "Sehrys... the others."

Sehrys looked up at him, trying to remember what other people could possibly exist.

"The other humans... they're planning to sell them. We have to help them." Brieden leapt to his feet to take action; his legs promptly failed him. He fell to the floor in a heap.

"Brieden!" Sehrys knelt beside him.

"Sorry," Brieden mumbled, looking embarrassed. "I'm a little dizzy... I guess I haven't really had much to eat or drink for a while."

"I don't imagine you did," said Sehrys, his brow furrowed. "They probably fed you as little as possible to keep you alive and used the compulsion to keep you from passing out."

"But the others, they—"

Sehrys pressed the bottle into Brieden's hand. "If anyone comes back here and tries *anything* with you, use this. And... don't look them in the eye."

Brieden dropped his gaze to the floor, looking ashamed. "I'm sorry, Sehrys," he whispered.

"Don't, Brieden. Just... I'll be right back. I love you."

With those words, Brieden looked up and met his eyes again. "I love you, too."

AS SEHRYS LEFT THE ROOM, BRIEDEN CLOSED HIS EYES AND felt as if he was spinning. He was overwhelmed with emotion, incredibly light-headed, and he had never been so thirsty.

God, what in the Five Hells had he *done*? He had let himself fall under another's control; he had let other people touch him. People who weren't Sehrys. He had almost let himself get sold, had almost lost himself completely.

But. Sehrys loved him.

Sehrys *loved* him.

And even if they couldn't be together...

No. Brieden wasn't going to think about that. He had time to figure out why Sehrys didn't believe they could be together, time to figure out a way to make it work regardless. Because he loved Sehrys. And Sehrys loved him. And what could possibly be more important than that?

SEHRYS RETURNED TO THE ROOM, HIS HEART HEAVY WITH guilt. The three sidhe and the rest of the humans were gone. They had left the inn, taken the wagon and, according to a few people who had seen them leave, they were heading out of the city.

He wasn't going to find them. Not without leaving Brieden alone in that filthy inn for Gods knew how long. The true extent of his body's distress from being under compulsion for so long would catch up to him soon, and he may not be able to cling to consciousness for long when that happened. Leaving him alone and defenseless simply wasn't an option, no matter how it weighed on Sehrys to leave the others to their fates.

When Sehrys reached him, Brieden's eyes were closed, his breathing was shallow and his skin was unnaturally pale. Sehrys knelt and picked him up.

"Sehrys," Brieden muttered. "The others—"

"They're gone, Brieden, I'm sorry. But I've got you. I'm going to take care of you. It's all right to sleep now, okay?"

Brieden murmured softly against his chest and slipped out of consciousness. Sehrys kissed his forehead gently and carried him out of the room. He and Brieden were not going to sleep in this filth-hole. Sehrys would find them a sidhe-run inn, and maybe they would just have to stay in Lasemik for a little while. Sehrys had never dreaded going home more.

CHAPTER NINETEEN

BRIEDEN AWOKE TO A WARM BREEZE AGAINST THE skin of his back. He opened his eyes slowly, attempting to take in his surroundings.

He was lying on his stomach on a deep, plush bed of—something... moss, perhaps?—covered in a soft fabric. The room he found himself in appeared to be made of wood, but there was something strange about it. Slowly, he realized that the walls seemed to be crafted from a single, unbroken piece of wood, unfinished but smooth. The room was round, and the floor was marked with ever-decreasing rings as if it were made from one enormous log. Round, glassless windows circled the room, which smelled of green leaves and fresh wood.

Brieden heard faint movement off to one side and angled his head toward it. Sehrys stood with his back to him, wearing form-fitting breeches and nothing else. He was doing something at what appeared to be a wooden table growing out of the floor. Brieden remained silent, enjoying the view.

He had a few muddled memories of Sehrys gently urging small sips of water and bites of something food-like on him and pressing his warm body against Brieden's as he drifted in and out of dreams. He also faintly remembered Sehrys wrapping his arms around him and filling him with soft, cool light, which would explain how utterly wonderful Brieden felt. It wasn't quite the same way he'd felt after waking up at the inn in Okosgrim, though. This felt mellower by far, and Brieden had no desire to climb out of bed or even move at all.

He felt a smile creep across his face as Sehrys bent to pick something up from a basket on the floor. God, he had missed watching him.

And then he remembered that he had missed it because he hadn't been with Sehrys. He'd been with Sir. And Madame. And Milord.

He had let them take him, let them control him. They half-starved him and tried to make him have sex with two of them, including a *woman,* and they had been planning to sell him.

God, if Sehrys hadn't—

Sehrys.

Sehrys *loved* him. He hadn't been dreaming that part, had he?

He was fairly sure he hadn't been, but he was also having a difficult time determining what exactly had been real and what hadn't. Being under compulsion had felt like a dream, and breaking free from it had *still* felt like a dream because he'd been so weak and dizzy...

Brieden didn't realize he'd emitted a panicked whimper until Sehrys turned abruptly with a wedge of melon in one hand and a knife in the other.

His soft expression shifted into one of concern. "Brieden? Are you—"

"I love you," Brieden croaked desperately, his heart all but lurching to a halt in his chest as he waited for a response.

Sehrys's face broke into a wide smile. He deposited the fruit and knife on the table, and then walked over to Brieden to kneel by the side of the bed. He took Brieden's hand in his.

"I love you, too," he answered, and his gaze obliterated any possible doubt.

They both moved into the kiss at the same time, each reaching out to cup the cheek of the other, the sweetness of the contact making them sigh and melt closer together.

Brieden smiled as he pulled back, feeling somehow shy.

"I was worried for a moment that I might have dreamt it."

"It was real," Sehrys assured him, stroking Brieden's chin with his thumb. "And it still is."

Brieden swallowed. "Sehrys, I... I knew what he was going to do. Sir. Or whatever his name actually is. I just felt so lost and sad and..." He sighed and winced as he attempted to run a hand through his tangled hair.

Sehrys climbed onto the bed beside Brieden, pulled his hand away from his hair and reached up to smooth the tangles with gentle, nimble fingers. "Brieden, I know. I understand."

"I... I'm so sor—"

"You have nothing to apologize for," Sehrys cut in, stilled his hands in Brieden's hair and held his gaze. "You were vulnerable and you had a moment of weakness. You were a person with a heart. That is your only crime. If anyone is to blame, it's me."

Brieden gaped as Sehrys resumed working on Brieden's hair. "*What?* Sehrys, no. I left you at the cafe, I didn't give you a chance to—"

"I should have followed you. I should have come after you right then and there. Well, no. What I should have done was never give you cause to leave in the first place. I should have told you everything and not been such a coward."

"You're not a coward," Brieden insisted, stroking Sehrys's cheek. "You're the strongest person I've ever met."

Sehrys swallowed and lowered his hands to his lap. "Brieden, I'm not. I—do you have any idea how much you terrify me? I can't stay with you—I can't *let* myself even consider it, because—" he wrapped his arms around himself, drew an unsteady breath and began to tremble.

Brieden pulled Sehrys into his arms and held him, stroking his back in soothing patterns. More than anything, he wanted to ask, to respond, to *argue,* but he held his tongue, because this was as close as Sehrys had come to contemplating a life with him. The confession was so delicate Brieden was afraid it might tear in half if he so much as let a whisper of breath touch it.

"I'm not... just a normal sidhe, Brieden." Now his voice was shaking too.

"I didn't imagine you were," Brieden said softly, breathing out.

"If I belonged to a different caste, I could go with you. Even then it would be terrifying because your life is so much shorter than mine, and I don't know how I'm ever going to survive losing you, and it seems so much less painful to lose you now, even though I'm not sure how I'm going to survive that either..."

He clutched Brieden tightly. His skin had grown even paler than usual.

"It's all right, Sehrys," Brieden soothed. "It's all right to be scared. I'm here. I'm right here."

Sehrys drew a deep, shaking breath and squeezed Brieden even tighter.

"But, Sehrys, if it were me..." Brieden ventured. "If I could either lose you now or lose you years from now, I would take the years. I would take every second I could get. I... I know it isn't fair. But the only thing in the world that I know I want is you."

"It's... it's about more than what I *want*, Brieden." The despondency in Sehrys's voice was enough to make Brieden choke back tears.

"What else, then?" Brieden murmured, burying his nose in Sehrys's hair and breathing deep.

"I... Brieden, I just got you back. I don't want to ruin it. If I promise that I'll tell you soon, can we just... celebrate right now? That we're here and free and together? Maybe just love each other and put the rest on hold?"

Brieden closed his eyes, pulling Sehrys even tighter into the circle of his arms as if holding on tight enough could keep him there forever, keep every problem and complication and unanswered question at bay. "All right," he finally answered. "I... I can do that. Yes."

"Thank you," Sehrys whispered. His tears were warm against Brieden's neck.

The moment was interrupted by a loud rumble from Brieden's stomach, and Sehrys laughed, loosening his ferocious grip on Brieden. He tilted his head to meet Brieden's eyes.

"Come on. There's plenty to eat, and I believe you are long overdue for a good meal." He wiped his eyes; a sweet smile spread across his face as he rose to his feet and held out his hand to Brieden, who moaned and fell backward onto the mattress, pulling the blanket more tightly around his body.

"But... couldn't you bring it here? This bed feels so good."

Sehrys raised an eyebrow; his eyes brightened into mirth. "Brieden, the table is literally ten paces away."

"True. But the bed is *right here*. And it's even more comfortable than the one we had in Silnauvri."

"You have been lying in that bed since yesterday. Now get up or I will throw the painstakingly hand-picked selection of cheeses I bought for you out the window."

Brieden quickly pushed himself back up to a sitting position. "Cheese?"

Sehrys chuckled as he walked to a cluster of branchlike hooks growing from the wall and pulled down a lightweight robe. "Yes. Cheese." He tossed the robe to Brieden. "I knew you would be in the mood for more than fruit and leaves after your ordeal."

Brieden stood, and as the blanket slipped away, he found himself naked. He looked down at himself and then gave Sehrys a cheeky grin.

Sehrys threw his hands up. "The more exposed skin there is, the faster I am able to heal you. I assure you that my actions were completely honorable."

"Of course they were," Brieden answered smugly, pulling on the robe.

"I take no responsibility for any... indecorous thoughts that may have occurred during the process."

"Oh no?" Brieden asked, moving to sit next to Sehrys.

"No. That would be entirely your fault. For looking so..." Sehrys tilted his head.

"Indecorous?"

"I was going to say delicious." Sehrys bit into a piece of melon slowly, then held Brieden's gaze as he licked juice from his fingers. Brieden sucked in a ragged breath as he watched Sehrys suck one slender finger completely into his mouth and then pull it free with a loud pop.

"Eat!" Sehrys urged with a playful smile, gesturing to the bounty spread across the table, He had outdone himself. The table was laden with sliced melon and berries, various cheeses, tender salad greens and a large, crusty loaf of fresh bread. Sehrys poured Brieden a cup of water from a glass jug while Brieden ripped a large chunk of bread from the loaf. Feeling as if he were tasting food for the first time in years, he moaned with pleasure again and again as he sampled everything he laid his eyes on. The fruit was sweet and succulent and perfectly ripe, and Sehrys had chosen the best assortment of cheeses Brieden had ever tasted, which was especially impressive since Sehrys never ate it himself.

"You're too good to me." Brieden sighed, popping a berry into his mouth and gazing at Sehrys.

"Says the man who rescued me from slavery and saved my life," replied Sehrys with a small smile.

"I could say the same of you. Except that you've saved my life far more often."

Sehrys laughed. "After the first time, it hardly makes sense to keep track."

Brieden smiled, drinking in every bit of him.

"I missed you so much." The words came softly, like a confession, and there was a slight blush on Sehrys cheeks when he looked up to meet Brieden's eye. "It was only a few days, but..." Sehrys shrugged. "I missed you."

"I missed you too," Brieden said. "Even under compulsion. You were still the last thing I thought of every night."

They stood up together, abandoning the meal. Their hands caught and their fingers laced together naturally as they moved toward the bed.

As they sank into the soft mattress together, Brieden let his hand slide down the smooth, soft skin of Sehrys's back and threw his leg across Sehrys's hip. Brieden's robe began to slide back, and Sehrys lifted Brieden's arm gently to ease it off of him completely.

"I love you," Sehrys said, and that was all it took. Brieden's lips found his, and they became lost in one another's bodies.

Brieden unlaced Sehrys's breeches and peeled them off, then grabbed his buttocks and pulled their bodies flush against each other. They slid together for a few moments before Sehrys pulled back, pushed Brieden down onto his back and straddled him.

"I don't care who else has touched you, Brieden. You're perfect and I love you and you're mine. Will you let me show you?"

Brieden simply stared up at Sehrys, who was straddling him naked and aroused and glowing with slight perspiration, and nodded, helpless.

Sehrys began pressing tiny kisses to Brieden's neck, moving his lips across the sensitive flesh of his throat while his hands gently caressed Brieden's chest. Brieden moaned softly while Sehrys worked his way downward, mouth and hands progressing ever lower.

When he reached Brieden's stomach, Sehrys skimmed his fingertips up and down his legs, the lightest touch imaginable, making Brieden shiver. He moved his mouth to Brieden's erection, teasing it lightly with his tongue before crawling up the length of Brieden's body. Sehrys paused to kiss Brieden delicately on the lips before moving his mouth to Brieden's ear.

He traced the shape of Brieden's ear with the tip of his tongue before whispering, "Brieden, would you please turn over and close your eyes," and kissing his earlobe.

Breathing heavily, Brieden complied. Sehrys moved away from the bed for a brief moment and then returned, his lips back upon Brieden's ear almost immediately. Brieden shuddered at the rush of sensation that the tickle of his breath sent through his entire body.

"Tell me if you don't like this, but I—"

"I'll like it," Brieden gasped out. "Anything you want to do, Sehrys... I'll like it."

Sehrys smiled against his ear. "All right. Just lie there. Keep your eyes closed. Let me take care of you."

Brieden expelled something between a whimper and a sigh as the familiar drizzle of tingling liquid fell across his back. Sehrys straddled him, and Brieden could feel the strain of Sehrys's erection pressing into the cleft of his ass. He shifted slightly and groaned at the sensation as Sehrys began to massage his shoulders.

It was undeniably erotic, but also just... incredibly relaxing. Sehrys kneaded the muscles of his neck, shoulders, and biceps and then moved down his back; the oil not only heightened the sensation of Sehrys's touch but seemed to speed the relaxation of his muscles as well. When he reached Brieden's tailbone, Sehrys lifted himself from his seat on Brieden's rear and moved his oil-slicked hands there instead. He kneaded the firm cheeks and began pressing light kisses to them.

Brieden sighed with pleasure. He felt Sehrys shift off of him, and then felt a gentle nudge at his hip.

"Brieden," Sehrys said softly. "Would you lift...?"

Brieden lifted his hips and allowed Sehrys to stack pillows beneath them, ever mindful of his groin as he shifted Brieden into position.

Brieden's heart pounded as he contemplated where this might lead.

He felt Sehrys settle between his thighs, gently pushing his legs further apart with his hands. And then Sehrys's hands were on his buttocks again, hot breath mingling with cool air as Sehrys spread him open.

"Oh. God," Brieden whimpered, and felt himself shamelessly arching up toward Sehrys's mouth.

It was all the encouragement Sehrys needed. He spread Brieden's cheeks even further, and then the slick tip of an oiled tongue was teasing Brieden's entrance.

Brieden bucked slightly, and even though Sehrys's hands were holding him gently in place, the movement caused Sehrys's tongue to dip slightly inside. Brieden gripped the bed coverings and howled.

Sehrys began darting his tongue in and out, moving it from side to side and in hard tight circles around Brieden's rim; the tender flesh throbbed with sensitivity and made Brieden writhe, alternating between grinding down into the pillows and arching into the searing wet heat of Sehrys's tongue.

Brieden had tried this before, with other boys, but he had never gotten past wrinkled noses and giggling experiments. Sehrys lapped at him as if he was *hungry* for him, as if there was nothing he would rather taste, moaning and licking and kissing until Brieden was nearly delirious with need.

"Sehrys, *Please.* I want you... I want you inside me."

Sehrys pulled his tongue out of Brieden, and Brieden tilted his ass up even higher, knees digging into the mattress, legs spread so wide the muscles in his thighs screamed for relief, but he'd never felt better. Never felt more beautiful or aroused or desperate to be claimed and *taken* and filled.

"Please," he repeated, a tiny, broken plea, and Sehrys gave a deep moan, settling his hands on Brieden's hips.

"Gods, look at you," he murmured. "You're the most gorgeous thing I've ever laid eyes on."

Brieden groaned with relief when slender fingers slipped inside him, the stretch so satisfying he could probably have come from that alone, even before Sehrys's fingertips grazed the spot inside where he'd been yearning for contact.

When Sehrys finally thrust into him, he breathed, "I love you" against Brieden's neck, and his lithe, strong arms wrapped tight around his waist. Brieden reached back to loop an arm around Sehrys's neck, then turned for a sweet, awkward kiss so that he could whisper the same words back.

They made love slowly, gasping out their love, and one another's names, and the names of deities, as their bodies rocked together, warm and close and tight and so, so deep. Sehrys's hand trailed up Brieden's body, splaying flat across his heart as he pressed kisses into the sweaty valley between Brieden's shoulder blades. Brieden could feel his love at every point of contact.

The buildup was so slow that they didn't notice precisely when soft noises of bliss turned to heavy grunts of passion, but as the pleasure built, their breath became more ragged, their bodies sweatier. Brieden thrust his hips up roughly as Sehrys ground him down into the mattress until finally he came, screaming, with Sehrys buried to the hilt inside him and shuddering through his own release only seconds later.

"Mine," Sehrys whispered against Brieden's hair, still inside him and holding him tight as their breathing slowed. Brieden closed his eyes and smiled.

"Yours," he agreed, and let himself believe that it would always be true.

CHAPTER TWENTY

"**H**OW ARE YOU DOING THAT?" BRIEDEN ASKED, as he watched Sehrys light candles with a single flame produced from his fingertip. "Don't you need an anchor?"

Sehrys smiled. "I have one." He gestured around the room. "Or haven't you noticed that we are inside a tree?"

Brieden opened his mouth and then closed it, pulling himself up from the bed so that he could look out the door.

He *hadn't* realized they were inside a tree, although it did make sense now that he looked around. He had been distracted because he and Sehrys had spent the entire day making love.

Brieden pulled on his robe and parted the curtains that hung over the entrance to the room, and his eyes widened as he stepped out to the landing and looked around. The tree was enormous, and their room seemed to be about two-thirds of the way to the top. A spiral staircase circled the trunk from top to bottom, broken by landings like the one outside their own door and interspersed with foliage that seemed to come from a hundred different species of trees. Four other trees of similar design surrounded them, towering high over the city.

Off in the distance Brieden saw something... odd. It was almost like looking down into the sea from atop a cliff, but the rippling surface was entirely vertical, stretching as high and wide as he could see, and obstructing Brieden's view of anything that lay beyond it. "What's that?"

Sehrys came outside to join him, but the answer dawned on him a moment before Sehrys responded.

"That's The Border."

Brieden was speechless. The sheer magnitude of it was overwhelming, even at such a distance, and he didn't know whether he would be able to walk up to it without falling to his knees in awe. "It's..." he finally began, trailing off.

"I know," Sehrys agreed.

"What's it like, Sehrys? Is it completely different on the other side?"

"Not completely different, no. Some of the plants and animals are different, although some animals can cross The Border at will. It's only meant to keep humans out."

Brieden glanced at him. "But why? I mean... why is it like this?"

He didn't need to explain what he meant because it was clear that he meant *all* of it: the slavery, the compulsion, the abandoned ruins, the religious persecution. The Border itself.

"I don't know," Sehrys sighed, easing himself onto the wide bench on their landing. He sat facing the lush green landscape that disappeared into shimmering blue-gray. "I *should* know," he continued, frowning, as Brieden sat next to him. "I... I was a different person before I left the feririar, Brieden. I wasn't terribly responsible. I neglected any and all studies that weren't directly related to sharpening my power."

Brieden smiled slightly. "That doesn't sound like you."

"Yes, it's amazing what slavery can do to a person," Sehrys said, his eyes going cool. "I never used to have a care in the world. I used to just flit around kissing boys and eating flowers."

"You still do that," Brieden pointed out.

Sehrys laughed. "Yes, I suppose I do. But... I never thought about deeper truths, Brieden. I never thought about what any of it meant. I led such an easy, comfortable life, and I chose not to learn about the ugliness in the world. I lost my sister far too young, and it was horrible, and that was all the ugliness I cared to acknowledge."

Brieden took his hand, watching Sehrys as he gazed at the undulating Border with a faraway look in his eyes. He wanted to ask Sehrys about what would happen when they crossed that Border, and why Sehrys was fighting the idea of staying with Brieden. He wanted to know what made Sehrys different from other sidhe, although he couldn't imagine it actually making a difference. He would want to be with Sehrys no matter what.

But knowing the truth could also mean knowing, actually *knowing*, that that this journey across Villalu really was all they could have.

So Brieden didn't ask.

"So..." Brieden said, searching for a topic. "Do plants... trees, I mean—do they count as earth? I mean, as far as anchoring goes."

Sehrys nodded. "If they are growing out of the earth, yes. Some aquatic plants function as water."

"Hmmm," Brieden mused. "One thing I don't understand, though."

"Yes?"

"Sir—he could compel me no matter where we were. He didn't seem to need an anchor or essence or anything like that."

Sehrys nodded. "There is a fifth anchor, for those sorts of powers."

Brieden stared at him for a moment. "Are you... going to tell me what it is?"

Sehrys rolled his eyes as if it should be obvious. *"Life,* Brieden. Any power that relies on a direct link to another source of consciousness uses life as its anchor. Healing works in a similar manner. When I healed you and he compelled you, we drew the power from your life-source. That's why you retain a bit of power for a week or two afterward. It's kind of a give-and-take."

Brieden was incredulous. "So I... retained some of his power after I broke the compulsion?"

"I cleared you of it," said Sehrys in a disgusted tone, as if he were referring to cleaning a pile of vomit. "You do still have a bit of my essence lingering, though, from the healing."

"So," Brieden mused, "Do I have enough of your *essence*," he punctuated the word with a lewd expression, at which Sehrys rolled his eyes fondly, "so that I can grow our flowers?"

Sehrys considered this. "You know, I'll bet you could."

Brieden smiled. "Show me how?"

Sehrys nodded happily and stood up to lead Brieden back inside.

THEIR TIME IN LASEMIK WAS FAR TOO SHORT.

As much as he wanted to linger with Brieden in the soft bed at the tree inn, Sehrys was unsettled. He knew he wouldn't feel entirely safe until they had crossed The Border, and the only way they were going to be able to do it with any degree of safety was to bypass the other border cities and cut through the forest.

Objectively, it was the safest route. But it made Sehrys's heart pound, made him wake up and pace in the middle of the night. Because the safest way he could think of to go back in would be to follow the path he had taken out. To travel back through that clearing where he had been caught. The place where he had been raped for the first time, the place where he had first been treated like a thing rather than a person.

But it would be different this time. This time he would travel it with his eyes open, and with Brieden beside him.

But still... to go back there...

ON THEIR THIRD NIGHT IN THE TREE, BRIEDEN AWOKE TO soft sobs. Sehrys wasn't beside him. Brieden sat up and looked around, finding himself frozen in horror when he finally located him.

He was curled up tightly against the wall, naked, with moonlight flooding in through the windows and making his pale skin glow. Sehrys's face was pressed into his knees, and he was crying so hard his entire body shook. It reminded Brieden so vividly of that first night in Dronyen's castle that he thought he would be sick. He moved across the room as fast as he could and knelt beside the elf.

"Sehrys," he whispered, placing a gentle hand on his shoulder. Sehrys looked up at him, unable to stop sobbing, unable to speak. Brieden pulled him into his lap and held him tightly, stroking his back and planting occasional soft kisses on his forehead. They stayed like that for a long time, until Sehrys cried himself to sleep and Brieden carried him back to bed.

WHEN SEHRYS WOKE UP IN HIS ARMS, BRIEDEN DID NOT ASK what it had been about, although Sehrys could see the fear and concern in his eyes.

Over breakfast, Sehrys told him.

"There has to be another route we can take, Sehrys," Brieden insisted.

Sehrys sighed. "There is. There are. But you don't understand, Brieden, The Border is *chaos*. It wasn't nearly this bad when I was a boy, but the last time I crossed..." Sehrys shuddered. "The Panlochs wouldn't even bother with it, none of the rebel cities want to claim it, and the eastern feririars want nothing to do with it because all of the trouble is on Villaluan soil. The humans and The Sidhe... they *hunt* one another there. And then there are all the humans desperate to get into Khryslee, willing to do anything to get through, and all the recently exiled sidhe starting floods and fires because they're terrified of humans and because their power goes a bit... haywire when they're forced across. The only way to get through quickly and somewhat safely is to use one of the lesser-known routes. And the one I came through the first time... it's the only one I know."

"We'll find another," Brieden said, crossing his arms over his chest and sitting up straight.

"Brieden, it's too dangerous. We just—it's all right. I'll be all right, as long as you're with me."

Brieden looked thoroughly unconvinced.

Sehrys rubbed his swollen and red-rimmed eyes. "We can't simply stroll through The Border anywhere. We have to go through a portal. It's the most secluded one I know of... it's logical, Brieden. I'm just being..." Sehrys waved a hand dismissively at his own emotional reaction.

"Sehrys. You are planning to revisit the site of the most horrible thing that has ever happened to you. I'm sorry, but that doesn't sound *logical* to me. Can't we ask around? Look for another way? I don't want you to do this."

Sehrys shook his head, tracing a grain of wood in the tabletop. "I can't—if we start to ask, people might figure out where we are going. Who I am. I just need to get you to Khryslee before I can go home, Brieden. Please."

"Sehrys—"

"Please, Brieden." Sehrys closed his eyes and bit his lip, voice small and broken. Brieden pulled his chair closer and held him, but the stiffness of Brieden's embrace betrayed his frustration.

THEY LEFT THE NEXT DAY.

It had become clear to Brieden that any argument with Sehrys about their route would end with Sehrys curled up and sobbing while Brieden tried to suppress the guilt and anger wrestling inside him. So he gave in.

He did, however, secure one very important promise. Sehrys had agreed that after they crossed The Border, he would answer Brieden's questions, even though Brieden wasn't entirely sure he wanted to hear the answers.

But that would be after they crossed The Border.

After they followed the path that Sehrys had been led along in chains.

After they found the clearing where Sehrys had been held down and taken by force for the first time.

Brieden very much wanted to introduce the men who had done it to his sword. With his bare hands, he wanted to destroy every man who had ever hurt Sehrys. The more Sehrys cried, the more Brieden itched for a good spot of justified violence. It was slightly unsettling, but nothing seemed to quell it.

"We should get some more weapons," Brieden said abruptly as they readied the carriage.

Sehrys gave him a noncommittal look.

"If it's really as dangerous as you say, we need to be prepared. And if anything happens to… compromise your power, I want to be able to fight. We need more than a sword."

Sehrys sighed. "Yes, that probably makes sense."

"*No one* is going to hurt you again, Sehrys," Brieden said. Sehrys flinched at his tone.

Brieden wrapped his arms around him. "I hate this," he murmured. "I know it's nothing compared to how you're feeling, but I don't want to take this route any more than you do. When I think about what they did to you—"

Sehrys nestled against him. "I hate it too. But Brieden, I meant it when I said that I'll be all right as long as you're with me. Before, when I was caught... I've never felt so lonely in my life. But I've never felt *less* lonely than when I'm with you."

"You have me," Brieden whispered, and kissed him again. *At least until Khryslee.*

On their way out of the city, they bought bread and cheese and fruit and butter and weapons: in addition to swords, they now had several throwing stars, a quiver of iron-tipped arrows and a bow, a set of iron knuckles studded with jagged spikes, a double-sided battle axe and a whip. Brieden had the least expertise with the whip, but he was sure he could handle it with reasonable competency if the need arose.

Maybe the arsenal was overkill. But he wasn't taking any chances, and he could think of no better use for the last of their money.

Because after they left Lasemik, there would be nowhere to spend it.

CHAPTER TWENTY-ONE

BRISSA ADJUSTED HER CROWN AND SMOOTHED the white lace of her gloves before opening her parasol against the midday sun. The gown she wore was one of her favorites: seafoam-green Ryovnian silk edged in stark white lace and dotted with tiny polished pearls at the sleeves and waist, with pale green slippers to match.

"Are you sure you wouldn't prefer to take a carriage, Your Majesty?" Vyrope asked, after weaving through the group of ladies to fall in step beside Brissa as they made their way out of the castle. "It's rather warm out today." She stood nearly as tall as Brissa in her own pale peach dress, her green-brown eyes shining with excitement. The ladies all looked their best that afternoon, but Vyrope looked particularly lovely, with her glossy black hair freshly plaited and her dress perfectly tailored to her voluptuous curves. The soft smattering of freckles across her nose was unusually visible in the sunlight.

"I am sure I'd rather walk," Brissa assured her with a smile. "It is a short way, and the day is beautiful. It reminds me of springtime in Ryovni."

Vyrope closed her eyes and breathed deep. "That it does. It bodes well. How do you feel?"

Brissa cocked her head as they moved onto the stone pathway to the palace gates. "I feel like a queen."

The ladies approached the gates at a leisurely pace and flanked Brissa when she came to a stop. The outer stone gates were thrown wide, but the thick bronze bars of the inner gate remained in place. Brissa nodded to the guards who stood poised to defend the gate and handed her parasol to Vyrope as those in her path parted to let her through.

"What is the meaning of this?" came the demand from the other side of the gate.

"The meaning of what?" Brissa inquired, tipping her head to the side and smiling at Drayez. "I was notified that you had arrived in an attempt to seize the throne. Surely I am not expected to throw the gates open to a usurper, am I?"

Drayez stared at her. Behind him, his small entourage of a dozen guardsmen clad in breastplates and chainmail exchanged uneasy glances.

"I am patriarch of the House of Panloch, as you well know, and it falls upon me to see to the running of the kingdom until Thieren is crowned," he said. "Have you gone mad, child?" The arrogance and irritation in his eyes made him look more like Dronyen than usual, despite his weathered skin and the gray hair at his temples.

"Not as such, no," Brissa replied. "I simply have no desire to marry another of your sons, nor do I desire to return the throne to the House of Panloch."

"*Return?*" Drayez roared. "The throne has been ours for ten generations. I had imagined you would require the customary grieving period before the wedding, but instead you stand before me looking fit to sit down for tea with your *ladies,* attempting to deny me access to my own castle so that I might properly lay my son to rest?" Drayez looked around at the guards stationed at the gate. "Subdue her immediately and raise the gate. That is an order."

"It is too lovely a day to wear black," Brissa commented, smiling at the guards, all of whom remained perfectly still. The ladies murmured their agreement; their gowns created a veritable rainbow of gold and blue and peach and green and cream and crimson. "And that veil was *stifling*. No matter, though. The Panloch rule has come to an end, and your son's remains are of as little concern to me as the contents of last night's chamber pot. I recommend that you walk away now and allow this to end peacefully."

Drayez snorted, his gray eyes settling into cool steel. "My dear, although I will admit that this is one of the more adorable coups I have witnessed, I hardly think you understand the trouble you are getting yourself into. You may have convinced a few guards to do your bidding, but you have nowhere near the resources to challenge me. Now stand down and let me through."

Brissa's smile broadened, and she moved even closer, laying a delicate gloved hand against one of the bars of the gate.

"If anything is *adorable*, Lord Panloch, it is how utterly blind you have been. You were all too pleased to offer your son a Ryovnian bride, and from a trade perspective, I can see the advantage in it. But you have never been to Ryovni, and it seems to me that you know little of our people. If you had, I can't imagine that you would have allowed *this* many ladies to accompany me to court."

Drayez laughed mirthlessly as he cast a skeptical eye across the ladies assembled behind Brissa, even as each lady pulled a sword from the folds of her dress. The guardsmen assembled behind him joined in his laughter, but wasted no time in pulling their own swords from their scabbards.

"If I am to entertain the possibility that you are telling me the truth, what you are saying is that this has been planned all along. That your parents—"

"My parents have sent several more ships. They will be arriving any day now. Those loyal to the House of Panloch within the palace walls are dead. It's over."

Drayez lunged forward, and Brissa caught his arm neatly through the bars of the gate, twisting his wrist until he yelped in pain. "My mother is queen of Ryovni, my father king. The Keshells have *never* served your House. We have merely bided our time." Brissa released Drayez's arm, as his nearest guardsmen raised their swords and strode forth to his aid. She leaned closer, bracing both hands on the bars. "And this place? *Villalu Proper?* The arrogance of your family is truly staggering. I am giving this territory back its ancestral name, and my first act as queen is to strip you of your nobility and exile all Panlochs from within its borders. So, *Mister* Panloch, I hereby cast you, your brethren and all your heirs out of Miknauvripal. If you wish for mercy, you will retreat to your own lands at once."

Still cradling his wrist, Drayez narrowed his eyes. "You have just made the most terrible mistake of your little lifetime, my dear. I will personally see to it that you watch your entire family die before you, starting with that abomination of a twin sister of yours."

Brissa clutched the bars tighter. "My sister is worth five dozen of your sons," she informed him, her eyes narrowed and her tone cool and flat.

"I should have known better than to poison my line with the sea hags of yours," Drayez snarled. "I was suspicious when your father offered me your hand rather than your twin's, and when she arrived here, with her hair clipped short and dressed like a man—"

"My sister is a Ryovnian warrior," Brissa hissed. "And if you must know, Mister Panloch, she is not the abomination. *I am.* Now, shall you leave or shall you die?"

Drayez snorted. "My men prefer not to harm ladies, but we will do what we must. I will not leave, but neither will I die."

"I am sorry to say that you are very much mistaken on that count, Mister Panloch," Brissa replied. She turned and made her way through the crowd of ladies and guards. She retrieved her parasol from Vyrope and turned to face the gate. "Open the gate," she commanded. She fixed her eyes on Drayez as the crank turned and the bars began to rise. "And kill them all."

CHAPTER TWENTY-TWO

Sehrys reminded Brieden more and more of the elf he had been at the beginning of their journey. He was both hypersensitive and aloof, crying into Brieden's arms one moment and refusing to look him in the eye the next.

Brieden was very worried.

As he drove them along the winding road toward The Border, Brieden held Sehrys's hand and tried desperately to keep him entertained with near-constant chatter. He told Sehrys about Ravurmik and his grandmother and the river where he and his brother had liked to swim. He told Sehrys about the Academy and all the mischief he had gotten up to with the spoiled boys of Villalu Proper. He told Sehrys about the different weapons he had learned to use there, hoping that might give Sehrys some comfort. He asked Sehrys if he would make them stew when they set up camp, and then talked about which root vegetables he preferred.

Then he asked if Sehrys would play his pipes while they rode. At first Sehrys demurred, but he smiled when Brieden fetched them from the carriage after they stopped to water the horses, and when he finally began to play, Brieden knew he should have just asked him to play in the first place. The tension rolled from Sehrys as he wrapped himself in the music. The fear was still there, but Sehrys seemed to breathe it out into the notes, releasing it from his body as he filled their path with music.

Brieden let Sehrys lose himself in the music and close his eyes as it washed over him. It neutralized what little effectiveness he had as a lookout, but it was worth the sacrifice to soothe some of his pain. And, it also seemed to distract Sehrys from the many grisly details Brieden noticed around them as they passed through the countryside and into the forest, drawing ever-closer to The Border.

Things like trees embedded with iron-tipped arrows and smeared with plum-colored sidhe blood.

Or the leathery, discolored human ears nailed to a fencepost.

Or the shriveled, graying sidhe ears nailed to another.

Brieden was very glad that Sehrys was too absorbed in his pipes to notice the large boulder with a message smeared across it in dark purple blood. The message was a passage from the T'aukhi Scrolls, the sacred writings of the Followers of Frilau:

To tame the mighty sidhe, to bind him in iron and use him for the service of man is a kindness, for only through this may he pay penance for his cruelty and find his way to Summerland.

The Frilauan faith had been gaining traction, especially in the few generations since the House of Panloch had converted. But this was the first time since the bloody raid on his village all those years ago that Brieden had seen evidence of exactly how far the followers of the mysterious prophet were willing to go in their quest for religious dominance.

He quickened their pace, gripping the reins tight enough to turn his knuckles white until the boulder and its message was far behind them.

BY THE TIME THEY MADE CAMP, SEHRYS SEEMED TO HAVE relaxed a bit, even humming to himself as he selected herbs from the carriage for their evening meal. He made stew, but he didn't eat much of it. He didn't even seem excited when Brieden mentioned that he thought he had seen some honeysuckle a little way back along the path. It seemed that food was the last thing on Sehrys's mind.

"How much farther?" Brieden asked, setting his bowl aside to study the map he'd brought to the fireside.

"Probably two or three days, if we continue at our current rate and don't run into any trouble," Sehrys replied, as he pointed out their location to Brieden.

"You... you really seem to remember the route quite well."

"It's not the sort of thing you forget, Brieden. I spent the entire time in a wheeled iron cage, trying to memorize everything I possibly could about the landscape because I was sure I would find a way to escape. I was *sure* of it." He sighed heavily and looked away.

Brieden decided to stop making observations about Sehrys's uncanny powers of recollection. "The stew is delicious, Sehrys," he said, then rolled up the map and reached for his bowl once again. The stew had gone cold and his voice sounded weak even to his own ears.

Sehrys looked at him. "I'm sorry, Brieden. I know I must make for miserable company right now. It's—I know it's completely irrational, but I keep thinking that *they're* around here somewhere. That they're going to find us while we're sleeping and it's going to happen all over again. Except it will be worse because they'll get you too."

Brieden took Sehrys's hand. He didn't need to ask whom Sehrys was talking about.

"I won't let anyone hurt you again, Sehrys, and you won't let anyone hurt me. Or have you forgotten how good we are at rescuing each other?"

Sehrys smiled. "We are quite good at that."

THEY SLEPT IN SHIFTS.

Neither of them was particularly enthused to sleep without the solid warmth and soothing breath of the other, but they were in dangerous country, even without Drayez and his men to worry about, and couldn't afford such an indulgence. Sehrys in particular didn't sleep well without Brieden to cling to, and although it embarrassed him to admit it, he confessed that he was afraid to fall asleep because of what he had awoken to six years ago. But he did manage to drowse for a few hours while Brieden sat by the opening of the tent with a bow and a quiver full of iron-tipped arrows. An arrow buried in the heart would kill a human just as well as a sidhe, after all.

After he almost nodded off a few times on watch, Brieden finally decided to wake Sehrys rather than chance falling asleep. He crawled into the tent and touched Sehrys lightly, and Sehrys flew bolt upright with a blood-curdling scream. Brieden leapt back but grasped Sehrys's hand. Brieden's eyes were wide as Sehrys panted and looked around wildly, squeezing his hand until Brieden sucked in a sharp breath of pain.

Sehrys finally seemed to realize what he was holding and relaxed his grip. "Brieden... oh, Gods, I could *smell* him. He was the one who kept—even the others told him not to do it so much, that it would drive the price down, that it would *ruin* me, but he..."

Sehrys pulled Brieden to him so hard that Brieden almost lost his balance. He buried his face in Brieden's chest and inhaled deeply.

"Gods, Brieden, I don't want to smell him, I want to smell *you*. I don't want to remember what it felt like, I just... I... Brieden..." Sehrys nearly *clawed* at Brieden's tunic while he wrapped his arms and legs around him and began kissing his neck fast and hard. He mumbled half-sentences as his hands roamed. Straddling Brieden, he ground hard against his lap and panted desperately, as if trying to burrow inside Brieden's flesh to escape the sense memory of the long-buried attacks that the dream had awoken.

"Sehrys," Brieden soothed, running his hands slowly up and down Sehrys's arms, and then moving them down to his hips to gently still them. "Sehrys. Stop. Look at me."

Sehrys continued to claw and grab until Brieden took Sehrys's hands in his.

"Sehrys."

Sehrys slumped against Brieden's neck, his breath ragged. "Gods, Brieden," he whispered. He wasn't crying. He sounded as though he was beyond tears.

"It's all right, Sehrys. I'm here. You're safe. You're *safe.*"

Sehrys shuddered against Brieden and then went pliant as Brieden wrapped his arms around him. They stayed like that for a long time, just holding each other.

Finally Sehrys pulled back a bit and let out a shaky laugh. "I suppose it's my turn to stand watch for a while. I'm certainly in no state to sleep *now,* anyway. I'm sorry I... sort of attacked you like that." He looked sheepish.

Brieden shrugged. "It was one of the more pleasant attacks I've had to fend off in my lifetime," he said and smiled.

"I..." Sehrys began, "Do you... think you would be able to sleep outside? I can keep the bugs away." He was still looking a bit shame-faced and quickly added, "You don't have to, I just—"

"Of course." Brieden gave him a gentle squeeze.

SEHRYS SAT WITH HIS BACK AGAINST A WIDE, SMOOTH TREE trunk. Brieden slept with his head in Sehrys's lap, his lips parted slightly. He was beautiful. Sehrys listened for danger and watched Brieden sleep.

He let the image of Brieden fill his mind: It was the image of all that was good and noble and sweet and kind and earnest and perfect and beautiful in the world.

He held the image in his mind like a treasure. He tried to lock it in his memory, secure every detail, just as it was right now.

Sehrys would have to memorize his eyes later, and the rest of his body, because Brieden was wrapped in a blanket. But this image was worth remembering despite the lack of clear brown pools and sculpted limbs. This image was nothing more or less than pure, distilled *Brieden.*

He noticed the sunrise only because of the way the rosy hue fell across Brieden's features.

SEHRYS HAD LET BRIEDEN SLEEP FAR TOO LONG, AND THEY didn't head out until very late the next morning.

"You should have woken me up sooner," Brieden groused.

Sehrys gave him an apologetic smile. "I couldn't. You looked far too lovely and peaceful. And you needed the rest."

"*You* need the rest more than I do," Brieden argued, as Sehrys stifled a mighty yawn. By afternoon, he had convinced Sehrys to nap in the carriage while Brieden drove.

"You'll be my secret weapon," Brieden assured him, handing Sehrys his own dressing gown and blanket, both imbued with Brieden's scent. "If anyone gives me trouble, you can burst out of the carriage and rescue me."

"You are aware that I cannot rescue you if I'm asleep," Sehrys pointed out with a wry smile, accepting the blanket and gown.

"You sleep lightly. I am confident you will come to my aid if the need arises."

When he picked up the reins to carry them on their way with Sehrys nestled securely in the carriage, Brieden began to sing. He chose soothing lullabies and lilting love ballads and continued singing until he was fairly certain that Sehrys had fallen asleep.

The day was bright and clear; the trees dappled the sunlight along the wide dirt path. Were it not for Sehrys's associations with this route and the occasional evidences of bloody battle, it would probably be an incredibly pleasant road to travel.

Lost in thoughts and daydreams—alternating between living together in a flower mound on a dairy farm in Khryslee and making love against moss-covered rocks under a trickling waterfall—Brieden didn't notice the sound of the approaching carriage until it was close.

When it finally registered, he squared his shoulders and did a quick mental check of his weapons: sword at his hip, quiver on his back, dagger in his boot, throwing stars tucked under the perch, bow securely in his lap, and—he eased them on—iron knuckles on his fingers.

Brieden arranged his face into the most innocent, serene and unconcerned expression he could muster and carried on.

A wave of relief come over him when he saw two human men at the helm, neither of whom bore the seal of the royal guardsmen. His relief ebbed, however, as he noticed something else attached to the back of the carriage.

It was an iron cage. On wheels. And it was occupied.

Brieden swallowed the lump in his throat when the carriage pulled abreast of his and slowed to a stop. He was incredibly grateful that Sehrys was hidden from view.

"Afternoon, traveler," said the driver of the other carriage in a jovial voice. "Where might you be heading?"

"Lekrypal," Brieden answered automatically. "Of a mind to trade some spices."

"Spices, eh?" the second man said with a leer. "You look like a man with coin. Sure we couldn't interest you in some quality sprite flesh? No open market for it this far west, you know."

Brieden stiffened. "I know. I'm... not interested, thank you." Brieden's mind raced. Were these the same men who had kidnapped Sehrys all those years ago? Could they possibly be? The iron cage wasn't unique; most slave traders had them. It was the best way to keep sidhe docile until they had enough verbena in their bloodstreams to control them. But on this path, this *very path*...

What could Brieden do? He had to free the two sidhe in the cage. But how? Should he wake Sehrys? But what if they were the same men? Would it strengthen Sehrys to see them, make him unleash his full power, or would it put him into a state of shock, giving the men the upper hand? There might be another three or four men in the carriage. Brieden doubted he could take them all on his own. But would waking Sehrys just give them a third sidhe for the cage?

Brieden shifted his gaze to the cage, trying to appear as if he was considering its contents. But the second his eyes locked with one of the sidhe, all sound dulled into background noise, although he was certain the men were still talking to him.

Because he knew those eyes. They belonged to Sir.

And with him was Milord.

CHAPTER TWENTY-THREE

It took Brieden a moment to realize that he was not under compulsion.

Looking into Sir's eyes and feeling no loyalty, no tug of love for him, nothing to battle or submit to... it was odd. So odd that Brieden couldn't entirely grasp it.

It was also kind of sad.

Sir was kind of sad. He looked waxy and older than he had when Brieden had last seen him, although it had been less than two weeks. His hair seemed more olive than emerald; his face was gaunt; his violet eyes were tired and dull. Of course, it was possible that he had *always* looked that way, that the compulsion had merely kept Brieden from seeing it.

But Milord did not look well either, which made Brieden recall how Sehrys had looked when Dronyen had him draped in iron chains, as if the iron sucked something vital and life-giving from their bodies.

Brieden tried not to pity them. If *anyone* deserved such a fate, it was Sir and Milord. But that was exactly the problem. No one did.

"Friend?"

Brieden was startled out of his thoughts. His first instinct was to snap at the flesh-peddler for calling him *friend*, but he managed to hold it in.

"I'm... I'm sorry. I—where did you find them? How did you catch them?"

The driver gave a broad smile, obviously proud of himself. "Honeysuckle bush just up the road. Rigged up some chains. Easy as a lass from Lasemik, and works every time."

Brieden shuddered, remembering the honeysuckle he'd tried to tempt Sehrys with just the night before.

"Pretty things, ain't they?" the driver's companion added. "Even prettier when you get them on the verbena and take away the iron. You *sure* you're not looking to buy? There's nothing better than being the first to break in a wild one."

"I don't believe in slavery," Brieden said coldly before he could stop himself.

The driver snorted. "Oh, here we go. You a religious man, friend?"

Don't you dare call me friend, you—"If you're planning to use the T'aukhi Scrolls to defend yourself, don't bother," Brieden replied. "I was raised to revere the Dragon God, not the false words of a blasphemer."

"Frilau was the Dragon's *prophet*!" the driver's companion snapped, eyes alight with righteous anger. "The blasphemy is in denying the truth of his scrolls!"

"We didn't stop to get into a theological debate," the driver cut in before Brieden could retort. "We were merely wondering if you might have something to trade. You said you trade in spices? Salt, perhaps?"

"Sorry, no," Brieden muttered. "I should... I should probably be on my way." He looked back at Sir and Milord. Sir looked utterly resigned, but Milord looked beseechingly at Brieden. It was a look of pure desperation, a look that said *please don't leave me please don't leave me please don't leave me.*

Brieden swallowed. "You know you can't bring slaves into the border cities, don't you?"

The driver laughed sharply. "Son, we've been doing this a long, long time. We have everything we need to get us far enough east to make a profit."

A long, long time.

How long? Longer than six years, perhaps?

"Sehrys!" Brieden barked suddenly, loud and sharp.

The two humans stared at him. *"Excuse me?"* demanded the driver.

"I... um... nervous tic. Just... you know, I believe I might have some salt after all. If you'll give me a moment..."

The men exchanged suspicious looks. Brieden started to climb down from the perch, carrying his bow.

"You know what, friend? Why don't you stay right there? And we'll be on our way."

Brieden bit his lip. The driver's companion looked ready to nock an arrow in his own bow as he glared at Brieden, and Brieden was pretty sure that this could turn ugly if—

"I think you should let them go." The voice beside him was soft but steady. Brieden looked at Sehrys in surprise. He hadn't even heard him move out of the carriage.

Sehrys stared at the men with a neutral expression, and his voice betrayed nothing of the fear he must have been feeling.

The men back stared at him. Then the driver's companion quickly nocked an arrow. He screamed when both bow and arrow burst into flames.

"No," Sehrys said. "I did not ask you to shoot me with an arrow. I asked you to—" his eyes flickered over to the cage and widened when he saw Sir and Milord. "Let them *go*." He returned his gaze to the two humans in front of him.

The driver snapped the reins to set the horses in motion, but Sehrys gave a quick, sharp cry, *"Cho!"* and the horses stopped, watching him.

"Thank you," Sehrys said, smiling at the horses. "You see? *Some* people actually listen to me when I speak. Now, I *could* kill you—" He flicked a wrist, and the three men who were attempting to crawl out of the carriage fell to the ground as the earth shook violently. "*All* of you. It would be quite the... what did you call it, Brieden? *Catharsis.* Yes, that's it. But the trouble is, killing people seems to *do* something to me." Sehrys frowned. "And killing you would feel exceptionally good, but it would also *hurt* me. So..."

Sehrys glanced back at Brieden. "Brieden? What do you think?"

"I... I don't know, Sehrys. These—are these the same men who—"

Sehrys cut him off with a laugh so cold it made gooseflesh rise up on Brieden's arms. "No. If they were, they would all be dead by now."

Eyes wide and shoulders trembling, the men looked from Sehrys to Brieden, .

Sehrys sighed. "All right... why don't you start by unloading the carriage? Completely. Leave the... the prisoners where they are."

SEVERAL HOURS LATER, SEHRYS AND BRIEDEN CONTINUED along the trail, Sehrys now sufficiently refreshed to sit beside Brieden and hold his hand. They were mostly silent, their chosen course of action heavy between them. Brieden could tell that it sat no easier with Sehrys than with himself.

Their carriage was much more heavily laden. They had relieved the slave traders of all forms of iron and verbena, as well as weapons and most items of value. The heavy iron cage on wheels trailed behind them, still holding its two occupants.

The slave traders had gone in the opposite direction and had not been stripped of either horses or carriage. Brieden was not entirely at ease with their decision, and he knew that Sehrys wasn't either, but he didn't know what else they could have done. Leaving the men without a carriage would only encourage them to steal one from someone else, Sehrys had reasoned. Killing them would have been simple, but neither Sehrys nor Brieden had it in them to simply kill the men execution-style, especially not when they grovelled and whimpered and pled for their lives.

He *had* done his best to instill deep fear in them. He had glowered at them with green-fire eyes, surrounding them in flames. He had spoken words into his cupped hands and then cast them into the fire, where the words grew hot, and swirled around the men relentlessly, bounced like sparks off the wall of flame surrounding them, and grew in volume until they shook the earth: "*There are more like me, and they are coming for men like you. Most are not so merciful. Change is coming to The Border, men, and if you are trading slaves when it comes, you will scream for the mercy of your Five Hells.*"

Sehrys's words had chilled Brieden to the bone, because there was not even the barest hint that this might have been an exaggeration or an empty threat. Sehrys had sounded like a man with a *very* specific plan in mind.

It didn't sound like a bad plan, but it sure as hells sounded like a bloody one.

They finally pulled into a suitable clearing as dusk approached. Sehrys leapt down and began cooing over Crow and Raven, who were exhausted from pulling the extra burden of the cage. Brieden meandered to the back of the carriage, stopped in front of the cage and folded his arms across his chest.

"Well. This is—"

"Ironic, yes," Sir cut him off. "Congratulations, boy. We are completely at your mercy. Now either kill us or spare us your gloating, if you don't mind."

Milord's eyes widened. "No... he just... no. Don't listen to him. He's—he's tired. And upset. And..."

Brieden narrowed his eyes at Sir, who seemed to be shifting uncomfortably on the floor of the cage.

"S—did... did they hurt you?"

"What do you think?" snapped Sir. "They dropped iron chains onto us. Or is that how you take your pleasure? I never took you for one who—"

"That's not what I mean and you know it," Brieden said. "Do you need—did they—" He let his words trail off as Sir looked away pointedly. Milord flinched.

"I'm sorry," Brieden said.

"Spare us your pity," Sir snarled. "Coming from an animal like you, it—"

"I should think you'd be rather grateful for his pity," Sehrys said, stalking over to join them. "Seeing as how it's just about all that's keeping you alive right now."

"Sehrys..." Brieden said gently, "You don't understand. Those men, they—"

"I know," Sehrys said. "They did exactly what slave traders do. I *remember.*" Milord's eyes widened at that, and even Sir's gaze flickered over to him.

"It shouldn't have happened, and I'm sorry for you that it did, but it doesn't make either one of you innocent. You've done exactly the same thing to the humans you've enslaved, and I don't want to know how many times."

"It wasn't the same!" Milord protested. "They, they liked it—"

"They were compelled," Sehrys corrected.

"They were compelled to *like* it!" Sir exploded. "Gods, are you really doing this? *You?* Humans experience compulsion as pleasure. Their bodies enjoy it. It isn't *rape!*"

"Yes, it *is*!" Brieden's fists clenched into balls at his side.

Sir looked at Sehrys. "*Hukes nau esperanga—*"

"Speak Villaluan," Sehrys cut in, "so that Brieden can understand you."

Sir narrowed his eyes and glanced at Brieden with a sneer. *"Esil lek drestocono esiles ad es linge grimog perabo efa nauefa berishkintanit,"* he said.

"If you call him that again, I'll cut your tongue out of your head!" Sehrys stopped just short of lunging at the cage.

"He doesn't mean it. He's just old-fashioned." Milord's eyes shifted nervously between the two other sidhe.

Sehrys raised an eyebrow at Milord. "Is that what you're going to call it?"

"You know what I mean," Milord muttered, looking at his feet.

"No, I really don't," Sehrys said.

Milord looked puzzled. Sir simply snorted. "He doesn't *know* what you're talking about because he probably flitted about doing whatever he pleased while the other children were learning. I imagine it was all just *beneath* you, wasn't it, you precious little thing?"

Sehrys glared at him.

"Um, Sehrys?" Brieden walked away from the cage, gently pulling Sehrys with him. Sehrys allowed it, his expression still dark. When they were out of earshot, Brieden sighed and turned to Sehrys.

"Let me kill them," Sehrys blurted.

Brieden gaped at him. "Sehrys, no."

"Why *not?* Is this some sort of official let-slave-trading-rapists-go-free day? Some sort of Villaluan holiday I was never told about?"

"That holiday is observed every day in Villalu," Brieden answered bitterly. "But we can't kill them in a *cage,* Sehrys. We need to figure out what to do."

Sehrys sighed. "I know what I need to do." He walked back to the cage. "Tell me your names."

"Tash Tirarth Valusidhe efa Lesette efa es Zulla Melleva Feririar ala es Fervishlaea efa es Sola Pelzershe," Milord answered immediately. Sehrys nodded and turned to Sir, who pressed his lips together and

glared. Sehrys folded his arms across his chest and stared. After a solid minute of thick silence, Sir sighed heavily and complied .

"*Brec Nauerth Valusidhe efaf Iric efa es Swesta Vurule Feririar ala es Fervishlaea efa es Sola Pelzershe,*" he muttered, refusing to meet Sehrys's eye.

"Thank you, so that would make your *nomkinli* Tash and Brec, correct?" Sehrys asked. "Pet names," he clarified for Brieden's benefit.

"Yes," Tash replied. Brec glared at him.

Sehrys exhaled. "All right. Now I don't want to kill you quite so much. Brec, I'm going to bind you."

For the first time, Brieden saw fear in Brec's eyes.

"Kill me instead," he whispered. "You may as well. I'll be defenseless."

Sehrys rolled his eyes. "You *must* have something else."

Brec sighed, and waved a hand dismissively. "Earth," he said, sounding unimpressed.

Sehrys's lips twitched into something that was almost a smile. "You were a home-grower," he said with an edge of unmasked delight.

Brec glowered at him. "What of it? Too low-caste an occupation for your taste?"

"Of course not. It takes great skill to do it well. Much more respectable than being a slave-trader."

"I was *never* a slave-trader," Brec insisted.

Ignoring Brec's statement, Sehrys turned to Brieden to explain. "Sidhe with the power to compel usually have an elemental power as well. One of the *non*-abhorrent ways one can use compulsion is to direct it through that element. Those who command earth can use the combination of the two to grow homes and other structures. Like the sidhe inns we stayed at." Sehrys turned back to Brec. "It's a talent I've always envied," he admitted.

"Then why don't you go ahead and *do* it?" Brec said.

"Sehrys can't compel," Brieden pointed out.

"Oh, is that what he *told* you?" Brec asked and laughed.

"It's true, I can't," Sehrys said, looking at Brieden. "I was bound," he added, turning back toward Brec. "By choice."

Brec looked incredulous. "You expect me to believe—"

"Look. I may have been a precious little thing that *flitted about* while the other children were learning, but I did have a basic sense of right and wrong." Sehrys walked closer to the cage, got as close as he could without touching it.

"I know what it can do to people. I understand the constant temptation, Brec, I do. And I will admit that I loved my power, that I still love my power, but no good would come of the compulsion for me. I knew I didn't have a future as a home-grower or a light-keeper or a water-bearer. I only would have used it for control."

"But *you*... you could have controlled *sidhe*," Tash breathed, staring at Sehrys with something very much akin to wonder. "You could have done anything."

"I... yes." Sehrys conceded. "And now, thank the Gods, I can't."

"Don't you miss it? Can't you feel it... *itching* at you when you aren't using it?" Brec searched Sehrys's face desperately.

"Yes," Sehrys answered softly. "But if I can live with it, so can you."

SEHRYS DID NOT TRUST BREC AROUND BRIEDEN, NO MATTER how ardently Brieden swore that he would avoid his eyes. He led a miserable and resigned-looking Brec into the forest on his own, leaving Brieden with Tash.

"Are you hungry?" Brieden asked, suddenly realizing that it had probably been a good long while since the elf had eaten. Tash nodded mutely.

Brieden picked a variety of leaves that he'd seen Sehrys eat and brought a flask of water to the cage as well. He sat beside the cage as Tash settled in to eat.

"Tash... what is Sehrys going to do?"

Tash sighed. "He's going to bind him. Suppress his power to compel. Permanently. Keep it locked under his skin, where he'll always feel it, but it can never get out."

"And Sehrys... feels that way too?"

Tash shrugged. "Sehrys has quite a bit more power than Brec in other areas. In *every* other area. It probably isn't as much of a hardship for him." Tash chewed thoughtfully. "Or... maybe it's worse," he corrected himself. "Because his ability to compel would have been so much stronger than Brec's. Suppressing something like *that* could be pure torture. I don't really know."

Brieden swallowed hard. So Sehrys was suffering constantly. Perhaps that was why he had endured so much without breaking. Because he had had so much practice. Because he had already learned to live his life withstanding what most people couldn't imagine feeling for even a day.

Another thought struck Brieden before he could force himself to push it away:

Tash knew who Sehrys was. Or at least *what* Sehrys was with respect to other sidhe. Brieden could end his frustration and agony right now, could just ask Tash exactly—

Brieden stood up abruptly, heart pounding as he realized how close he'd come to violating Sehrys's trust. "I'll get you a blanket." He quickly strode away.

BRIEDEN AND SEHRYS LAY TOGETHER IN THE TENT THAT night, each lost in thought.

Sehrys finally sighed. "That was... hard. The binding. I didn't enjoy it."

Brieden glanced up from where his cheek lay pillowed on Sehrys's chest. "Tash said that having a power bound is akin to living in a constant state of torture."

Sehrys laughed softly. "That might be a bit dramatic."

"Sehrys, why didn't you tell me?"

"I didn't hold it back on purpose, Brieden. I suppose I... I don't know. It seemed simpler that way."

"You need to stop doing that." Brieden kept his voice gentle and punctuated the statement with a kiss to Sehrys's chest. "I know you're not ready to tell me everything, but please stop holding things back from me like it's instinctive. I want to know everything about you. Even the complicated parts."

Sehrys exhaled slowly. "I went a long time without having anyone to trust, Brieden, so I suppose it has become a bit instinctive. But you're right. And I do trust *you*."

Brieden traced whisper-soft circles around Sehrys's nipple. "I know you do. Would you tell me what it's like? Having part of your power bound?"

"It's unpleasant, but I've grown accustomed to it. There are even times when the pain stops altogether."

"Mmm. Like when?"

"Like when you're inside me," Sehrys whispered into Brieden's ear, making him shiver. Brieden turned his face up to Sehrys just in time to find his lips caught in a gentle kiss.

"I'm sorry you had to do that today," Brieden whispered. "I know S—Brec, I mean, probably deserves far worse, but it must have been difficult to cause that kind of pain."

"It was. It is. But now he can't hurt anyone else the way he hurt you, Brieden. I'm not sorry I did it."

"Neither am I."

"And now I don't want to think about him anymore." Sehrys trailed his fingers below the back of Brieden's waistband.

Brieden smiled. "You're trying to seduce me."

"Yes, Brieden, *trying* would seem to be the appropriate choice of word."

Brieden's smile turned into a laugh, and he rolled over until he was on top of Sehrys. "Don't stop now. You've got me almost convinced."

THEY TRIED TO KEEP QUIET, BUT THEIR MOANS AND CRIES easily carried to the cage behind the carriage, where the two men huddled under blankets tried not to notice the sharp and familiar scent of a certain flower that was most certainly *not* indigenous to this area.

Tash sighed heavily and decided to try and drown out the noises of pleasure coming from the tent with simple conversation.

"What are we going to do, Brec?"

Brec glared stonily up into the night. He felt as though he had been neutered. *Neutered.*

"I'll tell you what we're going to do. We are going to kill his fucking human and make him watch, and then we are going to bleed him dry until he's weak as a kitten and we're swimming in essence, and then we are going to sell him to the first brain-dead sadist of a wealthy human we can find, sell the essence and live like kings."

Tash stared at him with wide eyes. "But... what—we shouldn't— we can't just—he's going to—but... *how?*"

Brec laughed bitterly, his voice cutting into the darkness around them. "I don't know. But we've got all night to come up with something."

CHAPTER TWENTY-FOUR

"I DON'T KNOW THAT I SEE IT THAT WAY, BRIEDEN," Tash said. "Personally, I'd rather find myself under the *impression* that I was enjoying myself, even if it were false, than go through what those slave traders did to us."

Brieden winced. It was his turn on watch, and as Tash couldn't seem to sleep either, they had found themselves in conversation once again. Brec was lying in the cage with his back to Brieden, giving all appearances of being asleep, although he may have just preferred to ignore their conversation.

"I don't want to negate what happened to you, Tash, but that doesn't make what you did—or I suppose what you *tried* to do to me any better. If Sehrys hadn't stopped us—"

"Your body seemed to be responding to it," Tash said softly, not meeting Brieden's eyes.

Brieden flushed. "Yes... I—that isn't the point. In fact, that's precisely the problem. Have you ever experienced compulsion?"

Tash sighed. "No."

"Well, trust me. After the compulsion breaks... it feels *very much* like a violation."

"That's precisely it, though. Usually it never does break. Most humans that are compelled simply stay that way forever, happy and unaware."

"And destroyed. Emptied out like a shell. Dead inside."

"Did you feel dead inside?"

"I think I would have, eventually. I could feel the corrosion start-ing. In retrospect, I think I would rather lose *anything* before I would give up my free will. It was as if my *selfhood* were being taken from me."

Tash smiled slightly. "You sound like one of the L!Khryauvnian devotees." Brieden gasped as Tash named his grandmother's Sand God; his heart thrummed at the prospect of new information.

"My grandmother was a devotee! At least, I believe she was. Do The Sidhe worship him differently than the humans? What do his devotees believe? Tell me what you mean."

Tash rolled his shoulders, his lips quirking into something almost like a smile. "You are very inquisitive. Quite like a child."

Brieden scowled. "Don't condescend."

Tash studied him. "How much has Sehrys told you about how Villalu came to be?"

Brieden furrowed his brow. "Villalu was breathed into being by the Dragon God in the Age Before the World. Sehrys never spoke of it, but everyone knows *that* story."

"I don't." Tash leaned forward. "Tell it to me."

"Only if you swear to tell me about L!Khryauvni."

Despite Brieden's muddled pronunciation of the God's name, Tash didn't laugh. "You have yourself a deal," he said.

"All right. So the Dragon breathes worlds into being and then burns them into cinders if they displease Him. Some of the ashes from His last creation escaped on His breath when He created Villalu, and there were bits of magic in the ash. The ashes became The Sidhe, of course, and they were too beautiful for the Dragon to destroy. So He created The Border to keep them contained. But, being magical, sidhe sometimes escape the Faerie Lands and slip into Villalu to dance beneath the moons." Brieden shrugged, giving a short laugh. "I... that's what my people believe, anyhow. The Frilauans—"

"There is no need to speak to me of the Frilauans," Tash cut in. "And the story is quaint, but everything your people believe is wrong."

"The more educated among us do not presume the creation story to be a literal truth, Tash," Brieden said, aware that his tone sounded defensive. "But neither do we presume to know the absolute truth of how the world came to be. Do *you* presume to know such truths?"

"Of course not," Tash admitted. "But I know quite well how *Villalu* came to be, and despite what you people may believe, Villalu is hardly the world. Did you know, for example, that The Sidhe owned humans—well, you would consider it ownership, most of us would think of them as pets—long before humans owned sidhe? Before The Border was even in place?"

Brieden stared at him. "I thought... I thought The Border had always been there. To keep us separate from the Faerie Lands."

"It is there to create a separation, yes. Because you humans run around like wild dogs, destroying everything you touch, unless you are properly compelled."

Brieden snorted in indignation.

"You *do*, you know. Brieden, tell me what exists in this world other than Villalu?"

Brieden frowned. "The Faerie Lands, but—"

"What else?"

"I don't understand."

"What would happen if you were to set sail south from Ryovni and simply kept going?"

"I would sail until I reached The Winds at the edge of the world."

"What if you set sail eastward from Lord's Isle?"

"The same."

"And what *are* those winds?"

Brieden sighed in irritation. "They keep objects from flying off the edge of the world and into space. Are you trying to prove me ignorant? Because every child who grows up in a fishing village is well aware of such things."

"I am not attempting to prove you ignorant, but I *am* attempting to reveal your ignorance."

Brieden narrowed his eyes at Tash suspiciously. "What exactly is the difference?"

"What I mean to say is that you are no more ignorant than nearly any other human in Villalu, but that does not mean you understand the truth. The world does not have edges. The world is round, like a ball. And there are many lands beyond Villalu. And many lands beyond Laesi—that which you would call the Faerie Lands—as well. Villalu is nothing more than a tiny bit of land surrounded by borders on all sides."

Brieden blinked. "*What?*"

"It's the truth."

"It isn't. It can't be. There is your country and my country and space above. A *ball?* Do you have any idea how absolutely ridiculous that sounds?"

"A *twirling* ball," Tash added, his eyes twinkling with mirth.

Brieden stood, scowling. "You are mocking me, and I believe I am done listening to it tonight." He brushed the dirt from his trousers.

"The followers of the Blessed Guardian of the Sands instigated the first uprising," Tash said, his voice serious now, and edged with something very like desperation. Brieden paused and looked down at him. "They were the first to refer to the keeping of human pets as slavery. The first to insist that humans were *people,* members of the elfin races just as much as The Sidhe. A prominent queen became a devotee, and the pets were freed. Which of course led to swarms of wild humans running about and causing more trouble than anyone could argue they were worth. But the thinking at the time was that

The Sidhe owed the humans their own lands governed by their own choices. So a portion of the Eastern Sea Lands was sacrificed to the cause; all of the humans were rounded up and sent there; and The Border was created. Those lands are called the Eastern Border Lands now, and its easternmost peninsula and surrounding islands, now circled by a border, is Villalu. This Great Change is known as *Es Muchator* on the other side of The Border, and every school child knows of it." Tash made a broad sweeping motion with his arms. "And that is the shortest possible history I can give you of the past fifty thousand years."

Brieden sank back down into a sitting position, eyes wide and mouth slightly agape.

"The Borders aren't there to keep The Sidhe *out,* Brieden. They are there to keep the humans *in.* To grant them their freedom while safeguarding the rest of the world against their destructive tendencies."

"But... that can't—"

Tash rose to his knees, scooting closer to the bars between Brieden and himself. He stared at Brieden.

"Do you really think we couldn't just do whatever we wanted to you? Do you really think we couldn't simply *swarm* Villalu and compel the lot of you, destroy all the iron and verbena and free all the slaves?"

Brieden swallowed hard, his throat suddenly dry as bone. Because that was a *very* good question.

Tash barked a short, wry laugh. "Two reasons. First, when The Border was built, a Non-Interference Doctrine was put into place. The doctrine states that humans are the free and rightful masters of Villalu, and that in Villalu alone, only humans may establish laws. And second, we don't have prisons or dungeons on our side of The Border. The Council of Nations knows *exactly* what happens to us over here, and they don't do a thing about it because *this* is *prison.* This, Brieden, is *hell.*"

Tash's cheeks had become flushed and his breathing seemed labored. He slumped to the floor. "We were only trying to get by," he muttered. "That's all we were trying to do."

Brieden stared at him. He hadn't known it was like this at all. He hadn't known *anything.*

"There are other ways to get by," he managed to argue, but his voice was barely a whisper.

"We can never go back. We are *exiled.* We can live in the border cities, but we're still at the mercy of human governance, even there. And the competition for resources in the cities can be fierce. It's no kind of life for a sidhe with weak powers. Following Brec was working. He was taking care of us. But now..."

Brieden watched him intently. Tash looked downright forlorn. "What happened to Madame? I know that isn't actually her name, but—"

"Aehsee," Tash murmured. "Her name was Aehsee. Her pet name, anyhow." He shrugged and looked off into the distance. "Sold," he said. "Pretty quickly, too. Women are in much higher demand."

They sat in silence for a few moments.

"Brieden?"

"Yes?"

"Do you think—could you let me out for a bit, so I can... uh, eliminate?"

Brieden blushed at the request. "There is a chamber pot right there, Tash."

Tash's nose wrinkled in disgust. "You want me to spend the entire night sleeping with *that* in here? Sehrys took us out earlier. I don't see why you can't."

"Probably because you could set me on fire with a flick of your wrist if I let you out," Brieden reasoned. "But if you really need to... I mean, I could wake Sehrys."

Tash sighed. "Yes, I suppose. But... do you *really* think we should wake him? He seems to need the rest. And I wouldn't want him to get angry and decide to—"

"Tash, what are you doing?" Brieden was looking at him through narrowed eyes.

"Brieden, I just have to—"

"No. You're trying to soften my resolve so that I will take pity on you and give you a chance to overpower me. Do I honestly seem that naïve to you?"

Tash pursed his lips, heaved a sigh and allowed his shoulders to slump. "Yes," he admitted sullenly.

Brieden gave a soft laugh, touched by the slightest edge of bitterness. "You might want to start thinking for yourself before Brec gets you killed, you know," Brieden said, staring at Brec's supine form. "I don't care how bitter he is or how elaborate a scheme he may have cooked up. There is no *way* the two of you could overpower Sehrys." Brieden stood once again. "Use the chamber pot, Tash. Or wait until it's Sehrys's turn on watch and he can take you out. But I'm done talking to you."

Brieden walked back to the tent to watch over Sehrys while he slept.

"Nice job," Brec muttered from his corner of the cage.

"ALL RIGHT, THAT'S *IT*!"

Tash blinked against the harsh morning sunlight, taking a moment to realize that it was Sehrys who was yelling and storming toward the cage. Brieden ran after him with a nervous expression, his sword swinging from his belt.

"No, Sehrys, I didn't mean—*think* about this. Please. It's not even him! He's just following along, it's B—"

Brieden's words died in his throat as Sehrys's eyes brightened into an unnatural glow and a section of bars began to sizzle and melt, forming a large hole on the side of the cage directly in front of them. The very second he was close enough, Sehrys pulled Brec out by the throat. A few of the fragmented, weakened iron bars clattered to the ground at the sheer force with which Sehrys seized the other sidhe.

Brieden and Tash stood dumbfounded.

"Of course it's Brec, Brieden. I know that," said Sehrys evenly, his blazing-fire eyes boring into the horror-struck sidhe in his hands. He took a deep breath and closed his eyes for a moment, and then shoved Brec away. The shocked sidhe stumbled backward and fell to the ground.

Sehrys opened his eyes and knelt in front of him. "Why? Can you please just tell me? We saved you from *slavery,* you ingrate! We were planning to let you *go!* And then you have your lackey attempt to manipulate Brieden, and to what end? So you can kill him and drape me in iron and bleed me of essence? Was that your little plan?"

Brec's fear had cooled into open disgust. "More or less," he sneered. "We had to have *some* sort of plan. We had to *try.* Go ahead and kill me if you please. You've already left me impotent."

"I've left you perfectly *intact,* lacking only the ability to *enslave* people with your *eyes!*" Sehrys grated.

"Humans," Brec muttered, almost too low to hear.

"Excuse me?"

Brec whipped his head around, meeting Sehrys's gaze without a flinch. "I said *humans.* Not people, *humans.* Or are you going to start binding homegrowers so they are unable to compel *plants?* In the name of the Gods, where does it *end?*"

"Humans are people," Sehrys said, his tone dangerously calm. "*Brieden* is a *person*!"

Brec's lips curled into a chilling smile. "*Brieden* is your *fucktoy*."

Sehrys lunged at Brec, hauling him up by his arms and slamming his back into the bars of the cage. Brec flinched at the iron digging into his skin.

"Okay," Sehrys said softly. "All right. This is how we are going to do this. I am not going to use anything against you except a measure of earth that is even in strength with your own, and, of course, my fists. And we are going to *settle* this."

Sehrys let go of Brec and turned to Brieden. "Brieden, ready the horses. Arm yourself. If I lose this, I want you to ride away as fast as you can."

Brieden choked on his own breath. "Sehrys. No. This is insane. Let's... let us just leave. Come with me. He can't compel, he can't do anything. He is *trying* to provoke you. Don't give him the satisfaction."

"Brieden, please trust me when I say that the *satisfaction* here is going to be all my own." Sehrys was still staring at Brec, cracking his knuckles, his eyes manic.

Brieden touched Sehrys gently on the shoulder. "Sehrys, please," he said softly. "I don't know why you think you have to do this. Whatever threat he may have posed has already been contained. He's... he's really nothing more than *pathetic* now. Please walk away from this."

"Brieden..." Sehrys's eyes flickered into something a bit softer when he looked into Brieden's eyes. "I—the things he said about you. About *us*. I can't simply let him—"

Brieden moved his hand from Sehrys's shoulder to his cheek. "Be the better man," he soothed, stroking Sehrys's cheek with his thumb. "He can say whatever he wishes to say. It has no bearing on me. On *us*." They gazed at one another for a moment.

It was only a moment.

It was enough.

From his vantage point near the cage, Tash only saw Brec standing behind Brieden for a split second before he saw the look on Brieden's face.

The look of shock.

The gasp of pain.

Brieden fell to the ground on his side, his own sword lodged in the back of his ribcage.

"*Brieden*!" Sehrys screamed, scrambling down to try to catch him as he fell.

Brec laughed, deep and rich. He raised a severed bar from the cage over his head, his hands covered with torn fabric from his own shirt, and brought it down swiftly across Sehrys's back.

Sehrys fell forward with a cry. Brec pushed the bar into Sehrys's flesh with the heel of his boot, so hard that the flesh began to sizzle.

"Oh, that was *too* easy," Brec chuckled, luxuriating in a sense of victory. "I knew I could count on your boy to soften you up. Tash, will you—" Brec stopped speaking abruptly, and Tash could feel the other man's eyes on him. But he wasn't looking at Brec.

He was looking at Brieden, bleeding on the ground. At Sehrys, screaming as the iron burned into his skin.

At Brec. Tormenting those who had freed him, even after all he had put them through.

Tash met Brec's eyes and both men immediately sprung to action. Brec moved fast. He flicked his wrist and the earth beneath them began to tremble, cracks forming beneath Tash's feet.

Tash moved faster. With barely a twitch of his hand, he transformed Brec into a shrieking, writhing column of flame, burning fast and loud and blue-hot, acrid smoke dancing across the clearing on the warm morning breeze.

Tash rushed to move Sehrys and Brieden away from the fire.

It was difficult to wrench the iron bar from Sehrys's flesh without being able to touch it himself, but Tash finally managed. The bar had weakened as a result of its deep contact with sidhe flesh, and broke apart as Tash removed it, leaving several small shards behind. Sehrys scrambled to his knees and fell upon Brieden in a panic, trying to heal him even with jagged splinters of iron protruding from the gaping wound in his own back, even without removing the sword.

Tash had never been good in a crisis. His instinct had always been to give up, to run, to hide, to seek protection from someone stronger than himself. But Tash did not have those options, not now. He couldn't just kill Brec and then leave Brieden to die, too. What would be the point?

Tash moved over to Brieden and gently urged Sehrys away. It wasn't easy; Sehrys was hysterical. But Tash broke through with gentle, repeated messages: *I'm going to help him. You can't heal him until you have healed a bit more yourself. You need to let me look at him. Sehrys, I'm going to help him. I'm going to help him. I'm going to help him.*

Tash examined Brieden. He still had a pulse, although it was growing faint. He was still breathing. He didn't seem to have lost too much blood. It was probably safest not to remove the sword yet, but they didn't have a lot of time.

"Sehrys." Sehrys sat beside Brieden, rocking back and forth, and whispering Brieden's name over and over again. "Sehrys," Tash repeated, touching his arm gently and looking at his face. "I can help you. I can help *Brieden*. But you need to listen to me, all right? Do you have a medical supply kit in the carriage?"

Sehrys looked at him, blank and uncomprehending face white as a freshly bleached sheet. "*Brieden*," he whispered brokenly.

"Sehrys, if you don't communicate with me, *Brieden will die.* Now. Medical kit. Do you have one?"

Something seemed to snap into focus behind his eyes, and Sehrys nodded. "Under... under the seat. In a wooden box. I... I should have been watching. I should have—what have I—"

Tash bit his lip. He had never seen a creature as powerful as Sehrys look so utterly annihilated. Especially not because of a simple human boy.

"Sehrys, I need you to do something, all right? I need you to stay with Brieden and... and hold his head in your lap. I'm going to be right back."

When had he and Sehrys slipped into Elfin tongue? He was fairly sure that Sehrys hadn't noticed either.

Tash returned to find Sehrys holding Brieden's head in his lap, stroking his hair and whispering to him fervently. He appeared oblivious to the charred remains of Brec's body only a few feet away. Tash shuddered and willed himself to ignore the smell of death and burning flesh as he hurried over to Sehrys and Brieden with the kit.

Tash knelt behind them. "Sehrys," he said softly. "This is going to hurt, all right? Just keep talking to Brieden." He extracted long, slender aluminum tweezers from the kit and began extracting Sehrys's splinters one by one. Sehrys shuddered and yelped with pain a couple of times, but mostly his attention stayed trained on Brieden. When the last splinter was out, the wound closed.

When the wound was but a faint pink scar, Tash touched Sehrys lightly on the back.

"All right, Sehrys. When you're ready... I think you can heal him now."

Tash didn't add that he sincerely hoped it wasn't too late.

SEHRYS FOUGHT TO CALM HIMSELF. HE WOULD NEED ALL OF his focus for the task of healing Brieden. It was difficult: When he reached out to anchor his power in Brieden, he sensed how incredibly faint his life-force had become. Fainter by far than it had been at the inn in Okosgrim. Almost too faint for Sehrys to save him.

He fought to keep the frantic fear at bay. If he panicked, Brieden's life would slip away even more, and then it really *would* be too late. Instead, he concentrated.

It was a long time before Sehrys felt his power take root. He wasn't sure that it was going to, but he *had* to be sure. He had to *know* that it would work, even if it seemed impossible. It was the only chance he had. When he finally felt the power latch on in the form of a tiny, delicate tendril wrapping itself around the faintest glimmer of life, he couldn't stop the tears. He didn't try.

It took a long, long time. It took every shred of energy he had. It might have taken years from his life. Sehrys didn't care. He had plenty of years to spare. He would give Brieden every single one of them if he could.

When the power was strong enough, he wrapped it around the sword in Brieden's body and slowly pushed it out, mending organs and muscles along the way, until the sword fell to the ground. The power mingled with Brieden's blood, some of it *becoming* blood, until his veins once again thrummed with vitality.

When Brieden's pulse was strong and his breath was sure, Sehrys finally allowed himself to stop.

And then he passed out beside him.

Tash stared at the two men. He wondered if Sehrys realized that he had been chanting *esil vorn nau,* the Elfin expression of deepest love, in a trance-like voice the entire time that he worked on Brieden. By the end, his voice was hoarse.

Tash thought about what he should do. It would be some time before they awoke, but he was fairly certain that they would both survive. Brieden was calm and insightful, and Sehrys was quick and powerful. Both were very intelligent. Even if they were left with nothing but the clothes on their back, they *would* survive. Tash was sure of it.

He looked at the horses and the laden carriage.

He looked back at the two men on the ground.

Tash carried first Brieden and then Sehrys to the tent and laid them down.

He walked to the carriage and paused for a moment, considering.

"Oh, very *well*," he muttered irritably. He rummaged about until he found a flask of water and a couple of apples, and then settled himself against the trunk of a large tree to keep watch.

CHAPTER TWENTY-FIVE

BRIEDEN KNEW RIGHT AWAY THAT SOMETHING had happened.

He was lying next to Sehrys in the tent, daylight streaming in through the parted entryway. His mind was a strange jumble of confusing information, and his body was warm and energized.

Brec. Tash. Sehrys. Pain. The flashes came to him sharp and disconnected. He shook his head to try to achieve some clarity.

When clarity didn't present itself, he stood up; his limbs flowed like liquid. The specks of dust in the beam of sunlight at the entryway were unusually detailed. The familiarity of the sensation startled him: Had Sehrys healed him? But why? What had happened? And why were they *both* asleep at the same time? Surely that couldn't be safe.

Brieden stretched, his breath catching at a slight tenderness in his side. He moved his hand to his back and found a smooth stripe, like a new scar.

And then he remembered. He'd been stabbed.

Brieden cast his eyes around the tent, looking for his sword.

When he didn't see it, he grabbed the dagger he hid at the bottom of his satchel and crept outside. The first thing he noticed was the broken cage. Yes. Of course. Sehrys had done that.

Then there was the smoking pile of something... or *someone*. Yes, that would cause the smell of burning flesh in the air.

And then he saw Tash. He was sitting in front of a small fire, humming to himself as he looked through their supply of herbs and dried mushrooms.

Tash looked up; he laughed when he took in Brieden's befuddled expression.

"Come here and I will fill in the blank spots in your mind. I imagine you're feeling quite well, so you can help me make a stew. Sehrys is going to need something hearty."

Brieden stared at him.

Tash sighed. "I'm on your side now, if I'm on anyone's side other than my own. At least until I can get to Lekrypal. I figure that's the closest of the border cities."

Brieden's hand flexed around the dagger in his hand.

"Oh, for—I'm not going to *burn* you, Brieden! I already took care of Brec. Isn't that enough?"

"You—you did that? I thought Sehrys—"

"Sehrys was in no state to do *anything*. Brec damn near killed the both of you. And then Sehrys damn near killed *himself* when he healed you. He shouldn't have tried to see it through. You were too far gone. Hence the stew."

Brieden swallowed, his throat suddenly tight and dry in the face of this information.

"He's going to be weak for a little while," Tash continued, "and he's going to need you to take care of him. But he will be *fine,* Brieden, I promise you."

Tash's eyes had gone almost soft.

Brieden smiled through his inevitable tears. "Thank you," he whispered, before sitting down next to Tash and staring into the fire.

SEHRYS DIDN'T AWAKEN FOR SEVERAL MORE HOURS.

Brieden had been checking on him regularly and almost didn't hear the soft, pleading cry that came from the tent as evening began to spread across the sky.

"Brieden?"

Brieden wasn't sure whether he heard the quiet sound with his ears or his heart, but he leapt to his feet and was beside Sehrys in an instant.

Sehrys's eyes were heavy and he seemed weak. He struggled just to raise his head.

"Sehrys," Brieden whispered, throwing himself onto the blankets beside him and squeezing him tight. Sehrys hugged him back with as much energy as he could manage.

Brieden eased Sehrys back down onto the blankets. Sehrys simply stared up at him. "You're alive," he murmured.

Brieden laughed. "Yes. You saved me. Again. But it was dangerous, Sehrys, you shouldn't have—"

Sehrys groaned. "Hush. Brieden, please kiss me." Brieden did.

"I love you so much," Sehrys sighed. "Stay here with me?"

Brieden smiled, settling down beside Sehrys. "Of course. You should eat soon. Tash and I made stew."

"Tash..." Sehrys murmured. "Killed Brec, you know. Tash did."

"I know."

"Not sure we can trust him, though."

Brieden stroked Sehrys's chest gently. "I think he just wants a ride to Lekrypal. He stayed here and kept watch until I woke up. He could have left with the horses."

"Mmm, I suppose."

"And do you know what else?" Brieden asked with a sly smile.

"Hmmm?"

"Having a third person to rotate watch with means that we can sleep together again." Brieden kissed Sehrys's cheek. "I've missed holding you at night."

"Me too," Sehrys sighed, attempting to snuggle closer. Brieden pulled him in so that he wouldn't have to expend his energy. Sehrys sighed contentedly and closed his eyes again. His stomach rumbled as Brieden slid his palm across it.

"You need to eat, Sehrys. Healing me took a lot out of you."

"Too tired to eat," Sehrys mumbled.

"You won't get any less tired until you eat. Come on."

Sehrys whimpered, flopping his head onto Brieden's chest with exaggerated effort. "Don't want food. Want *you*."

Brieden kissed Sehrys's forehead. "What if I carry you outside, and hold you while you eat? Then you can have both."

"Not a helpless *child*," Sehrys grumbled.

"No, you are most certainly not a helpless child. You are my hero. Please let me take care of you the way you've taken care of me."

Sehrys managed a mischievous grin, as his hand slid under Brieden's tunic and across his stomach. "Mmm... I can think of *another* way to take care of me."

Brieden laughed. "Sehrys, if you're too tired to eat, you're *definitely* too tired for that."

Sehrys sighed. "I know. Just want to keep touching you, though. So *warm*."

"Are you cold?" Brieden asked. Sehrys shrugged slightly, but burrowed closer to Brieden.

Brieden moved to fetch their warmest blanket, which was folded up at the foot of their makeshift bed. Sehrys whined pitifully. "You're too far away."

"I'm right here, Sehrys," Brieden said softly, crawling back toward him with the blanket.

"You're alive." Sehrys looked at him. "Brieden, I truly thought... I just need you close right now. Please."

Brieden planted soft kisses across Sehrys's face. "I'm not going anywhere."

Brieden wrapped Sehrys in the blanket and carried him out to the fire Tash had started. Sehrys's protests were half-hearted. Before long, he was snuggled against Brieden with an expression of pure bliss, appearing to forget any objections he may have had. He even allowed Brieden to feed him as they sat by the fire. Brieden was touched that his fierce and acerbic lover was willing to put himself in his hands, yielding and vulnerable and trusting Brieden to care for him completely.

After he had eaten what Brieden deemed a reasonable amount, Sehrys rested his head in the crook of Brieden's neck and sighed deeply. The warmth of the blanket and the fire and Brieden, together with the bit of stew in his stomach, lulled Sehrys back into an easy sleep.

Brieden looked over at Tash. "You... you can stay in the tent when it's your turn to sleep if you want to..." Brieden began, his cheeks heating.

Tash snorted. "Thank you, but no. That tent is, uh... I believe it is strictly a two-man tent. Let us leave it at that."

Brieden dropped Tash's gaze, slightly abashed.

Tash shrugged. "If you can spare some blankets, I'm happy to sleep outside. I can always clear some space in the carriage if it rains."

Brieden smiled. "If you're sure."

Tash nodded. "It will be a delight after sleeping in that cage. Why don't you go ahead and lie down with Sehrys right now? I'll wake you when I get tired."

"I... thank you. But be sure to wake me as soon as you want to get some sleep. You've had less rest than I have recently."

Tash shrugged. "I haven't been able to truly move and breathe freely for some time. Please believe me when I say that nothing restores a sidhe's energy like a lack of proximity to iron. Go on. I'll be fine."

Brieden pondered Tash as he carried Sehrys back to the tent. If the sidhe had an angle, Brieden certainly couldn't figure it out. Still, he would be glad to deposit him in Lekrypal. Having him along was making Brieden uneasy.

Sehrys roused when Brieden eased him onto their nest of blankets. Seeming afraid that Brieden might leave him there alone, he murmured Brieden's name and grabbed at his arms. Brieden was pleased to note that his grip seemed a bit stronger.

Brieden pulled Sehrys into his arms and simply lay there, enjoying the solid warmth of Sehrys's body against his. "I love you," Brieden whispered into Sehrys's hair.

"Esil vorn nau," Sehrys replied softly, his voice slurred with sleep.

A FEW HOURS LATER, BRIEDEN AWOKE TO TASH'S VOICE AND carried Sehrys back outside so that Tash could get some sleep. He sat by the fire holding Sehrys, his sword beside him, which had thankfully been mostly cleansed of his blood.

The warmth of the fire and Sehrys's soft breathing against him created a strong, but undeniably false, sense of safety. Brieden fought the urge to sleep, focusing instead on the way that the firelight danced across Sehrys's delicate features and running his hands through Sehrys's soft violet-red hair. The last thing he could afford to do was let his guard down; the threats posed by slave traders and sidhe criminals aside, the royal guard would no doubt be combing the border lands in search of them. Drayez had to know that they planned to cross into the Faerie Lands, and he had to know that his time was running out.

Sehrys finally woke up, and Brieden helped him find a place to relieve himself. There was no awkwardness or embarrassment, nothing but the complete comfort that they had come to feel with one another. Brieden laughed. It had taken Sehry's full bladder to make him realize he'd never been more intimate with another person.

Sehrys insisted on walking back to the fire, although he moved slowly and leaned on Brieden. After he had settled in front of the fire, Brieden hung the cauldron and brought Sehrys some fruit and leaves while they waited for the stew to heat.

"You've really become quite the nursemaid," Sehrys said, snuggling back against Brieden, who had sat down behind him.

"I'm just glad that I finally have the opportunity to take care of *you*. And I'm glad that you're letting me do it."

Sehrys turned his head to kiss Brieden as his arms wound around Sehrys's waist. "You always take care of me, Brieden. We take care of each other."

Brieden pulled him even closer. "Yes, we do. And I don't want us to stop. I want us to take care of each other forever."

"I want that too," Sehrys said softly, leaning his head back onto Brieden's shoulder.

They sat in silence until the stew began to bubble, letting their last words sway and echo between them. Now was not the time to finish this conversation, after all. Now was the time to keep things gentle and tender between them.

Brieden was encouraged when Sehrys took two helpings of stew, and they sat in comfortable silence with occasional murmured conversation until the sky began to turn pink with the rising sun.

Before long, Tash began to stir on the other side of the fire, and then he was up, heating more stew and telling them to go back to the tent to get some more rest.

They did go back to the tent, but to Brieden's surprise, rest did not seem to be the first thing on Sehrys's mind.

He had barely closed his eyes before warm lips pressed against his neck and a smooth hand slid up his bare abdomen. He blinked and turned his head to find himself staring into lust-darkened eyes.

"Sehrys, aren't you..."

Sehrys smiled and pressed a kiss to the hollow at the base of Brieden's throat. "If you would be amenable to taking a more active role this morning, I... I want you so much right now. I want to be as close to you as possible."

"I want that too," Brieden murmured, turning to face him. "But only if you're sure."

Sehrys laughed softly. "I'm quite sure. Just don't expect me to move too much."

Brieden smiled into a soft kiss. "I think I can work with that," he murmured against Sehrys's lips.

Given the magnitude of Sehrys's most recent healing and the residual power it had instilled in Brieden, he produced the red flowers quite easily. He was grateful that Tash did not look over at him when he crept out of the tent to do so.

Sehrys had finished undressing himself by the time Brieden returned, and Brieden quickly shed his own clothing as well. He stretched out onto his side beside Sehrys, head propped on an elbow, running the furled tip of a red flower in a light, teasing path over Sehrys's supine form. Sehrys reached up to still the movements of Brieden's hand even as he murmured with pleasure at the tickle of the flower and his nipples stiffened into hard buds. He tipped the flower upright in Brieden's hand, twisting the tip open with nimble fingers. Brieden smiled down at him and drizzled the contents of the flower across Sehrys's chest, stomach and groin, and then down his thighs. Sehrys closed his eyes and sighed as Brieden began to massage the oil into his skin, starting with his shoulders and slowly working his way down. By the time he reached the downy hair between Sehrys's legs, they were both fully aroused.

"We should probably try to keep quiet," Brieden whispered into Sehrys's ear. "Tash—"

Sehrys nodded his assent, eyes still closed, breath ragged with pleasure.

Brieden took Sehrys's length into his hand and stroked him slowly. Sehrys arched his back and moaned softly. Brieden would *never* get enough of seeing Sehrys this way; it simply wasn't possible to lay eyes on anything sexier or more fulfilling.

He paused just long enough to unfurl a second flower, and then resumed stroking Sehrys with his right hand while he dipped three fingers of his left into the newly opened flower. He nudged Sehrys's thighs apart with the back of his hand, and Sehrys complied by spreading them wide. Brieden began to gently stroke Sehrys's entrance, and the elf's breath caught on a stuttering squeak of pleasure.

As he began to push the first finger inside, Sehrys groaned, low and deep, and opened his eyes to gaze at Brieden, glassy and unfocused. "Brieden," he breathed. "Oh, Brieden, that feels... I love you... Gods..."

Brieden leaned in to kiss his lips as both hands continued to work between Sehrys's legs.

"I love you," Brieden said when he pulled back. "I just want to make you feel good, Sehrys."

"So good. *So* good, Brieden. Please... more..."

Brieden slipped in a second finger, thrusting more deeply and stroking the little pleasure-nub when he found it. Sehrys let out a piercing cry, and Brieden quickly kissed him again in an effort to swallow the sound. Poor Tash had *definitely* heard, but there was nothing to be done about it now.

Besides, he really couldn't ask Sehrys to stop making noises. Not when those noises kept racing straight to Brieden's cock.

Brieden added a third finger, thrusting and stretching until Sehrys began whimpering and pleading for more, and then slicked himself up quickly, gasping at the feeling, knowing that he would never get used to the sheer intensity of it. He gently ran his hands up Sehrys's long legs, hooking his ankles over Brieden's shoulders as he pressed forward, sliding completely into Sehrys in one fluid motion.

Sehrys threw his arms behind his head and arched his back impossibly high. His moan of pleasure blended with Brieden's own; their joined voices were loud, clear and unrestrained.

Brieden grunted as he thrust into Sehrys and scattered kisses down his neck and chest and face; his lips shimmered with flower-oil. He was utterly lost in the taut, slippery heat inside Sehrys's body, in the slick, silken skin of his thighs against Brieden's hips as Sehrys cried out again and again, and clutched desperately at Brieden's back, his sides, his hips, his buttocks.

With a gasp, Sehrys slithered a hand between their bodies to squeeze himself at the base of his erection, whimpering as Brieden's thrusts grew harder and deeper and more erratic. "Brieden," he panted, "t-tell me when you're getting close."

Brieden responded with a deep moan, pressing his face into Sehrys's neck. Sehrys immediately buried the fingers of his free hand into Brieden's hair, gently holding his head in place and gasping as Brieden continued to slide in and out. Toe-curling pressure built at the base of Brieden's spine.

"Sehrys," Brieden groaned, muffled, against the flesh of his neck. "I'm... I'm going to—"

"Yes," Sehrys whispered, and released the grip on his own erection, giving himself four firm strokes before completely coming undone, wailing Brieden's name and clenching down around Brieden's final, deep thrust.

Brieden came with a loud groan, gasping Sehrys's name against his throat as he ground their hips together, chasing every last morsel of pleasure before gently lowering Sehrys's legs with shaking arms and falling on top of him. Their hearts were thudding against one another.

Their breathing slowly returned to normal, their heartbeats calmed to a soft, comfortable rhythm. Brieden almost fell asleep soft inside his lover's body, but he eventually had to move when Sehrys shifted uncomfortably beneath his weight.

He cleaned them with water from their flask and their last clean cloth, and then lay beside Sehrys and pulled him close. Sehrys was almost asleep, but moved into Brieden's embrace by instinct.

"Brieden," he mumbled, his voice thick and dreamlike. "When Brec stabbed you... you almost left me. Don't... please don't leave me again."

"I won't," Brieden replied, "but you have to promise me the same."

Sehrys was silent, save for steady, warm breaths across Brieden's chest. Because Sehrys was already sound asleep.

CHAPTER TWENTY-SIX

TASH WAS SURPRISED TO SEE SEHRYS EMERGE from the tent before Brieden, several hours after the sounds of their lovemaking had ceased.

Sehrys still had a blanket wrapped around him. He yawned deeply as he sat down next to Tash by the ever-present fire.

"Why did you tell Brieden you were weak?" Sehrys asked, watching the flames dance. "You made this fire, after all, and it's really quite good."

Tash shrugged. "It's more or less the truth. I'm good with close-range fire, but that's about it. I excelled at teaching, but there isn't much opportunity for that here."

"No," Sehrys agreed thoughtfully, "although that may be changing sooner than you think, Tash. At least if I have anything to say about it."

"You... you're not going to stay with Brieden, then? I thought, I mean it seems like you two are..." Tash trailed off as he studied the look on Sehrys's face.

"I love him," Sehrys admitted. "But before... all I knew of Villalu came from border city excursions as a child, and I didn't even see what was really happening there, let alone outside the city walls. When I was captured, I eventually started to believe that I was going to die in slavery. I was considering how I might take my own life when Brieden found me. If it hadn't been for him..." Sehrys drew his knees to his chest and propped his chin on them. Tash watched him silently.

"No one deserves it, Tash. I don't care what they may have done. *No one* deserves slavery. The Non-Interference Doctrine is too severe."

Tash tilted his head and made a noise of assent. "That may be true, Sehrys, but do you really think you can change *that*? It's been in place for millennia. It's an immutable doctrine."

"Tash, tell me this. How long have humans kept sidhe slaves?"

"Not that long, really. About two thousand years, since the Followers of Frilau began to seize power. The practice has truly blossomed over the past few hundred years, though, under the rule of the Panloch dynasty."

"But why? What could be the justification?"

"How much do you know about the Followers of Frilau, Sehrys?"

Sehrys sighed. "Very little. Brec may have been wrong on many accounts, but the picture he painted of me at home in my feririar was uncomfortably accurate. When it comes to historical knowledge, particularly that of Villalu, I'm as ignorant as a pixie."

Tash pursed his lips. Would that he were lucky enough to be so ignorant. "You should be grateful for your ignorance. The Followers of Frilau believe that slavery is the only way to save the souls of sidhe. Frilau was the leader of a militant fundamentalist group that splintered off from several closely linked human religions several thousand years ago. The Frilauans believe that we are an evil folk, and that suffering slavery is the only way to pay penance. They were nothing but a small, fringe cult for a very long time. No one took them seriously. At least not until they slaughtered half the Devotees of L!Khryauvni in Villalu and rose to power, anyway."

Sehrys stared at him. "This all happened *after* the Non-Interference Doctrine was established."

"Yes."

"But... didn't anyone—?"

"Of course. A group of sidhe devotees of the Blessed Guardian went so far as to establish their own republic in protest, where they welcomed humans as equal partners in governance. Of course, the only way to keep such a place truly safe was to build it in Laesi. So it's always been a bit of a struggle for humans to get to it, and it doesn't really do the sidhe in Villalu much good. Lovely idea, though."

"Are you... you're talking about Khryslee, aren't you?"

Tash laughed. "See now? You're not as ignorant as you thought."

"Don't patronize me."

Tash smiled and shrugged. "Oh come, now. How often does someone like me get the opportunity to patronize someone like you? Have some compassion."

Sehrys rolled his eyes. "Surely there must have been more outcry than that? How was the Non-Interference Doctrine maintained when the humans were making us into *slaves* over here?"

Tash's smile shot chills down Sehrys's spine. "The execution of the Non-Interference Doctrine comes down to the Queendom of the Eastern Border Lands. And lovely Queen Loq believed ever so strongly that because the only sidhe in Villalu were either those who chose to live with the risk or those who had been exiled for severe crimes, there was no reason to formally protest the policy. In fact, she seemed to believe that it created an added *deterrent* to crime. Her daughter Gira was of the same mindset."

Sehrys swallowed hard. "And Gira's son—?"

Tash smiled. "Ah, yes, the child king. Pity about dear Gira, wasn't it?" His was a tone of vicious delight. "You know, I was exi—that is, I *left* shortly before she died. I only learned about it from other sidhe in the border cities. I don't know much about her son at all, other than the fact that he was painfully young when he was crowned." Tash sighed. "But what concern is it of mine anymore? Let the whole realm burn down for all I care."

Sehrys tried to breathe normally.

Tash had just confirmed everything that Sehrys had suspected. He tried not to allow himself to feel sick at the flood of disappointment and heartbreak that washed over him. He had no right to think about his own happiness. This was not about him. This was much bigger than him. This was about all the sidhe in Villalu.

Tash studied him, his lips twitching.

"You're really going to do it, aren't you?"

"What are you talking about?"

Tash rolled his eyes. "You're going to try and cozy up to the child king."

"Um, something like that, I suppose," Sehrys said, failing to fight against a wry smile of his own.

"Well, you're pretty enough. Powerful enough, too. It will never work, though."

"Why not?" Sehrys asked, still amused.

Tash gave Sehrys a level look. "Because you're never going to be able to leave Brieden."

In the tent, Brieden lay and listened to the elves' voices. Their native tongue really was beautiful. It didn't even matter what they were saying; Brieden could listen to it all day.

THEY WOULD LEAVE FOR LEKRYPAL THE FOLLOWING MORNING.

After the three of them had eaten, they prepared to wash their bedclothes and garments in a nearby creek. When the task was underway, however, Sehrys suddenly grew much weaker, sighing that perhaps he hadn't fully recovered his strength from *saving Brieden's life* after all.

Brieden smiled to himself as he and Tash took the washing down to the creek, leaving Sehrys to prepare the next meal. He only regretted his easy compliance with Sehrys's obvious manipulation when he asked Tash about the reason for his exile from the Faerie Lands.

"Murder," Tash said simply. "My husband took a lover."

Brieden blanched. "You... you killed your husband?" Would Tash still be able to light Brieden on fire if he submerged himself completely in the stream?

Tash looked aghast. "No! Of *course* not! I would never do that to *him*. I... I loved him. It was that horrible boy he was cavorting with. I killed *him*. Burned him alive."

Tash sounded terrifyingly calm. Brieden very much wished that Sehrys was with them. He didn't like being alone with Tash when he had that glint in his eye.

"You—but—that's just so—you actually *killed* him?" Brieden had killed before too, but only to defend his own life or that of someone he loved. It was hardly the same as what Tash had done.

Tash looked confused. "Wouldn't you kill anyone who touched Sehrys?"

"If they were *hurting* him I would, but if he chose to... to be with someone else, I would be heartbroken, but I wouldn't kill anyone. Perhaps I would hit the man he chose once or twice, but I wouldn't kill him."

Tash snorted. "You, my friend, are *not* a sidhe."

"True, but—"

"If it were the other way around, Sehrys would kill the man. I'm sure of it."

"He didn't kill *you*, though."

"Brieden, why do you think I ran so fast when I saw that bottle of essence? Do you realize that I ran halfway to the city walls in nothing but my undershorts?" Tash laughed. "And *you* were only his human. I didn't even realize that he thought of you... like that."

Brieden raised his eyebrows. "Like what?"

"Like... like a husband. He hasn't even gone on a soul-walk and he already looks at you like you're his lifemate."

Brieden felt his breath catch. Husband. *Lifemate.* He found himself stunned into a dreamy silence, absorbing the impact of hearing another person say it.

Brieden didn't know what he wanted to do with his future. He had settled on Khryslee because it sounded like a place free from many of the societal ills that couldn't be avoided in Villalu, and on the thin hope, before Sehrys had shown any truly romantic inclination toward him, that he and Sehrys might somehow end up there together. But when he heard Tash's words, something became clear. Something that he had known was true for a very long time but hadn't let himself say, even inside his own head.

He wanted to be Sehrys's lifemate. It was the only thing he wanted with complete conviction. Absolutely everything else in his life was negotiable.

But then something else Tash had said drifted back to him: *He hasn't even gone on a soul-walk.* Because Sehrys *had* gone on a soul-walk. Six years earlier, he had gone on a soul-walk and emerged completely and utterly ready to marry another man. A man who wasn't Brieden.

A man who was also a sidhe, and probably gorgeous, and who had grown up with Sehrys and knew far more intimate things about Sehrys's life than Brieden ever would. A man Sehrys was going to see again when they crossed The Border.

And for a brief moment that he wasn't proud of, Brieden had nothing but the deepest empathy for Tash's crime.

"Brieden?" Tash had the look of someone who only just realized that Brieden wasn't listening to him.

"Oh... I apologize, Tash. I was a bit lost in thought. What did you say?"

Tash smiled self-consciously, focusing on getting a spot out of the cloth he was cleaning. "I was just saying—what I mean is, I've been *wanting* to say... that I'm sorry, Brieden. For... you know."

Brieden looked at him. "Are you?"

Tash sighed and ventured a glance at Brieden out of the corner of his eye. "Yes. I am. I—this isn't an excuse, so don't treat it like one, all right? I just... I truly didn't think of it as—as—"

"Rape?"

Tash flinched. "Yes. That. I never did. I always thought—or I suppose the truth is that I never thought about what it might be like. For you. Humans just seem so *happy* when they're compelled, and you're such an *unhappy* people most of the time, and the only other people I've known to call it slavery are religious zealots, so I just... I didn't know, Brieden. I'm sorry."

Brieden's face softened into an almost-smile. "Thank you, Tash."

Tash's gaze darted to the now-nonexistent spot on the cloth he was washing.

"I'm just glad you didn't get any further before Sehrys stopped you," Brieden added, "or he *would* have killed you."

Tash let out a bark of laughter. "I know," he said, and though Brieden joined him in his laughter, they both knew that it wasn't truly a joke at all.

SEHRYS WAS HOLDING BACK HIS POWER UNTIL IT WAS FULLY restored so that he didn't strain himself, so he gratefully allowed Tash to take over the fire when he and Brieden returned from doing the washing.

They ate a supper of stale bread that tasted quite good after it had been toasted, as well as fried mushrooms and sliced apples and pears.

Tash talked about Lekrypal, having spent time there before, and considered his options with regard to possible employment. He seemed nervous to be going forth alone, but he also had an edge of excitement in his voice.

It wasn't clear if he noticed how quiet Brieden and Sehrys had become.

The next day, they would reach Lekrypal. After they parted ways with Tash, it would only be a day's journey to the clearing where they would cross The Border.

They ate one-handed, fingers interlaced, ignoring the awkwardness in favor of the prolonged physical contact. Suddenly every question, every fear was climbing toward the surface, pushing at the skin of this delicate thing that they had created together.

They knew they were destined to part once they crossed The Border. Both of them had shed tears over it. Each of them had lost sleep over it. But it had been an eventuality. Something they could push to the back of their minds and hearts because right *now* they were together.

They didn't let go of one another's hands. They wouldn't. They couldn't.

They were all too aware that before long, they could be grasping at nothing but air.

CHAPTER TWENTY-SEVEN

THEY LEFT TASH IN LEKRYPAL WITH A SIZEABLE share of the weapons and other items of value they had stolen from the slave-traders. He could trade the items to support himself until he was able to find work.

It was an odd farewell. Tash hadn't exactly become their friend, but he was certainly no longer their enemy. Neither of them completely trusted him, but neither wished to see him come to any harm.

Brieden believed that Tash had changed and would continue to change, and he gave him a tight and sincere hug when they said goodbye. Sehrys was less sure, but Tash had saved him, which had allowed him to save Brieden. He had also saved Sehrys the trouble of killing Brec. For that, Tash deserved a chance, if nothing else, at a better kind of life. He gave Tash's shoulder a firm squeeze before he and Brieden departed.

"Thank you," Tash said, with his head bowed. He looked up and took a deep breath.

"Take care of each other," he added. Brieden smiled and squeezed Sehrys's hand. Sehrys bit his lip and tried to smile, but didn't quite succeed. Tash sighed and turned to Brieden. "My apologies," he said, before setting his eyes on Sehrys and slipping into Elfin tongue.

"Sehrys, please soul-walk about him before you make a decision," he implored. "I would do anything to be with my lifemate again,

Sehrys. *Anything.* This isn't the sort of thing you can simply walk away from. Just... be with him while he lasts in this world. The ills of the world will keep for a century or two."

Sehrys couldn't bring himself to respond, but he knew the resigned grief in Tash's eyes was most likely reflected in his own. After a moment, Tash shrugged and nodded. "Good luck to both of you," he finished in Villaluan. He smiled, perhaps a bit sadly, and headed toward the inn.

"WHAT DID TASH SAY TO YOU?" BRIEDEN ASKED AS THEY headed out of Lekrypal.

Sehrys shrugged. "Just... advice about going home, I suppose."
Home.

It wasn't the first time he had heard Sehrys call it that. Of course, it *would* be home for Sehrys—that much should have been obvious—but Brieden hadn't really thought of it that way. For him, home was simply *Sehrys.*

Brieden had already lost every other home he had known. Now he might lose Sehrys, too.

"What... kind of advice?" he ventured.

Sehrys sighed, looking away.

"Sehrys, we're going to have to talk about this sometime."

Sehrys turned back to face him. "I know, Brieden. I already told you, after we cross The Border—"

"Of course," Brieden mumbled. "I know. I just... how far is it, Sehrys? I feel like I'm riding along, trying to enjoy the scenery on the way to my own execution."

"Don't say that," Sehrys said quickly, tightening the hand that was holding Brieden's while he held the reins in the other.

"I'm sorry, I just—"

"Brieden, I know. I'm sorry too. I'm not trying to be cruel, but—well, Tash and the detour to Lekrypal provided a distraction.

But the truth is that now we're back on the path that I know, and the answer to your question is that we aren't far at all, and I can really only manage one source of emotional overload at a time."

Brieden swallowed and looked at Sehrys, ashamed. "Oh, Sehrys, I didn't mean... I know how hard this is for you. I shouldn't have..."

"It's fine, Brieden," Sehrys assured him with a soft smile.

Brieden disentangled his hand from Sehrys's and wrapped his arm around Sehrys's waist.

They rode in silence for most of the day. Neither could think of anything to say that wouldn't make everything hurt more.

Late that afternoon, Brieden woke without realizing he had been sleeping. Sehrys's arm was curled around him and Brieden's head lay on his shoulder. Brieden groaned at the stiffness in his neck as he straightened.

Sehrys gave him a fond smile, eyes glittering with amusement.

"What?" Brieden mumbled as he stretched.

"You just... your face is pink where you were lying on me, and I can see the weave of my tunic pressed into your skin. And your hair is..." Sehrys didn't have to say. Brieden knew how his thick black waves flattened into odd shapes when he slept. Sehrys laughed softly as Brieden tugged it back into shape.

"It's very cute," Sehrys said and kissed Brieden's cheek where it was still warm and tingling.

Brieden pursed his lips, but the fondness in Sehrys's eyes was nearly a tangible thing. It made Brieden's heart drop to his knees and then leap back into his throat.

Their hands found one another.

Brieden squinted and rubbed his eyes with his free hand, convinced that they were still clouded with sleep. Because what he saw ahead of them was... incredibly strange. It looked like a dome, the size of a large palace, made of something like water but more like steam, and a bit like the way that air takes on a wavy appearance on a hot day.

It was hard to look directly at it, but impossible to look away.

When the dome was still there after he'd blinked several times, Brieden turned to Sehrys.

Sehrys gazed at the dome with a strange expression, between dread and longing. He guided them directly toward it.

"Sehrys, what…?" Brieden allowed his voice to trail off. As they got closer to the dome, more details became apparent, such as the swirls of violet that raced across the dome's surface, if you could call it a surface, and the strange rhythm to the warm breeze that began to pulsate around them, and the sleepy feeling that seemed to be washing over him, even though he had just taken a long nap…

Sehrys squeezed his hand. "Brieden, do you remember when I told you about what I was doing when the slave traders got me? The Nuptial Rite?"

Brieden nodded.

"This was my destination." Sehrys smiled. "It's the safest place I know. I think we should sleep here tonight."

Brieden fought to keep his eyes open. "I… thought you said it was a sacred site?"

"It is a sacred site, but that doesn't mean we can't stay here. I think you might like it very much."

Too exhausted to hold his head up, Brieden slumped against Sehrys, his head falling onto Sehrys's shoulder. "So *tired,* Sehrys," he sighed.

He was half-asleep when Sehrys shook him violently. Brieden's eyes snapped open.

They had pulled to a stop. Sehrys grasped Brieden by the shoulders and stared at him.

"Brieden. Listen to me very carefully. You *cannot* fall asleep until we get inside the dome."

Brieden groaned. The dome seemed so far away. Sehrys may as well have told him not to fall asleep for a solid week.

Sehrys brought one of his hands to Brieden's chin, nudging it upward until he looked him in the eye. "I've heard this can happen, and given how easily you were compelled, it doesn't surprise me that it's affecting you this much. It's going to be the same at The Border, but even stronger. You need to hold my hand *tight* and not let go, and you need to stay awake. Do you understand?"

Brieden nodded miserably.

"Okay," Sehrys said, but he sounded nervous.

Brieden held onto Sehrys's hand as they started moving again. Sehrys urged the horses faster as Brieden struggled to stay conscious. Whenever his grip slackened, Sehrys squeezed Brieden's hand hard.

Sehrys's skin started to glow. Brieden must have accidentally lapsed into sleep after all. This was a dream. Then he remembered that Sehrys glowed sometimes when he was using his power, and then Brieden was glowing too, and then the horses and the carriage were also enveloped in the soft green glow. Sehrys squeezed his hand almost hard enough to break bones. Brieden's half-lidded eyes popped open.

"Sehrys! You're *hurting* me!"

"I'm sorry. I don't want to hurt you. But I don't want you slipping off into another dimension either."

Brieden whipped his head around to gape at Sehrys. "*What?*"

"Just hold on tight," Sehrys said through clenched teeth, and he gripped Brieden's hand even harder as they surged forward.

For a moment there was nothing. No color, no texture, no depth and no sound. They had no bodies.

Except they must have had bodies because Brieden's hand definitely hurt.

Because Sehrys was squeezing it.

And then a blur of every color imaginable, and endless, screaming tunnels whipping out in every direction...

And then they were in the most beautiful clearing Brieden had ever seen.

He could see the walls of the dome from the inside, but here they had taken on a much calmer and more muted quality. They looked more like heavily frosted glass, blurred around the edges, than something writhing and pulsating and alive. The clearing consisted of a carpet of soft, vivid grass of green and violet and amber and rust. Off in the distance was a babbling brook of which Brieden had seen absolutely no evidence outside the dome. And there were the strangest trees...

No. They weren't trees. They were flowers. The entire clearing was filled with flowers, from the tiniest and most delicate blossoms imaginable, hiding shyly behind blades of grass, to towering stalks as thick around as ten men and reaching almost to the top of the dome.

And there was birdsong all around them. Rustling among the trees—among the *flowers*—hinted at other forms of animal life as well. Brieden gasped when a creature that he at first presumed to be a dragonfly landed on his finger. Because it wasn't a dragonfly. It looked like a miniature cross between a sidhe and a human, but with round black eyes barely rimmed by the thinnest band of gold, and no visible body hair whatsoever. It was dappled blue and green and yellow, with delicately patterned translucent wings.

It sat on Brieden's finger, swinging its legs like a child on a tree branch, hands braced on either side of its hips, and gave Brieden a look of earnest appraisal.

Brieden remained absolutely frozen, afraid that the slightest twitch might somehow crush the tiny creature.

"What *is* it?" he breathed, barely moving his lips.

Sehrys gave a small, delighted laugh at the wonder in Brieden's eyes. "It's a pixie, Brieden."

"Does it—can it talk?"

Sehrys shrugged, and then rested his chin on Brieden's shoulder, peering down at the little faerie.

"Not so that you or I could understand. There are those who study them. They do communicate, although their language is much, much simpler than yours or mine. They tend to be very curious. I imagine that you are the first human this one has ever seen."

Sure enough, the pixie fluttered to Brieden's ear, tugging insistently at the top of it. The pixie's ears were pointed like Sehry's, and it seemed utterly intrigued by the rounded shape. Brieden squirmed as the tiny hands prodded at him and the fluttering wings tickled his ear.

"Hey!" he cried out, laughing, as the creature climbed inside his ear to look around.

Sehrys reached over to pull the creature out between two fingers when it seemed determined to explore more deeply.

"Sehrys! Be careful!"

Sehrys laughed lightly. "They're tougher than they look, Brieden. I'm not hurting it."

The pixie did not appear injured when Sehrys dropped it into his palm. It did look somewhat indignant, however, and Brieden laughed at the haughty expression on the tiny face. The pixie opened its mouth and apparently launched into a tirade, which registered as barely audible squeaking to Brieden. Appearing satisfied that it had made its point, it turned and flew off.

Brieden turned to Sehrys, beaming. "Sehrys... this *place...*"

Sehrys smiled back. "I know. And you haven't even seen the best part yet."

The horses led them toward the center of the clearing at a steady walk, and Brieden realized he was no longer tired. If anything, he felt energized. In fact, he felt *more* than merely energized. He looked at Sehrys. He absolutely couldn't believe that they weren't both naked, that he wasn't spread out beneath Sehrys on the impossibly soft-looking grass. Barely even realizing he was doing it, he placed his hand on Sehrys's upper thigh and squeezed gently.

Sehrys turned to him with a giddy laugh, his eyes just as dark with lust as Brieden's must have been. "I know, Brieden," he murmured. "You can feel it too, can't you?"

Brieden's throat was dry. He swallowed hard. "Yes," he said, his voice rough. "What is—I mean, I always want you, but what is this?"

"*M!Ferauvise*," Sehrys replied.

It was one of the most erotic things Brieden had ever heard.

"Say that again," he purred, sucking gently at Sehrys's neck.

"*M!Ferauvise*," Sehrys gasped out and groaned .

His lips still firmly attached to Sehrys's neck, Brieden let the hand on Sehrys's thigh slip between his legs, and was unsurprised to find him fully aroused.

"Brieden... Gods... no, we have to stop."

Brieden moved his hand to Sehrys's knee, pulling back to look at him with a raised eyebrow.

"Are you serious? Why don't you just stop the carriage? That grass looks nice and soft, though I frankly wouldn't care if it were full of thorns right now."

Sehrys shook his head, although he shook from the self-control it took to deny Brieden.

"We will, I swear it. But this is a very important shrine. It requires a specific sort of offering, and the ritual behind it is important."

Before Brieden could express the frustration and confusion elicited by this answer, he was struck silent by the sight before him.

They had rounded a cluster of flowering shrubs and flower-trees to reveal an enormous statue of a sidhe woman.

If *statue* was the correct word. She seemed to be crafted of stone, but the flowering vines that wrapped around her seemed as essential a part of the structure as the stone itself. The vines wove themselves into an immaculate multicolored flowing robe that hung off her shoulders artfully to reveal her plump and voluptuous breasts, hips, stomach and thighs. Brieden had never seen such a curvaceous sidhe. True, he had seen far fewer females than males, but they had all been slim and lithe. The curves suited the statue quite well, however, and Brieden supposed that he might find the image arousing if he were differently inclined.

Brieden was finding more or less *everything* to be arousing.

The statue's face was soft and rounded, her eyes managed to look both dreamy and piercing, and her lips were parted as if in pleasure. Her hair flowed around her and bounced in the wind. It was made of flowering vines that seemed to grow directly from the statue's head. It was intensely scarlet, heavy with *hubia rija* flowers, though these particular flowers were larger, redder and more swollen with oil than those produced by either Sehrys or himself.

Sehrys was obviously not surprised by the statue, but he looked as awestruck as Brieden felt. Sehrys climbed down from the perch, gently pulling Brieden behind him, and they approached the statue hand-in-hand.

She was at the top of a small hill, and they climbed a set of low stone steps to reach her. Before her was a bed of mosses and flower petals. Sehrys knelt and Brieden mimicked the action. "*Esil supalin vormikente nau'at,*" Sehrys said, seeming to address the statue. "Her name is *M!Ferauvise,*" he added, turning to Brieden. "She is The Mother of All. The Sacred Whore. I always felt a special affinity for Her, but I suppose... even more so now."

"Sehrys..." Brieden said gently, squeezing his hand.

Sehrys glanced at Brieden, but did not let his gaze linger long enough to gather heat. He smiled.

"I don't say that to criticize myself. The word "whore" doesn't have the same connotation among The Sidhe as it does among humans. Whores are among our most powerful and revered spiritual leaders. To be with one is an honor that few ever experience. I was referring to Her story."

Brieden smiled encouragingly, also making sure not to look at Sehrys for too long, even though his head was literally spinning at the notion of whores being *revered spiritual leaders.* It was almost as alien a concept as Tash's claim that the world was a spinning ball.

"Legend tells that She came from another world," Sehrys continued. "She was a slave there, used for the pleasure of men. She suffered for many, many years, slowly storing away bits of power in the prison where She slept. One day, She overpowered Her captors and killed them all without mercy." Sehrys laughed shortly. "The original story is quite a bit more descriptive, but I think you've already seen what that kind of thing looks like."

Brieden gave a small, bitter smile and nodded. That he had.

"She found a doorway into another world and slipped through. When she found Herself in this world, She was alone and heavily pregnant in a barren, empty landscape. But even though the world was ugly and Her situation was desperate, She was *free.* And She was so happy to be free that she began to pleasure Herself. And Her pleasure was so powerful that She began to birth all the beauty in the world. And then, when the world was full of streams and flowers and stars and sunsets, She began birthing all the elfin races. Humans, too, Brieden. You *are* one of us, you know."

Brieden gazed at the statue as Sehrys told the story, amazed at how She almost seemed *alive.*

"And then," Sehrys continued, "after a thousand years had passed, She began to mate with The Sidhe, and from those unions, She birthed all the other creatures of the world, and that is why we do not eat animals. Because they are our children." He smiled, face awash with reverence.

"It is our very first and most sacred story. Most do not hold such an affinity for The Mother after childhood. However, I always have...

278

I suppose it might be because my own mother was not suited to family life, and I never really knew her. The Mother was always such a comfort to me, especially after I lost my sister. And now I think my affinity for Her is even greater. After—"

Brieden pulled Sehrys to him instinctively, to comfort him, momentarily forgetting about that *something* that seemed to permeate the area around the statue, alighting all their nerves with urgent desire. "Oh... I... I'm sorry..." Brieden stuttered, unsure whether he should let Sehrys go or keep drawing him closer.

Sehrys took a deep breath. "We should... make our offering."

"Is it... a sexy offering?" Brieden asked.

Sehrys laughed. "Very much so."

"Sehrys, *what* is causing this feeling? It is as if I have never known arousal before."

Sehrys pointed to the vines trailing from The Mother's head. "Those vines have been growing there since that statue was built, a hundred thousand years ago or more. The flowers replenish when they are plucked, but the power in the vines..." Sehrys shuddered. "The vines emit that feeling, whatever it is. And everyone who visits must give a gift of pleasure to The Sacred Whore. Some believe the offerings themselves strengthen the feeling." Sehrys turned to Brieden then, and Brieden's breath caught at the intensity in his gaze.

"I've always wanted to come here with someone, Brieden."

"What—did you do when you came here on your own?" Brieden almost couldn't stand to ask the question. He was fairly sure the heat between his legs wouldn't withstand the answer.

"I pleasured myself."

Brieden groaned and fell forward, clutching at Sehrys. The thought of Sehrys lying on a bed of mosses at the foot of this statue, naked and touching himself, very nearly caused Brieden's body to seize into orgasm on the spot.

Sehrys stood up and pulled Brieden with him, and then headed toward the steps, away from the statue. "Come on."

Brieden looked at him. "But... I thought we were going to—"

Sehrys stepped back and looked at the ground, breathing heavily. "Gods, Brieden, you sound so—" Sehrys took a few more deep breaths. "We are. But we must start with the ritual bathing."

"I *hate* the ritual bathing," Brieden complained. "I wouldn't care if we were completely filthy. I *like* it when we're filthy."

Sehrys choked back what sounded like a sob. He bit his lip and headed down the stairs, apparently too overcome with blind lust to respond to or even to look at Brieden.

When they got to the creek, they were far enough from the statue that they suffered decidedly less from uncomfortable arousal. They freed Raven and Crow and climbed into the cool creek near a cluster of bushes covered in puffy white flowers. Sehrys grabbed a handful of the flowers and rubbed them between his wet hands, creating a lather. He began to smooth it across Brieden's chest and then his arms, lifting them and scrubbing thoroughly.

"These are the flowers that were in those elfin soaps we got in Silnauvri," Sehrys said as he washed his lover's body. He looked into Brieden's eyes. "This ritual isn't meant to be taken lightly, Brieden. The Mother is only appeased by acts of beauty and love. Self-love or lovemaking. Just sex won't do."

Brieden smiled. "Then it's probably for the best that we never have *just* sex."

"Yes, but I very much would like to do this properly. It means a lot to me that we do."

"I know, Sehrys," Brieden answered, kissing him softly and quickly. "Tell me what we're going to do."

"All right," Sehrys said, sounding a bit breathless. "First we wash each other. Then we anoint each other with oil from another type of flower."

"You sidhe and your flowers," chuckled Brieden.

Sehrys smiled. "Then... then we make love at the base of the shrine."

"And that shall be my favorite part," Brieden whispered into Sehrys's ear.

"Brieden, I should warn you... those flowers on the shrine, they're extremely intense."

"Sehrys, please stop talking about it while you're naked and wet and I can't do anything about it," Brieden groaned. "It's cruel."

Sehrys gave him a playful wink as he lathered up more blossoms, then moved around Brieden to wash his back. Brieden could feel the heat of Sehrys's body, and, once or twice, the brush of what *had* to be Sehrys's erection. He groaned again, because really, everything Sehrys did or said would feel cruel until he was buried as deep inside of Brieden as he could get.

After they had finished bathing, Sehrys led Brieden back toward the shrine. They stopped at a flower-tree with a sunburst-yellow canopy. Coiled around the trunk—Brieden couldn't think of it as merely a *stem*—was a vine bearing deep blue flowers that looked quite a bit like the *hubia rija* that aided in their lovemaking.

"Are these the same as the red flowers?" He asked, plucking a particularly large one from the vine.

"They're definitely related," Sehrys said, shooing away a pixie. "But this one will help... keep things steady."

Sehrys began first, rubbing the oil into Brieden's skin, not skipping an inch between his throat and his toes. This was considerably more torturous than the bathing, of course, because Sehrys gave his cock several firm strokes, clearly struggling not to continue when Brieden shuddered against him and made soft sounds of pleasure.

The oil did have an effect, though. It didn't dull Brieden's senses; it simply quelled the urgency and made him feel more sensual. It didn't make his skin tingle the way the red flowers did, but settled into his skin and made each of Sehrys's touches feel deep and rich, as though he could just keep melting into them forever and ever.

He understood what Sehrys meant about this oil helping to keep things "steady." He and Sehrys could probably make slow, gentle love for hours and hours with this oil settled into their skin.

Sehrys sighed into Brieden's touch when it was his turn to anoint Sehrys. Brieden noticed the difference as he rubbed Sehrys's silken skin and made it gleam. If he hadn't been rubbed into relaxation himself just moments before, he was fairly sure he would have come simply from running his hands across Sehrys's body this close to the shrine.

When they reached the foot of the statue, it was if they were in a shared altered state; the lust induced by the vines from the statue rolled through them in waves, deliciously tempered by the mellow, sensual contentment in their oiled bodies. Sehrys stood on The Mother's foot and reached up to pluck a single plump red flower from one of the vines flowing from Her head. When he turned around, Brieden was already spread out on the bed of mosses in front of the statue. Sehrys's breath caught in his throat and he closed his eyes for a moment while Brieden gazed up at him. Sehrys was beautiful.

No matter what happened between them, and no matter what happened in Brieden's life, he would always have this. *They* would always have this.

Sehrys lowered himself into the soft moss beside Brieden, and they finally allowed their eyes not only to meet but to linger. Sehrys touched Brieden's face with his fingertips, tracing its contours. Brieden sighed happily, but did not close his eyes as he normally did. He kept his eyes fixed on those of his lover as he ran his fingertips down Sehrys's side, ghosting across his hip, dipping around to lightly trace the crease where his thigh began. They continued stroking softly with fingertips, their eyes locked as if by some physical force, the torture of it hanging sweet and strong and timeless between them.

Their lips finally met, and with the connection came a shift in the urgency . Brieden surrendered to it first, and when he pressed his lips to Sehrys's, he felt it in waves throughout his entire body. He groaned and pulled Sehrys flush against him and opened his mouth. Their tongues slid together with such perfection that neither of them could imagine, let alone remember, what it felt like to be less connected to one another than they were in that moment.

The kiss deepened impossibly; neither of them was entirely aware that their hands on one another's bodies were becoming decidedly bolder and needier. Brieden held the back of Sehrys's head with one hand and cupped his buttocks with the other, pulling Sehrys against him closer, closer, *closer,* trying to find a way to create more contact between them. Sehrys's hands mirrored his own, except that he had also allowed a finger to drift toward the heat of Brieden's entrance, and he began to softly stroke the puckered opening, making Brieden shake and clutch him tighter and moan into his mouth.

There was nothing sudden about the need. It built up slowly, achingly so, as each nerve ending was prodded from softly glowing coal to snapping, writhing ball of flame, as touches turned to licks and bites, and rocking turned to grinding and thrusting. When Sehrys finally pulled away from Brieden and steadied his hands enough to unfurl the bright red flower, Brieden was whimpering and writhing and bucking his hips, unable to hold still even if he had wanted to. Just *moving,* even without Sehrys against him, relieved a small edge of the desperation boiling in his bloodstream.

Sehrys dipped his fingers in the oil, gasped at the sensation and stared at Brieden, stared shamelessly as Brieden writhed and made tiny cries of need that only grew more urgent as Sehrys's eyes on him grew darker and hotter and ever more ravenous.

"I love you," Sehrys whispered.

"I love you," he returned, his voice a strained croak.

It was good that they said it then. Because when Sehrys touched Brieden's opening with a single oil-slicked finger, words instantly became far too complex to contemplate.

Sehrys stroked slowly, and Brieden panted in short, harsh gasps, overwhelmed and almost unable to withstand the magnitude of pleasure he was experiencing. Sehrys slowly moved the finger inside Brieden, and Brieden tossed his head back and screamed, throwing his legs as wide open as he possibly could and arching into Sehrys's touch.

Sehrys worked him open slowly; his deep, measured breaths escalated into ragged panting as he stared at his fingers at work. Brieden watched his face, transfixed, until he couldn't stop his eyes from rolling back in his head. His body squirmed and his erection dripped onto the hot skin of his stomach as Sehrys massaged that gorgeous spot inside him with perfect pressure.

When Sehrys finally knelt between Brieden's legs and slicked himself, he let out a yell at the sensation of the oil on his member. He lifted Brieden slightly as he sank into him; the sensation was so intense that Brieden couldn't hold back a scream of wild joy as he wrapped his legs around Sehrys's waist and gripped his shoulders. When Sehrys was buried deep inside, he paused long enough to let their eyes meet and lock. When Sehrys began to thrust, they didn't break eye contact.

Their gaze deepened as Sehrys increased the force and speed of his movements, sliding hard and fast in and out of Brieden's body. He hit Brieden's sensitive spot over and over again, and even as Brieden writhed and screamed beneath him, even as Sehrys moaned and yelled with each thrust, their eyes remained locked.

It was as if their minds had merged into one seamless thing. It was as if they could see into one another's very souls. It was as if the true depth of their connection was finally presented to them, unmasked and delicate, yet somehow strong as steel. It would be so easy to break what they had, but on some essential level, it was completely and utterly untouchable. No destructive force in the universe could find its way to the true heart of their love and their bond, and that was utterly terrifying and neither one of them looked away. Their eyes were naked and open and they let each other all the way inside.

They clutched each other. Deep grunts were wrenched from their throats as Sehrys slammed into Brieden, hard and fast and deep, Brieden rocking his hips up sharply to meet every thrust, to try to pull Sehrys as far inside him as possible. The intensity was so overwhelming that all they could do was try to express it with their bodies while they sobbed and gasped and convulsed and held each other's gaze through a blur of sweat and unshed tears.

Sehrys grasped Brieden's cock with an oiled hand and stroked him tight and fast. They both cried out as Sehrys snapped his hips and flicked his wrist three final times before he let go, bracing himself on shaking arms as Brieden seized up and they both came, so hard that they regained consciousness only several moments later, lying in a tangled heap.

Words were not allowed. Anything they said would be bitter-sweet. So they kissed, for a long, long time, before allowing themselves to fall into a messy sleep.

Chapter Twenty-Eight

It was early afternoon by the time Sehrys and Brieden left the shrine. They had spent the night at the foot of the statue and had made love five times—although to think of it that way would be to separate the experience into pieces, to compartmentalize it, and that wasn't strictly possible. They hadn't stopped touching each other, hadn't emerged from their pleasure-trance even through their bouts of sleep; the crackle of lust in the air rendered them downright insatiable.

It was entirely possible that they had just given The Mother of All the best offering She had ever received in all the thousands of years that such offerings had been made.

When they finally summoned the strength to leave, they were sore and spent and ravenous and desperately thirsty. They managed to gather the horses and make their way to the far side of the dome, as far from the statue as possible, in order to bathe, eat and get a bit of uninterrupted sleep before leaving their tiny oasis and venturing out into the harsh reality of western Villalu.

Sehrys clung to the memory of it: of the depth of Brieden's eyes, the sounds that he made, the feel and scent of him as they fell over the edge together again and again; of the miniature universe that they had created consisting of only their bodies and their pleasure and their souls and their love. The time they had spent in that little universe carried the weight and meaning of years, even though it had only been hours.

But try as he might, other memories crowded in, vying for a position at the forefront of his mind, memories that grew more vivid as the scenery around them became horrifically familiar. Before long, they found themselves on the specific route that Sehrys had taken a handful of times in his life, most of them in a state of peace and reflection.

Sehrys had chosen The Mother's shrine for his Nuptial Rite because she was so meaningful to him. Few others chose her because the shrine was technically on Villaluan soil. In fact, few made the trek at all anymore—not since the humans had begun taking sidhe slaves.

But Sehrys hadn't been afraid. Sehrys was too young and powerful to be afraid. And he couldn't imagine any other God guiding him on his soul-walk.

But all of that had changed.

His time at the shrine with Brieden would be his last visit to The Mother. Sehrys could not make this journey again. The shrine itself was unmarred in his mind—even more exalted, in fact, since he'd made the offering with Brieden—but the path that led between his home and the shrine was forever poisoned.

He gritted his teeth as they emerged from the forest path to drive through a sunlit clearing, the very clearing that had lived a long and well-fed existence in his nightmares.

It was such a nondescript place: pleasant enough for a nap, but nothing special. It was still rife with that sweet grass that Sehrys had always liked so much: a variety that was rare in eastern Laesi, but abundant in Villalu.

Sehrys couldn't imagine ever wanting to eat it again.

He gripped Brieden's hand tightly and felt his body tense, and Brieden didn't ask what it was. He simply stroked gentle circles into Sehrys's back with his free hand and allowed him to guide the carriage through the clearing at a brisk pace. By the time they were back on the wooded path, Sehrys had both the reins and Brieden's hand in a white-knuckle grip.

"Sehrys," Brieden said softly, flexing his fingers.

"Sorry," Sehrys whispered, letting go of Brieden's hand.

"Sehrys, we should stop for a bit. Give you a chance to—"

"I'm fine, Brieden."

"Sehrys, you're not. Please at least let me drive."

Sehrys sighed heavily, but thrust the reins into Brieden's hands. When he began to curl in on himself, forcing himself to hold the tears at bay, Brieden eased the horses to a stop, and Sehrys wasted no time in nestling himself tightly into Brieden's embrace. Brieden brushed a light kiss across his forehead.

"I'm never going back there, Brieden," he swore, and the mere words, spoken aloud, seemed to melt something hard and cold and heavy inside. Because it was finally true.

"Never," Brieden agreed softly, cupping Sehrys's cheek.

"We have to be careful." Sehrys sat up straight and fixed Brieden with an overbright smile, desperate to leave the clearing, and all it represented, firmly behind him. "Soon we'll be close enough to The Border that we'll be in no danger from slave-traders or the royal guard; their minds become muddled, iron melts, verbena sours and wilts and loses its potency. But in this stretch here—" Sehrys swept his hand to indicate the area around them "—you should probably arm yourself, Brieden. There could be trouble."

And sure enough, there was.

No more than an hour later, Brieden pulled the carriage to an abrupt halt, barely missing a veritable wall of iron chains pulled taut between two trees across their path.

"Good job, my darlings," Sehrys whispered to Raven and Crowe, as he and Brieden looked around them to assess any further danger.

The flash of movement in the bushes alongside the road caught Brieden's attention almost too late. He lunged for Sehrys and pulled him down just as two iron-tipped arrows flew past them and narrowly missed them both.

Crouching on the footrest in front of the perch, they scanned the area, but whoever had shot those arrows was nowhere to be seen.

"Brieden, I have to get down," Sehrys whispered. "I need the ground for an anchor."

Brieden nodded. "I'll cover you," he whispered, gathering his bow and quiver of arrows from beneath the seat. He grabbed the back of Sehrys's head and gave him a quick, hard kiss before he jumped to the ground.

But before Sehrys could even begin to follow him, there was a dagger at Brieden's throat. The man who grabbed him wore armor emblazoned with the Panloch crest.

"Brieden Lethiscir, you are hereby under arrest for crimes against the crown."

"No," Sehrys gasped, readying himself to leap to the ground as the king's army emerged from the surrounding trees to encircle them.

"Move, slave, and I will kill him where he stands. King Thieren would prefer to see to it himself, but he does not suffer from his brother's passions or his father's pride. If you look to your left, you will see that my companion holds an iron collar. Take it and put it on."

Sehrys swallowed and turned to see the solder in question holding out an iron collar at the end of a long wooden pole. Sehrys reached for it.

"No!" Brieden croaked, wincing as the blade pressed to his skin more tightly. "Sehrys, go. You are so close. Please. They're going to kill me either way. *Please* just keep going!"

Sehrys shook his head; the movement freed silent tears from his eyes. "Not while there is still a chance on earth that I can save you. Nothing is more important than—"

His words were cut off with a sharp gasp as a splatter of blood covered Brieden's face, followed by a wretched choking sound. "*Brieden*!" he screamed, leaping to the ground by instinct and throwing his arm up as the men surrounding the carriage surged toward him. He barely heard their screams as every bit of metal that touched their bodies began to melt: swords, armor, earrings, daggers and shields, all dripping like butter near a flame. The men yelped as they dropped their weapons and wrenched the armor from their bodies, palms blistering at the contact. Those who failed to move quickly enough fell to the ground and howled in pain, their melting jewelry and armor causing their skin to bubble and blacken.

Those who were able attempted to flee into the surrounding forest, but stopped short at the edge of the road, raising their arms in surrender.

Sehrys barely registered any of it.

What he did see, the *only* thing he could see with any degree of clarity, was that Brieden, although visibly shaken, seemed somehow unharmed. The man who had held the dagger to Brieden's throat slumped with the point of an arrow stuck out the front of his own throat as his blood flowed down the front of Brieden's tunic, soaking it through. The man's eyes were wide, and his blade fell to the ground with a clatter. As Brieden shook free and ran to Sehrys, the man collapsed to the ground.

The man's assailant was revealed the instant he fell; her small stature had been hiding her from view. "Really," she said, lowering her bow. "Weren't you boys getting a bit sick of that whole song and dance?"

Sehrys wasted no time in pulling Brieden into his arms, squeezing him tightly enough to feel sticky, cooling blood seeping through to his own skin. The woman was the very one who had helped in their escape from Dronyen all those months ago, although she had clearly left the comforts of palace life far behind. Her hair had grown out just long enough that she had to hold it in place with a strip of cloth to keep it out of her eyes, and her cheeks and breeches were streaked with dirt. She wore chainmail and a blue and silver breastplate over her tunic, and she had gathered an army.

All around them, a veritable sea of warriors clad in blue and silver had crept out of the forest, surrounding the remaining members of the king's guard.

"Oh, please, sacrifice me so that you may live. For you, my love, *you* are he who matters in this life," the woman crooned, with hands clutched to her chest and her voice shrill and dramatic. "No, my love, it is you who must sacrifice *me*," she continued, her voice now absurdly deep. "For if you are to perish, the birds shall never sing another song, and the sun shall collapse into a cold and lifeless thing."

Sehrys raised an eyebrow as Brieden turned to face her, eyes widening when he saw who stood before him. "Are you *quite* done?" he finally asked, crossing his arms over his chest.

"Nearly!" she assured them with a broad grin. "Just a bit more, I swear." She cleared her throat and launched back into the shrill voice.

"But my darling, I have heard tragic news: that all things must sometime die." She threw the back of her hand against her forehead and gave a loud, shocked gasp. Several of her warriors twittered with laughter. "All things must die, my sweetest one?" she wailed, her voice once again mockingly deep, "Say it cannot be so! Well then, let us perish together, so that we do not live to see how the world could bear to continue without us!" She bowed low before springing back up to face them. "There. Now I am done."

"Who are you?" Sehrys blurted.

"Cliope Keshell, at your service," she replied, holding her hand out to the pair. Brieden and Sehrys exchanged glances.

"Oh, for—my flesh is not poison, boys, just because it covers a woman's bits."

"No, I—" Brieden shook his head. "Forgive me. And thank you. Again." He reached out and shook Cliope's hand. "You are... sister to Brissa Panloch, are you not?"

"I am sister to Brissa *Keshell*," Cliope corrected. "Elder by a full ten minutes, in fact."

"Twins," Sehrys mused, unable to help how the information made his heart throb for the twin he had lost.

"Twins," Cliope confirmed, her voice proud. "Fraternal, of course." Sehrys jumped as Cliope grasped his hand and gave it a firm shake.

"What do you want from us?" He demanded before things could grow too comfortable between them. "And—yes, thank you of course, but—"

Cliope held up her palms. "I understand. You have no reason to trust me, even if I *did* assist your lover in rescuing you from slavery without getting himself killed in the process."

"Which you did with no eye to self-interest, I am sure," Sehrys responded.

"Does it matter why I did it, when it saved your lives either way?" she asked.

"It does if you require our trust," Brieden said.

She considered his words. "Fair enough. But first things first." She held up a finger and turned to her soldiers. "All right, best to kill them now."

Before Brieden or Sehrys could utter a syllable of protest, every member of the king's guard was slain, even those who screamed out their surrender.

"But—the king will—" Brieden protested weakly.

"There is no king," Cliope countered, "no matter what Thieren wishes to call himself."

"Thieren?" Brieden asked, eyebrows raised.

"Yes. Drayez is no more, although it appears his remaining sons are not yet prepared to surrender and allow the queen to rule in peace. Speaking of which, the reason I am here is to deliver to you a message from the queen."

"Quite a lot of bloodshed for a simple message," Sehrys commented, casting his eyes across the carnage.

"It is rather important."

"I should hope so."

Cliope unbuttoned a pocket on the left hip of her breeches and pulled out a small scroll. It was yellowed with age, on parchment nearly as thin as the wing of a pixie. Sehrys's eyes went wide.

"That—that looks like an *Imervish* scroll," Sehrys whispered. Brieden frowned at the scroll in confusion. "Incorruptible," Sehrys translated. "A sort of spell scroll of The Sidhe. Such scrolls are rare. And powerful. And... unstable." He took it from Cliope and stared at it.

She nodded. "Very astute. Aren't you going to open it?"

Sehrys ran a finger along the broken wax seal at the open end of the scroll and raised his eyebrows. "You have opened it already?"

"It was opened by human hands before I was born. But don't worry, it's quite stable."

Sehrys gave her a measured look before carefully unrolling the parchment.

He furrowed his brow. "This looks like the old tongue." He looked up at Cliope and Brieden in turn. "The old language of spells. I—I was to begin learning it after I was married, but... " He sighed, neatly rolling up the scroll and returning it to Cliope. "I am sorry, but it is no more than gibberish to me. I cannot understand it."

Cliope's face fell. "But you are *Aldevucavish*. Are you sure you cannot… cannot *summon* some sort of understanding?"

Sehrys's eyes went wide at the elfin title. "Who are you?" he demanded.

"I told you—"

"No. Who are you *truly*? Some sort of *puca*, or—"

"I *told* you. I am Cliope Keshell from the island of Ryovni. I am twenty-two years old, and my blood is as human as my disposition, I assure you."

"Then how on earth do you know who I am?" he hissed, shooting a furtive glance back to Brieden before moving closer to her.

Cliope tapped the scroll against her chin. "This scroll and others were found in the caves of Ryovni many generations ago. We… we have received help in deciphering most of them and coming to understand what they represent, but this one eludes even those who have helped us. But they knew who you were."

"And who are *they*?" Sehrys demanded.

"It is not my place to share that information just yet." Cliope's face was mild. "To be plain, my sister and I had hoped that freeing you would serve the dual purpose of getting Dronyen out of the way and enticing you to help us win this war. From what we understand, this scroll is truly the key to it all." She sighed. "But if you cannot help us—"

"I did not say I cannot help you," Sehrys corrected her. "Simply that I cannot read the words. But first you must tell me why I should help you at all."

Cliope gaped at him. "Other than the fact that I have saved your lives twice apiece now?"

"Yes." Sehrys narrowed his eyes at her. "You have helped us, it is true, but you have made it plain that it was in service to your own self-interest. You seek to convince me that your cause deserves my help, but you will not reveal to me how you have come to know things that no human should know. You murder those who displease you without a second thought—"

"Sehrys," Brieden interrupted, stepping forward to touch his arm lightly. Sehrys turned to face him, and Brieden gestured to the soldiers who stood watching them. "Look."

Sehrys glanced around at the assembled warriors. "Yes, Brieden, I have noticed—"

"No. *Look* at them."

Sehrys looked. And as his gaze fell across the soldiers' individual faces, he saw for the first time exactly who stood before him clad in silver and blue. A large handful were Brissa's ladies, hair tied back and delicacy abandoned, but he recognized many others as well. Men who had fought in the king's army during Sehrys's time at Dronyen's castle, men who had served as palace guards, young men and women who had tended the stables and the kitchens, and even a few women Dronyen had favored from the brothel in the village. This was not merely an invading army, to be sure.

This was an uprising.

Sehrys's heart caught in his throat. He had never anticipated something like this. He had never imagined humans could be willing to take such a risk. That so many would stand behind the woman who helped to free him, understanding full well how much damage he could do to them all if he so chose, in defiance of a ruling House that could very well still have them all killed.

"We assessed the loyalty of all," Cliope informed him, her gaze following Sehrys's. "We had many good warriors, to be sure, but not nearly enough to take Panloch castle without the assistance of those who best knew the palace and the ruling House." She turned her eyes back to Sehrys, her voice serious. "This is not merely one House overtaking another. This is not merely a play of politics. We seek to change Villalu, and to do that, we must decipher this scroll. Please. If you can help us—if there is anything you can do, you—you were our last hope. Our only hope." Her voice, reduced to little more than a threadbare whisper, cracked slightly.

Sehrys allowed his gaze to linger on a wiry boy who still bore marks on his face from the time Dronyen had beaten him within an inch of his life for dropping a plate of meat. The boy had never dared look at Sehrys before, but he was looking at him now. And there was nothing in his gaze but warmth and something almost like reverence. Sehrys would never have thought a boy like this would care so much, that so many humans felt the same sort of stir within themselves that Sehrys did. The stir to do something *more.* The stir to be a part of something important and difficult and beautiful.

It was strange to think that Brieden was perhaps not such an exception after all, that there could be more good in the human realm than he had let himself contemplate. He gave the boy a small smile and a nod and turned to face Cliope once again. Her eyes throbbed with quiet desperation despite her unyielding composure and she held the little scroll clutched tight in both hands.

He did not know how she had come to possess that scroll. He did not know what might happen if she and her sister learned the truth hidden in the words on the whisper-thin parchment. What he did know was that Imervish scrolls were used to unlock incredibly powerful magics. Magics that could do terrible damage in the wrong hands.

He also knew that the wiry boy with the marks on his face had risked everything to follow Cliope to the very edge of the world as he knew it, all on the thin hope that Sehrys would be able to help them. And so he made the choice to trust her.

"As you wish," he finally conceded. "I know someone who can help you."

CLIOPE AND HER GUARD ACCOMPANIED THEM ALONG THE
road to The Border to help ward off any thieves or slave-traders
who may have been lurking about. Sehrys and Brieden learned
from Cliope about the changes had already begun to take place
in Villalu since Brissa had seized the throne, and the challenges
she faced in keeping it. So far, only three of the ten Houses of
Villalu had pledged their loyalty to the Keshells. Most remained
undecided. At least two remained openly loyal to the Panlochs.
Despite Cliope's near-hubris at the certainty of their victory, the
war had truly just begun.

When the humans' eyes began to grow heavy from the hum of
The Border, Sehrys and Brieden took their leave.

"I will send word as soon as I can," Sehrys promised. He led
Cliope a few paces away from Brieden, who was engrossed in a
conversation with a young woman he knew from the palace staff.
"Cliope, I am sorry that I cannot offer to stay and be of further
assistance to your efforts. And... and I truly do appreciate all that
you've done for us. More than I can ever express."

"We could use a secret weapon like you in our army," Cliope
interjected, "but perhaps it is for the best. Securing loyalty from
enough of the other Houses is challenge enough as it is. If our role
in the escape of Dronyen's prize slave, let alone the fellow-feeling
between us, were to become public knowledge, our battle could
become tilted quite sharply uphill."

Sehrys smiled. "True. But I do want you to know that after I
cross The Border, I may be in a better position to help than I am
now. Expect word. I will not forget."

Cliope threw her arms around him in a brief, shocking hug.
"Thank you. May the Gods speed you safely home."

After all goodbyes were said, Sehrys escorted a sleepy Brieden to
the carriage perch and continued west. The queen's guard waved
and cheered even as they yawned into the backs of their hands.

"Why can't I fall asleep?" Brieden muttered into Sehrys's shoulder as they drew nearer to The Border. "Why can't you just hold onto me and let me sleep?"

"Because The Border guards against human entrance in two ways. You need to be physically connected to me, physically protected, and you need to be mentally present and conscious. The Border is... it's a gateway between worlds. It is almost a living thing, and it wants to pull you in. You'll *want* to go where it beckons you, and the closer you are to sleep, the harder it will be to resist the pull. And if you don't resist it you could end up... anywhere."

"What do you mean by *anywhere*?" Brieden asked, intrigued, as he forced his eyes to remain open.

"There are innumerable worlds, Brieden. Some much better than this one and some much, much worse. But if I lost you in the void, I'd..." Sehrys inhaled sharply. "I would never find you. And the chances that you would end up somewhere safe are very, very small. So *please* stay with me through this."

Brieden sighed dreamily, his head dropping from Sehrys's shoulder to his chest. "I'll stay with you forever, Sehrys," he murmured.

Sehrys fought back the prickle behind his eyes and the jolt of pain in his chest at the sweet, simple and half-wakeful statement. The statement that he knew Brieden meant with purity and intensity. The one beautiful thing that Sehrys could not say back.

Sehrys shook Brieden awake. "Brieden. Listen to me. I am going to keep talking to you, and you are going to answer me, all right?"

"Mmm."

Sehrys squeezed Brieden's hand until he yelped. "God, Sehrys, that still hurts a bit from *yesterday*!"

"Good. That means I won't have to exert as much pressure to keep you awake."

"That's horrible. Why are you being so mean?"

"Because I'd rather hurt your hand than send you into a world of seven-foot-tall carnivorous insects and noxious gases instead of air!"

Brieden sat bolt upright at that. "That... that isn't real, is it?"

Sehrys shrugged. "I've only heard rumors. Very few sidhe have successfully traversed worlds and returned to tell the tale."

"But... it can be done?"

"It *can* be. It rarely is. It takes powerful magics and years of study."

Brieden looked at Sehrys thoughtfully. "I'll bet you could do it."

Sehrys flushed slightly and shrugged again. "I suppose I could, were I so inclined. But as I see it, there are problems enough in this world without having to go out looking for an additional world's worth."

"Mmm," Brieden said, his eyelids growing heavier. The path they traveled was overgrown this close to the border; the forest around them closed in on all sides, making the world feel cozy and small.

"Brieden, I haven't told you much about Laesi, have I?" Sehrys asked, desperate for a conversation topic to keep Brieden awake.

"Um... what? No, not really. I mean you said your fer... uh..."

"Feririar."

"Mmm. You said some people live in plant houses there. Like the ones in Silnauvri."

"Yes. And in tree houses too, like that inn we stayed at in Lasemik. Do you remember that?"

"Mmm."

"Brieden!" Sehrys squeezed his hand hard.

"What! I am! I mean, yes. I remember."

"There are flowers as big as trees, just like those at the shrine, but there are actual trees there, too. Trees like none you've ever seen before, Brieden."

"Mmm."

"Brieden, ask me a question."

"Ummm, what sort of question?"

"Any sort. You have to stay awake, remember?"

They passed beneath the first of a series of crumbling stone archways that meant they were getting close to the portal. Very, very close. Sehrys tried to keep the nervousness out of his voice. He slowly spread a pulse of binding energy around himself, Brieden, the carriage and the horses. He wasn't worried about Crow or Raven; horses were never drawn to the wormholes the way humans were, but keeping them all together gave them an extra measure of security. It certainly couldn't hurt.

"Brieden! *Ask me a question!*"

"*Ow!* All right! Ummm... where did you live in your feririar?"

"I lived in a Great Hall of Flowers."

"Like the plant houses?"

"Similar, but much grander in size, and made *entirely* of flowers. The home-growers who created it wove it together from *srechelee* flowers. They are some of the biggest flowers you will ever see. And the surrounding gardens had flowers of every variety known to The Sidhe. It was magnificent. I lived there with Firae."

Brieden couldn't disguise the gasp that escaped him. Sehrys winced. He hated to do it. He hadn't wanted to do it. But they were nearly there and he needed Brieden awake. And he knew that mentioning the name of his former betrothed, and of the fact that they had shared a home, would jar Brieden awake.

Brieden didn't seem to notice how close they had become. He didn't even seem to notice the blue-gray glittering wall that rose up before them. The Border was enormous. It was oppressive. It loomed like a frozen tidal wave, as tall as the heavens. But his eyes were fixed on Sehrys, wide and shocked and overwhelmed from nothing more than hearing Firae's name.

"I'm going to tell you, you know," Sehrys promised, meeting his eyes for as long as he dared. "I'm going to tell you everything, just as soon as we cross. But you need to stay awake, Brieden."

"I'm awake," Brieden said steadily. He was now grasping Sehrys's hand just as hard as Sehrys was clutching his.

"Who are you, Sehrys?"

"You know who I am, Brieden."

"No, I mean... at home. In your feririar. Who are you there?"

"I told you, I will tell you as soon—"

"Tell me now."

Sehrys looked straight ahead. "If I tell you now, you might let go."

Brieden opened his mouth to respond, but his words were lost in the sudden impact, the vacuum suction, the writhing tunnels that screamed at them, sang to them, terrifying and so intriguing.

They couldn't see one another. All they could do was feel. Feel their hands clasped tight, tight enough to see them safe through this void, no matter how badly Brieden wanted to sleep. Sehrys knew how much Brieden wanted to give in, to surrender to the pull of the countless worlds that reached out for him, to the colors swirling a sinuous dance around the wormholes that pressed in on every side.

Sehrys squeezed Brieden's hand more tightly. He couldn't lose him. Not like this.

Brieden squeezed back.

And then they were struck by a wall of sunlight.

CHAPTER TWENTY-NINE

BRISSA GROANED IN FRUSTRATION AT THE KNOCK on her bedchamber door. "Shall I tell them Her Majesty is indisposed?" Vyrope asked, releasing Brissa's nipple from between her teeth. Lerekhe made no movement to stop her ministrations between the queen's thighs.

"No," Brissa answered with an irritated sigh, giving Lerekhe's forehead a gentle nudge until she lifted her head to meet Brissa's eyes, lips glistening and eyes dark, looking as if she hadn't heard the knock. The sight was nearly enough to make Brissa reconsider Vyrope's offer.

"Stay here." Brissa rose to her feet and wrapped a robe around her naked form. She padded across the cold stone floor and opened the door just far enough to reveal Bachuc standing on the other side. He was perhaps only ten years her senior, but he carried himself with a precision that made him seem much older. He was short and sturdily built, with a neatly trimmed beard and excellent posture. Brissa was pleased to see him wearing his own charcoal waistcoat and cream-colored tunic. She hoped he'd elected to burn the heavy crimson robes he'd been forced to wear while in the employ of the House of Panloch.

"Your Majesty, please forgive me," he begged, looking scandalized at seeing her in a thin robe that hid little from the imagination. She smirked, unable to tamp down the delight his discomfort caused her. The years under Frilauan rule had made the people of this region so very repressed, and it gave her pleasure to fluster them.

"Not at all, Mister Bachuc. Please come in and have a seat and share your news."

Bachuc appeared hesitant, but followed Brissa into the room. His eyes widened when he saw two of her ladies lounging in her bed, partially covered by rumpled bedcovers, breasts and legs exposed. He stuttered helplessly, face red as an apple, when they greeted him as if nothing were amiss.

"I fear that you have caught me in the middle of taking pleasure with my ladies, but no matter," Brissa said, gracefully sliding into one of the chairs at the little tea-table by the window. "There are many hours left yet in the day for us to enjoy ourselves. Now, Mister Bachuc, what news?"

Bachuc nearly stumbled into his seat across from her; he closed his eyes and shook his head before clearing his throat and addressing her.

"Lord Thieren is most displeased, Your Majesty."

"As I imagine he might be. I plotted to destroy his brother, I killed his father, and I took the throne from his House. I would probably be quite displeased myself were I in his position."

"Your Majesty, I do implore you to understand—the throne is far from secure. The Panlochs were cruel masters and few of us regarded them with true loyalty. But Villalu is vast, and there are more Followers of Frilau than perhaps you know. And in my estimation, Thieren is more formidable than Dronyen and Drayez combined."

Brissa considered him. "Tell me *specifically* what you fear."

"Specifically, Your Majesty, I fear that your men—that is, your *soldiers*—are at great risk. There are whispers that your sister's regiment encountered the fugitives at The Border and allowed them to pass."

"I fail to see what it would matter if it were so. We are at war, after all."

Bachuc took a deep breath, visibly fighting back frustration. "Your Majesty, may I speak plainly?"

"Of course. In fact, I insist that you do. My name is not Panloch, Mister Bachuc. You have been loyal to me at great risk to yourself, and I vow that you will never be punished for expressing what is on your mind."

"Thank you, Your Majesty," Bachuc said on an exhale. "I fear, Your Majesty, that your own customs may have granted you an incomplete view of the role that slavery continues to play on the mainland of Villalu. Even those who are not devout Followers of Frilau would tend to agree that the Panloch family has the right to blend the elf's ashes with that of his deceased master."

"The right to murder the elf and encase his remains in iron, you mean."

"Yes. I implore you to understand that I am not expressing my own opinion, but rather that of the heads of most of the Houses."

Brissa furrowed her brow. "But the House of Panloch is our *enemy*. Surely we can't be expected to see to the comforts of our enemies?"

"Surely not," Bachuc agreed. "And if you had captured the elf for yourself, even if you had burned him and cast his ashes into the sea out of spite, your actions would be held beyond reproach. But you must understand that Frilau's influence is greater than may be evident at first glance. Many see the creature as worse than a demon. Especially this one, having murdered a king. To send such a creature back to the Faerie Lands..." Bachuc held his hands up and sighed.

"I see." Brissa chewed her lip pensively. "Thank you for sharing your thoughts with me, Mister Bachuc. This could indeed create a problem. But what is to be done about it?"

Bachuc took a deep breath. "I know Your Majesty finds such things unsavory, but if you were to make a statement of open support for the keeping of sidhe slaves—"

"That is not an option," Brissa cut him off, eyes snapping up to meet his own. "I will wait until my rule is secure to ban the practice outright, as I see the prudence in that, but I will *never* condone it."

Bachuc bowed his head. "Very good, Your Majesty."

"Tell me, Mister Bachuc, whose support do we most risk in light of this terrible rumor?"

"The Lajecs, for one. And the House of Chrill already leans Frilauan."

"I've heard the Jichyns are uneasy allies at best, Your Majesty," Vyrope added from where she and Lerekhe sat listening on the bed. "They have no allegiance to Frilau, but they are a slave-owning House."

"As were the Ellechetts," Brissa pointed out, "but they were quite easily persuaded in the end."

Bachuc nodded his agreement, but his brow was furrowed and his lips pressed into a thin, tense line.

"Mister Bachuc, your concerns are valid and I thank you for sharing them. If you will allow me to finish with my ladies, I will have the clear head necessary to discuss strategy with you and come to a solution."

"Of course, Your Majesty," Bachuc replied, scrambling to his feet and into a deep bow to disguise his blushing cheeks. "Shall I meet you in the Council Room in a quarter of an hour?"

All three ladies in the room fell into a fit of laughter. "Better to make it the full hour, Mister Bachuc," Brissa said and winked, fighting to hold in more laughter as he scuttled out.

Brissa smiled at Mister Bachuc's retreating form and then turned back to the women on the bed, untied the sash on her robe and let the garment slide to the floor.

She tried not to concern herself with Bachuc's misgivings or the fact that Cliope should have sent word by now, but slipped back into soft warm arms and let the weight of the world slide off her shoulders for the bliss of an hour.

CHAPTER THIRTY

BRIEDEN WAS SLAMMED BACK INTO HIS BODY AND time and space so forcefully that it made him dizzy. His body spasmed and he ripped his hand from Sehrys's and hurled himself off the perch. When he hit the ground, he fell onto his hands and knees and vomited.

Brieden emptied his stomach and then dry-heaved for some time, taking noisy, shuddering breaths. His skin was damp and cold. When his breathing began to even out, he felt a warm hand on his back.

He let Sehrys help him to his feet and wipe him off with a soft, dry cloth. Then Sehrys led him to the shade of an enormous tree— or perhaps flower—and brought him water from a flask and some blossoms to eat. Brieden was suspicious of the blossoms, but he relented and found that they had a pleasant taste and settled his stomach considerably. With a deep sigh, he closed his eyes, leaning his head back against the trunk of the tree behind him.

"That was *awful*."

Sehrys brushed a lock of hair out of Brieden's eyes, sighed and sat beside him. "Yes. I'm sorry. I knew it would be bad, but I've never brought a human through before. I didn't realize it would be *that* bad."

Brieden dropped his head onto Sehrys's shoulder. "We did it," he said softly. "We're here."

"We are," Sehrys agreed.

"Sehrys," Brieden looked up at him with a broad smile. "You're *safe.*"

Sehrys smiled back.

"Let's find a place to set up camp," Brieden said. "And then we can make some tea, and we can talk."

Sehrys's smile faded, but he nodded resolutely. "Yes," he agreed. "That sounds like a good plan."

Laesi was beautiful.

Brieden was reminded strongly of the shrine, but everything was... *more* so. The broad valley was carpeted with lush grasses of green and blue and gold and violet, creating a vast patchwork of color that was so vivid and beautiful it made his eyes water. Copses of trees and flower-trees dotted the sloping plain. In the near-distance, Brieden could make out a stone bridge over a river bend. Many of the flower-trees were even larger here than in the dome; without a roof to contain them, some seemed as tall as mountains. Laesi was a veritable world of grass and flowers, and everything smelled sweet and pure.

He recognized some things from Villalu: elder and willow trees, and some very normal-looking toads and rabbits. He also saw some creatures he had never dreamed of.

He saw a small, fluffy creature that looked a bit like a cat, but with the long snout and pointed quills of a hedgehog. Its coat shimmered and shifted in color. It flushed green as it ran through green grasses, and then shifted to pink when it wandered into a patch of pink flowers.

He saw something that looked like a large, silver fish swimming through the air. It moved past them at incredible speed and dove upward into the tightly clustered canopy of a scarlet flower-tree, causing thousands of tiny blossoms to rain down in its wake.

And he saw a lizard with brilliant orange and gold wings like a bird's. Its skin was vivid green and it seemed to be pursuing a pixie. Brieden gasped and clutched Sehrys's arm.

"Sehrys, that lizard is going to eat that pixie!"

Sehrys looked. "Yes, it very well may," he agreed.

Brieden's mouth fell open.

"Brieden, they keep the pixie population under control. Trust me, you do *not* want to see the results when they overbreed."

Brieden averted his eyes from the chase.

"They just... they look so *human*."

"I know," Sehrys said gently. "But... *all* animals have that spark and individuality, Brieden. You just saw it more clearly in the pixies because they are shaped something like you and I."

Brieden swallowed. "Do you think we could set up camp soon?" he asked, eager for a distraction from the flying lizard, who had caught the pixie. The tiny creature let out a chilling shriek before it was devoured.

Sehrys nodded. "Perhaps just over that next hill? There is a grove of trees there that looks agreeable, and a little pond for the horses to get some water."

It took them little time to reach the spot in question, and Sehrys wasted no time making a fire and setting the kettle on to boil once they had arrived. His body seemed alight with nervous energy, and Brieden was grateful for the calming tea he chose to brew.

"All right, Sehrys," Brieden said when he had a cup of tea between his hands. "I believe it's time for you to tell me some things."

Sehrys sipped his own tea delicately and then sighed. "Yes. Thank you for giving me this long. So. I suppose... do you have any specific questions to start out with, or shall I just—"

"You're some sort of royalty," Brieden blurted out. "Is that it?"

Sehrys smiled slightly and looked down at his cup. "No. Not exactly."

Brieden raised an eyebrow, but he sipped his tea and waited for Sehrys to continue.

"Brieden, sidhe society is a caste system. The castes are not determined by bloodlines, although there can be a genetic component to the powers that manifest. The royal family, however, *is* determined by bloodline or marriage line. To add some diversity to the ruling class, royals are allowed to marry others of particular castes."

"Like... yours?" Brieden asked, his throat going dry.

Sehrys nodded. "Like mine. My caste is *vishli Aldevucavish*. I suppose the best translation into Villaluan might be... Spiral caste."

"Spiral?" Brieden couldn't contain his fascination. Sehrys had rarely mentioned the sidhe castes.

"The name in Elfin essentially means spiral. The spiral is a sacred shape. It contains all, expands and contracts, repeats itself indefinitely. It is fluid and fixed and unbroken all at once. Spiral caste sidhe are... well, we are extremely rare."

"And... what does it mean?"

"It means I have a full range of power. It means that I possess every power a sidhe can possess. Every manifestation of it. And the strongest possible manifestation, too. The strength of each power feeds the others, moving like a spiral, so that I can focus my energy on the most minute, precise task or the most large-scale and complex maneuver. And sometimes... sometimes it can be so much that it's difficult to control."

"I honestly can't say that I'm surprised," Brieden replied, voice steady. "I did imagine that your power was on a different scale from most other sidhe. But I don't understand why that means you can't stay with me."

"There is this law," Sehrys replied, "called *es lemeddison rubrio*. The Non-Interference Doctrine."

Brieden nodded. "I know about it. Tash told me."

"Oh. Well. That law is the reason The Sidhe haven't done anything about the slavery in Villalu. Or the treatment of women and children in Villalu, for that matter. It is the reason that the Council of Nations has chosen to simply ignore human society and put up walls and cast our criminals among them, as if doing so were some sort of great kindness on our part. And, at present, there is really only one person with the power to—"

Sehrys stopped in mid-sentence, looking up in alarm.

"Sehrys, what is it?"

Sehrys had gone pale, paler than Brieden had ever thought possible. "Brieden, we have to—"

He looked around wildly, and then grabbed Brieden's hand, both their cups of tea falling to the ground as he ran toward a grove of trees, pulling Brieden behind him.

"Brieden, we have to hide. We can't let them—"

But it was too late.

Seemingly out of nowhere, they swarmed.

Enormous dragonfly-like creatures, larger versions of the one Brieden had seen in Silnauvri—*grimchins*, Sehrys had called them grimchins—were flying at them from every direction. Astride each grimchin was a sidhe.

Most were women, although a few men were peppered throughout the group. Some had swords at their hips and others carried bows and quivers full of arrows. All were dressed in glossy green, skirt-like garments; their feet and chests were bare. Clearly they were warriors. Brieden stared in amazement.

Sehrys stopped running. He stood in front of Brieden protectively, reaching behind him to grasp Brieden's hands.

"Don't move a step away from me," Sehrys whispered, voice fierce and urgent. "I'm going to keep you safe."

Brieden squeezed Sehrys's hands and pressed himself tightly against the other man's back.

"*Esilog esvih lek muradog wa esilog perita kaloba per es zershe!*" Sehrys called out after the first of the sidhe had landed and dismounted. "*Esil esvish nautollanga esmet sidhvalu ad Khryslee wa fali nauefa Rigday silves silarija mandrubog!*"

A woman walked toward them, her gaze shifting between Sehrys and Brieden suspiciously. "*Nau hafalt falasa. Wa nau alt lastolle sil berish,*" she replied.

The rest of her group wore simple flowered headdresses, but hers was ornate and impressive. She wore a sash across her torso with something indecipherable written in rich gold lettering.

The lilt of her voice made it sound as if she was asking questions, and Sehrys was speaking in the tight, impatient tone that he used when he became evasive. He gripped Brieden's hands more fiercely, and his voice turned angry.

And then he heard it. *Sehrys Silerth Valusidhe efa Naisdhe efa es Zulla Maletog Feririar ala es Fervishlaea efa es Vestramezershe.* Sehrys's full name. This woman used it, and the *way* she used it...

She knew Sehrys. She *knew* him. So why no hugging and tears of joy to see that he was safe and alive and home?

The atmosphere suddenly shifted and Sehrys gasped. Brieden saw another group approaching on grimchins.

Brieden saw that the central figure seemed to take up more space as a matter of pure presence. His grimchin was noticeably larger than any of the others. He wore a look of lazy superiority. He was clad in a garment similar to those worn by the other sidhe, but his was a deep shade of blue, and he wore boots to match. He was beautiful.

His skin was golden and his hair was long, silken and nearly coal-black. Across his shoulders was a magnificent cape, woven through with flowers of every color: tulips and lilacs and roses and cherry blossoms and violets and orchids and dozens more that Brieden couldn't identify. The cape seemed to be a living thing, not losing a single petal as it whipped in the wind behind him. His headdress was incredibly intricate and simply gorgeous. It was a crown of vines and flowers and leaves and berries and looked as if it had been crafted by an artist of inhuman capabilities—which, Brieden supposed, it had.

The six others in his group surrounded him and landed with synchronized precision. One of his guards reached out a hand to help him down from his grimchin, although he could clearly have managed quite well on his own. As he strode across the grass, every sidhe from the first group knelt.

Brieden had spent enough time in a royal court to know a king when he saw one.

The king advanced on them, wearing a look of pure disbelief, and finally came to a stop a few paces before them. He stared. His eyes were burgundy shot through with red and gold, like a shock of autumn leaves, and there were tears gathering in them.

"Sehrys," he whispered.

"Firae," Sehrys said, his voice shaking with emotion. He pulled his hands free from Brieden's and threw them around Firae's neck.

CHAPTER THIRTY-ONE

"DON'T MOVE A STEP AWAY FROM ME," SEHRYS whispered. "I'm going to keep you safe."

Brieden squeezed Sehrys's hands and pressed himself tightly against Sehrys's back. Brieden's heart pounded against him, and all Sehrys could think about was how fragile Brieden was. How much Brieden was going to need him. And how far he really was willing to go to keep him safe.

The first members of the royal guard landed and dismounted.

"We are unarmed and seek passage through this land. I am escorting this human to Khryslee and wish your king only pleasant tidings," Sehrys called out.

The Marshal walked toward them, and Sehrys's heart sank when he saw who it was. Her pet name was Sree, and she had always been one of Firae's most trusted advisors. She hadn't yet achieved the rank of Marshal when Sehrys had left, but things had clearly changed.

Sree had once been suspended from service for telling Firae that Sehrys was frivolous and not worthy to become his lifemate.

"You have returned," she said, her eyes shifting between Sehrys and Brieden. "And you brought... a pet."

"He isn't a pet," Sehrys answered, trying to keep his voice even.

"So you are escorting humans to Khryslee now? In direct violation of the Non-Interference Doctrine?"

"The doctrine says nothing about escorting humans to Khryslee."

"It does, however, say a thing or two about bringing humans across The Border, does it not?"

"I had to bring him across," Sehrys said. "He risked his own life to save mine, and the king of Villalu is out for his blood because of it."

"And why would the king of Villalu care about *you*?"

"Because I was his brother's slave, that's why," Sehrys spat. "Where did you imagine I was these past six years? Drinking nectar in the border cities?"

Sree shrugged. "I always figured you decided not to marry Firae and couldn't face him. But if you were actually enslaved as you claim—"

"As I *claim*? Do you have any idea what goes on across The Border?"

"Not my concern," Sree said flatly. "But your human will have to go back."

Sehrys glared at her. "No."

"Then we'll have to kill him. He can't stay here, and the Khrysleans can't keep using our lands to transport fugitives."

"*Fugitives*?"

"You said he was wanted by the Villaluan king. That makes him a fugitive, wouldn't you say?"

Sehrys gripped Brieden's hands even harder. "Sree, he is *not* going back to Villalu. I am bringing him to Khryslee and I am going to personally see to his safe arrival there. After I have done that, I will come back and explain everything to Firae. But if you so much as try to touch a single hair on his head, if you so much as *think* about hurting him, I swear I will—-"

"What, *Sehrys Silerth Valusidhe efa Naisdhe efa es Zulla Maletog Feririar*?" she taunted. "What exactly will you do to me in front of an entire guard of armed soldiers? Even if you managed to survive, your human certainly wouldn't."

Sehrys's eyes narrowed. Why was she trying to provoke him? If she attacked Sehrys, Firae would never forgive her. He would probably kill her. That is, of course, assuming that Firae wouldn't prefer to kill Sehrys himself.

Did Firae think the same thing that Sree did? Had he spent the past six years thinking Sehrys had abandoned him? Had he foregone the customary grieving period and already taken another lifemate? Sehrys felt his insides twist with a barrage of confusing emotions. He had assumed Firae would still want him, that he had been grieving him. But the fact that perhaps Firae *wouldn't* want him anymore meant that he could stay with Brieden.

But then nothing would change in Villalu.

But then he could stay with *Brieden.*

Before Sehrys could figure out how to respond to Sree, he caught sight of a familiar-looking group of grimchin-mounted sidhe.

In the middle of the group was one of the largest and finest grimchins Sehrys had ever seen. She was just as Sehrys remembered her.

And then he saw the man who rode her. He gasped at the sight.

Because it had been six years. Six years since he had seen anyone from his childhood. Six years since he had seen his family.

And this far east, Firae was the closest thing to family that Sehrys had. After he was sent to the Eastern Border Lands following his sister's death, Firae had been Sehrys's rock. He understood what it was like to be different, to be isolated from others his age in the name of privilege. He knew what it was like to see fear and awe in the eyes of the people around him, and he knew what it felt like to hate himself when he sometimes secretly enjoyed that awe.

But most of all, he knew what it felt like to lose the person you loved the most in all the world. And when Firae spoke of his mother and Sehrys spoke of his sister, they had looked each other in the eyes and never had to pretend to be okay.

Firae couldn't hate him. He *couldn't.* Firae had been his best friend. Firae had been his first love. At one time, Firae had been his everything.

But that had been a different time, and Sehrys had been a different man.

That was before he truly understood himself. That was before he saw what true strength looked like. That was before he knew that it was possible to love someone as much as he loved Brieden.

Firae was still beautiful. He had barely changed in the last six years. He dismounted and walked toward Sehrys, a look of pure disbelief on his face.

And warmth. And tears.

Firae stood before him and simply stared. "Sehrys," he whispered.

And suddenly it hit him. He was safe. He was *home.*

Sehrys had never truly believed that he would see him again. That he would see *any* of them again.

"Firae," Sehrys said, his voice shaking with emotion. He launched himself at Firae, throwing his arms around the king's neck.

"You're alive," Firae sobbed. "You're *alive!*"

"I never thought I'd see you again," Sehrys whispered, tears rolling down his cheeks. "I missed you so much."

"Sehrys—where—what—when the sentry reported that she'd seen you, I thought she had to be mistaken. I had to come see for myself because I never would have believed—what happened? What *happened?*"

"I was captured by slave-traders," Sehrys answered softly. Firae let out a wail of despair.

"I never would have gotten out alive if it hadn't been for Brieden," he added.

"Who is—" Firae froze, and suddenly seemed to notice that Sehrys wasn't alone. He broke the hug, and Sehrys instinctively turned back to Brieden.

When he did, his heart nearly shattered.

Sehrys had never seen Brieden look like this before. Not when he had realized the true difference in their lifespans, not when he had left Sehrys in the cafe in Silnauvri, not even when he was at Brec's mercy, refusing to fight the compulsion.

Brieden looked utterly broken. His face was awash with pure, unmasked anguish.

"Oh, Brieden," Sehrys murmured, reaching for his hand. Brieden gripped it so hard Sehrys thought he was going to break his fingers. And he wanted nothing more than to take Brieden into his arms, to hug him and kiss him and tell him how much he loved him. But he was fairly sure that the rest of Brieden's life would take place in the next five minutes if he attempted any such thing.

Firae's Villaluan wasn't perfect, but it was too good for Sehrys to try to communicate anything reassuring to Brieden. So he tried desperately to do it with his eyes.

"I thought you had your compulsion bound," Firae said. Sehrys could hear the frown in his voice.

"I did," Sehrys replied, turning back to face him without letting go of Brieden's hand.

"Then why is he looking at you like that?"

"He... I..." Why hadn't he prepared himself for this? Even knowing that he might not get Brieden to Khryslee without running into the royal guard, he hadn't expected to run into Firae himself.

His frown deepening, Firae strode forward and grabbed Brieden by the collar. Brieden's eyes widened in terror.

"*Firae!*" Sehrys shrieked in alarm.

Firae pulled Brieden close and pressed his nose to the base of his throat, inhaling deeply. When lifted his face, his eyes were blazing with burgundy-gold fire.

"He defiled you," Firae growled. The earth began to shake around them. Brieden yelped as if in pain; a hand flew to his chest.

"No," Sehrys insisted, his voice hard. His eyes met Firae's, green fire lashing against burgundy, and the earth stilled. Brieden let out a breath and lowered his hand slowly.

"You *stink* of him, Sehrys."

"We've been traveling together for months!"

Firae gave a harsh, mirthless laugh. "Sehrys. Have you forgotten who I am? You stink of *him*. It's in your pores, your musk, it's all through you. There is only one way for that to happen, and you know it."

"He didn't defile me," Sehrys repeated firmly, his voice soft.

"Sehrys—" Firae began.

"Would you like to know how many men *did* defile me?" Sehrys shouted. "It might take some time, you know, because I lost count within the first year. I'm sure you'd *all* be interested to know!" He directed his wrath at the attendant guards. "It will just confirm what some of you have thought all along, that I'm not good enough to be your other king. Because now I've been *defiled*. Used. Wasted. *Ruined*!"

Sehrys shot his flashing eyes back to Firae, who was staring at him.

"Sehrys, no..." he began, "I didn't mean—"

"Brieden is the one person, the *one person* who never made me feel like I'd been defiled, Firae. He never made me feel as if there was something wrong with me, no matter what other men had done to my body. And yes. Yes, I have been with him. Many times. But it was entirely mutual, and it was I who initiated it."

Firae's face was unsettled, lingering somewhere between rage and guilt and overwhelming sorrow.

"I... Sehrys... I didn't—I am so sorry. Of course there is nothing wrong with you. I just... it shouldn't have been *him*." He looked at Brieden, a look of near-hatred in his eyes. "It should have been me."

"Yes, well," Sehrys replied, his voice soft again. "It has been six years, Firae. Have you remained chaste all that time?"

Firae flushed and looked at the ground.

"Sehrys..." The voice was so small, so pained that Sehrys acted on pure instinct. He pulled Brieden into his arms, hugging him tightly.

"It's going to be all right," he whispered.

"It shouldn't have been him," Firae repeated, the rage seeming to win out in his voice.

"It was, though," Sehrys said defiantly, moving out of the embrace but keeping a hold on Brieden's hand. "He saved my life, Firae, and I owe it to him to see him to safety. I promised him that I would bring him to Khryslee, and that's what I am going to do."

"It most certainly is not. That thing is going back to Villalu or into the void or he is dying by my hand this very day. But you are *not* bringing him to Khryslee."

Sehrys clenched his jaw and looked into Firae's eyes, his gaze ice-cold. Firae gave a slight shiver.

"And how exactly do you propose to stop me?" Sehrys hissed.

Firae looked dumbfounded. "Sehrys, you wouldn't—"

"Firae, try me. I'm not the same boy you knew six years ago. I have spent those years living in hell, fighting to keep hold of a trace of sanity and a will to live. Brieden saved me from that, and he almost got killed in the process. Several times. If you harm a single hair on his head—" Sehrys advanced on Firae, pulling Brieden behind him, and grasped a strand of Firae's hair for emphasis— "a *single hair,* Firae, I will never speak to you again. I will never so much look at you. If you hurt Brieden, Firae, I will *hate* you."

Firae swallowed, struggling to keep a superior look on his face. "Fine, then. We shall send him back to—"

"No. He will be killed if he returns to Villalu. There is war there and he is wanted and he won't be safe. Just... just let me bring him to Khryslee, Firae. Please."

Firae sighed. "You really expect me to let you bring him to Khryslee?"

"Yes."

"In direct violation of the Non-Interference Doctrine."

"Yes."

"In direct opposition to the choices I have just presented you regarding his fate."

"Yes."

They stared at each other, their eyes burning into one another.

For that moment, no one else took a breath.

Finally, the corners of Firae's mouth began to twitch. He fought for a moment before allowing himself to surrender to laughter. "Sehrys. Oh, Sehrys, you *are* the same boy I knew six years ago! I don't care how else you may have changed. No one else would ever dare to speak to me that way."

Sehrys smiled a little too, in spite of himself.

Firae sighed deeply. "All right. I don't want our reunion to continue like this, Sehrys. You're finally back, and I... all I wish is to be alone with you. But I can't let you take him to Khryslee."

Sehrys opened his mouth to argue, but Firae held up a hand.

"I cannot, Sehrys. Even if he is accepted into Khryslee, he will remain free to roam the Eastern Border Lands. And I simply cannot allow that when... when it is clear to me that he holds a piece of your heart. But I will allow him to be kept in a holding cell for now. And then we can calm down and discuss this further."

Sehrys studied him for a moment. "It has to be a *nice* cell. In the Northern Tower."

"Fine."

"And I need your oath that he will be treated well and afforded all the reasonable comforts."

"You have it."

"And you have to assign him guards that speak fluent Villaluan. And I have to approve them personally."

"Sehrys—"

"These are my conditions, Firae."

"I am still your king, you know."

Sehrys held his gaze, with his lips pressed tightly together.

Firae sighed. "You're lucky I love you," he muttered.

"I'll take that as a yes," Sehrys said and smiled. "And I have to be the one to escort him to Alovur Drovuru."

Firae crossed his arms over his chest. "Now you're just making a mockery of me altogether."

"You have to let me *talk* to him! Explain what's going on."

"All right, Sehrys, but under no circumstances are the two of you to be alone together. And tonight..." Firae lifted Sehrys's free hand to his lips and kissed it. "Tonight, I want you all to myself."

"Agreed," Sehrys answered softly.

BRIEDEN WANTED TO DIE.

The moment when Sehrys had pulled his hands away from Brieden and thrown them around Firae had felt, unequivocally, like the end of the world. The end of all hope. The end of color and vitality. The very end of Brieden's heart.

It all had made sense, and it had emptied him of everything.

Sehrys wanted to help the Keshells and end the slave trade. If Sehrys married Firae, he would be in a position to do exactly that. And no matter how much Sehrys might love Brieden, Sehrys was not selfish enough to walk away from that opportunity.

It was clear that Firae wanted Sehrys, and it was also clear that he wanted to rub Brieden out of existence. And the more heated their exchange became, the more Brieden's heart surged with fear. Because even though he couldn't understand the words, Brieden could see that underneath Sehrys's anger was affection. He and Firae seemed to have something akin to passion dancing between them.

The fire in Firae's eyes didn't scare him nearly as much as the fire in Sehrys's.

But even in the midst of the confrontation, Sehrys had hugged Brieden. He had reassured him. Sehrys had told him that everything was going to be all right.

And now, as they sat in the carriage together, a tiny seed of hope tentatively planted itself in a hidden corner of Brieden's heart.

Maybe it really *was* going to be all right. Maybe, somehow, it still could be.

They were going to Sehrys's feririar. Or rather, to Alovur Drovuru. Sehrys told him that the community of sidhe who lived there made up the feririar, but that the name of the place itself was Alovur Drovuru. Brieden didn't entirely understand the distinction, but it didn't matter. What he did understand was that he was going to be a prisoner. That technically, he already was.

The king had promised that he would come to no harm—that he would be well cared for. Sehrys promised to visit him as often as he could until he and Firae had "figured things out," but he didn't say much more than that. They were not alone in the carriage; two members of the royal guard accompanied them, one beside each of them, as they sat facing each other.

The royal guard that served the king. Firae. Sehrys's first love, and perhaps his future husband.

Firae was a beautiful elfin king with burgundy eyes who lived in a Great Hall of Flowers. Brieden was a simple peasant from a tiny fishing village who badly needed a bath and a shave.

Between the two of them, the choice was obvious.

When the carriage pulled to a stop, Sehrys managed to get close enough to Brieden to whisper a soft "I love you" into his ear. And then Brieden watched him walk away, toward Firae, who had already dismounted from his grimchin. They strolled off into the night, hand in hand, completely at ease with one another.

They were beautiful together.

Brieden didn't take in the village, although it was surely full of the wonders of the Faerie Lands. He didn't even pay attention to where the carriage was taking him. His heart was smashed and his life was broken.

Even if there *could* be a way, Brieden realized, he had been counting on Sehrys loving and wanting him as much as he loved and wanted Sehrys. But Sehrys obviously cared for Firae. Maybe he even loved him. Maybe, even if he loved Brieden best, he loved Firae enough.

The guards led him up a long set of steps that spiraled around a mighty tree. It was much like the inn where he and Sehrys had stayed in Lasemik. Brieden didn't care.

He didn't even know how long he had been there, curled into a ball and crying, when he suddenly realized he was alone.

There were bars on the windows and the door.

FIRAE LED SEHRYS TOWARD HIS BEDCHAMBER, SPEAKING excitedly about all of the people who were going to be thrilled to see Sehrys the following day.

Sehrys paused in the doorway. Firae looked back at him with a raised eyebrow. "Problem?"

"No. No, of course not. I was just wondering... is my old room occupied, or should I use one of the guest chambers?"

Firae frowned. "Sehrys, I was hoping that you might consider staying with me tonight."

Sehrys inhaled sharply. "I... Firae, it's just... it's too soon."

Firae walked back toward the door, taking both of Sehrys's hands in his.

"Sehrys, I would argue that it's been too *long*. I don't mean to suggest that we have to... do anything. Just stay with me? Hold me?"

Sehrys pulled Firae into a tight hug. "Firae," he whispered. "Please, just don't push. It's me. I'm here. But... I need my own sleeping chamber right now. I just need some time to myself. Please understand that."

Firae sighed, but gave Sehrys a gentle squeeze. "I understand. I'm just so happy to see you again. I suppose I'm afraid that if I let you sleep somewhere else you'll be gone in the morning."

Sehrys gave him a light kiss on the cheek. "I'm not going anywhere. Now, can we please get some tea and honeysuckle? I want to hear about *everything* that's been happening."

Firae laughed. "That may take all night."

Sehrys smiled. "We have time."

Firae went to find a hand servant to fetch their tea and flowers. Sehrys walked to the window. He looked to where the Northern tower stood, shrouded in darkness.

"Brieden," he whispered. "Please... I..."

He couldn't find the words.

Sehrys wiped the tears from his eyes and plastered a smile on his face as he heard the door open behind him, and turned to face Firae as he strode back into the room.

BRIEDEN MOANED AS THE MORNING SUN INVADED HIS EYES. Despite the luxurious-looking bed, he had slept curled up on the floor.

He rolled onto his back and threw an arm across his eyes to blot out the light. He didn't want to be awake. Being awake meant facing reality. And facing reality meant facing the fact that he had lost Sehrys.

Sehrys was probably still sleeping, exhausted from a night of passionate lovemaking with Firae. They were probably tangled up in the sheets of Firae's obnoxiously large bed with obnoxiously soft sheets and Firae was probably an obnoxiously perfect lover, and Sehrys was probably thanking the Gods that he finally knew what making love with a real man was like and Brieden simply wanted to die.

He wasn't going to move all day. He ignored the sound of the door unlocking and creaking open. Let them kick him or kill him or leave food for him that he couldn't even eat because it was probably just flowers anyway. Brieden didn't care about anything anymore.

"Wow. Uh, were you sloshed when they brought you in last night? Because Sehrys didn't mention anything about that."

At the sound of Sehrys's name, Brieden contemplated moving his arm away from his eyes.

"Or... are you sick? Do I need to get a healer? Or... Gods, did Firae do that thing where he burns you on the inside without it showing on your skin? I *hate* it when he does that."

Brieden was pretty sure Firae *had* started to do that before Sehrys stopped him. He hadn't known what was happening at the time, but now he did, and it was just another obnoxiously impressive thing about the smug, arrogant, gorgeous king. Somehow Brieden didn't think that his skill with a bow and arrow would quite measure up to burning someone from the inside out with a look.

"Hey, friend." The voice was closer. *Too* close, really, as if the person were kneeling beside him. Brieden really wished that who-ever it was would just go away.

When it was clear that his new companion had no intention of leaving, Brieden sighed and shifted his arm to his forehead, peering at the figure above him.

The sidhe was young, not a child but barely a man, and almost certainly younger than Sehrys. He was a slip of a thing, small and slender, with pink cheeks and a mop of wild cerulean curls. His face was narrow, his ears had pronounced points even for a sidhe and his silver eyes danced with mirth. He fixed Brieden with a cocky grin. "Man, you *are* pretty. No wonder Sehrys boned you all across Villalu."

Brieden felt his eyes widen. Who *was* this man? What was wrong with him? Who spoke in such a way?

"What do you want?" Brieden asked, surprised by the gruffness in his own voice.

"Hey. No need to snap at me, my friend. You are my new *idol.* You fucked Sehrys raw and then walked right up to Firae holding his hand. And Firae not only *didn't* kill you, he put you in the nicest cell in the Northern Tower, and he let Sehrys send *me* to stand guard. The Gods will be singing your tale across generations!"

So this man knew Sehrys. In fact, it sounded as if Sehrys had specifically asked for this man to look after Brieden. He tried to imagine Sehrys having any sort of amicable relationship with this man and he simply couldn't. He seemed far too lewd, for one thing.

He reached a hand out to Brieden. Brieden stared at it.

"Am I not doing it right?" he asked, his brow furrowed. "Don't Villaluans clasp their hands together and shake them vigorously when they meet one another for the first time?"

"Oh," Brieden muttered. "Yes. Of course. Sorry." He sat up. This may be the worst day of his life, but the man was trying to be friendly. Personal misery was no excuse for poor manners.

He shook the man's hand. "I'm Brieden."

"A pleasure, Brieden," the sidhe said, shaking Brieden's hand so hard he almost wrenched his arm out of the socket. "You can call me Jaxis. I can tell we are going to be the most *wonderful* of friends!"

CHAPTER THIRTY-TWO

"YOU'RE THINKING ABOUT HAVING SEX WITH him right now."

Brieden looked over at Jaxis and raised an eyebrow. The elf had roused him from a very pleasant dream. Brieden was now thoroughly awake and sitting on the edge of the bed, but it was true that lingering wisps of the dream remained on the edges of his mind.

"It's a bit of a talent of mine. It's not officially recognized in the registry of powers, but I think that's just because they're threatened by it," Jaxis explained from where he sat at the small table in the center of the room. "Married officials especially, because they're probably worried that I'll know when their lifemates are thinking about fucking me. Which, I'll be honest, is *often*. Not that I can blame them."

Jaxis's cocky smile was turned up to full blast. Brieden rolled his eyes.

Besides the table and the bed, Brieden's cell held a modest cabinet containing small comforts such as extra blankets; thin, soft robes; and materials with which to clean his teeth, shave and wash. The room also held two features that had fascinated Brieden enough to distract him from his pain for at least a few minutes these past three days.

The first was a shallow bowl of water that protruded from the wall at a level with Brieden's waist. The bowl held a drain connected to a copper pipe that disappeared into the wall. There was also a spout, flanked by a triangle formation of three smooth stones. If Brieden touched the left-most rock, cold water came out. If he touched the right-most rock, hot water came out. And if he touched the rock in the center, warm water came. Jaxis had explained that it was the water-bearers, those sidhe who possessed both the power to summon water and the power to compel, who created and sustained the water basins throughout the feririar.

The second feature that fascinated Brieden was thanks to the lightkeepers, who possessed both compulsion and the ability to manipulate fire. There was a dial made of wood on the wall next to Brieden's bed. When he turned it slightly, four oil-lamps mounted on the walls burst into tiny flames, like those of a candle. The more he turned the dial, the larger the flames became.

"That's why I don't believe Sehrys is truly Spiral," Jaxis continued, as Brieden toyed with the fire dial. "Spiral caste is supposed to have every power possible, whether it's in the registry or not. But before, when he and Firae were supposed to get married, Firae was practically executing people in his sleep, he wanted it so badly. And Sehrys didn't have a single clue. His legs were sewn up so tight he... uh... you probably don't really want to hear this, do you?"

"Actually, the idea of Sehrys *not* having sex with Firae is a perfectly acceptable topic of conversation. Please continue."

"You *were* thinking about boning him though, weren't you?"

Brieden sighed. "Yes."

Jaxis studied him for a moment. "He and Firae aren't doing it, you know."

Brieden tried not to let his head snap up or his eyes widen with hope. He didn't succeed at either.

Jaxis smirked.

"How do you... uh... are you quite sure?"

Jaxis laughed. "Am *I* quite sure? I can smell sex a mile away, friend. Besides, Firae is behaving like an absolute asshole. Which only happens when his isn't getting filled, if you know what I mean."

"Jaxis? Can I ask you something?"

"Of course."

"Has anyone ever told you that you are absolutely *disgusting*?"

Jaxis laughed. "You humans are prudes. But yes."

Brieden almost smiled.

"Seriously though, friend, Sehrys has been... strange since he got back."

"What do you mean, strange?"

"He isn't acting coquettish with Firae, which I suspect is probably because you've got him cockwhipped, but still—it's strange. It's as if... before he disappeared, the last topic he ever wanted to discuss was politics. He was atrocious about it, in fact; he would act incredibly bored and sigh a lot when Firae tried to engage him in talk of policy, but now it seems like the *only* thing he wishes to discuss with Firae."

"Yes, I imagine his experiences over the past six years could have changed his priorities a bit."

"I suppose—I just—I wonder..."

Brieden furrowed his brows and looked back up at Jaxis, not realizing that he'd allowed his head and shoulders to droop once again.

"It just seems like Sehrys is trying to influence Firae politically."

Brieden shrugged. "He probably is. Like I said, I'm sure his experiences have—"

"Of *course* they have. Sehrys is so madly in love with you that he would rather sit in his room and sigh than climb between the thighs of a very willing partner, which is something I am not cursed to understand, but his plan is fairly obvious. He'll marry Firae even though he'd rather be with you because he suffered tremendously in Villalu, and others suffer still, and if he becomes king, he'll be in a position to do something about it. We both know all that."

Brieden moved to turn off the lamps in favor of the sunlight streaming through the windows. "I don't know. I'm not sure how Sehrys truly feels about either one of us."

Jaxis rolled his eyes. "Don't be an idiot. What I'm *saying* is, it looks to me like he's attempting to influence Firae politically *now*. Before marrying him. Perhaps even *without* marrying him. I wouldn't give up just yet, friend."

Brieden realized that he had been holding his breath. He let it out slowly. "Are you saying... I don't think..." He paused, considering Jaxis's words. "The thing of it is, Sehrys hasn't even come to visit me yet, and it's been three days. I know he won't let Firae kill me, but I don't know. I figure he's probably feeling conflicted, and—"

Jaxis laughed. "You do realize that Firae has been keeping Sehrys as busy as possible so he can't find time to come and see you, do you not?"

Brieden sighed. "Sehrys is not a prisoner, though, is he? If he truly wanted to see me, he could."

"It is not as easy as you might think to defy the king," Jaxis pointed out. "And I don't imagine you would have enjoyed a visit from your beloved if it came with Firae tagging along behind him and frowning at you the whole time."

Brieden considered this. He might be so desperate to see Sehrys that even Firae's presence would be worth it.

"But today you are in luck, my friend," Jaxis continued. "Firae has an important meeting with some delegates from the High Midlands. And Sehrys is my friend. He tells me things."

"Such as?"

"Such as the fact that he's coming to see you this afternoon. So I think you should give yourself a shave and then let me take you to the community baths. You are starting to stink, and you don't want Sehrys to go soft in his breeches when he sees you."

Brieden didn't even give Jaxis a disgusted look at his choice of language. He was frozen where he sat, trying to wrap his mind around what Jaxis had told him.

He's coming to see you this afternoon.

Sehrys was coming to see him. Sehrys was actually coming to see him.

Brieden ran to the mirror and flinched at his own reflection. "Jaxis," Brieden said desperately, "I look like the Third Hell."

"Yes, you do," Jaxis agreed. "Which is why I suggested that you bathe."

Brieden began taking things out of the cabinet next to the stone bowl with the water spout.

"What should I use? What does this do? Can I shave with this?" Brieden held up a bottle of rose-tinted fluid.

Jaxis raised an eyebrow. "I would not recommend shaving with that, no."

"Why not?"

"It's oil of *hubia rija*. I don't know what the Villaluan name for it is."

"I'm... not sure there is one. But I know what it is, yes."

Jaxis's face spread into a filthy smile. "Yes, I'll just bet you do. Well, you are free to make use of it; even if Sehrys won't bone you right now, you can take care of your own needs, can you not? But shaving with it is not a good idea. Here, if you use this powder, you can mix it with water and it makes a foamy paste..."

Jaxis familiarized Brieden with all of the products, and then graciously changed Brieden's bedding and set a simmering pot of something fresh and sweet-smelling on top of the cabinet while Brieden shaved. Then Jaxis brought Brieden out of his cell for the first time since he had set foot in Alovur Drovuru.

"I'M MERELY SUGGESTING, FIRAE, THAT IT MIGHT BE A GOOD idea if I start to attend some of these meetings with you," Sehrys said casually as the two took a morning stroll through the gardens of the Great Hall.

Firae chuckled. "You never cared about policy before," he said for what seemed like the eight-hundredth time.

"Yes, I know. And now I do," Sehrys snapped.

Firae's smile faltered. "It's just... it is a strange thing to grow accustomed to. Before, you always said that I could worry about affairs of state and you would worry about keeping our home filled with music and flowers."

Sehrys sighed. "There is more to life than music and flowers, Firae. I wish I could have learned that lesson through some other means, but I have learned it nonetheless."

Firae squeezed his hand. "No one should have to learn any lesson through such means," he said softly.

Sehrys squeezed back. "Firae, if you still want me to be your other king—"

"Of course I do," Firae said without hesitation.

"Then wouldn't it make sense to familiarize myself with what a king *does?* I'm not the sort to just host luncheons and plan concerts anymore, Firae. And if that means I'm no longer the sort of man you wish to be with—"

"Sehrys," Firae said gently, "stop." He tugged on Sehrys's hand to quiet him. "You are exactly the sort of man I want to marry. You are the *only* sort of man I want to marry. But Sehrys... affairs of state, they—what I mean to say is, you—"

Sehrys glared. "Are you trying to say that I'm not clever enough to participate in the running of the Queendom?"

"No. I am not trying to say that at all. I—all right, Sehrys, I am going to be honest with you. You were an excellent student of magics, but a poor student in nearly every other discipline. You paid little attention to your history and social policy classes, and you never paid any mind to current events besides which flowers and perfumes were in fashion, and don't look at me like that, because you know what I'm saying is true."

"You're saying I'm too *frivolous* to participate in the running of the Queendom."

"I'm saying I'd like to assign you a tutor. If you truly wish to delve into the sort of complex and delicate matters that affect hundreds of thousands of lives, you will need a solid grasp of the social sciences and the ability to draw context from historical events."

Sehrys sighed, stroking a petal on the tall orange flower beside him with his thumb. "How long will that take?" he asked.

"Are you in some sort of hurry?" Firae asked, his tone fond and teasing.

"I suppose I am, yes. Sort of."

Firae arched an eyebrow.

"It's the Non-Interference Doctrine, Firae. It's... it's the slavery in Villalu, and the mess at The Border, and—"

"It's an immutable doctrine, Sehrys."

Sehrys scoffed. "So-called immutable doctrines have been overturned before, Firae."

"Such as?"

Sehrys scowled at him.

"Let's find you a good tutor, and then we can come back to this discussion, all right?"

"Fine. But you had better find me an excellent tutor. I plan to study hard and work fast."

"In that case," Firae responded with a smirk, "I know *just* the person."

THE BATHS OF ALOVUR DROVURU, LIKE SO MUCH OF LAESI, were like nothing Brieden had ever seen.

It took Jaxis and him about ten minutes to walk to the baths. Brieden often lost the thread of Jaxis's monologue but never found it difficult to disguise his daydreaming. Jaxis's topics never strayed far from sex, drinking or his prowess at everything, the two aforementioned subjects included. But the walk was far from boring.

Alovur Drovuru was beautiful. Some houses reminded Brieden of the plant-mounds in Silnauvri, but they were larger and more complex. There were also homes built into the enormous stems of flower-trees, and even a couple of small rock caves.

The most impressive structure by far, however, was the Great Hall. Six enormous flower-trees anchored the Hall, their canopies of translucent white petals joining together into one mass against the vivid blue sky. Each trunk-like stem comprised a tower, and between the trees were innumerable vines, laced together with nearly seamless precision to form the Hall itself. The flowers that dotted these vines were of every color Brieden had ever seen, and some that he had never seen before. The vines grew to just below the canopy of white petals, high enough to allow for three floors within the Hall.

Brieden desperately wanted to see inside of the Hall, partly out of a pure sense of curiosity and wonder, but also to secure proof that Sehrys was indeed staying in his own room instead of sleeping with Firae.

Unable to completely look away, he kept the Hall in the corner of his vision until he and Jaxis paused at the crest of a large hill.

"Beautiful, aren't they?" Jaxis asked, forcing Brieden to turn away from the Hall to look. As soon as he caught his first true glimpse of the baths, all thoughts of the Hall fled. He had seen them from a distance, obscured by foliage, from his cell in the tower, but he hadn't understood what he was seeing.

Jaxis chuckled at Brieden's gasp, at his wide eyes and open mouth.

From their vantage point, Brieden could see the baths in their entirety. To his right was another large hill, the crown of it almost entirely consumed by an enormous crater. The crater was filled to the brim with sparkling water the same green-blue color of Jaxis's hair. On the left side of the crater, several rivulets and small waterfalls veered off, traveling down the hill and pausing to feed sparkling water into several smaller pools before continuing on their path. The gentle slope of the hillside was dotted with too many little pools for Brieden to count. After leveling off, the rivulets joined into one large stream, feeding the sparkling water into a second large crater pool at the base of the baths. After gazing for a moment, Brieden noticed something odd about some of the figures he saw frolicking in the pools.

Some sidhe were using the streams to float downward, from stream to stream. And some, in other streams, seemed to be floating *upward.*

"Jaxis... how—"

Jaxis laughed again. "Thank the water-bearers, Brieden. I dare say we have the most talent east of the Western Midlands. Our baths are world-renowned."

"Not in Villalu," Brieden muttered, bitter that he had spent his life in such a harsh, bland place.

"Villalu isn't really the *world*, Brieden. It's more like—"

"More like someplace you all would rather not think about."

"Exactly," Jaxis responded brightly. "Now come on, let's get wet, wench!"

Brieden tried not to snort with laughter as Jaxis took off at a run. He would have to find out exactly who had taught Jaxis to speak Villaluan. Did Jaxis really understand what he was saying half the time?

The baths were lovely: even prettier up close than from the hill-top. The heady scent of flowers filled the air. Brieden saw bushes

336

of the same puffy white flowers that Sehrys and he had used for soap in the stream at the shrine, as well as vines of plump golden flowers snaking around the trunks of flower-trees. Several sidhe were rubbing the fragrant oil from these flowers into their skin, and several more were walking about, all of them naked and unself-conscious beneath the midday sun.

Brieden blushed and averted his gaze. He fidgeted with his own clothing before quickly pulling his tunic over his head.

"Brieden!" Brieden glanced up without thinking, horrified to see Jaxis bounding toward him completely naked, his cock bouncing with each footfall. Brieden looked away.

"Oh, Gods, Brieden. Just strip already. You're behaving like a virgin at Beltane."

Brieden was about to ask what Beltane was when Jaxis leaned a little too close.

"All right, see here. Chances are, a lot of these ladies are going to think you're the most adorable thing they've ever laid eyes on. This is your chance to convince me to give you and Sehrys a little alone time later today. So just look for red bracelets, all right?"

Brieden blinked. "Red bracelets?"

Jaxis held up his wrist. Brieden supposed he had noticed the bracelet before, but he hadn't paid it much attention. It was simply three small red gems threaded into braided twine.

"It's... uh... an indicator of relationship status? Your people do something like this, don't you?"

"We have wedding rings," Brieden ventured with a shrug. "To signify marriage. It's usually only the women who wear them, though."

"Then how do the ladies know whether a man is available?"

"Villaluan society involves a lot of... navigating for women."

Jaxis snorted. "No, *thank* you. This pretty little bracelet has fetched more bedmates than your tiny human mind could *handle*, friend."

"What does it mean exactly? That you've committed yourself to a life of random, anonymous sex?"

Jaxis laughed heartily. "More or less. Without the commitment part. We of the red bracelet avoid commitment in all forms, even to the red bracelet itself."

Brieden wanted to ask what the other indicators of relationship status were, but they could just as easily have this very conversation in the water. Without giving himself a chance to think, Brieden untied his boots and peeled off his trousers and undershorts.

The water was warm, and clear as mountain air. Small creatures, including what looked to Brieden like aquatic pixies, flitted about beneath the surface, but none seemed to be the biting kind. Soft white sand carpeted the crater.

Jaxis was absolutely right about how Brieden would be received. Before they could get into a discussion of relationship signifiers in Laesi, Brieden found himself enveloped in a crowd of cooing young sidhe, both male and female, as well as some whose sex Brieden was unable to pinpoint.

Most of his admirers couldn't speak a word of Villaluan, giving Jaxis the opportunity to translate.

"I *wish* it were still legal to keep pets," Jaxis translated for a honey-haired woman. "You are the cutest thing I've ever seen." Jaxis winked.

Brieden scowled. "Tell her I'm very glad that keeping pets *is* illegal, and if she's so nostalgic for slavery, she would probably just *adore* all that Villalu has to offer."

"That answer doesn't inspire me to give you time alone with Sehrys, friend."

"Fine," Brieden ground out. He smiled, placing a hand on Jaxis's shoulder and winking at the honey-haired sidhe. "Tell her whatever will impress her, Jaxis," Brieden said in a cheerful voice, looking at the woman. "But could you please just ask all

338

of them to stop touching my ears? It's making me feel a bit like an object."

"If you have to feel a bit like an object so that I can feel a *lot* like an object, so be it, friend," Jaxis said, steering Brieden slightly to the right. "Now, straight ahead, violet hair, brown eyes. See her? Go let her play with your ears. I'll be right over to chuckle and good-naturedly scold you."

"Like I'm a *dog*?" Brieden demanded, deeply offended.

"I don't even know what that is."

"Dogs are kept as pets."

"Oh! No, then. Not like a dog."

"I don't mean pet in the sense that you probably imagine I do. There is no... mind control, or... or any sort of sexual aspect to the relationship. They're just simpler creatures and we train them and care for them keep them as companions..."

Jaxis looked confused.

"Kind of like... grimchins?" Brieden guessed.

"Oh. Then, yes. Go behave like a house grimchin with cute ears. Do dogs have cute ears?"

"Um, actually, yes. Most of the time."

"A dog it is, then. Go be a dog."

"I think I might have preferred Brec," Brieden muttered, as he went over to let yet another woman with a red bracelet play with his ears. He sighed, then smiled in an effort to mask his irritation. The things he would endure for a bit of time alone with Sehrys!

WHEN JAXIS BROUGHT BRIEDEN BACK TO HIS CELL, SEHRYS was sitting at the table waiting. He wore a soft green robe that looked as if it could have been crafted from a single enormous flower petal, with jeweled amber buttons up the front and flowering vines winding like bracelets around his forearms. His ears were adorned with amber and silver cuffs and his feet were bare. His eyes were

339

tired, but there was something easier and more natural about him. Brieden had never realized just how out of place Sehrys had looked in Villaluan boots and breeches until he saw him like this. As he truly was. Among his own kind. *Home.* It was the most wonderful thing Brieden had ever seen, even if it reinforced just how much he, Brieden, didn't belong here.

Brieden had brought his own change of clothes to the baths, and was now looking reasonably fresh and presentable, and as fetching as he could manage without turning himself into a burgundy-eyed sidhe king.

"Hi," Brieden said softly, as he and Jaxis joined Sehrys in the cell.

"Hi," Sehrys returned with a smile.

"All right, then," Jaxis said, glancing between the two of them. "So, I'm going to go have a little visit with the lovely young woman you introduced me to at the baths, Brieden."

"Mmm." Brieden didn't so much as roll his eyes or snarkily inquire as to *which* young woman Jaxis was referring.

"And... you both know that if Firae finds out I left the two of you alone—"

"Uh-huh," Sehrys responded dreamily.

"*Sehrys!*" Jaxis grabbed his arm and pulled him around to look him square in the eyes.

"Jaxis, do not *manhandle* me!" Sehrys said huffily, pulling his arm free. "Yes, I heard you. Thank you for doing this. I will make sure that Firae doesn't find out, and now I would like you to please *go away.*"

"All right. I'll be back a little before Ki'iz's shift," Jaxis mumbled, referring to one of Brieden's two other guards.

"The Gods will be singing your tale across generations," Sehrys responded absently, waving Jaxis away with his hand.

As soon as the sound of Jaxis's footsteps had receded, Brieden flat-out launched himself at Sehrys. Sehrys caught him in his arms without a second's hesitation. Their lips came together like magnets; their kisses were feverish and desperate from the very start.

"Sehrys," Brieden murmured, as Sehrys's lips moved to his neck. Sehrys began to steer Brieden toward the bed. "Sehrys, I—do you—I don't know if—oh, *God,* Sehrys—"

The backs of Brieden's knees bumped against the edge of the bed and they tumbled onto it, tangling together, and he was lost.

He was so lost, it was nearly impossible to claw his way out of the beautiful haze that had settled over him the very moment he laid eyes on his lover again—the haze that was entirely comprised of the sight and scent and feel of Sehrys, real and solid in his arms.

But he had to try. He *had* to. Because he understood exactly what Sehrys was to him, but he didn't know what he was to Sehrys at *all.*

With focus and self-discipline that would have stunned his instructors at the Academy, Brieden pushed Sehrys off of him, his palms flat against his chest to keep him an arm's length away. Sehrys's eyes burned wild with equal parts lust, shock and confusion.

"Sehrys," Brieden said evenly, forcing himself to take measured breaths. "We can't just—I need to know what is this is. You and me and... and you and Firae."

Sehrys's eyes flickered, and Brieden's heart sank when he saw the familiar retreat: iron gates crashing down behind the gorgeous pools of green, locking him up tight, rendering those expressive eyes utterly and completely unreadable.

"Brieden, I told you... from the very start, I *told* you that it was complicated. I told you that I couldn't stay with you. I just—what do you want from me?"

"You find it necessary to ask me that question again?" Brieden responded softly, his voice bruised with pain. He dropped his hands from Sehrys's chest and pushed himself up into a seated position, scooting backward until his back was flush against the curved wooden wall.

Sehrys bit his shaking lip as recognition flashed across his face. It was clear that he remembered the first time he had asked Brieden that question, trapped in his own cell in Dronyen's castle. There had been no trust, no reason for Sehrys to believe that Brieden wasn't simply another human man who wanted him for one twisted purpose or another. At the time, it hadn't occurred to Sehrys that Brieden might honestly want only to help him. And to love him.

And now? Now, after all Brieden had risked for him, after everything Brieden had done to earn his trust, he was demanding the same explanation yet again, as if Brieden hadn't spent the past three days in a cell without any communication from Sehrys. As if the last time Brieden had seen him hadn't ended with Sehrys walking away from him, hand-in-hand with his former fiancé, while Brieden was led into captivity.

It was as if Sehrys had slapped him, and even the guilt rising in Sehrys's eyes did nothing to soothe the sting.

"I'm sorry," Sehrys said with a sigh, and reached for Brieden's hand. He winced when Brieden drew it back from him. "Brieden, please."

Brieden clenched his jaw, closed his eyes and took a moment to breathe before responding. "Please what?" he finally whispered, opening his eyes to look at Sehrys. "Please *what*, Sehrys? Please just shut up and while away the hours in this fucking tree trunk while you traipse around making wedding plans and stop in to see me every now and again when you want your cock stroked?"

"Brieden!"

"Why didn't you tell me?" Brieden very nearly roared.

"Because I didn't… I didn't want to *ruin* everything! I just wanted to be with you while… while I could."

"So you were doing it for yourself, without regard to how it would make me feel."

"Brieden, no. I... I *told* you it couldn't last! I told you that my love for you didn't change anything. I tried not to tell you how I felt, but you pushed and pushed—"

"All right. So I pushed. But I just..." Brieden trailed off, and a thick blanket of silence fell across them. They didn't look at one another. Neither could bear it.

"Sehrys," Brieden finally said gently, when his anger had ebbed until only the deep sorrow at its heart remained. "When we were together in Villalu, even though you knew that you would return here—that you would return to *him*—you were mine, weren't you? Completely?"

"Yes," Sehrys whispered.

"And now?"

Sehrys wiped a tear from his cheek. "I don't know."

"But... is there even a chance, Sehrys? Even the tiniest chance in the world that we might find a way to be together?"

"Brieden... I'm sorry. But I don't even know that. I don't think—I can't see how—I just don't know."

Brieden nodded, fighting back his own tears. "Very well. When you do know, Sehrys, let *me* know. But in the meantime... if I'm going to be trapped here, I do want you to visit, but just... just to talk. I won't share you with him, Sehrys. I love you so much that it physically pains me sometimes, but I can't share you because that would probably kill me."

Sehrys nodded silently and stood up to leave. In the doorway, he paused to look at Brieden. Brieden avoided his eye.

"I understand," Sehrys said. "And I... I never wanted to hurt you. But I think you're right, and I have been selfish. Because even though I didn't *want* to hurt you, I knew that I would. And I gave myself to you anyway because I wanted it. Because I wanted *you*. I'm just... I'm so sorry, Brieden."

"It was worth it," Brieden murmured. "Even if this is how it ends, it was worth it to be with you, Sehrys."

Sehrys swallowed. "Of course it was worth it. It was more than worth it. I don't think I'll ever stop loving you, Brieden."

Brieden finally looked up and met Sehrys's eyes. They only held the gaze for a few seconds before it became far too painful to endure.

And then, held together by the most frail and delicate threads imaginable, Sehrys left, closing the cell door firmly behind him before allowing himself to completely fall apart.

CHAPTER THIRTY-THREE

"MAY... I ASK A QUESTION ABOUT YOUR STRATEGY concerning the scroll, Your Majesty?" Bachuc's words were slow and careful despite his pink cheeks and the cider on his breath.

Brissa smiled at him. They had finished discussing local strategy some time ago, and Brissa had declared it time to pass around the wine and cider to celebrate a particularly productive Council meeting. Those present for the meeting had relaxed into informal conversation, and even Bachuc was growing bold. It was a side of him Brissa hoped to see more as their trust in each other strengthened.

"You may ask any question you like, Bachuc," Brissa assured him, sipping her wine. "I have told you that before, and my answer will not change. It is important to me that you know that. You will face no retribution for your questions."

"Thank you, Your Majesty. It's simply that... you had the elf. He was here. At the palace. If this scroll is as important as you say, why did you not demand that he read the scroll then, as a condition of assisting in his escape?"

"It is a fair question," Brissa acknowledged, casting her eyes around the polished chestnut table in the center of the council room. In addition to Bachuc and herself, she had chosen her four most insightful and trusted ladies—Vyrope, Cesmi, Alia and

Seshen—to serve on the Queen's Council, as well as Tepper, her newly appointed head of the palace guard. All regarded her with bright eyes and keen interest.

"The first reason, quite simply, is that it is unlikely the elf would have helped us with something so powerful and potentially destructive as the scroll without having any reason to trust us. He hadn't even come to trust Mr. Lethiscir yet; he was hardly going to trust Dronyen's sister-in-law. We had to *earn* his trust, and there was no way to do that while he was Dronyen's slave."

Seshen nodded and hummed her agreement from across the table, helping herself to another cup of cider.

"The second reason is that neither Cliope nor I were sure that he would be able to read the scroll properly while his powers were bound. It is written in a language of spells, after all. False information could be more harmful than none at all."

"He still may not choose to help us," Cesmi pointed out from beside Bachuc.

"True, but this is probably the best chance we will ever have."

"If Cliope doesn't manage to offend him too badly in the process," Vyrope muttered. The table broke out into laughter.

"You know, our very first plan was for Cliope to accept Dronyen's proposal," Brissa said after a moment's lull in the conversation. "Bachuc approached our father about her first, as she was the eldest daughter of our House. She was going to stab him in his sleep on their wedding night and stage a coup."

"Do you honestly think she would have held off stabbing him until the wedding night?" Alia asked, eyebrows raised.

"Of course not," Brissa scoffed. "That was the first reason of many that led us to change our plan." The table erupted in laughter again.

"That might have saved me a bit of trouble, at least," Tepper interjected, rubbing his forehead. "Brieden is stronger than he looks,

I'll tell you. The boy knocked me out cold. I still get headaches when I think back on it."

Brissa gave him an apologetic smile. "He tied you up most thoughtfully, though, Mister Tirchin. Cliope said she'd never seen such tender care given to a captive's comfort." Alia and Seshen covered their mouths, failing to hide their laughter. "He's quite the gentleman, that one. And it really wasn't so long before she found you."

Tepper heaved a sigh, but his eyes belied his mirth as he took a long pull from his mug of cider. "That is true, Your Majesty. I will have to remember to thank her for choosing not to slit my throat the next time I see her."

"Did she really threaten you?" Cesmi asked and winced.

Tepper chuckled. "She was not yet sure of my allegiance. But it all turned out well in the end."

"I would have to agree," Brissa said, raising her glass to Tepper before taking another sip. "You are a most invaluable part of this Council, Mister Tirchin. I hope you know that."

"Thank you, Your Majesty," he said, his cheeks going a darker pink.

"And as the wine has loosened my tongue and tilted me toward the sentimental side of my nature, I might as well make use of it." Brissa cast a wry smile around the table. "You are each of you invaluable to me, every one. Cliope and I could never have gotten this far without you. Please do not ever forget that."

Vyrope dared to squeeze Brissa's hand on the table. "We won't, Your Majesty," she murmured, eyes soft.

"We will win this war, Your Majesty," Bachuc added, voice fierce and steady.

Brissa nodded, letting the confidence of all those gathered wash over her, with the fortifying warmth of Vyrope's hand still firm around her own. She fought against the knot in the pit of her gut, the constant niggling reminder that she still had not heard from Cliope.

"We are winning this war already," she said, shoulders squared. She would not surrender to worry. Cliope would not want it, and there was too much at stake. "To victory," she added, raising her glass.

"To victory," her council echoed, loud and joyful, and the knot in her gut loosened just a bit.

CHAPTER THIRTY-FOUR

"**D**O YOU LOVE HIM?"

Sehrys looked up from the flowers he was arranging and sighed when he saw the stack of books in Sree's arms. It was bad enough that Firae had insisted upon Sree as Sehrys's tutor, but he had hoped they could at least restrict their conversation to the topics of his lessons.

"Pardon?" Sehrys tried to keep his voice as pleasant as possible.

"The human. Do you actually love it? Him, I mean. Do you actually love him?"

Sehrys quirked an eyebrow. "Why are you asking me that? Why do you even care?"

"I care because I care about Firae," Sree said firmly, setting the books down on the table. "He was almost over you, you know. Less than a year before the grieving period would have ended, and he was already discussing possible suitors."

She searched Sehrys's face for signs of anger or jealousy. Sehrys did his best to approximate them, but he wasn't fast enough, and Sree was shrewd.

"You don't love him," she said pointedly, tossing a book at him with far more force than necessary.

Sehrys flinched, but managed to catch it before it hit him in the face. "I—what? You just asked me—"

349

"Firae. You don't love him. You're using him because you wish to be king."

"No."

"Really. So you have suddenly just taken an interest in hundreds of thousands of years of history because it suits your fancy?"

"Yes, really. I care about Firae very deeply. He's *family*, Sree. He's—I'm not using him. But I won't deny that I want to be king, and I want to be an educated one. Important changes need to be made and I want to see them through."

Sree rolled her eyes. "So you had a few rough years, and now you want to be the next savior for the poor, exiled criminals in Villalu. Let's see how devoted you still are after you're used to proper baths and pretty clothes and regular massages, Sehrys."

"Sree, why are you such a—" Sehrys stopped himself and sighed. "I appreciate that you care about Firae, Sree," he said, keeping his tone as kind as possible. "But this really isn't any of your concern."

"This is *completely* my concern. I'm not the only one with some concerns about you being appointed king. Many are politically opposed to this union, and if you love someone else better, maybe you ought to just—"

"It's not that simple."

"Actually, I would argue that it *is*. It's precisely that simple. And you know that there's only one way out of a marriage to a royal after you've been mated." Sree placed her palms on the table between them and leaned close to him. "And I know how fond you are of your pretty neck, Sehrys," she added in a low voice.

Sehrys simply glared at her, and then went back to arranging the flowers when it became clear that she had no plans to begin their lesson.

"Just stop treating Firae like a *pet*," Sree admonished. "That's what you've got your human on hand for, right?"

Sehrys swore softly as he pricked his thumb on a thorn. He pushed the flowers aside and sat down. "Sree, you may wish to consider the way you choose to speak to the man who will soon be your king. Perhaps we should begin our lesson, unless you would like to see what happens to *your* pretty neck if you continue to address me in such a threatening and disrespectful manner."

Sree held his gaze, her bright green eyes chilled with suppressed hatred. "Fine, then," she finally replied, pulling out a chair and sitting down. "Let us discuss Queen *Tyzva efa es Pura Ovni Feririar's* handling of the Sylph wars. Open your text to page twelve hundred and nine.

SEHRYS ALLOWED FIRAE TO KISS HIM. IT WAS A PERPLEXING experience on a number of levels.

He had always loved kissing Firae. They had skipped lessons in order to kiss for hours when they had been younger. They had played games, chasing after one another so that the boy in pursuit could tackle the other and kiss him breathless, gasping nervously at the eager way their bodies responded.

But now... he didn't love it. He didn't hate it because Firae was a very good kisser, and his touch was tender with love. Sehrys felt safe with him. But he did not love it. It didn't send a thrill down his spine. It didn't send a tingle across and beneath his skin until all he could do was shiver and melt into a state of blissful surrender.

Those things only seemed to happen when he kissed Brieden.

Too, he found himself disengaging from the kisses he shared with Firae.

When Sehrys had been enslaved, he had been used in many different ways by many different men. To keep himself sane, to keep some part of himself free from their abuse and control, Sehrys had disengaged. He had imagined that his body was one entity and his mind was another, and he had pushed himself into memories and daydreams. He had clung to them as tightly as possible. Often, especially in the early years, they had been memories of Firae.

And then Brieden had rescued him. Sehrys had grown to trust him. And when he and Brieden had begun to kiss and touch each other, he had found that it was different from being used in every way, and he had remained present for every moment that they shared. For the first time since being enslaved, Sehrys had stayed fully in his body while being kissed and touched. He had assumed that it would be the same when Firae kissed him. After all, Firae was kissing him tenderly, and he had been careful to make sure that Sehrys was comfortable. When they were younger, he had never disengaged; when they were younger, being with Firae was all he wanted to think about most of the time.

So why was this happening? Why, while Firae kissed him, did Sehrys feel the familiar tug to follow his mind elsewhere, to think about songs from childhood and his mother's eyes and the sparkle of the moonlight on the baths of Alovur Drovuru?

He tried not to linger on the question because he already knew the answer. It was because he didn't want to be here. He didn't want to be doing this.

He wanted to be with Brieden.

"Do you love him?"

Sehrys did not look up from Brieden's lute, which he held in his hands as he absentmindedly stroked the strings. He had brought it to Brieden because he thought he might like to have it with him. It had also been an excuse to visit.

"I..." Sehrys couldn't look at him. If he looked at him, he would shatter into a million pieces. He continued to study the lute.

"He's family, Brieden," Sehrys finally answered softly.

"So is that a yes or a no?"

"How can I not love my family?"

Brieden heaved a sigh of frustration.

"Sehrys, you *know* what I am asking. I think the least I deserve is an answer."

Sehrys sat down, still not meeting Brieden's eyes. "I love him," he admitted.

There was a moment of heavy silence. It stretched between them like years.

"Oh," Brieden finally said, his voice cracking slightly even on the single syllable, and Sehrys forced himself to keep his eyes trained on the instrument he held. He could *not* endure the look on Brieden's face right now.

Sehrys bit his lip to hold back all of the additional information that Brieden didn't need to hear, because really, how could it help the situation? Brieden didn't need to know that while Sehrys loved Firae very much, it was only a fraction of the love he felt for Brieden. He didn't need to know how much Sehrys wished he could marry Brieden instead, how much he wished that he could be selfish and have what he wanted and ignore the rest of the world.

Brieden didn't need to know that walking away from him was making Sehrys die inside. He didn't need to know because it would change absolutely nothing, and would only make Brieden cling harder to a possibility that had never really existed.

"I... I brought you your lute," Sehrys whispered, almost too quietly for Brieden to hear, before setting the instrument down on the table and quickly heading out the door.

Brieden didn't reply.

FIRAE PULLED AWAY FROM THE KISS, FROWNING.

"Sehrys, what's wrong?"

"Nothing," Sehrys said, attempting to sound dreamy and breathless. But Firae knew him far too well.

"Please don't lie to me, Sehrys," Firae said softly, pain evident in his voice. He rose from garden bench they had been sharing.

Sehrys sighed as he blinked up at him. "I'm sorry. I just—it's hard, Firae. You know what I've been through. It's difficult to—I think the physical side of things is just... it might take some time. That's all."

Sehrys willed Firae to simply accept his words, to squeeze his hand and say he understood, to do or say anything other than ask him—

"But what about *him*, Sehrys? It didn't take very much time for you to become physical with him, did it?"

"It's... different, Firae," Sehrys offered lamely.

"How *precisely* is it different, Sehrys?" Firae began to wander around the corner of the garden they were occupying, a nervous habit he'd had for as long as Sehrys had known him. He approached the birdbath, a structure growing out of the earth with a thick stem that matched the vibrant green of the grass beneath his feet; the bath itself was cupped inside a bowl of joined peach-colored petals edged in blue. He ran his fingers across the surface of the water, avoiding Sehrys's eye.

Sehrys sighed deeply, searching his mind for an answer that wouldn't be a lie and wouldn't get Brieden killed.

"You were going to be my husband, Firae."

"Yes, Sehrys, and I hope that will still come to pass." A pixie landed on the lip of the bath and chattered at him noisily. Firae withdrew his fingers and turned to face Sehrys.

"I... I wanted to wait until our wedding night. It was important to me. It still is. Isn't it important to you?"

"You didn't wait until the wedding to kiss me the last time."

"I was *just* kissing you! *Minutes* ago!"

"Only in the strictest sense. You were a galaxy away, Sehrys." Firae resumed his pacing, pausing to pluck a handful of berries from a bush at the edge of their little garden clearing.

"I... no, I—"

"And you used to let me touch you," Firae added softly, popping the berries into his mouth and chewing them slowly. "You used to like it when I touched you."

"I'm sorry," Sehrys said sadly.

"I'm not looking for an apology, Sehrys, I'm looking for an explanation."

Sehrys chewed his lip.

"It's him, isn't it? You're in love with him."

Sehrys studied his hands. "If I say yes, you'll kill him. Or have him killed."

"Then say no." Firae looped around the birdbath again before heading back to the bench where Sehrys sat.

"Firae... I've never lied to you, have I?" Sehrys implored, looking up at him.

"Not to my knowledge, no."

"I haven't. So why are you trying to... trap me like this?"

"I'm not trying to *trap* you, Sehrys. I'm just trying to get the truth out of you."

"Why does it even *matter* how I feel about him, Firae? Shouldn't how I feel about you be the only thing that matters?"

"And how *do* you feel about me?" Firae asked, coming to a standstill in front of Sehrys.

"I love you," Sehrys answered simply. "I've always loved you. Can't you see that?"

"It's different now."

Sehrys sighed, turning his head to catch a glimpse of the North Tower. "Yes. It's different now."

Firae turned to follow Sehrys's gaze with his own and resumed his pacing.

"Couldn't you just let Brieden go?" Sehrys said, after silence had stretched between them for a bit longer than was strictly comfortable. "He's no threat to you, Firae. If you just let him go, we can... move on."

Firae frowned at the tower, but sat down beside Sehrys once again and took his hand. "We can't move on anyhow? Right now? Even while he remains here?"

"It would be quite difficult."

"And if I—"

Sehrys looked him in the eye. "If any harm comes to him while he is in your care, Firae, no matter how 'accidental' it may appear, I will leave you. But if you let him go to Khryslee, our problems are over and I am yours."

Firae looked thoughtful. "All right."

Sehrys blinked at him. He hadn't imagined that Firae would yield so soon. "Really?"

Firae sighed irritably. "Yes, really. As long as he stays in Khryslee. I make no promises about what I might do if he comes back for you."

Sehrys turned his face away slightly so that Firae wouldn't see the tears in his eyes. "He won't."

"All right. Sooner rather than later, I suppose. I'll let Jaxis know that he and Ki'iz can set out with the human in the morning."

Sehrys furrowed his brow. "I don't think we'll need Jaxis *and* Ki'iz to accompany us, Firae."

Firae narrowed his eyes at Sehrys. "We? Us? I don't think so."

"What is that supposed to mean?"

"Say your goodbyes here, Sehrys. You are *not* accompanying him to Khryslee."

"What? Of course I am!" A thread of panic began to rise in Sehrys's chest. "I have to see him safely there, Firae. I *have* to!"

"And you don't trust Jaxis and Ki'iz? I thought they were your friends. I thought that was why you asked them to watch him."

"I trust them. That isn't the point. I need to get him there. I need to see, with my *own eyes,* that he is safe. I can't completely be with you until that happens." Sehrys did not add that neither would he be able to completely *trust* Firae until he saw Brieden safely to Khryslee.

"That is not happening before you marry me, Sehrys."

Sehrys glanced at Firae, and then back at the North Tower. He couldn't deny that Firae was giving him precisely what he'd been asking for. "Well, then," he said. "I suppose we should go ahead and get married."

Firae smiled. "Yes. We should. I will speak to the priestesses about arranging soul-walks and a ceremony next week."

Next week? Sehrys's head spun. He had been so good at holding off the inevitable, but there it was. Firae wasn't wasting any time.

"Do we really need to soul-walk again?" Sehrys asked around the lump in his throat. "The last time I was on my way home with the firm intent to marry you, Firae, and I imagine you came to the same conclusion, so—"

"Sehrys. We must soul-walk again." Firae spoke firmly, leaving no room for argument. "It is tradition, it has been six years, and things are more complicated now than they were the last time. We need to know that this is still the right thing for both of us. This is forever, Sehrys. We need to take it seriously."

Sehrys drew a deep breath, but then nodded. "Of course. You're right."

"Now, who would you like to visit? The Mother again?"

"No," Sehrys answered. "No, I... uh... don't particularly care to travel through Villalu."

"Of course not," Firae bowed his head slightly. "I'm sorry, I didn't think about—"

"Firae, it's fine. Just... tell the priestesses I'll be visiting the shrine of someone new this year."

"Have you any idea who it will be?"

Sehrys smiled in what he hoped was a nonchalant fashion.

"Yes," he answered. "The Blessed Guardian of the Sands That Carpet the World."

CHAPTER THIRTY-FIVE

"**T**HIS IS NOT HEALTHY, BRIEDEN."

Brieden didn't open his eyes. He was lying on top of his bed, his untouched dinner on the table to his left.

I love him. I love him. I love him.

It was a droning background noise inside Brieden's head, making it impossible for him to concentrate on anything else. Sehrys loved Firae. Brieden knew this to be true. Sehrys wasn't just going to marry Firae because he believed he must. Sehrys was going to marry Firae because it was what he *wanted*.

Brieden hated his life. He didn't care if he never left his cell and he hoped Jaxis would go away.

"I'm not going away."

Brieden sighed, but didn't open his eyes, even when Jaxis sat down on the bed next to him.

"This is growing pathetic. You're not even a useful means of attracting ladies anymore. You've become too depressing."

Brieden ignored him.

"Brieden, snap out of it. Your whole life can't be about one person. There are probably *plenty* of men to bone in Khryslee. You don't see me lying about in my own filth and moaning about some woman."

Brieden opened his eyes and propped himself on his elbows. "First of all, Jaxis, I am not lying in my own *filth*, thank you very

359

much. And second—" Brieden held up his wrist dramatically—
"note the absence of a red bracelet. I don't just want a willing partner.
I want... I want someone to be in love with. Someone who loves
me just as much."

Brieden let his arm fall back down to his side.

"All right, I get it. I know you're miserable right now, and if I
enjoyed fucking men, I would certainly do what I could to make
you feel better, but seriously, friend, there is a world beyond Sehrys."

Brieden stared at Jaxis, unsure which part of the statement he
should react to, or what his reaction should be.

"What I mean to say is, what did you wish to do with your life
before you met him?"

That was a very good question. He could certainly tell Jaxis what
he had been *planning* to do—work for Dronyen and continue to get
promoted and then maybe buy a better house for his mother when he
could afford it and... things got a bit fuzzy after that. "I don't think
I ever really knew," Brieden answered honestly. "There was never
anything that I really *wanted* for my future until... until Sehrys."

"But what if you'd never met Sehrys? Or what if he had died?"

"Jaxis! Don't even *say* that!"

Jaxis raised an eyebrow. "Really, Brieden? Because you know that
even if you and Sehrys married and went off to spend years fucking
each other and... I don't know, watching sunsets and exchanging
flowers in Khryslee, *he* would have to experience that. You're human,
and you are going to die much, much sooner than any of us. Sehrys
has no choice but to think about a future without you no matter
what happens. So perhaps you should, too. It's only fair."

Brieden sat up, his hand drifting absently to the lamp dial on the
wall. He spun it between his fingers as he thought.

"I think you may have a point, Jaxis," he finally admitted. "But
I honestly have no idea what I want to do."

"Maybe I can help you. I'm actually quite good at this kind of thing."

"Oh? Did you always want to be a guard for the king?"

Jaxis laughed. "Nah, I'm actually just a reservist, but I'm doing this as a favor to Sehrys. My real job is helping to manage the baths. I'm a water-bearer."

"Oh. Wow. That's... amazing, Jaxis. I had no idea." That Jaxis had a hand in compelling such a complex and renowned system of waterways was impressive.

Jaxis shrugged, but made no attempt at humility. "Yeah, I am rather amazing at it. And it's a great way to meet ladies."

"But... why did Sehrys ask you to guard me? If there are so many other guards and you already have a job, I mean."

Jaxis grinned. "Sehrys is my friend. Most members of the guard are quite loyal to Firae, and some of them aren't such big fans of Sehrys. Sehrys wanted you with someone he could trust."

Brieden nodded, wondering how anyone could dislike Sehrys.

"Also, I speak flawless Villaluan, and Sehrys wanted you to be around someone you could talk to. There are only three members of the guard who speak Villaluan and whom Sehrys also trusts. Ki'iz and Vrac you know," Jaxis said, referring to Brieden's other two guards who watched him when Jaxis was off-duty, "and Runa... but Sehrys didn't want Runa spending time with you."

"Why not?"

Jaxis laughed. "He didn't offer an explanation, but I'd wager it's because Runa is a rather stunning man who would *definitely* want to bone you, and I don't think Sehrys wanted him to... uh... you know... *bone you.*"

Brieden felt his face creep into his first small smile of the day.

"Sehrys was jealous?" he asked softly, not sure if he should be admonishing himself for the comfort it gave him.

Jaxis laughed. "Of *course* Sehrys was jealous. But, Brieden, I can't help but notice that we're talking about Sehrys once again. I thought we were going to talk about *you*."

Brieden sighed. "I know. But what else do I have?"

"You *don't* have him anymore." Jaxis winced at his own harsh statement, but didn't back away from it. "I'm sorry. I don't mean to be cruel. But... what are some other things you like besides Sehrys?"

Brieden continued to fiddle with the dial on the wall, casting the room into shadows and then back into light, pausing occasionally between the two extremes. It was true, he didn't have Sehrys anymore. And short of taking his own life, there was no solution except to move forward.

Not that he hadn't thought of taking his own life. Initially he had dismissed the idea because it would upset Sehrys. But the truth was that Brieden wasn't through living. He was still only twenty-three, and he had learned there was a place in the world where he could be himself, with or without Sehrys. He did still want to go to Khryslee.

But the question was a good one. What *did* he like besides Sehrys?

"You like having sex with men," Jaxis supplied helpfully. "There's always a living to be made in that."

"No," Brieden answered firmly.

"At least I'm *trying* here, friend."

"I'm good with weapons," Brieden ventured. Jaxis looked thoughtful for a moment before shaking his head.

"Probably wouldn't do you much good in Khryslee, to be honest. Even *hunting* is prohibited there."

"I... I like cheese," Brieden muttered feebly.

To his surprise, Jaxis's eyes lit up. "Hey! That's an idea! You could be a cheesemaker or a dairy farmer. I hear the dairy trade is *lucrative* in Khryslee. I've even heard that people there ride bulls and retired dairy cows instead of horses."

"But Jaxis, I don't know anything about actually *making* cheese or raising goats or cows or—"

"But you know you like cheese, and that's as good a place to start as any. Think of it this way: Before you had sex, you didn't know what you were doing, but you knew you liked cock, so you learned. It's no different." Jaxis smiled, looking satisfied with the analogy.

Brieden also smiled, in spite of himself. "Thank you, Jaxis. But even so, I don't know where I'm going to sleep at night, much less how to get started on learning a new trade. I haven't got any money, or—do they even use money in Khryslee?"

Jaxis shrugged. "Mostly they barter, I believe, although there may be some sort of coinage in circulation too. I can't really say. But you don't need to worry about things like that; Sehrys will set you up with everything you need at least three times over. You saved his life and brought him home and fucked him senseless the whole way here. He won't hang you out to dry."

Brieden sighed. No, Sehrys wouldn't hang him out to dry. He did still seem to care about Brieden, at least enough to help him get situated in a new life.

A new life that could only be hollow and colorless and gray.

Would his heart ever heal? Would he ever get over Sehrys? Would he ever be happy again? He had lost Sehrys forever, and it made him restless. Restless to get out of this cell, to get out of Alovur Drovuru, even to get away from Jaxis simply because he was connected to Sehrys.

"I wonder if Firae is ever going to let me go."

"Oh. Didn't Sehrys tell you?"

Brieden looked at him. "Tell me what?"

"Firae said he'll let you go. He even said Sehrys can bring you to Khryslee—" Brieden's heart leapt— "after the wedding." The leap ended in a crippling crash.

"Oh," Brieden whispered, barely audible. He took a deep breath. "But does that mean—when is the wedding? Do you know?"

Jaxis paused a bit too long before meeting Brieden's eyes.

"Yes," he finally said, and Brieden had never heard him sound so serious or sad. "They are taking their soul-walks tomorrow. And the next day—"

"They'll be married," Brieden finished in a whisper.

"Yes."

"I just thought—do you think—I thought Sehrys would visit me before—why didn't he tell me himself?"

"Most likely because he's spent the last two days pretending to meditate, but in fact he's been crying his eyes out in his room," Jaxis answered softly, still in that serious tone. "Brieden, I don't know if he *can*. Tomorrow night, the betrothed are allowed to interact only with one another after the soul-walk, and tonight—I've just never seen him like this."

Brieden nodded; a tear slid down his cheek. It gave him no relief to know that this was painful for Sehrys as well.

"Jaxis?"

"Yes?"

"Could you—I don't mean to be rude, but could I have some time to myself, please?"

Jaxis nodded and stood. "Of course," he answered gently. "But only if you agree to go to the baths with me this afternoon. Heartbreak is awful, friend, but it's no excuse for allowing yourself to become an unfuckable mess."

Brieden nodded in response. "Okay."

He waited for Jaxis to leave his cell before burying his face in his pillow to muffle his loud, shuddering sobs.

SEHRYS TOOK A DEEP BREATH AND TRIED, ONCE AGAIN, TO push through the constant throb of heartache and center himself.

He had been in his chamber all day and couldn't remember the last time he'd eaten. He needed a bath badly and was nowhere near mentally prepared for his soul-walk tomorrow.

This was it. This was his life. He had no choice but to behave like an adult and accept it.

Sehrys forced himself to pick at the honeysuckle bush outside his window, looked across the moonlit gardens of the Great Hall and sighed. He definitely needed to bathe, but he didn't want to go to the royal baths for fear that he might see Firae or Ki'iz or, Gods forbid, Sree. The walk to the public baths would probably do him good anyway, and the larger pools were likely to be quite empty. Not many elves bathed at night, save for couples who sought small, secluded pools for their activities.

As he immersed himself in a clear pool, Sehrys looked up at the moon, doing his meditation exercises for his Rite the following day. He was actually able to attain the proper level of trance for a few moments before thoughts of Brieden again invaded his placid inner world.

He tried not to let the trickle of the waterfall remind him of the time that he and Brieden had made love beneath a waterfall in Silnauvri. When he reached for the puffy white flowers along the banks in order to wash himself, he pushed away the memory of how he and Brieden had ritually bathed one another before making love at the foot of the Great Mother's shrine. And when he noticed a shrub dotted with large red flowers close to the line of trees behind the baths, Sehrys bit his lip and fought away the tears.

As he walked back to the Hall, Sehrys found himself taking an entirely unnecessary detour.

All right. So he was going to walk past the North Tower. That was fine. But he was absolutely *not* going to stop.

Sehrys swore under his breath when he realized he was standing in front of the tower. He willed his legs to move him back toward the Hall, but a strange flickering caught his eye. The window of Brieden's cell dimmed and brightened in a strange rhythm.

He puzzled over it before remembering how Brieden had fiddled with the lights the last time he was there. And then Brieden's expression when he had seen his first pixie was in Sehrys's mind, and the innocent wonder that filled Brieden's eyes whenever he encountered something new and exciting from Laesi, and *Gods,* they must have sparkled with that same wonder when he first discovered the lights. Sehrys was sorry he'd missed it because he *loved* how excited Brieden became over such things, and Sehrys had no idea precisely when he'd begun to climb the spiraling staircase toward Brieden's cell.

He had to stop. He had to go back to the Hall. What was he doing? Why did his traitorous feet refuse to bring him back to his room? Seeing Brieden would only make everything worse for them both.

When he stopped, he was just a few paces from the entrance to Brieden's cell. He leaned his forehead against the wall and took several deep breaths. There was still time. He could leave. He didn't have to do this.

Sehrys walked to the entrance of the cell. The heavy outer door stood open, but the inner barred door was in place, and Brieden and Jaxis were sitting on the bed in soft conversation.

Sehrys paused before lightly rapping his knuckle against the bars.

They both looked up at him. Jaxis smiled. Brieden's eyes widened slightly but Sehrys couldn't read the emotion there. No one said anything.

Finally, Jaxis stood up. "Come on in, Sehrys," he said. "It's unlocked."

Sehrys didn't smile: He wasn't sure he remembered how just now. Despite the dull sadness that had slowly become his new emotional baseline, he was very happy that Firae had agreed to let Jaxis stay with Brieden. No one else in Firae's employ would dare grant him such liberties.

Sehrys pushed the barred inner door open and stepped into the room. He tried not to look Brieden in the eye, but he felt something akin to a magnetic pull, forcing him to meet Brieden's gaze, to bear the pain he saw there, to endure the intensity and the longing.

Jaxis cleared his throat. "I'll just… I'll give you some time alone," he muttered, squeezing Sehrys's shoulder on his way out of the room and closing both doors behind him.

Sehrys tried to tell Jaxis that he didn't need to go. He tried to say that there was no reason for Jaxis to go, that he hadn't meant to come, that he couldn't stay—

"Brieden," he heard himself say.

Brieden continued to hold his gaze. "You're getting married in two days," Brieden said softly, his tone begging Sehrys to refute the statement.

"Jaxis told you."

"Yes. But why didn't—you should have been the one to tell me."

Sehrys nodded. "I should have. I just… I… it's too much, Brieden."

"You're telling me it's too much, Sehrys? At least you'll be happy. At least you'll be able to spend your life with someone you love."

Sehrys's face crumpled, and he tore his gaze away from Brieden's to sob into his hands.

Even in his anger, even in his hurt, Brieden was with him in an instant, his arms wrapping around Sehrys and rubbing his back to soothe him. Because that was the man Brieden was. That was the man Sehrys was giving up. He clutched Brieden and breathed him in and cried until he could once again form words.

When his first attempt at coherent speech failed, Brieden pulled away slightly and looked at him. "It's all right, Sehrys. Slow down. What did you say?"

"I *said*," Sehrys managed between shaking breaths, "of course I won't be happy, you *idiot*!"

Brieden's eyes widened. "But... you said you love him, Sehrys. I thought—"

"Brieden," Sehrys said, their eyes locking once more, "I do love him. But I'm *in* love with you. And there is most definitely a difference."

Neither of them were exactly sure when it happened. But it quickly became apparent that they were no longer looking at each other because they were kissing, and it was passionate and raw, and when Sehrys tried to pull back and mutter an apology, Brieden dove at him and kissed him even harder.

Every second of contact was as sharp, clear and intentional as it was desperately fast. Brieden pulled Sehrys toward the bed, their clothing falling away in a trail behind them, until they fell onto the mattress together, naked and pressed close.

Every touch was urgency. Every touch was fire. There had been too many words and too many tears and everything else was broken, but this, *this* was whole and unruptured. This was Sehrys and Brieden, their essences mingled, what they created together that could never be replicated or destroyed.

Brieden reached under the mattress and pulled out a bottle of rose-tinted fluid. Sehrys didn't fight the soft laugh that escaped him, but he didn't comment either. They didn't speak and they didn't cry.

Urgency melted into reverence and they took their time, kissing each other all over, stroking one another as they sighed with pleasure. Each man gave extra attention to his favorite parts of the other, memorizing lines and curves and tastes and textures. They did the things that they knew would produce the most delicious noises, drawing them out, making each other blind with arousal but holding off on anything that could lead to release.

And every few moments, whatever they were doing turned into kissing. The intimacy of their faces pressed close, their breath becoming one, was the very heart of all that they needed right now.

They kissed while Brieden moved his fingers in and out of Sehrys's body, and they kissed as Sehrys lifted his legs to wrap around Brieden's waist and pull him inside. They made love slowly, more slowly than they ever had, eyes locking tenderly between kisses, holding on to the moment for as long as possible.

And even after the lovemaking ended, the kisses continued, hands caressing each other's necks and shoulders and faces, fingers running through sweat-dampened hair.

They kissed until they fell asleep, naked and tangled together.

BRIEDEN WASN'T SURE HOW SEHRYS HAD MANAGED TO SLIP out without waking him. Even so, he wasn't surprised to wake up alone.

Brieden moved onto his side, gazing out the window at the pink-and plum-colored sunrise. Had Sehrys already left for his soul-walk? He wondered what the soul-walk really *was*. He had never gotten a full explanation, but then, he had never asked for one.

Sehrys had told him it was just a formality. A part of the marriage ritual. The next time he saw Sehrys, Sehrys would be king.

He would also be married to another man.

Brieden didn't cry. He was still heartbroken and he was still miserable, but he felt strangely calm as well.

Because last night with Sehrys had been exactly what he needed.

It had been absolutely incredible. It had been indescribably beautiful.

And it had also been goodbye.

CHAPTER THIRTY-SIX

THE SHRINE WAS IN A SMALL VALLEY FULL OF ROSES, lilies and other flowers native to Laesi. It was surrounded by a forest of *tashlivija* flower-trees, with pale green stems and a canopy of deep purple blossoms. The diffused sunlight made Sehrys's skin glow violet as he made his way along the rarely-used winding path. Few sidhe visited L!Khryauvni's shrine anymore; He had become inexorably linked to human rights and the abolition of slavery, and not many sidhe wanted their spiritual lives flavored with politics.

Of course, *everything* was flavored with politics, regardless of whether one chose to live in ignorance of that fact.

Ignorance was a luxury Sehrys had lost on the way home from his last soul-walk.

It was midmorning when Sehrys arrived, bearing a small bottle of sand from the Western sea. He grew a patch of lilies at the foot of L!Khryauvni's statue and gazed reverently at the vine-draped figure, which held a stone carving of connected bivalve shells in His palm. If this had been a conventionally planned marriage, Sehrys would have had time to procure shells for his offering too. As it was, he had been lucky to find a trader with sand to sell on such short notice. Sehrys poured the sand in a circle around the lilies, his eyes still on the connected stone shells.

They represented the connection that remained even after the death of the creature within: two halves that can exist separately, but mean so much more when that delicate bond between them remains.

Schrys ran his fingers along the shells in the statue's palm, tracing the connection as gently as possible.

He murmured a request that the Blessed Guardian allow him this soul-walk, and then kissed the statue's toes and rose to his feet when he received no sign that his request had been rejected.

He found the flowers he was looking for: dark-blue glossy petals cupped around a sticky golden center. The center held the hallucinogen that would assist him in his trance, but he ate the petals too. They offset some of the bitterness of the drug.

Sehrys undressed and settled himself cross-legged before the statue, placing one palm on the sun-warmed stone. He closed his eyes and breathed deeply, working himself into as deep a trance as possible, making himself empty and receptive so that he could slip out of his body easily when the walk began.

"YOU NEED A DRINK."

Jaxis strode into Brieden's cell and thumped a large bottle of pale blue liquid onto the table. Brieden looked over at him from the window.

"What's that?"

"Nectar of *zula sopor rija*," Jaxis said. He poured two glasses and walked over to Brieden, handing him one.

"To us of the red bracelet," Jaxis said, clinking their glasses together.

"To true love that never dies," Brieden responded, knocking back the beverage in one swig.

It may have been nectar, but it was obviously *fermented* nectar, and decidedly quite alcoholic. Still... the flavor was sweet and delicate and undeniably appealing. When Jaxis brought the bottle to the window, Brieden held his glass out for more. Why in the Five Hells not? If ever there were a day to wallow in drunkenness, this was it.

WHEN THE DRUG BEGAN TO TAKE HOLD, SEHRYS FELT HIMSELF move and ripple inside his own skin. Tentatively, he climbed out.

He paused for a moment to observe his body, deep in trance at the foot of the statue. Then he looked up into the now-intelligent eyes of L!Khryauvni.

Without speaking in the manner of flesh-beings, the God asked him why he had chosen to visit His shrine instead of any other. What could L!Khryauvni offer Sehrys that no other Goddess or God could?

Guidance, answered Sehrys. *The path to Unity.*

How do I fix what Your followers lost? How do I achieve a common understanding that may never have existed at all between such different peoples?

And finally, painfully, *How do I sever the ligaments that hold us together? How do I let him go?*

The Blessed Guardian looked at him thoughtfully. Finally, he signaled that he would send a guide.

Sehrys couldn't help but feel a pang of mild frustration. He didn't *want* a traditional Nuptial Rite for this soul-walk. He already knew that he and Firae had already been perfectly content together in at least a handful of lives. He had seen those lives the last time. All the answers Sehrys needed right now were the sort to come from the Blessed Guardian Himself. A guide could only show him what he had already seen. Or, quite possibly, show him things he didn't *want* to see. Sehrys began to protest, but paused when he felt a cool mist-like whisper of a hand on his shoulder.

He turned around to behold his guide, and all of his arguments against having one evaporated.

"Sister," he breathed softly, taking her hand.

Nehaisa was just as he remembered her, small and pale and not even close to fully grown, with long scarlet hair and eyes like his own. He took a moment just to drink her in.

She stood on her toes to kiss his cheek, and he felt that same cool mist-like touch again as her lips brushed against him.

"This way," she said, her voice as musical as he remembered.

She led him into the forest of purple flower-trees. The world around them faded from deep purple into black, until he felt as if he was stepping into the night sky. Galaxies swirled around him, growing larger than he could perceive and then shrinking until they were smaller than a grain of sand. Sehrys had no way to gauge his own size or density, or even whether his consciousness was clinging to the illusion of a corporeal body at all. He let himself drift until he found that place: the one place in all of the universe reserved for him, his soul, his very essence. Nehaisa nestled beside him, and yes, the illusion of corporeal form was back so that he could fully appreciate her presence.

"You have already seen your lives with Firae," she said, and he nodded.

"But there was something else last time, wasn't there?" she continued. "Something that you chose to ignore."

Sehrys looked at her uneasily. "I just... I knew I could be happy with Firae. I *saw* it. I didn't see any need to... make it more complicated."

"And yet it has become more complicated."

"No," Sehrys insisted. "It isn't. I want to marry Firae. I... I care for him a great deal, and if I am king I can change things, Nehaisa. I could leave a legacy of—"

"Sehrys," she admonished gently, "is there no other way?"

Sehrys gave her a puzzled look.

"You chose to ignore the other because it scared you." It wasn't a question. "And yet so few in any world are given such a gift. Do you really choose to deny it? Out of fear?"

"It isn't—it's not—he isn't—"

She stroked his cheek. "He found you anyway, didn't he?" she asked softly. "Even though you tried to keep him lost to you in this life. He still found you."

Sehrys felt a flush of sadness. He was sure that, back at the shrine, his body was shedding tears.

"I miss you," Sehrys whispered.

"I miss you, too," his sister replied. "Please don't resist this, Sehrys. You have to look this time."

Sehrys considered the glittering points around him and drew a particular set of them toward himself. These were the lives in which he and Firae were together. Past, present and future, scattered across universes, they did have a connection. That much was undeniable. Firae's life fit his, perhaps more like a mitten than a glove, but it fit nonetheless.

He tried to ignore the heat at his back. He tried not to turn around and see what he knew was there, what had always been there.

He had successfully ignored it the last time. Why had L!Khryauvni not simply answered his questions? Why had He sent him a guide who embodied his sister in every way? Why had He made him come back *here*?

He had ignored what was behind him last time. This time, it was even more difficult.

"Sehrys, turn around," Nehaisa urged.

"I can't," he whispered.

"Jaxis, what *is* this?" Brieden slurred after his fourth glass of nectar. "I feel strange."

"You're drunk," Jaxis said idly.

"I've been intoxicated before. Jaxis, this feels different."

"But you've never had *this* to drink before, have you? You're probably just unaccustomed to faerie nectars. You'll be fine."

Brieden furrowed his brow. "You only had one glass. And you didn't even finish it."

Jaxis smiled. "I'm on duty, friend. Besides, I thought you might need it more than I do today."

Brieden looked at him suspiciously. "Jaxis, what did you—" His eyes rolled back in his head before he could finish, and Jaxis caught him as he fell. He carried Brieden to the bed and laid him down gently.

Jaxis paused before leaving the room to look down at Brieden with a smirk, his eyes dancing with mischief. "You'll thank me later," he said cheerfully, as he sauntered out the door whistling to himself.

NEHAISA SQUEEZED HIS HAND GENTLY. "IT'S TIME FOR ME TO go."

"No!" Sehrys swore he could feel his physical heart beating with alarm. "You just—it hasn't been long enough. Don't leave me yet."

"Sehrys, there is nothing else for me to show you. You're choosing the path of least resistance, and there doesn't seem to be anything I can do to convince you otherwise."

"No! I'm choosing—you can't truly claim that my choice is the path of least resistance!"

"It is the path of least pain, Sehrys," his sister amended.

"But if you understood how painful this is for me—"

"Is it more painful than letting yourself love as deeply and freely as you are truly capable, knowing that he will leave you alone in this world when he dies?"

Sehrys stuttered before finally responding. "It nearly killed me when you died. I don't know if I can do it again."

"Brother, you can. You are so strong."

"I don't feel strong," Sehrys whimpered brokenly. "I'm just trying to do what's right, and... even if I am afraid, and even if the fear is part of my decision, I can't let the brutality in the world continue. Not when I have the power to do something about it."

"I know you care about your world, Sehrys. You will continue to care, no matter what happens. But marrying Firae... you can't think it is the only way."

"What other way is there for me?"

"What other way have you considered?"

"I..." Sehrys didn't know what to say. All he knew was that his sister simply didn't understand. If there was another way, of *course* he would have found it.

Wouldn't he?

"Sehrys, turn around. You owe it to yourself to at least see what it is that you are rejecting."

"I know what I am rejecting," Sehrys said sadly.

"You know a piece of it. You have the opportunity to know more."

Sehrys swallowed, and Nehaisa hugged him. "It is your choice now, Sehrys," she said, giving him another kiss on the cheek. "I trust you can find your own way back."

"But I... no... I..." Sehrys was so distraught that he didn't notice the familiar presence at his side. The presence that was so familiar, it was like another part of him. Connected by the finest ligament.

His sister's eyes shone with what appeared to be tears. Her smile was dazzling.

"Oh, Sehrys, he's *beautiful*," she said, and then she was gone.

Sehrys glanced at the spot where Nehaisa had been looking and was stunned to find Brieden standing beside him.

"Sehrys?" Brieden ventured.

"What are you doing here?" Sehrys whispered. This was absolutely *unheard* of.

"I was looking for you." Brieden wrapped his arms around Sehrys's waist. "I found you."

Brieden was obviously dreaming. There was no other way that he could be here. But even in the dream state, how could he find Sehrys? This place, this reality that Sehrys currently occupied was deeper than the world of dreams, and only sages and elder priestesses could reach it without—

Jaxis. Of course.

Sehrys hoped he remembered to thoroughly throttle his friend when he returned to Alovur Drovuru.

"Sehrys, where are we?" Brieden asked dreamily. "I feel like if I let go of you, I'm going to disappear."

"We... we're someplace you probably won't remember, Brieden. We are at The Heart of All Worlds."

"What does that mean?" Brieden asked, his arms grasping Sehrys more tightly as he nestled his head against his chest. Sehrys was surprised by Brieden's warmth and solidity, almost as if they had never left their bodies.

"I'm not sure anyone really knows. But we sidhe believe that this is where all souls are born. And this is where we come to connect to our other lives."

"Other lives?"

"Yes. This life is one of many that you have lived and will continue to live. Your essence is not bound by your flesh."

"Are you in any of my other lives?" Brieden asked, kissing Sehrys's shoulder.

"Yes," Sehrys admitted softly, all too aware of the heat pressing in behind him.

"Can you show me?" Brieden whispered, and Sehrys felt his resolve crack.

He didn't turn around. He couldn't. But he did glimpse over his shoulder just long enough to find a cluster of the light-points. He reached behind himself and drew them to his chest.

The small, bright entities swirled before them, and Sehrys held them carefully, because they were the most precious things he had ever touched. "These are lives we have lived together, Brieden. Just a few of them."

Brieden peered at the tiny star-like lights that seemed to dance in the cup of Sehrys's palms.

Brieden reached to touch one tentatively and gasped as a bolt of light shot through him. "Sehrys, that was... it was... it was *us*, but..." Without finishing his thought, Brieden touched another light and then another. He stared up at Sehrys.

"Is this real?" he asked in a whisper.

"I suppose that depends on what you mean by real," Sehrys answered. Brieden sighed and wrapped his arms back around Sehrys's waist.

They stayed that way for a measureless space of time, until Brieden began to fade, back into the world of dreams, back toward waking life.

Sehrys felt so cold and empty when he'd gone.

Brieden had not been afraid to let the visions wash through him. If Brieden had only known what it was that was really pressing in from behind them...

No. Brieden would not have feared that either. Of this, Sehrys was certain.

The Blessed Guardian had sent him here for a reason. And with or without Jaxis's interference, the Blessed Guardian had allowed Brieden to find him because He wished it to be so.

Sehrys took a deep breath.

"Have courage," he whispered to himself and turned around.

The multitude of tiny lights was so intense it nearly blinded him. There were too many to differentiate, too many to count even if he had the rest of his long life to try.

Nehaisa had been right. So few in any world were given such a gift. Such a terrifying, humbling ocean of a gift.

Centering himself, Sehrys made a choice.

He allowed his defenses to melt, surrendered all semblance of control. The edges of his form began to blur and drift, and he cast himself wide across the heavens.

The millions, or perhaps billions, of twinkling lights surged forth, rushing through him, permeating him completely.

And he saw it all.

He saw worlds much like the one they lived in now, and worlds that were different in every conceivable way. There were worlds in which they were both human, worlds in which they were both sidhe, and worlds in which they were some other kind of creature altogether. Lives in which they found and lost each other quickly, and lives in which they stayed together for years upon years. In some lives they loved free and proud, and in others the love they shared got them both killed. There were lives of misery in which they never truly saw what they were to one another, and a few lives like precious jewels in which they found each other so, so young and saw one another with clear eyes from the very first moment.

There was every kind of barrier and every kind of victory. And in every life, in every world, their essences were unmistakable. They were Sehrys and they were Brieden, in any language, in any interpretation. It was always them.

No matter what happened in any world, they would always find their way back to one another. And no matter what happened in this world, no matter what Sehrys chose to do, he and Brieden would belong to each other forever.

With that final realization, everything around him reverberated with a loud, echoing snap, and he was thrown into a blanket of light and sound.

Sehrys's breaths came thick and heavy and hard, his limbs were a weak, trembling mess and it took him several dizzying moments to realize that he was back in his body. He slumped to the ground, aware that the sun had already set and that he had a long walk back to Alovur Drovuru.

He allowed himself to lie in the grass as he readjusted to having a body, to time and space and width and depth and shape and size and color. He closed his eyes and heaved a deep sigh.

His soul-walk had not left him with the sort of firm confidence he had been expecting. In fact, he still had some thinking to do on his journey home.

Sehrys ate a quick supper of berries and grasses and drank deeply from his flask of water. As he began the trek back to the Great Hall, back to Firae, who would be waiting for him by now, he pondered.

Two hundred years with Brieden or eight hundred with Firae?

A slow and currently unclear path toward change or a simple route to lasting power?

Fear and pain, or comfort and ease?

Searing passion and blinding love, or simple contentment and easy friendship?

Sehrys spent the entire journey home lost in thought.

When he reached the Great Hall, he had finally made his decision.

CHAPTER THIRTY-SEVEN

THE NIGHT OF THE NUPTIAL RITE

SEHRYS APPROACHED THE GREAT HALL SLOWLY, STILL TOO lost in his thoughts to bother reacting to Sree's scowl as she and the other guards moved aside to let him enter.

He approached Firae's bedchamber as if in a dream, although it was slowly turning into a gut-twisting and anxiety-filled dream. It was the sort of dream that made him wake up in a cold sweat, heart pounding. He was really going to do this. After the soul-walk... he couldn't believe that he was *really* going to do this.

He was surprised to enter Firae's bedchamber and find that he wasn't there. Sehrys sat on the bed and fidgeted before pacing around the room and mindlessly wandering to the largest window to gaze out at the North Tower. He needed to find Firae.

He wandered about the Hall, but no one knew where Firae might be. Yes, he had come back from his soul-walk. Last anyone had seen him, he had been in his bedchamber. Or in the music room. Or at the royal baths. Or in the garden.

Sehrys looked every place he could think of before finally retiring to his own chamber. Which was, of course, precisely where he found Firae.

Firae turned away from the window and smiled at him as Sehrys entered the room.

"There you are. Firae, I've been looking for you *everywhere*."

"Oh." Firae laughed softly. "I'm sorry. I suppose I thought you would just come back here."

They looked at each other for a long moment.

"So," Firae finally began. "Was it... the same as before?"

Sehrys shook his head. "No. You were right to insist that we do this again. Firae, I—"

"It was different for me as well," Firae said, moving to sit down on Sehrys's bed. "But Sehrys, I still love you. I still want to be with you. That hasn't changed at all."

Sehrys closed his eyes and inhaled deeply.

"I love you too," he said softly, opening his eyes and meeting Firae's. "And Firae, I would be *honored* to be your husband."

THE WEDDING DAY

BRIEDEN WANTED TO GIVE JAXIS A PIECE OF HIS MIND.

He had awoken in the middle of the night from the most bizarre sleep he had ever experienced, his head pounding and stomach full of bile, luckily managing to make it to the window before getting sick. But even after he emptied his stomach, something wasn't right. Solid lines waved and twisted in on themselves, and he kept seeing faces within folds of fabric and grains of wood.

That nectar had not simply been nectar. That nectar had *done* something to him.

When he woke again, it was morning; the world was back to its usual shape and continuity, but his head was still thumping and his stomach was still squirming. Yes, he would most certainly be having a word with Jaxis.

But of course, Jaxis was nowhere to be found. Ki'iz had been on duty all night, and she told him that she didn't think Jaxis would be back before Brieden left for Khryslee. She smiled and asked him if he had a message for her to pass along.

The look on her face when Brieden told her exactly what message she could pass along to Jaxis was one of absolute horror, but Brieden couldn't bring himself to feel the least bit guilty.

And when Jaxis surprised him by walking into his cell that afternoon, he opened his mouth to demand to know what Jaxis had been thinking, to find out why Jaxis apparently got so much pleasure out of kicking a man while he was down—but then he stopped.

The look on Jaxis's face was... unreadable. He looked oddly serious.

And then Jaxis's presence and Jaxis's actions and his still-pounding head all fell to the back of his mind because behind Jaxis was Sehrys.

And beside Sehrys, holding his hand, was Firae.

❦ THE NIGHT OF THE NUPTIAL RITE

"I HOPE YOU TRULY MEAN THAT," FIRAE SAID, SMILING UP AT Sehrys.

"Of course I do," Sehrys replied.

Firae studied his hands for a moment, and then looked back at Sehrys. "And what about... Brieden?"

Sehrys blinked. Firae had never called Brieden by his name before.

"I... I've chosen you, Firae. But I do still want to bring Brieden to Khryslee. Like... like you promised I could. After the wedding."

Firae smiled. "Of course," he responded gently. "After the wedding."

❦ The Wedding Day

This was odd. Odd and awkward, and Brieden wasn't enjoying it one bit.

He was sitting in the carriage with Sehrys and Firae while Jaxis drove, and for some reason, Firae had insisted on sitting directly beside him.

The seats weren't that large. They were quite close to one another.

Sehrys sat across from both of them, avoiding Brieden's eyes. Mostly, he kept his gaze trained on his lap, where he wrung his hands mercilessly. Occasionally, he looked up and smiled nervously at Firae.

Having Sehrys there was the worst kind of torture: He loved and hated it with equal ferocity. He couldn't decide if he wanted this carriage ride to end as soon as possible or if he wanted it to last as long as possible, just so he could spend a few more moments close to Sehrys, able to see him and almost to touch him, even if Sehrys refused to look at him.

"Brieden," Firae said.

Brieden jumped, he was so startled at being addressed by the king.

"I... I want to tell you that I am sorry. I should not have held you prisoner. I am a very passionate man, and I can sometimes be..." Firae looked to the roof of the carriage, and then let out a frustrated sigh. "*Teksil abdor 'grimval' ala lingefavillalu?*" he said, glancing at Sehrys.

"Impulsive," Sehrys provided softly. It was such a blessed treat just to hear his voice.

"Sometimes I can be *impulsive*. But you saved Sehrys's life. You brought him home to us. I should have treated you like an honored guest, not a prisoner."

Firae glanced at Sehrys. "I was jealous," he added, looking strangely self-conscious. "I hope that you can forgive me."

Brieden didn't look at him directly, but he tilted his head slightly in Firae's direction. Was he serious? Was this man who was taking the love of Brieden's life away from him actually asking Brieden to *forgive* him for almost killing him? For holding him prisoner? For *taking the love of his life away from him?*

Still, the fact that Brieden was no longer a prisoner was not to be taken for granted. And besides that, Firae could burn him on the inside just by looking at him, with the full and complete blessing of the law.

"Yes, I... suppose so," Brieden mumbled.

Firae frowned. "Brieden, I had hoped you'd be a bit more... gracious than that."

Sehrys's eyes flickered to Brieden for the merest instant, and he looked...

He looked *confused.*

Brieden was beginning to get the distinct impression that he was missing something.

Something big.

☙ THE NIGHT OF THE NUPTIAL RITE

SEHRYS WAS BEGINNING TO FEEL UNCOMFORTABLE UNDER the scrutiny of Firae's gaze.

"Sehrys, my soul-walk..." Firae stood up and began pacing slowly. "Last time it was about you. Only you. But this time—"

"Was there someone else?" Sehrys asked softly. He certainly couldn't fault Firae for something like that.

Firae turned and looked at him. "No."

Sehrys watched Firae searched for words.

"It—for the most part, it was actually about me. My role as king. My *legacy*. And... and what sort of a man I want to be. What sort of a *person*."

Firae paused at the window before turning back to look at Sehrys.

"Sehrys, I need you to be completely honest with me. If the Non-Interference Doctrine weren't in place, if there were no slavery in Villalu and no exploitation in the border cities... would you still marry me?"

Sehrys stared at him. "Firae, I—that isn't—that's not—"

"Sehrys." His tone was soft and vulnerable, his eyes open and beseeching, desperate for honesty no matter what the cost.

"No." Sehrys couldn't look at him when he said it. His cheeks burned with shame.

"You don't love me, do you, Sehrys?"

"Of course I—" Sehrys sighed. He had no taste for half-truths or intellectual dishonesty, and it was time to be done with them once and for all. He owed Firae that much.

"Firae, I love you. But I love you like family. Like my dearest and most precious friend. When I was sent to Alovur Drovuru for training, I was so alone, and you... you breathed life back into the world for me, Firae. You made me feel so special and you *understood* me. That's never going to change and I don't think I could bear to lose you."

Sehrys looked up when he felt a warm hand on his shoulder. He smiled sadly at Firae through wet eyes.

"You won't lose me, Sehrys. You'll never lose me. But I can't marry you."

Sehrys stared at him, unblinking.

"I can't marry you because you didn't choose me. Not in your heart. You chose Brieden."

"I... but—"

"Sehrys, I don't want a political marriage. I want a love match. I want a lifemate. The fact that you were willing to sacrifice that for yourself to help so many others, to bring the world closer to a place of justice—I was so selfish and so blind. Because what you're planning to do *is* important. There is nothing more important. But Sehrys, *I* should be making that sacrifice, not you."

Sehrys was rendered absolutely speechless. He wasn't even sure he was hearing Firae properly. He didn't dare to dream that he was. As subtly as possible, he actually pinched himself on the thigh.

He felt it.

This was real.

It was as if an enormous band of iron was cut free from his heart, and it felt so good that it *hurt,* bursting out of him in loud tears that shook his body. He leapt to his feet and threw his arms around Firae, hugging him as tight as he could. "I'm sorry," he managed between sobs. "Firae, I'm so *sorry.* I wish..."

"I know, Sehrys," Firae said, and held him.

🪷 THE WEDDING DAY

"BRIEDEN, I UNDERSTAND THAT YOU MAY NOT CARE FOR ME," Firae said in his slow, careful Villaluan, still sitting far too close to Brieden for comfort in the carriage, "but Sehrys is the most important person in the world to me, and he wants us to at least be..." Firae seemed stuck on a word. "*Teksil abdor ala 'nauvonanga'?*" he asked Sehrys, who supplied him with "amicable."

"Yes. Amicable. He would like—*I* would like for us to be amicable. And if *I* can try, I believe you can also. After all, you are the one he has chosen."

Brieden froze, wondering briefly if he were still under the influence of the strange nectar that Jaxis had given him the previous night. "I... what?"

"Didn't..." Sehrys cleared his throat. "Didn't Jaxis give you my note?"

Brieden stared at him.

And then everything slid into place.

Sehrys wasn't avoiding Brieden's gaze because it was too painful or because it would make Firae angry or because he wanted to spare Brieden. He was doing it to be kind to *Firae*. He was doing it because he didn't want to force Firae to witness the way he looked at Brieden. He was doing it because he didn't want to make Firae suffer more than he already had.

Because Sehrys had chosen *him*. Sehrys had chosen *Brieden*.

"Brieden?" Sehrys asked tentatively, still not meeting his gaze.

"Oh. No. Jaxis never gave me a note. I... I thought you two had gotten married this morning."

Sehrys swore in Elfin under his breath, and yelled something to Jaxis, who responded with a peal of laughter. Firae also laughed softly, but now that Brieden knew the truth, he saw the pain in the king's eyes.

"Well," Firae said, "that explains a few things. I didn't read Sehrys's note, but I can tell you at least some of what it said."

Brieden nodded, still too deeply in shock to do much more.

🪷 THE NIGHT OF THE NUPTIAL RITE

"I AM GOING TO NEED YOUR HELP," FIRAE SAID, "EVEN IF YOU aren't my king."

They had gotten through the worst of the tears and the raw emotion and were sharing a pot of fragrant, calming tea on the garden terrace behind Sehrys's room.

Sehrys looked at him. "With what?"

"Sehrys, I can stop the enforcement of the Non-Interference Doctrine as far as sending sidhe into exile goes, but there's a lot more to it than that. I only have control of the Eastern Border Lands, and I'll need the cooperation of the other Queendoms as well as the Council of Nations to really see this through. It's going to be difficult and complicated, and it will probably take a very long time. This isn't just about ending slavery: This is about changing our relationship with the human governments in Villalu. This is about changing our entire criminal justice system. This is—"

"Long overdue," Sehrys whispered.

"Yes," Firae agreed. "And I'll need someone who has been through it firsthand. I'll need you to talk about it, Sehrys. What you went through. What it is actually like in Villalu." Firae studied him with nervous eyes. "I'm sorry, but—"

"I'll do it," Sehrys said softly. "Of course I'll do it, Firae."

"And I'll also need... we're going to need an ambassador to Khryslee. They've come the closest to what I think we're looking for. They've got sidhe and humans living and ruling together and they know how to make it work. We're going to need their help."

"Are you... you want *me* to do that? But Firae, I barely know the first thing about—"

"I know. You'll need to keep working with Sree. You have a lot to learn, but you're smart, Sehrys. People respond to you. And being Spiral doesn't hurt your standing either, truth be told."

"All right," Sehrys said slowly, willing himself not to make a face at the notion of working with Sree, especially now that he wouldn't be king. "That's... this is quite a lot to take in, Firae. Are you sure about all of this?"

"Of course," Firae answered. "I want to be remembered for this, Sehrys."

Ah, there was the ego that Sehrys knew so well. But he certainly couldn't begrudge Firae that. Not now.

"So," Firae continued, "we should go to Khryslee before you show up at the gates with Brieden. Speak with their Council and... well... if we can't get cooperation from the Khrysleans on this, Sehrys, I'm not sure what kind of chance we have."

Sehrys nodded. "That makes sense."

"If we leave first thing in the morning and go by grimchin, I imagine that we might be back in time for you and Brieden to leave before nightfall."

Sehrys gaped at him. "*What?* Are we in that much of a hurry, Firae?"

"Don't you want to get started right away?"

"Of course, but... *everything* has changed, Firae. Maybe we should take a few days to—"

"Sehrys, please." Firae's voice was soft. "It would be a kindness to me if you and Brieden could leave as soon as possible. I'm still in love with you, and I know that you were with him last night because his scent lingers on you even now." Sehrys stared into his cup, cheeks burning, unable to refute Firae's words.

"I want you to be happy, Sehrys. I truly do," Firae continued. "But to... to have to *see* the two of you, even just walking about together, to see you *looking* at each other and knowing that you're with him in *my* feririar—"

"I understand," Sehrys said quickly. "You and I will visit Khryslee in the morning. And I'll leave with Brieden when we get back."

"I still wish to see you and Brieden off," Firae assured him. "And... I want to speak with Brieden. I want to..." Firae sighed. "I suppose I'll have to stop trying to kill him and holding him prisoner if you and I are going to be friends."

Sehrys's lips twitched into a tiny smile. "It might be helpful. You don't need to be *his* friend, Firae, but it would mean a lot to me if the two of you were at least amicable."

Firae sighed. "I believe I can manage *amicable*," he said.

Sehrys stared up at the sky. It was late. He wanted to go see Brieden, to throw himself into his arms and tell him everything that had happened, to laugh and cry and talk and make love and know that they had years to fit all of it in. He *had* to let Brieden know.

But he also had to honor Firae. If Sehrys showed up for their morning trip to Khryslee reeking of Brieden and exhausted from too much lovemaking and too little sleep, he would never forgive himself. He had been willing to suffer for centuries for his principles, and now that he wouldn't have to, one night was certainly not going to kill him. Even if it seemed as though it might.

But he had to let Brieden know, even if he couldn't trust himself in his lover's presence that very night. "I'll have Jaxis bring Brieden a note," Sehrys said finally. "And I'll let him know that we will be leaving for Khryslee tomorrow afternoon. Assuming, of course, that all goes well in the morning."

They sat in silence for a while, allowing the intensity to dissolve a bit as they drank their tea and felt the warm night breeze on their skin.

"Sehrys?" Firae finally asked against the stillness of the night.

"Yes?"

"You *are* in love with him, aren't you?"

"Yes. Very much."

"And the years—?"

"Two hundred, perhaps, if his health is generally good and I extend his life."

"You'll lose some years that way too."

Sehrys nodded. "A few. It's worth it."

Firae nodded. "If you love him that much, I suppose it's worth it to me as well."

Sehrys took his hand and squeezed it gently. "Thank you."

❧ THE DAY OF THE WEDDING THAT WAS NEVER TO BE

FIRAE PARTED WAYS WITH THEM JUST OUTSIDE OF THE village; grimchins at the ready, members of the royal guard waited for their king and Jaxis.

After climbing out of the carriage, Sehrys instantly lunged at Jaxis, who danced away from him, giggling uncontrollably.

"I just had to! The lot of you were all so *dramatic* and *serious!* You should have heard yourselves before you realized Brieden hadn't gotten the note! Pure diamonds!"

Brieden couldn't care about Jaxis's cruel prank because the reality of the situation was finally beginning to sink in: He was going to Khryslee, and he was going with Sehrys. No one was chasing them or trying to kill them. No one was trying to keep them apart.

Sehrys looked as if any other circumstance might have led him to end Jaxis's life, but Brieden could see the truth dawning in him, too. The understanding and the excitement and the carefully repressed joy. Sehrys still wasn't meeting his eyes, but he sensed it there anyway.

Sehrys kissed Firae goodbye, and the kiss was not chaste. Brieden didn't mind. He *couldn't* mind, even if he'd wanted to, because Firae was getting one last kiss from Sehrys. Brieden would be kissing Sehrys for the rest of his life.

Jaxis pulled Brieden into a bone-crushing hug before he left, promising to come visit to see if there were any interesting women to bone in Khryslee. Brieden was touched. "Oh, and Sehrys has this note he asked me to give you," Jaxis added innocently, tossing a folded piece of parchment with a wax seal into Brieden's hand.

As the grimchins took off, Brieden and Sehrys stood side by side, watching them go. Sehrys waved at Firae, his fingers barely brushing against Brieden's as Firae moved farther and farther away. When the grimchins were nothing more than tiny dots on the horizon, their fingers tangled together. They stayed like that for a moment before turning to face each other.

They both opened their mouths to speak. Nothing came out.

Their eyes were fixed on one another and it was so much; it was everything; it was more than they could comprehend. They were still afraid to hold it too close for fear that it might break, that something else might wrench them apart.

"Oh, my God, Sehrys," Brieden finally whispered before their lips fell together.

And just like that, everything fell into place, and it was utterly, completely, and irrefutably real.

They held each other close, so close and tight that they could barely breathe, but they didn't care because it was real and it was solid and nothing was going to wrench them apart.

They kissed with intensity but without desperation, and let the tears fall, let the laughter shake them, let the grass tickle their cheeks as they tumbled to the ground together and rolled around with joy.

There was "I love you," whispered bright and fervent, against lips and palms and chests and thighs, right there in the grass and later in the tent, and over and over again until their voices grew hoarse with it. They said it and they said it and neither grew tired of hearing it.

But love had never been the question, really. Not between them.

And so that night, snuggled warm and sated in the tent, the question—the real question—was finally laid bare.

That night, they did something together they had never done before.

For the first time, they talked about their future.

CHAPTER THIRTY-EIGHT

"THEY HAVE JUST ENTERED THE PALACE GATES, Your Majesty," Vyrope informed her.

"Has she brought the elf?"

"I believe she has."

Brissa closed her eyes, exhaling slowly. She had been almost certain that Cliope's regiment would be too late.

"They'll be hungry and tired, I imagine. Could you see that some food and drink is prepared? And fresh honeysuckle for our friend, if there is any left in the garden."

"Of course, Your Majesty," Vyrope answered with a bow and a smile. She left to see that it was done.

Brissa drummed her fingers impatiently on the arm of the throne as she waited, mentally redecorating the room in her mind for perhaps the dozenth time. The Panloch aesthetic had been imposing, masculine and ornate, rife with carved golden this and crimson velvet that, thick, heavy blinds and looming dark-stained wood, and the throne room was the most offensive example of all.

Creating beauty couldn't be a priority, not yet. Not in the throes of war. But as soon as it became a practical reality, she planned to transform the room into a calming sea of cool blue and green, accented with clean lines of white and silver, and drenched in plenty of sunlight.

"Announcing Princess Cliope Keshell of Ryovni!" Vyrope called out, pulling Brissa from her daydreams. Brissa smiled at the formality of the introduction and stood to welcome her sister. Cliope looked worn and a bit thinner than Brissa would have liked, and she had dirt beneath her fingernails, but her face lit up the oppressive throne room. She bounded toward her sister, taking the steps up to the dais two at a time and throwing her arms around Brissa with a force that nearly made her stumble.

"Sister, how I have missed you! You will never guess what wonderful news I bring!"

"Perhaps not. I have heard barely a word from you since you set out in pursuit of the elf," Brissa admonished her, but didn't fight her smile. It never felt quite right to be separated from her twin for long.

They stepped back, holding one another at arm's length.

"You look beautiful as always, Brissa," Cliope said.

"And you look like you need a bath and a hot meal," Brissa returned with a smile. Cliope rolled her eyes fondly.

"I did not send word because I did not want to risk any message falling into the wrong hands," Cliope explained. "It... it is becoming less safe to travel through Villalu."

Brissa sighed. "I know. If we could convince the Darmons to swear allegiance, it would at least provide a nice buffer in the East, but—"

"But nothing!" Cliope interrupted. "I spoke with Lord Darmon personally just two days ago, and he has agreed to send five hundred troops."

Brissa gaped at her, sinking back down into the throne. "But... how?"

"Our new advisor!" Cliope beamed. "He has agreed to pose as a House Keshell slave in exchange for our protection."

"He *did*?" Brissa furrowed her brow in confusion. "He did not seem the sort to agree to any arrangement such as *that*."

"Oh. Yes. Not Sehrys. I imagine he would rather kill us both than ever pose as a slave again. I forget that you really know nothing of what has happened. Dronyen's elf is not here. He crossed The Border with his human lover some time ago."

Brissa's heart sank. "You did not reach him in time."

"No, we reached him at the *perfect* time. But he could not read the scroll and he would not stay."

Brissa narrowed her eyes at her sister. "What are you holding back, Cliope? I have little patience with riddles, you know that."

"There is no riddle. I am merely building *suspense*," Cliope scoffed. "But have it your way. Sehrys and Brieden met another sidhe in their travels, and they suggested that I might seek his help in reading the scrolls."

"He is of the Spiral caste as well?" Brissa asked in disbelief. The odds were nearly impossible.

"He is not. Common caste, in fact."

Brissa sighed. "Cliope—"

"Sister, just meet him. He has already been of great help, and I think you will find that he will be of far more use to us than any Spiral caste sidhe."

"Very well," Brissa assented, gesturing to Vyrope to fetch the elf.

"Announcing *Tash Tirarth Valusidhe efa Lesette efa es Zulla Melleva Feririar ala es Fervishlaea efa es Sola Pelzershe*," Vyrope called out a moment later, taking pains to pronounce the name as slowly and carefully as she could.

Brissa had thought that Sehrys was the least slave-like slave she had ever laid eyes upon. But when Tash Tirarth Valusi... well, whatever his name was, when *he* walked into the room, it truly struck her that she had never before laid eyes upon a sidhe who was completely free from human control.

He stood tall and lithe, with broad, muscled shoulders, shrewd dark green eyes, quirked lips, and hair like sunlight and tiger lilies.

His skin was kissed golden, a bit darker than that of most sidhe Brissa had seen in her own lifetime, but much lighter than nearly any human she had ever seen. He wore three silver hoops in one ear and two in the other and stood dressed in simple boots, breeches, tunic and jerkin, with a sword at his hip. The tunic was cut low in front and revealed a scar on his chest.

Brissa could not have explained her impulse to fall to her knees in front of the creature and offer him the throne if she had tried.

Instead, she cleared her throat. "Greetings, sir, it is an honor. Please forgive me if I struggle to pronounce your name, but it is like nothing I have heard before."

"An honor for me as well, Your Majesty," the elf replied. "And if it pleases you, you may call me Tash. It is my familiar name, and the one by which my own people most often call me."

"Tash it is, then. Please forgive me, Tash, for I am overjoyed to have you with us, but my sister tells me that you are of the Common caste."

Tash nodded. "I am. But much like your people, those with the most power do not always possess the most knowledge. If that were the case, after all, I don't imagine that the Panlochs would have fallen for your scheme and found themselves complicit in their own demise."

Brissa smiled. "That is quite true. But I have been lead to believe that translating my scroll requires such magical knowledge as comes only to the Spiral caste."

Tash's eyes glittered as if in challenge. He stepped a bit closer to the dais. "Your Majesty, I may not be powerful, but I studied and taught the known histories of The Sidhe in this world for nearly a century. I am fluent in forty-six languages. I understand your scrolls *perfectly*."

Brissa clutched the arms of the throne, her throat suddenly dry. "And what do they tell you?" she asked, her voice nearly a whisper.

Tash looked her square in the eye. "They tell me that we must set sail for Ryovni at once."

CHAPTER THIRTY-NINE

*B*RIEDEN.

I hate that I am writing you this letter. Not because I hate what it is going to say, but because I hate that it is a letter at all. I can't express to you the magnitude with which I yearn to speak these words to you in person, how painful it is, both in my physical body and in the depths of my heart.

However. Before I go any further, I believe I owe you the important part, and here it is: I am not going to marry Firae, and I want to go to Khryslee with you. I want to be with you in every way for as long as possible.

I have always wanted this, of course, for nearly as long as I've known you. But now I am asking if you will do it.

Will you?

Will you come to Khryslee with me, Brieden? Will you make a home and a life with me there?

SEHRYS AWOKE TO BRIEDEN TRACING THE FEATURES OF HIS face lightly with his fingertips. He smiled, impossibly shy, when Sehrys opened his eyes, continuing his movements.

"Good morning," Brieden whispered, and Sehrys was overcome with the sweetness of this, of how fragile it all still felt, of how neither of them completely believed that they could really have each other.

"Good morning," Sehrys returned, smiling at the feel of Brieden's roughened fingertips ghosting across his skin. He closed his eyes and sighed into the touch as Brieden gently kissed his eyelids.

"I read your note," Brieden said softly. "I do wish I had gotten it when I was supposed to, but it was nice reading it now, with you asleep right beside me. I shall keep it forever."

Sehrys smiled and pulled Brieden to him, kissing him softly on the lips.

"Just as long as I get to keep you forever," he murmured, and he could *feel* Brieden's smile against him.

Brieden wrapped his arms around Sehrys, pulling him into a tight hug, his arms shaking even as he pulled Sehrys closer. "Brieden?" Sehrys asked. "I thought we *weren't* going to cry anymore. I thought we—"

"I can't help it," Brieden managed, his voice trembling. "I'm so *happy*, Sehrys."

"I'm happy too," Sehrys whispered into the thick black waves of Brieden's hair.

Brieden sighed. "Let's just stay right here where everything is perfect."

"In this tent? On the outskirts of Alovur Drovuru?"

"Yes."

"But what about Khryslee? What about my ambassadorship? What about your *dairy farm*, Brieden?"

Brieden pulled back from the hug to look at Sehrys, their arms still draped around one another loosely.

"You're really going to let me have a dairy farm?"

"Isn't that what you want?"

"I mean, that's all right with you? Living that way?"

Sehrys kissed him. "Of course, long as you're kind to the animals, which I know you will be. It sounds nice, actually."

"I'm not going to know what I'm doing."

"That makes two of us because I barely know the first thing about political networking. But we figured out how to make it here from Villalu Proper in one piece. After that, I'm fairly confident that we can do anything we set our minds to."

Brieden chuckled. "That is a very good point."

They lay in silence, basking in the moment, as Sehrys began to trace patterns across Brieden's bare chest. It had been so long since either of them had had a place that truly felt like *home*. The promise of it was almost as exciting as the fact that they were going to have it together.

"What are you doing?" Brieden murmured, noticing that Sehrys's fingertips on his chest had become concentrated upon a small spot about two or three inches beneath his collarbone.

Sehrys blushed, his heart hammering as he considered what he was about to ask. "I—perhaps this is too soon," Sehrys began, "and I... I don't want to scare you, Brieden. I know that we should probably take our time, because the Gods know we have enough of it, but I... I just—"

"What, Sehrys?"

Sehrys locked eyes with him. "I want to marry you, Brieden. *So* much."

Brieden grasped Sehrys's face in his hands. "*Yes*," he said; the force of the word made Sehrys's heart surge. "Please Sehrys, yes. I'm yours and I want to be your husband and your lifemate, and I want it now."

Sehrys's laugh was wet with tears. "I don't know about *now*, Brieden. I want to get settled first, and I want a beautiful wedding. Nothing small and rushed. Not after everything we've been through.

But soon." Sehrys continued to trace the spot on Brieden's chest with his fingers while holding Brieden's gaze.

"So... I imagine that Jaxis told you, in emotionally damaging detail, the significance of the red bracelet."

Brieden laughed. "Yes."

"There are pieces of jewelry to signify other sorts of relationship status too," Sehrys said. "Bracelets are for those seeking a partner of some sort, but there are armbands and rings and pendants as well." He moved to sit up, crawling to the edge of the bed to fetch his satchel.

"When a couple is mated for life, they forgo jewelry in favor of something more permanent. A tattoo of the couple's own design... right on the chest in that place where I was touching you."

Brieden brought his own hand to the spot.

Sehrys fished the two small objects out of his satchel and moved back to Brieden, sitting in front of him cross-legged. Brieden moved to mirror him.

"But before that, when a couple pledges themselves to one another, some choose to wear a pendant of promise. The tattoo itself is meant to symbolize the pendant melting into one's body, imprinting itself there, when the promise is fulfilled."

Sehrys opened his palm. Brieden gasped. "That looks almost like—"

"Not almost. It *is* the same necklace, Brieden, and this other is the one that I used to try and find you. To *almost* find you. It would have worked, had you still been wearing the pendant. But they are cut from the same stone, and they are naturally drawn to one another. I imbued them with my own magic, so they may always be used in such a way."

One of the pendants was the very one that Sehrys had bought for Brieden at the market in Silnauvri, although it was nearly impossible to tell one from the other. The stones were still the same clear, glittering brown they had been when Sehrys bought them, still the same color as Brieden's eyes. But now they were also threaded through with bright, vibrant green. The color of Sehrys's eyes. The color of his power.

Brieden smiled. "They're beautiful," he said. "Even more beautiful than before."

"When a person puts this on, Brieden, it signifies that the promise has been made. It is very serious and it... it isn't something you just take off. It is almost as serious as the tattoo itself."

Brieden smoothed his fingers over both stones in Sehrys's palm.

"Brieden," Sehrys said, meeting his eyes. "Would you... would you wear my promise pendant? Be my lifemate?"

"Yes, Sehrys, of course," he whispered, fresh tears brimming. Sehrys placed one necklace on the ground and tied the other around Brieden's neck, securing the tough length of cord with a strong knot. When he drew his hands away, the pendant rested upon the very spot he had been tracing on Brieden's chest .

"You look amazing," Sehrys breathed, taking in the deep brown and vibrant green against Brieden's dark chest hair and chestnut skin and how the pendant reflected the sparkle in his lover's eyes.

But the most beautiful thing of all was what it meant. It meant that Brieden was *his*. The boys of Khryslee would be making no mistake about that.

Brieden smiled and picked up the second necklace, reaching to fasten it around Sehrys's neck.

"No!" Sehrys protested, stilling Brieden's hands in midair. "You have to *ask* me first."

Brieden rolled his eyes. "Sehrys, we already—"

"It's tradition," Sehrys explained.

Brieden smiled. "Sehrys," he said, his voice cracking on the single word and causing tears to spring to Sehrys's eyes. "Sehrys," Brieden began again, after clearing his throat. "Will you wear *my* promise pendant? Will you be my lifemate?"

Sehrys only managed the tiniest breath of a "yes," nodding his assent and crying softly as Brieden tied the necklace around his neck and then sat back to admire him.

"You look so beautiful," Brieden murmured. He leaned in to kiss the pendant before moving to kiss Sehrys's chest and then his stomach.

"Brieden..." Sehrys sighed softly, leaning back.

Brieden moved on top of Sehrys, straddling him, their pendants touching when he leaned forward to kiss him.

"One last time in the tent?" Brieden asked, before taking Sehrys's earlobe between his lips.

"I will... *oh...* be so happy to be done with this tent and have a proper bed again once and for all."

"Come, now. This is *our* tent. This was one of the first things I stole when I decided to help you escape from Dronyen. This was our first bed together."

"Are you referring to this pile of blankets?"

"Yes. *Our* pile of blankets."

"We are throwing these blankets away as soon as we reach Khryslee, and we are going to get some *proper* bedding."

Brieden kissed down Sehrys's neck, and then moved off of him to gently turn him over so that he was lying on his stomach. He proceeded to trail light kisses down Sehrys's spine.

"You're going to miss this tent," Brieden insisted. "You're going to miss making love with me on these blankets. I can tell."

"Mmm... the blankets aren't what appeal to me about the experience, Brieden."

"Do you remember the first time we made love in this tent?" Brieden whispered against the flesh of Sehrys's back.

"Of course I do," Sehrys murmured. "I remember *every* time with y—" His words were swallowed by something between a gasp and a moan when Brieden gently parted the cheeks of his buttocks to lick across Sehrys's entrance, hard and slow.

Brieden held Sehrys firmly in place with his strong, broad hands to keep him from writhing too much, and all Sehrys could do was gasp and cry out against the throbbing beat of pleasure that pulsed through his body as Brieden continued to work over and around the tiny, puckered hole with his tongue.

"G-gods, Brieden," Sehrys gasped out, trying to push up against Brieden's tongue, to draw it inside. Brieden flicked the tip in and then drew it out quickly, teasing him.

"Please," Sehrys groaned, desperate for so much more. There were *hubia rija* left over from the night before, and he managed to reach one and throw it back toward Brieden.

Brieden laughed fondly when the flower landed on Sehrys's lower back, wasting no time in unfurling its petals and working Sehrys open, giving him the gorgeous stretch that he had been craving, fingers twisting against the pleasurable spot inside him. Sehrys groaned softly, his breaths coming heavy, and he all but whined when Brieden pulled his fingers free and moved the heat of his body away from Sehrys.

"Climb on, love," Brieden breathed, and Sehrys looked over his shoulder at one of the most beautiful things he had ever seen: Brieden sitting back on his knees, hair loose and wild to his shoulders, eyes dark with lust, nipples peaked and skin gleaming with perspiration and arousal. His long, dark cock was flushed hard and full, damp at the tip, jutting up almost perfectly straight from the black curls between his legs.

Sehrys scrambled to his knees, letting Brieden clutch his hips and guide him backward until he could sink down onto Brieden's lap, his back flush against Brieden's chest, both men melting together with sighs of deep pleasure.

Brieden wrapped his arms around Sehrys's chest and held him; his fingers stroked the pendant below Sehrys's collar bone. Their bodies were connected in the most intimate way possible.

"I never imagined my life could be this perfect," he whispered and kissed Sehrys's shoulder. "I can barely believe you're truly mine."

"Always and forever," Sehrys whispered back, turning his head to kiss Brieden on the lips.

Brieden moved his hands back to Sehrys's hips and they began moving together, finding their rhythm easily as they moved at a leisurely pace. Their hips worked together, and Sehrys allowed his head to fall back on Brieden's shoulder; the shocks of pleasure running through him made him all but melt against his lover's perfect body. Every so often, one of Brieden's hands would leave his hip, sliding up Sehrys's chest to touch the pendant, as if making sure it was still there. After several such touches Sehrys closed his hand on top of Brieden's, feeling the press of Brieden's pendant against his back, as Brieden pressed Sehrys's own into his chest.

"I love you," Sehrys moaned, grinding down harder onto Brieden and clenching around him. Brieden cried out and pulled Sehrys closer, moving his hand from Sehrys's chest to grasp the flower and drizzle Sehrys with it. He began to pump Sehrys's cock in time with their movements, and it took only a few strokes before Sehrys was coming hard. Brieden rocked up into him as Sehrys collapsed against him, boneless, even as Brieden panted against his neck, still in a frenzy of building pleasure.

Brieden grasped both of Sehrys's hips and lifted and dropped him while thrusting into him hard, and Sehrys simply moaned at the saturation of pleasure and sensitivity, reaching back to wrap his arms around Brieden's neck and simply hold on until Brieden found his own release, wrapping his own arms around Sehrys's waist and placing one hand across his heart as he came, his cry muffled against Sehrys's shoulder.

They fell back onto the blankets, panting, and Sehrys let out a soft laugh.

"I suppose I will miss this tent a *little*. And I suppose it wouldn't be too terrible to save *one* of the blankets."

Brieden smiled at him. "I love you," he said.

KHRYSLEE WAS NOT EXACTLY WHAT BRIEDEN HAD EXPECTED. Actually, it more or less was, but the Khryslean border was what surprised him.

Yet another border.

He had not expected something very like a shantytown about a half-mile from Khryslee's border, near the bank of a creek. It was inhabited by all manner of human and sidhe and a few creatures that looked similar to both human and sidhe, but clearly belonged to a different species altogether.

There were tents and lean-tos and small one-room plant-mounds. Children ran about chasing pixies, and the older inhabitants of the settlement bustled around them, preparing food and repairing clothing and chatting animatedly. The people seemed reasonably content, but there was an unmistakable aura of melancholy about the place.

"It isn't always easy to obtain admittance to Khryslee," Sehrys reminded Brieden gently, as he drove them through the one road that intersected the settlement. "These are... refugees, I suppose. Most of them are from Villalu, but all of them would rather stay here and keep trying to live in Khryslee than go back to where they came from for one reason or another. As long as they remain in the settlement, they have been permitted to stay here."

Brieden looked around. There *did* seem to be more humans here than anything else. He turned Sehrys, unable to fight back his rising concern. "Sehrys, what if they won't let us—"

"Brieden. We have absolutely nothing to worry about. They have already accepted me as the king's ambassador. We'll be fine."

But Brieden could not meet the words with the level of confidence he should have. He looked at the people around him, some of whom had probably been there for years, and felt a pang of intense guilt.

"That's why we're doing this, Brieden," Sehrys said gently, as if reading his mind. "If Firae is successful, these people won't need Khryslee anymore. They'll have the whole world."

"Yes, but... I don't think they would let me in if it weren't for you, Sehrys. I don't deserve to live in Khryslee any more than these people do."

Sehrys placed a hand on Brieden's knee, and left it there. "Brieden, no one ever knows for sure whether they will be admitted to Khryslee. That decision is left solely to the Gatekeeper. And from what I know of her decision-making process, I think you stand a very good chance."

Brieden was going to ask Sehrys to explain further, but he was rendered speechless when he saw the gate.

He had expected something like The Border between Laesi and Villalu. Instead, they were confronted with a single gate. The top was visible, and the air was completely clear around it, offering a glimpse into Khryslee. It was obvious where Khryslee began and the Eastern Border Lands ended, however, because behind the gate, everything was *different*.

And of course there was the gate itself.

It was the largest thing Brieden had ever seen. He had no idea how it could have been built by any hands, human or sidhe. It consisted of a simple stone archway surrounding heavy wooden double doors with brass pull-rings. Each pull-ring was about three times the size of their carriage.

The gate extended so high that Brieden had to crane his head to glimpse the top. The doors had to be decorative. He couldn't imagine that it was physically possible to open them.

And behind the gate was a place even more beautiful than the Faerie Lands.

The sky seemed to have a slight rose tint, even in full daylight, and the cerulean grasses seemed to sparkle as they rippled in the breeze. Brieden saw more trees that were familiar from home than he had seen anywhere else since crossing The Border, and the array of flower-trees was simply stunning, casting a gloriously multicolored canopy across the mountain ranges visible in the distance.

Brieden was so transfixed by what he saw that it took a moment for him to realize that Sehrys had pulled the carriage to a stop about a hundred feet from the enormous gate. Sehrys climbed down from the perch and Brieden followed suit. After a few steps, the seeming lack of a proper border proved itself to be an utterly false impression. It was difficult to put it into words, even to himself, but Brieden simply *knew* that he couldn't pass through. No matter how hard he tried, he couldn't have forced himself to do it. There was no exhaustion or revulsion, just an absolutely clear and unmistakable inability to walk into Khryslee.

Sehrys looked up toward the top of the gate, and Brieden held his hand above his eyes, visor-style, and looked as well. What appeared to be a large bird spread its wings atop the gate and then dove.

The closer it got, the more frightened Brieden became. He clutched Sehrys's hand and leaned into him.

"It's all right, Brieden," Sehrys soothed. "It's only the Gatekeeper."

When she landed before them, Brieden wobbled, feeling his knees buckle, and Sehrys wrapped his arms around Brieden's waist and held him tight so that he wouldn't fall.

She was the most awe-inspiring creature Brieden had ever laid eyes on. Her wingspan was enormous; when fully extended, each wing was easily twice Brieden's height. The wings themselves were a gleaming bluish silver tipped with intense crimson. The lower half of her body was that of a large cat with a swishing tail. The tawny fur began to fade to near-naked skin around her chest, neck, and head, and those parts of her looked completely and irrefutably human, complete with small but unmistakable breasts. Her skin was a bit darker than her fur, a rich, light brown similar to Brieden's own, and the hair on her head was dark and curly, falling loose across her powerful leonine shoulders. Her lips were full and dark, and her eyes were an impossible shade of aubergine streaked with violet.

She was beautiful.

When she spoke, the earth seemed to vibrate. Brieden was sure that she could reduce him to dust with that voice if she so chose.

It struck him somehow, strangely, as a counterpoint to Sehrys's voice. While Sehrys's voice was high and soft and yet unmistakably male, this creature's voice was low and gruff but unmistakably female.

"Brieden Lethiscir," she said, and he almost passed out.

The creature waited, her eyes speaking of all the time in the world and then some.

"I... I... yes... um... ma'am," Brieden managed, his voice trembling. Sehrys held him and kissed his forehead softly to reassure him.

Though the creature did not smile, her eyes danced with amusement. Brieden wondered what she was. "I am Sphinx," she replied, as if hearing Brieden's thoughts.

Could she hear Brieden's thoughts?

"Yes," she said, and circled around them. Sehrys seemed completely calm and relaxed, so Brieden tried to force himself to relax as well. After all, if Sehrys wasn't afraid of her, she must not pose a threat.

"Oh, I can assure you, I could kill you both quite easily without even trying if I so chose," she said casually. "But I won't. You pose no threat to Khryslee, so I pose no threat to you."

Brieden let out a heavy sigh. That was certainly good news.

"Why are you here?" she asked in the tone of a teacher who is looking for a specific answer.

"I... I want to live here. With Sehrys. I... we... want to get married, and Sehrys—I'm sure you know about Sehrys's ambassadorship here, and I... I... I was thinking about starting a dairy farm."

The Sphinx settled in front of him, uncomfortably close. She smelled of lilies. "A dairy farm."

"Um, yes?"

"And what skills do you possess that would make this occupation a fitting one?"

"I... um... like cheese." She stared at him. "A... a lot. I like cheese a *lot,*" he amended, trying to put force behind the words. Unbidden, Jaxis's argument for why Brieden's love of cheese qualified him to become a cheese-maker popped into his mind, and the Sphinx roared—*actually roared*—with laughter.

Brieden blushed. "I... I... all I mean is that I want to learn. I'm *willing* to learn. But I'll do anything, really, to stay with Sehrys."

The Gatekeeper's expression softened and she looked at Sehrys and then back at Brieden.

"You love this sidhe."

"Yes."

The Sphinx returned her eyes to Sehrys. "*Sehrys Silerth Valu-sidhe efa Naisdhe efa es Zulla Maletog Feririar ala es Fervishlaea efa es Vestramezershe.* You know you will outlive this human by centuries."

Sehrys's arms tensed around Brieden.

"Yes," Sehrys said softly, and Brieden hated that choosing to be with him could make Sehrys sound so sad.

"Do you know how many years to expect together?"

"Well," Sehrys ventured, "I know that with the healing—I mean, I've heard... maybe... two hundred."

Brieden's eyes widened and he twisted in Sehrys's arms to look at his face, mute with shock. Two hundred years? *Two hundred years?* Was this real? Was she serious? Did Brieden misunderstand? Was Sehrys actually capable of keeping Brieden alive for another two centuries?

The Sphinx was still looking at Sehrys.

"I wouldn't say two hundred, no."

Sehrys's face fell, his arms growing limp around Brieden. He looked utterly devastated. "I'll take whatever I can," he replied shakily. "He will be my lifemate for as long as he is alive, and I will be his even after he is gone."

Brieden had no words, so he simply turned completely around in Sehrys's arms and hugged him tight. Sehrys's arms tightened in response.

"I am happy to hear that," the Sphinx said softly, more softly than Brieden had thought she was capable of speaking, "and I am sorry to have led you astray and caused you pain. Because what I meant is that two hundred years is probably the very least you can expect. You are of the Spiral caste, are you not?"

"Yes," Sehrys answered, excitement rising in his voice.

"I am far, far older than either of you, my dears, and I have seen exactly one relationship between a human and a Spiral sidhe. It was long ago. They are both gone now. But that sidhe gave her lifemate more than four hundred years."

And this time, when knees began to buckle, they both had to catch each other to keep from falling. Brieden was fairly certain that his brain was broken. None of this seemed possible.

"A-are you sure?" Sehrys stammered.

"Yes."

Brieden and Sehrys tightened their grip on one another, hugging fiercely. The Gatekeeper was quiet, giving them a moment to be speechless together.

When they finally pulled apart, Brieden pulled Sehrys to him and kissed him hard. They both had tears of joy in their eyes.

"Brieden Lethiscir," the Sphinx said. Brieden forced himself to turn away from Sehrys and face the creature. After all, he had just found out that he would have four hundred years to embrace Sehrys. He could spare a few moments.

"Sit."

Brieden obeyed as if guided by invisible strings. The Sphinx drew closer, so close that their faces almost touched. She looked deeply into his eyes.

Suddenly, his inner world opened up completely. His mind and heart and soul and memories were bared helplessly before this almost godlike creature. This creature that, although she could break him with the slightest thought, probed gently and thoroughly.

Brieden had no idea how long it lasted. Not very long, it seemed, although the sun was a bit lower in the sky when he finally came back to himself.

The Sphinx rested on her haunches and tilted her head at him in such a catlike way that he couldn't help but smile.

"You have a pure heart," she said. "One of the purest I've seen."

Brieden could actually *feel* Sehrys beaming with pride behind him.

"Sanya Forrester is looking for an apprentice at her dairy farm. She specializes in hand-crafted cheeses, and I think the two of you might work well together. I will send word to her to look for you tomorrow."

Slowly and silently, the enormous doors opened behind her. *An invitation.*

"Welcome to Khryslee, Brieden Lethiscir," she said, before leaping into the air and soaring out of sight, faster than anything Brieden had ever seen.

Sehrys looked down at Brieden. Ridiculous grins spread across both their faces. Sehrys reached out his hand to help pull Brieden to his feet, and then kept pulling him into a long, sweet kiss. When they broke apart, Sehrys lay his palm across Brieden's chest, over his promise pendant.

"Welcome home, Brieden," he said with a smile.

"Welcome home, Sehrys."

They climbed back onto the perch and drove into Khryslee, hand in hand.

At that very moment, thousands of miles away, a ship set sail for Ryovni.

And the journey continued.

Pronunciation Guide

Both Villaluan and the Elfin language are pronounced like English for the most part. However, several sounds occur in Elfin and not in Villaluan. For those, both the Elfin and Villaluan pronunciations are given. Elfin vocabulary words are in italics.

Aehsee. elf (A-ay-see)
Aldevucavish. an elfin caste (all-day-voo-ca-vish)
Alia. human (all-aye-a)
Alovur Drovuru. Elfin place name (All-o-vur Dro-voo-roo)
Arkeroft. a human ruling House and its province (Ark-ay-roft)
B!Nauvri'ija. elfin divinity (The ! is similar to the plain central alveolar Xhosa click sound. The ' is a glottal stop. Humans skip the first two sounds and the glottal stops and say Nay-oor-vri-ya.)
Bachuc. human (Bak-ewk)
Belloquei. a human Ruling house and its province (Bell-o-kway)
Beltane. elfin festival
Brec. elf (the final c is pronounced like the German ch in "ich" by elves and as k by humans); *Brec Nauerth Valusidhe efaf Iric efa es Swesta Vurule Feririar ala es Fervishlaea efa es Sola Pelzershe*
Brieden Lethiscir. human (Bree-den Leth-ish-ir)
Brissa. human
Busix. Elfin insult (The final "x" is similar to the Arabic voiced pharyngeal fricative. Humans pronounce it "ks." Boo-siks)
Cerade. human (se-ra-day)
Cesmi. human (Kez-me)

Cho. Elfin command to animals to stop

Chrillipal. human town (Krill-e-pal)

Chrill. a human ruling House and its province (Krill)

Cliope. human (Clee-o-pay)

Cochut. a pod (Ko-chut)

Darmon. human ruling House and its province

Drayez. human (Dry-ahz)

Dronyen. Panloch ruler

Ellechett. a human ruling House and its province (El-le-chet)

esil kryshi. Elfin honorific meaning "my sibling" (Ay-sil kry-shee)

es lemeddison rubrio. Elfin term meaning the Non-Interference Doctrine (es lay-med-dis-on ru-bree-o)

Es Muchator. Elfin term meaning "The Great Change." (Es Moo-ka-tor)

Feririar. socio-political elfin group (In Elfin, the final "r" is trilled as in Spanish. Humans who cannot pronounce the trill use simple "r" as in English. fer-ih-ree-arr)

Firae. elf (Fur-ray)

Frilau. Villaluan prophet, presumed deceased (Free-law)

Frilauan. Follower of Frilau, a human religion

Gira. elf (Gee-ra)

Grade. human (Grahd)

Grimchin. creature (grim-chin)

Herrett. human

hubia rija. a plant (hoo-bee-a ree-ja)

Huppah. Elfin command to animals to go (hup-pah)

Imervish. Elfin word meaning "incorruptible." (Im-er-veesh)

Jaren. human (Ja-ren)

Jaxis. elf (Jaks-is)

Jichyn. a human ruling House and its province (Jy-ken)

Jor. human name (Jor)

Keshell. a human ruling House and its province (Ke-shell)

Kessa. human

Khryslee. elfin province (Cry-slee)

Ki'iz. elf (Humans omit the glottal stop and pronounce Keez)

Kryshi. sibling, used as an honorific (Cry-shee)

L!Khryauvni. elfin divinity (Humans pronounce Cry-ah-oov-nee)

Laesi. elfin name for the Faerie Lands (Lay-ee-si)

Lajec. a human ruling House and its province (Lay-jek)

Lapyse. human (La-pie-see)

Lasemik. border city (La-see-mik)

Lekrypal. border city (Le-kree-pal)

Lerekhe. human (Le-ray-kee)

Lokosgre. human town (Lo-kos-gray)

Lottechet. a human ruling House and its province (Lot-eh-chet)

Loq. elf (The Elfin final "q" is similar to the Arabic laryngeal fricative. Humans who cannot make that sound, use simple "k." Lok)

M!Ferauvise. elfin divinity (Humans pronounce Fay-ra-oo-vee-say)

Merrowlee. human place name (Mer-row-lee)

Miknauvripal. human city (Mik-now-vree-pal)

Muirdannoch. human place name (Moo-ir-dan-nok)

Naurasvu. human village (Na-oo-ras-voo)

Nehaisa. elf (Ne-hay-sa)

Nomkinli. pet names, call names (nom-kin-li)

Oknaur. human village (Ok-na-oor)

Okosgrim. human village (Ok-os-grim)

Okoslajec. human town (Ok-os-lay-jek)

Panloch. a human ruling House and its provinces (Pan-lok)

Puca. Elfin word referring to a shape-shifting elf (poo-ka)

Ravurmik. village (Ra-vur-mik)

Ryovni. human province; the seat of House Keshell (Rye-ov-nee)

Runa. elf (Roo-na)

Sehrys. elf (Sare-is); *Sehrys Silerth Valusidhe efa Naisdhe efa es Zulla Maletog Feririar ala es Fervishlaea efa es Vestramezershe*

Seshen. human (Say-shen)

Sidhe, The. the Elfin name for the elfin race (In Elfin, the "dhe" indicates a voiced dental fricative. Humans pronounce Sheed.

Silnauvri. border city (Shil-na-oo-vree)

Sinchett. human (Sin-chet)

srechelee. elfin plant (Sre-kay-lee)

Sree. elf (Sree)

Tash. elf (Tash); *Tash Tirarth Valusidhe efa Lesette efa es Zulla Melleva Feririar ala es Fervishlaea efa es Sola Pelzershe*

tashlivija. elfin plant (Tash-lee-veeja)

Taukhi Scrolls. Frilauan religious texts (Ta-oo-ki)

Tepper Tirchin, aka Tep. human (Te-per Tir-kin)

Thieren. human (Thee-ir-en)

tochet. tree (Tok-et)

Tyzva efa es Pura Ovni Feririar. Elfin historic figure

Villalu. the human world (Vill-a-loo)

Villaluan. the human language and an adjective meaning "pertaining to Villalu" (Vill-a-loo-an)

Vishli. Elfin word meaning "caste" (Vish-lee)

Vrac. elf (Humans pronounce Vrak)

Vyrope. human (Vie-ro-pay)

Yestli River. (Yest-lee)

zula sopor rija. elfin plant (zoo-la so-por ree-ja)

ACKNOWLEDGMENTS

In 2011, after a years-long hiatus, I decided to write again. Just for fun, of course. I never expected the experience—and the incredible people I met along the way—to completely change my life. I cannot ever properly express my appreciation to those who found my rough-edged words amid a sea of fanfiction available for free on the Internet and decided to read it. I can never truly thank those who took the time to ask questions and offer feedback—or those who created art of their own that was in some way inspired by the stories I shared. The encouragement, support and community I found was priceless. From the most casual reader to the most prolific reviewer to the most dedicated fan artist, thank you. All of you.

I am also forever grateful to the many wonderful friends and family members who have accommodated my occasional lack of presence (both mental and physical) over the last year. And I thank them in advance for the years in the future that will be much the same. As anyone with a writer in the family knows, supporting someone through the process of birthing a book is not an easy task. This book would not have seen the light of day without tireless help and support from the brilliant minds behind Interlude Press, who helped me turn something good into something great, and the entire family of Interlude authors for being the most supportive cohorts I could imagine in this brilliant, terrifying, exciting new adventure.

But most of all I would like to thank Tilly and Pepper, for relieving my stress during every crisis, never expecting conversation when I'm focused on world-building and always keeping me company whenever I am compelled to get up in the middle of the night and write.

About the Author

CHARLOTTE ASHE IS A SOCIAL WORKER BY DAY AND A writer of romantic fantasy by night. A long-time fan of speculative fiction that skews feminist and features LGBT characters, Charlotte loves writing stories that are sexy, heartfelt and full of magic and adventure. She has put her BA in literature and creative writing to use over the years as a writer of fan fiction, and her most popular work has drawn more than one million readers worldwide, been translated into several languages and been featured in online publications including *The Backlot*.

Questions for Discussion

1. What are your thoughts on the role of women in *The Sidhe* and how that shifts from one culture to another in the book?

2. How do the two primary cultures depicted in *The Sidhe* approach the issue of slavery? Are they similar in any way?

3. How do humans and sidhe coexist in border cities versus in Khryslee, and how does Khryslee represent a different cultural point of view from either the Faerie Lands or Villalu?

4. Sehrys has extraordinary powers, more than the ordinary sidhe. How does that complicate his relationship with Breiden?

5. Brissa overthrows the government of Villalu and takes control of what had been a patriarchal culture. How does the shifting power structure of the human world parallel that of the Faerie Lands?

6. How is Villalu's world view shaped by the fact that humans are largely unaware that other worlds exist outside their borders?

7. What doctrine governs the sidhes' use of their powers, and what are the consequences of their policy of non-interference with Villalu? Is Villalu a form of prison?

8. What parallels exist between our world and the worlds of *The Sidhe* relating to world power, free choice, religious freedom and gender roles?

9. Brieden plans Sehrys' escape fully expecting to die. What, other than love, do you think motivated his actions?

10. Sehrys must choose between a life in service to others versus a much shorter period of personal happiness and love. Does he make the right choice, and how would you make this decision?

Charlotte Ashe

The King and the Criminal

The Heart of All Worlds, Book Two

What happens when the fairytale ends, but the journey continues?

SEHRYS AND BRIEDEN THOUGHT THEY HAD REACHED their happily ever after. But a compromised ancient spell puts their destinies and others into question when King Firae must cross The Border into Villalu in search of a convicted criminal. His departure leaves Sehrys to step into a role he had once coveted, and one that Brieden has always feared—that of ruler of the Eastern Border Lands. When the couple must ultimately confront the magnitude of their differences amid a storm of political upheaval, will love be enough to see them through?

Meanwhile, Firae confronts his own destiny when he must place his life in the hands of the very criminal he was seeking. Can he allow himself to place his trust in someone his own mother had exiled many years ago—especially when that criminal is also a beautiful and passionate man who awakens something far more potent in Firae's heart than a desire to fulfill his duty as king?

As each man struggles to understand his own destiny, devotion and legacy and the truth of his heart, a deeper and more urgent truth confronts them all. Their world is in far greater danger than any of them has realized, and each of them plays an integral part in what will ultimately be its destruction or its survival.

interlude press

Also from

interlude  press™

The Rules of Ever After by Killian B. Brewer

The rules of royal life have governed the kingdoms of Clarameer for thousands of years, but Prince Phillip and Prince Daniel know that these rules don't provide for the happily ever after they seek. A fateful, sleepless night on top of a pea under twenty mattresses brings the two young men together and sends them on a quest out into the kingdoms. On their travels, they encounter meddlesome fairies, an ambitious stepmother, disgruntled princesses and vengeful kings as they learn about life, love, friendship and family. Most of all, the two young men must learn to know themselves and how to write their own rules of ever after.

ISBN 978-1-941530-35-1

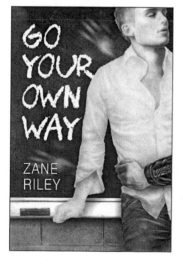

Go Your Own Way by Zane Riley

Will Osborne couldn't wait to put the roller coaster ride of his public education behind him. Having suffered bullying and harassment since grade school, he planned a senior year that would be simple and quiet before going away to college and starting fresh. But when a reform school transfer student struts into his first class, Will realizes that the thrill ride has only just begun.

Lennox McAvoy is an avalanche. He's crude, flirtatious, and the most insufferable, beautiful person Will's ever met. From his ankle monitor to his dull smile, Lennox appears irredeemable. But when Will's father falls seriously ill, Will discovers that there is more to Lennox than meets the eye

ISBN 978-1-941530-34-4

One **story** can change **everything**.

www.interlude**press**.com

interlude **press**

*One Story Can Change
Everything.*

interludepress.com

Twitter: @interludepress * * * Facebook: Interlude Press
Google+: +interludepress * * * Pinterest: interludepress
Instagram: InterludePress

CPSIA information can be obtained
at www.ICGtesting.com
Printed in the USA
FFOW03n1736140715
15142FF